DEAD AIR

A Cycling Murder Mystery

a novel by
GREG MOODY

VELO
press ®

BOULDER, COLORADO

Dead Air: A Cycling Murder Mystery
© 2002 Greg Moody

Printed in the United States of America

10 9 8 7 6 5 4 3 2 1

Distributed in the United States and Canada by Publishers Group West

International Standard Book Number: 1-931382-03-4

Library of Congress Cataloging-in-Publication Data applied for.

VeloPress
1830 North 55th Street
Boulder, Colorado 80301-2700 USA
303/440-0601; Fax 303/444-6788; E-mail velopress@7dogs.com

To purchase additional copies of this book or other VeloPress books, call 800/234-8356 or visit us on the Web at www.velopress.com.

Cover illustration: Matt Brownson
Cover and interior design: Erin Johnson

To Becky

For Cheryl

Contents

ACKNOWLEDGMENTS

With thanks to VeloPress, Amy Sorrells, and Theresa van Zante, as well as Tim Johnson and Steve Youngerman, all of whom helped immeasurably in the construction of this story. My thanks also go to those readers who had faith and patience, allowing me to break the rules of the form without their taking my head. For them, there is more to come. And finally, my thanks to Devon, Brynn, and Becky, who make each morning a new revelation and each evening a saving grace.

PROLOGUE

IN A WAY, THEY'RE BOTH CHILDREN, CREATED OUT OF NOTHING, THEN CAREFULLY nurtured to birth. Both bring pride, but for different reasons.

One brings life. One brings death.

One brings thoughts of a rich future; one brings memories of a tragic past.

One brings hope. One brings heartache.

And as such, they are both looked on with pride.

They both have a heartbeat.

They both have a brain.

They are both loved and adored and the centerpiece of dreams, rich in fantasy and desire.

Both exist for different reasons.

One exists to add to life.

The other exists merely to take it away.

Both exist in Denver today.

Both are immutably tied together.

Forever.

❦

SIX WEEKS. NOT SO VERY LONG, IS IT? YET IN THAT TIME, THAT PRECIOUS, SHORT space of time, the back of summer is usually broken and fall starts making itself known, despite the fact that it doesn't become official for another few days. Time hangs, hangdog, Sirius is in the sky, the world is baked but just out of the oven, steaming but cooling.

But not this year. The oven is still cranked high. The world continues to bake. The farmers complain. Too hot this year. Too dry. Too wet last year. No one is ever happy.

The meadows and forests burn with a look this summer. A cigarette. A campfire. A kid with a match and nothing to do other than toss it at a squirrel. An act of God. Every week another blaze.

The water table is low. It has been since last March. Restrictions abound, and no one pays the least bit of attention to them. City parks brown as an example to us all while lawns remain a rich, robust, chemically induced and water-sated green.

Leaves begin to show their edges, curled to the sky in search of a drop of rain, trying to decide if now is the time to change. The bike paths are empty. People have had their fill of riding and blading and walking the dog. They'll dream of days like this in January as they sit on Santa Fe for two hours trying to make it to work in a snowstorm, only to get there, talk about the drive, turn around, and begin it again in the opposite direction.

But for now, no more outdoor activities. They're sick of the bike and the blades and the dog and the little Baggies of dog poop, so carefully picked up and closed, then carefully tossed into the high grass beside the creek.

Besides, it's damned hot.

Too hot. Even Frightening Freddie March on TV6 has finally calmed down his usual predictions of "the-end-of-the-world-as-we-know-it weather" to just say, in his flat and plain Nebraskan tone, "It's hot, kids."

It's hot.

And yet, somehow, life goes on.

People read and write and listen, watch and pay attention to none of it, and continue on their merry way, stumbling over their own lives, confused and angry that the world is not wired to their own particular ass and their demanded comfort level.

They continue on.

Except those who have no lives anymore.

None at all.

No lives at all.

꙰

THE SWEAT TRIED TO HOLD HIM BACK, STICK HIM TO THE MATTRESS, BUT WILL was up again, sitting up, eyes wide and staring at nothing more than a window, a fan, not the figure he wanted to see.

"Is it you?"

"Are you here?"

"Is it …"

He shook his head and slumped back in bed again, the third time that night. It wasn't her. There was no figure. She wasn't there. She wasn't among the ghosts that crept through his dreams, crept through their room in the darkness. It wasn't her.

She wasn't there.

Will Ross wiped the sweat off the underside of his neck, then wiped that on the side of the mattress that had become positively soggy since he first lay down. He flopped heavily to the right this time, something new, moving back into the draft of the fan, curled up into his humid, heavy pillow, and drifted off, falling asleep again for another forty-five minutes, all that God would now allow, until he jerked awake and the questions popped out again.

"Ahh. Is it you?"

"Are you there?"

The answers were just as unsatisfying as before. No answer, no figure, no Cheryl.

No life.

No tears.

They were there, inside, building, constantly building, desperate to get out, to launch themselves from his eyes, his nose, his throat, his entire being at any time, the strangest times, but he held them in, he beat them back. It had been six weeks after all, callers on the radio said it was time for Will to move on with his life, to get over it, to forgive the killer, to move on, move on, move on—to where, for God's sake?

They could move on in a heartbeat. They were feeling all their emotions secondhand, delivered by anchors and reporters and writers and photographers who stepped into the mess but immediately stepped out into safety. They could all put it aside. But it was his. It belonged to him. It lived inside his head. They could move on, but where the hell could he go?

The bubble grew in his chest again. He stared at the ceiling and beat the tears back, again, third time tonight, three hundredth time in the past month and a half.

The baby cried in the other room, and within moments Will could hear Rose Cangliosi, his mother-in-law, rustle from the guest room down the hall to Elena's nursery. This was the last remaining connection to Rose's own family, her last connection with her own life, that of her daughter, now her granddaughter, and she was not about to let anything happen to her baby, disturb her baby, threaten her daughter's baby.

Rose and Elena, bonded at birth, bonded forever through death.

Elena grew quiet, and Will rolled back over, burying himself in Cheryl's pillow, cool and scented, and felt a sudden deep guilt. He should have gone.

"I know. I know," he whispered quietly to the darkness.

He should have gone to Elena. He should have gone to her baby. Our baby. But he didn't. He couldn't.

He didn't know. He didn't know why. Will still felt too goddamned sorry for himself, maybe. Still unsure of her. As if she was to blame, somehow. As if Elena was to blame for what had happened. As if it should have been her. As if it should have been him.

I am lucky to have her at all, I know that, he thought. I could have nothing, nothing at all to show for my life.

Nothing at all. But that doesn't change anything.

The worst part of the guilt, the heaviest part, the part that seized his heart and strangled his breathing, always came in the middle of the night when he lay trapped in bed and couldn't run from it.

I'm here, and the baby is here. And Cheryl is gone. That's all my fault, really my fault.

Will knew that. But he ran anyway.

He didn't know how long he could run from it, his own sin, his own failure, but he kept running anyway.

Fast and far away.

Cheryl's pillow still carried just the barest traces of her scent, and once more he turned and buried his face in it, breathing deeply of her. The teasing ache began again, and Will pulled himself away, turning on the light and throwing the room into a crazy quilt of shadows and GE sunbeams. The light shot straight up to the ceiling and straight down, the dark, mottled lampshade placing a gray stripe around the room between two pools of gold.

Will rolled back over and stared at the ceiling, trying to find the image of her face within the peaks and valleys of the textured plaster. Anywhere. She could be anywhere, he hoped.

Any sign. Look for any sign—in the quiet solitude of morning mass, in the face of the Virgin, in the clouds that played overhead, in the gentle rustle of the leaves of the oak beside her grave, hell, in his scrambled eggs.

Look for her, Will. Look for her constantly.

For a time, anyway, he had raged at God, begged and pleaded and prayed that God, in his infinite mercy, would turn back the hands of time. Just six weeks. Forty-two days. Yeah, that would be enough. Turn back the hands of time and let him be the one who found the ball. Let him be the one who kicked it away from the house. Let Will be the one who died.

Let her be here with Elena.

Let Will be strumming a harp on a cloud currently crossing over the Kansas state line, heading north-northeast toward New York City.

Change it around. Make it stop. Make it stop.

Make it stop hurting.

No? Then screw you, God. Take it away or go to hell. He closed his eyes tight and balled his fists and raged silently in the damp sheets.

The baby cried again. She was a fussy child, needy. Will relaxed.

Immediately, Rose Cangliosi's bed creaked, and he heard her hurry down the hall again. With barely a pause she shushed Elena in her bassinet. Will knew she was picking the baby up, stepping to the chair in the corner, and rocking her.

The baby cooed and grew quiet.

Soon the house slept again.

Except Will.

The empty feeling of uselessness crawled over him again, as it did each and every night. I was useless then, he thought; I'm useless now. The feeling fed upon itself. It grew, deeper and darker, pulling him down with it into some pit filled with snakes and spiders and discount-store bicycles.

"Is it you?"

"Are you here?"

The room was silent. Will drifted off for another forty-five minutes.

Dawn broke. Will smiled. Finally. Thank you, God. Sorry about what I said before. Time to start another day.

Without her.

Return to work. This was the day to return to work. Move his mind in a new direction. Get active again. Come alive again.

Without her.

No one to call. No one to see. No one to hear.

He folded himself up, twisting and unfolding his legs off the edge of the bed and onto the floor. He stretched. The pain lingered. The hurt remained.

No one to love. Don't you want somebody to love? Don't you need …

He pushed the tune out of his head. Easy. A thousand points of thought randomly floated through Will's head, colliding in his mind continually, a million per second. No one thought took over for more than a few moments at a time without being bullied to the side by a hundred others. The tune drifted away, out of his consciousness, back into the murk that twisted and frothed like eels in a pot.

Before stepping into the small master bathroom, he glanced across the hall into the tiny nursery. Rose and Elena slept quietly in the rocking chair, surrounded by Poohs of various shapes and sizes. One Tigger glanced warily out from the bottom of the pile, crazy and protective.

They looked good together, those two, Rose and Elena.

Cheryl would have looked even better.

Will slipped into the bathroom, stopping for a moment to glance in the mirror.

The man who returned the gaze was not Will at all but a man grown very, very old.

"Is she in there? Did she survive in your world? Were you able to save her? Were you able to ride up on your bike and save her at the last minute, save her by sacrificing yourself?

"Is she on your side of the mirror?"

The old man in the parallel universe on the other side of the glass asked the same questions as Will and received the same empty look in return.

"You poor dumb bastard," Will muttered, splashing cold water on his face in a daily ritual, filled with an empty hope of somehow coming alive once more.

*

PETER THE GREAT SAT UP SHARPLY, INSTINCTIVELY THROWING THE COVERS IN the direction of the threat. But there was no threat.

"Who?" he barked in fear.

There was no answer. The tiny open space of the minuscule bedroom was empty. He tried to catch his breath, but it was impossible. He was panting hard, soaked in sweat, hands shaking. Nightmares. No, worse, what had his mother called them?

Night terrors. They were back. And had been for the past six weeks.

He couldn't sleep. He couldn't bring himself to a state of quiet and calm, the quiet and calm he needed to work. He spent his days angry and agitated and constantly paranoid, looking over his shoulder, not for the police or the bomb squad, they had no idea, they were off on some wild-goose chase, the fools, but for something else, something he didn't understand, couldn't understand.

Something was following him. Not someone, but something. He had caught an old cartoon on cable and the cricket had said something about "always follow your conscience."

Bullshit. Always follow your anger. Conscience was for saps. Guilt was for losers. The meek. The cowed. Anger. Righteousness. Means to the end. Achievement. Revenge.

Those made life worth living as they drove the cattle into fear of your presence.

He took another deep breath.

He plucked at a corner of the dirty sheet and wiped the sweat from his face. Christ. What? A night spent at forty-five minutes at a crack? Twelve times down, twelve times up? Was that it?

He wiped his face again, the corner of the sheet already wet.

He threw the blankets back and sat on the edge of the bed, breathing deeply, as if he had just run a marathon after smoking a pack of Marlboros.

"Get a grip," he said aloud to the room, as if he was making sure it was empty by simply not getting an answer.

"Whoever you are," he wheezed, "show yourself and I'll kick your ass."

It sounded stupid. Moronic, even. The kind of stuff Mrs. Baker down the street, covered in her rosaries and scapulars to ward off the evil spirits, might say. Not him.

Not now.

"Fuck you," he whispered to the room.

He stood up, went to the bathroom, then stumbled out to the kitchen. He passed the door and stopped, turned, and stared back, first at the panels, then at the doorknob.

Maybe that was it. Maybe that was what had been bothering him all along. He had allowed them to change his pattern. He had stepped out of his element, owing strictly to fear. He had turned his back on his own reason for being. He had shown fear at the moment of his greatest triumph and run away from the consequences he had created, solely because of the headlines.

The basement had remained locked and empty for the past six weeks as the city had raised its head in fear and fury toward the perpetrator of what it called a horrid, senseless crime. *Beastly*, it roared. *Cowardly*, it raged.

Cowardly. That was what hurt the most.

There was nothing cowardly about it.

Peter wiped his face.

This was a war. A war waged against a man who two months ago had had it all and, now, thanks to certain talents and creativity found in this very room, had nothing. Nothing. No faith, no wife, no job.

An act of war, that was what it was, an act in a war declared by him. A war he had won. And to the victor went the spoils.

But not quite. There was collateral damage. Plenty to go around. And his way was not clear to victory.

It was his own damned fault, Peter thought. It was the fault of no one but Will Ross.

If he had only used the satellite phone, this wouldn't have happened. There would have been no need to set a surprise secondary. And it would all have been done. Six weeks of quiet, and the world would move on.

If only Ross had not noticed the vase, the vase weighted down with RDX and aluminum powder held in suspension by wax and oil and a clumsy detonator, too simple, too clumsy, then there would have been no need. No need at all.

But there was no choice. Will Ross had left no choice. And because he was the "stricken husband," he was the darling of the media. Odd how it all worked out. The man who caused it all became the martyr while the true martyr, the artist, became the pariah. They didn't understand that Will Ross had brought this on himself.

Not at all. They never understood.

And now, city editorials called Peter a coward. A radio-show host called him a psycho. While he was listening! He was called a creep, a deviant, antisocial, psychotic, and hate filled.

None of which was true.

He was just a man on a mission, with a goal to achieve, a place to shine, a curious need to have the world show its respect for his good works and his strong sense of self and his talents, his unusual, exceptional talents. His talents that rivaled and exceeded anyone else's.

He'd show them. He'd show them all.

Now they owed him an apology as well as the rest of it. The entire city. And Will Ross.

Will Ross still had a debt to pay. Will Ross was not free of him yet. Will Ross owed him. Big time.

"I'm not done with you yet."

He stumbled across the kitchen to the door, the magic door, took a deep breath, unlocked it, and looked down into the darkened basement, the corner of his world where he felt the most power and control, the space where his rage dropped away in a flurry of deadly creativity.

His element. His life.

For a short time, he had thought he wouldn't need it again. But he did. He needed it to finish the game, he needed it for his own sense of self-worth.

This should deal with the night sweats. A little pyrotechnic creativity during the day, and he would sleep tonight. Burn off the psychic memories of the past, if those indeed were the souls wandering through his room. Get back to work. That was the answer. That he knew. The answer to all of life's problems was a mere thirteen steps below where he stood right now.

He felt a delicious shudder run through him as he paused at the open door, then took a deep breath to steady his own sense of excitement and stepped back into his world.

The world of Peter the Great.

This wasn't over at all.

This had merely been a pause, a break, an intermission.

Relax, everyone. The danger is past.

Not by a long shot.

Will Ross was not out of the woods yet, nor was TV6, nor the city and county of Denver.

They needed to be amazed.

He was too close to success now. They owed him.

They owed him their fear. Their thanks. What was rightfully his.

He had a game to play. He had a job to do.

He stepped down the stairs and pulled the door closed behind him.

CHAPTER ONE

HEARTS AND MINES

WILL STOOD AT THE DOOR FOR WHAT SEEMED AN ETERNITY, ALTERnately shaking with chills and wiping the sweat off his face. There was really no reason for this, he kept telling himself, no reason at all, for it wasn't all that hot and there certainly was no danger within, no threat, just a tidal wave of sympathy to deal with, people trooping up, sullen faced, wringing hands, telling him oh how terribly tragic it all is ... how can you even bear to come back to work?

He'd have to come up with an answer.

Mortgage was good. That was the short answer—that he knew. Mortgage. No, honestly, that wasn't it at all. Money could wait. There was enough set aside. It was time. It was just time to move again. It was time to get his life moving in some direction, any direction, up, down, or sideways. And then there was the ache. The ache grew stronger whenever he sat alone or, especially, sat with Elena. It lightened, somewhat, whenever there was something to do: spin out a rim, tighten a bracket, even wrap a handlebar. So if he got busy, then, well, everything would eventually work itself out.

Right?

But what did he tell the faces? The faces that would swarm around him and expect an answer that he couldn't give and that wouldn't mean anything to them other than noise?

Will sighed. He could tell them *mortgage* and they'd all understand. You bet. Gotta pay the bills. Ain't life a bitch? Gotta pay the man. They'd understand and nod and get away from him as fast as humanly possible because widows and widowers, fresh-minted especially, are such incredible bummers.

It's a cancer of the heart. Sorry, pal. Don't want to catch what you've got.

Better you than me, pal; better you than me. There but for the grace of God go …

Will shook his head to clear the acid thoughts that piled on, one after another, and shook his arms and hands as if to loosen up. It didn't help, but it was something to do. It felt right. He took one step, then another and then another, one cascading now on top of the last, strode to the door, reached for the handle, pulled it, and stepped back into the world he had left so abruptly exactly six weeks before, left for a bicycle race that had changed his life.

Who could have imagined that?

Shirley at the door jerked in surprise, then gave Will a sad smile and a wave and buzzed him in. Her eyes glistened, but she never left her great glass booth. Smart lady. She was safe in there. She could show sympathy and express herself but not have to deal with it directly. Not have to hug or kiss or shake a hand or say a kind word.

Smart lady.

The others weren't so smart.

The word was out, mysteriously, quite obviously, that Will had returned. People poured out of offices on the first and second floors. The sales department, up top, looked to see if he was back for real and worth selling, adding a few waves for good measure. The production folks on the other side, lower, waved as well, keeping their distance.

Andy Andropoulos stuck his head out of his second-floor office door.

Will waved. Andy nodded and said, "Good to have you back, Will."

"Thanks, Andy."

Andy nodded again, waved, and stepped back into the safety of his office.

Nobody moved. The atmosphere carried the tension of a heavily armed standoff. Slowly, people melted back into office doors or turned, suddenly remembering something, and made for the back of the building, away from the unprotected openness of the atrium.

Will did the same.

He looked to his right and the double doors leading to the news department, hoping maybe there was safety in there, hiding out with the news of the day, hiding in a place where murder, death, and destruction were the norm, especially if there was compelling video.

Will stepped quickly to the doors and peered through the single square pane of glass set in the door, only to see a meeting under way, with Barbara Gooden and a bearded man Will didn't know quietly telling the staff something. It didn't look like a morning meeting, at least the ones Will had seen in the few weeks after he started at TV6. This was something different. More like a sermon, or a lesson, or rules for living.

A phone rang next to Barbara, catching her in midsermonette. The man beside her answered it, nodded, hung up, and whispered in Barbara's ear. Barbara nodded and brought her speech to a quick end. One last reminder of some kind.

She straightened her jacket and looked toward the doors, seeing Will's face framed in the square of glass. She donned a smile and quickly stepped off the assignment desk platform, the unknown man directly behind her, the staff then following the two of them like lemmings heading for the cliff. The look of love and concern on Barbara Gooden's face frightened Will to the point that he jumped quickly back from the newsroom door and for a second considered making a break for freedom.

Fifteen feet to the door. Keys. Car. Gone.

The newsroom doors burst open from the sheer force of Gooden's personality. She led the way, her hair, more golden than Will remembered it, actually shimmering as she passed through the streams of light that filtered in from various windows along the way. The effect was mesmerizing.

"Oh, my God," she moaned, trying to find the proper words, the proper tone to denote sympathy. Will steeled himself for the physical onslaught that was about to begin.

He forced a smile.

"Oh, my God, Will, it is so very good to have you back!" She sped up a bit so he couldn't run away, then wrapped her arms around him and crushed Will to her chest. He wiggled his chin into the nook between her neck and collarbone in order to breathe, then returned the hug, lightly, patting her on the back.

"Oh, God, Will, we are so sorry. ..."

"I know, Barbara," he said quietly. "I appreciate it. Everything. The time and the thoughts and prayers and everything you've done for me, us … us." Will kept forgetting to include Elena in his thoughts.

Other people were streaming out of the newsroom now. They were all wearing sad faces and sympathetic looks. There was safety in numbers. No one would have to deal with Will directly.

He suddenly realized what the meeting had been about. They knew he was coming back today. The meeting concerned how to act around the bereaved.

As each person shook his hand or hugged him and welcomed him back, he could hear the hum of their thought processes as they dealt with the moment, remembering tips, burying their honesty.

"Don't say, 'It was God's will,' don't cry, don't hug too long, don't say, 'You'll find somebody else,' don't ask for his wife's old tennis racket, make eye contact, but don't hold it for long, for God's sake, don't stare, and whatever you do, don't act like it's going to rub off and you're going to catch his bad mood, bad luck, or the death shadow that's hanging over him like a small-pox-infected blanket."

Will hugged, Will squeezed, Will nodded, Will thought, "Christ, I've got to get back to the sports department." He suddenly realized that deep in the heart of the great sports beast he was safe, as if the sports department was the one safe place in this building, at least for now, the one place in the world where the level of existing sympathy was tied directly to what had happened in the Major League Baseball pool over the weekend. His stomach was beginning to hurt.

He shook hands and nodded as quickly as he could, looking as accepting of their sympathies as he could under the circumstances, even those from people he didn't know, the bearded man, some heavily perfumed dame with a nasty look in her eye … Will's mind shut off. His feelings were buried. His consciousness was on hold. He blindly shook and nodded and shook and nodded and shook.

The nodding, smiles, and shaking continued until he felt like one of those bouncy-headed dogs in the back window of a Chevy with bad shocks on South Broadway. He shook and nodded and continued until suddenly he realized that the last handshake had already turned back toward the news-room and hustled through the safety of the heavy double doors.

Barbara Gooden and the unidentified bearded man stood silently beside him for what seemed like an endless streetcar ride into the night. Finally Barbara said, "Will, why don't you get set up in the sports department again and just take your time getting back into the swing of it. When you feel like it, drop by my office and we'll chat about getting you back up to speed, okay?"

She smiled, the desire to weep and crush him to her breast nearly overwhelming her sense of managerial professionalism. The walking beard beside her merely smiled and nodded. Barbara sighed. The beard sighed. Together they turned and walked, match step, back into the newsroom.

Standing alone in the lobby, Will swore he could hear crickets chirp. He turned and looked across the emptiness. The place was as dead as it would be at 7 A.M. on a Christmas morning. Doors were shut. His coworkers were in hiding. He took a deep breath and began the long, slow walk across the lobby to the sports office.

That door was still open. Always had been. Always would be. He stepped in.

"Welcome home, asshole."

Zorro.

The familiar voice began to cackle.

"I missed La Barbara's little meeting on dead-people etiquette, so don't expect me to do anything right, okay?" Clyde Zoromski never took his eyes off the four TV monitors set into the wall. "Goddamn it! Don't any of you assholes know how to play this game? Jesus Christ!"

Will leaned casually against the door frame, partly for a look of easy confidence, partly to simply hold himself up. He felt heavy.

Zorro turned back and forth between Will and the TV monitor, on which lurked the feed of an early-afternoon game from Shea. He was thinking, deciding something. His eyes widened, then narrowed, as if there was a great battle inside his head.

Zorro decided.

He stepped quickly across the short space of the sports office and bear-hugged Will, lifting him off the ground and squeezing him tightly. He set him down, hard, on the carpeted floor next to Will's desk.

"I'm sorry," Zorro said.

"Thanks," Will answered, rubbing the feeling back into his biceps.

"If you ever tell anyone I did that or that I had a tear in my eye—thank God you're back—then I'll break your goddamned neck. Understand?"

"Yeah, understand."

"Did Gooden kiss you? She loves kissin' people when they're sad. It's like she's the goddamned Good Witch of the North, and she kisses you to grant your every psychic wish."

"What the hell are you talking about?"

"Jesus, I don't know. Now, are you back for good, or is this just a check-it-out kind of session to see if you can handle living again?"

Will was struck by the audacity of the question, but also relieved. Zorro was the first person to not treat him with kid gloves since the funeral. It was a pleasant feeling to be seen as flesh and blood again and not some kind of bone china.

"Back for good, I think. Yeah, I think."

"Good. It's been me and Flynn for the last few weeks, and you can imagine the kind of work we get out of that son of a bitch. He goes on the road with the Broncos, he wanders off on a road trip with the Rockies, he's here, he's there, he's nowhere near this place, that's for goddamned sure."

"Didn't they hire any fill-in, any backup?"

"Some guy out of Mizzou, Denver kid, buddy of the new news director. You met the new news director? He's a pip, that's for goddamned sure. All beard and tough talk. Walked in the first day and threatened everybody's job. 'You don't want to be here and work my hours, you can get the hell out,'" Zorro bellowed in a tough, sarcastic tone. "He meant it, though. Shit, he meant it."

"What do you mean?" Will asked.

"You seen Sessions around anywhere?"

Will shook his head. Bill Sessions. Assistant news director. He had hired Will and supported him right through the bike race and its aftermath. No, Will hadn't seen Sessions.

"What happened?"

Zorro shook his head.

"Damnedest thing. Ransford, this new news director, was doin' the bully routine for the sake of the troops—'I'm gonna whip you into shape,' that sort of thing, you know the riff. ..."

"Yeah," Will said, smiling. "The new-coach scare speech."

"Yeah." Zorro nodded happily. "You know it. You've got it. Well, anyway, this asshole is doin' this speech and in the middle of it, Sessions stands up and challenges him, says that this is an experienced, veteran news operation that doesn't need to be talked down to and doesn't need to be 'belittled'— actually used the word—'belittled.' The guy just stared at Bill and within moments, moments, Sessions was fired, and two security guards escorted him out of the building. Can you believe that shit?"

"What did Barbara do? She let him get away with that?"

"She wasn't there. It was his show. And before she found out about it, the news director over at Channel 4 snapped him up and gave him a raise. That fast. Boom! Yer out. Boom! Yer in. Made everybody here sit up and say 'howdy,' that's for goddamned sure. Only person safe in here is the guy's new playmate. Jeeeezus. She's a piece of work. Anyway, he knew your replacement from some- place, and he'll be in about two-thirty to try and push you out of your desk. He took it over rather than use Ol' Jay's over there. I think he wants your job, which means I think he wants my job, which means I think he wants Flynn's job, and with his pal as news director, he just might get two of the three."

"Two?"

"I'll kill the little fucker if he tries to take mine. I'm trying to buy a new car."

Will stopped and thought for a moment, then shook his head as if to rat- tle the questions around to the proper place for processing.

"So, what's Barbara now if she's not news director? I mean, she was in the lobby. Came out of the newsroom like a house afire. She's not news director anymore?"

Zorro laughed.

"Oh, no. Miss Barbara, well, she's big-time management now. They've bumped her upstairs, title and everything. Got her a new office and every- thing. She's 'vice president of news and community affairs' for the whole chain of Stoval stations. She still runs the show here, don't you know it, but she flies out a couple times a month to consult the other stations in the chain on how to do the news and get great numbers."

Will was enjoying the rant. He encouraged it.

"And do they?"

"Get great numbers?" Zorro chuckled. "Look, we get good numbers, overall numbers. But we skew old. Our audience is damned near ancient. Old people love us. Old people and people with green teeth. Our audience is literally dying off. That's not just here, that's Cleveland and Atlanta and Jacksonville and Philly and San Diego. It's Barbara's job to keep those viewers happy and recharge their pacemakers once every six months.

"With your wife and the exploding basketball, we played the emotional angle—and the old people loved it. They'll just love you too. They'll look at you like an episode of *The Waltons*."

Zorro said it not maliciously but as a statement of fact, then realized what he had said and froze and stared, waiting for a reaction. Will froze for a moment as well, hearing the words, processing, the cogs whirring and meshing, the mind waiting for the moment when the heart bunched up and the tears gathered at the corners of his eyes. They didn't. There was nary a twinge.

He hadn't cried much at the time it had happened—shock, he guessed— and he hadn't done much, if any, weeping since. Now, faced directly with that moment in his life, he realized that the bottom hadn't dropped out, not completely, but that there was still a joist or two to balance on while he got his life back together.

Will sighed deeply, then nodded.

"I understand. So, uh, who's this news director?"

"Hugh Ransford. Some guy Barbara met at the Boinker Foundation."

"What's that?"

"It's some place in New York City where all the little news managers go to mentally masturbate for a couple of days in a row about how nobody in their newsroom appreciates their glorious grasp of the profession," he said, speaking through his nose, "before coming up with all kinds of great ideas that don't work in the real world but get imposed on stations nationwide."

Will turned to his desk and moved old and unfamiliar papers to new and unfamiliar piles. He nodded. He'd meet this guy soon enough, he figured.

"Did I miss anything while I was gone?"

Zorro scrunched his face and thought for a second, the images of the past month flitting through his head as quickly as they had flitted across the TV screen. "Oh, yeah, couple of doozies. Some guy at the state house chased his girlfriend down the street with a screwdriver—that was fun. I wanted to put it in as running, but Barbara snagged it for news. Then the goalie for the local hockey team knocked a door off its hinge during an argument with his wife. Didn't get that one either. Lead story that night. We crucified the guy."

"Did he deserve it?"

"Who knows? Everybody was so cranked about the fact he was a goalie, nobody bothered to see if it was really a story."

"Anything we had—like in the sports report?"

"Nah. Same old, same old. Win, lose, trades, players on pills—wait, no, that was news too—nope, just the scores."

He gave Will an "oh, well," kind of look.

"Gee, you're cheery. Uplifting even, given our chosen profession."

"Naw. Just realistic," Zorro muttered. "We're doing a job, nobody likes us for it, nobody takes us seriously. I just want to get along. Pay the mortgage, save for retirement, get the hell out."

"Then why do it?"

Zorro looked at Will for a long moment, then stood, took his Broncos '99 coffee mug, and headed toward the door. He stopped, turned to Will, and said in a hushed tone, barely audible, "Because I haven't had to sell one pair of shoes today."

He smiled and raised his eyebrows, then turned toward the hallway leading to the coffee machine. As he took big, galoomping strides toward his regular caffeine fix, Zorro cranked his head and shouted over his shoulder, "And remember—you didn't choose this profession, Willie—it chose you."

Staring at the empty door for a long moment, Will pondered the words and wondered why *he* was doing this. He tapped a pencil on the side of his computer and couldn't come up with an answer. A duck wearing a top hat nodded in agreement with no one in particular and dipped its head into a glass of water.

Much as Will had been doing for the past few weeks.

"LET'S TALK TO BARBARA AND GET HER TAKE ON THE IDEA."

Hugh Ransford made a face and shook the question away, then leaned back until the springs on the old wooden office chair groaned in agony. Ransford might have been the news director at TV6 since Barbara Gooden had moved upstairs, but though the title was his, the job and the office were mere show. Barbara Gooden ran the operation from her aerie on the second floor, and Ransford knew he'd better get used to that fact if he wanted to succeed here, make a name, and leap to a bigger market.

The springs groaned again as Ransford leaned forward, put his elbows on the desk, and pushed his eyeballs into the back of his head with the palms of his hands.

"No, she'd torpedo it right away, and if she torpedoes it, it's dead," he whispered. "We'd never get around her, we'd never get it on the air and she'd give him a high sign—she'd say something—which would ruin the story anyway. He'd know we were coming—it would never be honest. This one has got to be honest."

"Why do you let her run the show like that?"

Ransford pulled his palms away from his eyeballs, waited a moment for them to refocus, then stared at the woman across the desk, tall, brunette, long-legged, and good looking but with the sharp-edged air of a weasel.

"Because, my dear Beth, it's her show, and that's the way the game is played. We enjoyed free rein in Raleigh, but we're under the thumb of the Denver mafia now. And Barbara Gooden is the Godfather."

"Barbara Gooden is a bitch."

"Watch it. The walls have ears."

Beth Freeman leaned back with a sneer. "She's a bitch!" she shouted to the closed door.

"Done?"

"No. *Bitch!* Now I'm done."

"Good. You want this story. I think you should do this story. Barbara Gooden won't think so, and we'll both catch hell if we ask."

"Jesus. It's the story people want to hear. Give 'em what they want—even the Ice Queen says that on occasion."

"We've only been here a month."

"Yes, and in that month we've done jack shit in terms of stories. Is 55 really 55—or do they really ticket you at 65? How many breaks do city crews take in a day? Who parks where for Rockies games? Jesus. Your dead aunt could do those stories."

Beth Freeman shifted, looked out the window, curled her left index finger and buried it in her upper lip. She pulled it away quickly and turned back to Ransford, slapping her hands on the desk and slightly, ever so slightly, pushing her upper arms in, accentuating the line of her breasts.

"The stories we've got to do," she said, in a stern, almost schoolteacherish tone, "are pure emotional enterprise. The stories that piss people off, scare the shit out of them, or make them cry. You know that; I know that. Christ, even Lady Goodnews upstairs knows that. And you know—you know, Hugh—this one is going to make them cry."

She leaned forward for emphasis, drilling him with her eyes.

"The whole goddamned city is gonna weep 'til it barfs. You know that."

Ransford leaned back as if to run away and stroked his beard as if to hide from her. The action bought him some time to think. Beth Freeman might be a hard-ass, but she did have a point. Anger, fear, and tears were what made TV news work—local and national. Piss 'em off, make 'em weep, keep 'em up at night with new worries. Emotional peaks make the news, the show, the station, the career.

And she was right with this one.

This one was an emotional barn burner. Award winner, sure as shit. No doubt. But if Barbara Gooden got wind of it, then all bets were off. He stopped stroking his beard, picked up a pencil, and started tapping it on the cover of *Newsweek,* on top of the drawing of the killer asteroid that might be, could be, would be hurtling toward Earth in the next 10 minutes to 100 million years.

He turned the chair back to the desk with a squeak and leaned forward, his eyes following a line up past Beth's hands, through her cleavage, her throat, and her face, finally stopping at her eyes.

"How quiet can you keep this?"

"Even my dogs won't know. But I've got to have a photog I can trust."

"I haven't been able to bring in anybody full time yet. The shooters here have been here forever and are likely to remain so—not much turnover." He stroked his beard again.

"Fire one."

"Can't. After that asshole Sessions, Gooden has been watching me like a hawk. I've got to clear personnel through her."

"I wonder if we can hide a camera?"

"Without a photog?"

"Maybe. Maybe we can tell them we're working on another story. What about freelance?"

"It's gonna get back to Gooden," Ransford muttered. "She's watching the budget hard."

"So bring in Jeremy. Say he's visiting. Pay him on the sly," Freeman said, "out of some sideline budget. You've got those, don't you?"

Ransford leaned back in his grandfather's wooden office chair, the springs screaming again in protest.

"Gooden finds out, Andropoulos has a cow."

"He likes you," Freeman said with a knowing smile. "You're a guy. He likes working with guys—doesn't understand lady managers. He won't get pissed. And her—well, she'll find out only if we let her. Only if we let her."

Ransford grinned. "In other words …"

"It's better to ask forgiveness," Freeman said quietly, "than permission."

✳

WILL SHIFTED A PILE OF PAPERS TO THE RIGHT. HE SHIFTED A PILE OF PAPERS TO the left. He moved a pile of the new guy's personal effects from his desk to Jay's desk against the wall, then wondered why he had bothered. He hadn't been at the station or in any desk long enough to claim ownership on much of anything. But he realized that in such a territorial game, where you sat and what you claimed as yours played a big part in the life or death of your career: desk, stories, placement in a show, hell, even your chair. New producers got the shit chairs. Old-line anchors got the best. Since much of their day was spent sitting and thinking great thoughts, the choice of chair was important.

Besides, Zorro would have a fit if Will gave up his space, and Zorro wasn't worth the hassle.

He was still mindlessly moving things around an hour later, still opening mail and throwing away the letters, everything from "in deepest sympathy" to "we'll finance your new Ford," when a young man walked into the office, turned as if to drop what he was carrying on Will's desk, stopped, paused, cocked his head slightly as if considering whether he was in the wrong room, looked back at Will, paused again, and finally said, "Excuse me?"

"Huh?" Brilliant comeback, Will knew, but it was the best he could get off at the moment.

"I think you're in my desk."

"No. If I was in your desk, I'd be over there," Will thumbed over his shoulder at Jay's desk, "peering out of a drawer. The correct turn of phrase is, 'I think you're *at* my desk,' but that's not right either because I'm at *my* desk. That's your desk." He hiked the thumb again. Tough guy.

The young man pursed his lips, deciding whether to fight, then walked over to Ol' Jay's desk and put his stack of newspapers and a black shoulder bag on top of all the stuff Will had already put there.

He was about to say something to Will when Zorro walked in, full of caffeine and lunch, which might have included something liquid and alcoholic, Will wasn't sure, and brimming with attitude.

"Hey, hey, the gang's all here. Arthur Jackson, Will Ross, Will Ross, Arthur Jackson. I see you've lost the real estate battle, Art; that is too bad—but that's life in the big-city newsroom, now, isn't it?"

Arthur Jackson stared, hard, at Zorro for a moment, his lips tight, his face on the verge of going red. Zorro stared back, ready to punch the kid's lights out. The moment lasted maybe five seconds, seemed like ten, before Jackson broke, sat back, laughed, and nodded.

"Sorry. Sorry. Will," he turned away from Zorro and stuck out a hand, "I'm Art Jackson. Denver native, Mizzou grad, so I can't stand the CU Buffs, and I'm the fuckin' new guy here. Sorry I took your desk. That's the one Ransford pointed me into on my first day. My apologies."

Zorro snorted and walked out of the office. He couldn't stand *Father Knows Best* moments at the best of times. He probably wanted to punch somebody.

Will watched him go, turned back, and shook Jackson's hand.

"Nice to meet you. Will Ross."

"Sorry about …" Jackson got no farther before Will waved him off.

"Look, I appreciate that, but stop, okay? I've gotten so much sympathy today that I feel like I'm back at the funeral. And that's not necessary. I'm dealing with it. I'm okay. So let's just let it go—all right?"

"Sure. Sure. I'm sorry." Jackson nodded. "How's the baby?"

The question punched Will on the side of the head. He hadn't been expecting it. He hadn't been thinking of the baby at all. He hadn't included Elena in the psychic circle of his "I'm okay" statement.

"She's, uh, she's good. She's fine. Yeah." He recovered. "She's with her grandmother right now. She's staying with us. Yes. Yeah. She's fine."

Art Jackson nodded sympathetically. Behind the smile he had a single thought.

Bingo.

※

HUGH RANSFORD LOOKED OUT THE WINDOW OF HIS OFFICE INTO THE MURK OF A late-summer Denver brown cloud. It was like looking at a college boy's sheets six weeks after their last trip to the laundromat.

"When do you want to do this?" he asked.

Beth Freeman adjusted her jacket and touched the corner of her lips.

"I'm going to have to get to know him a bit first, but I'd say we can shoot in a week if you can get Jeremy here. Shouldn't be too hard. Widower. Looking for an ear. An idea that he's still attractive. Lady-killer."

"Bad choice of words."

"Ha. Yeah. Sorry," she said with exaggerated sarcasm. "But let's say a week. I can let you know by tomorrow if I'm going to need more time."

"Don't take too long. I like what Art is doing on the air, and I don't want to waste my time bringing along one of Sessions's hires if the guy can't cut it or pull himself together."

"Don't worry. Once we have the interview it's just a question of getting inside the house for video of the kid and pictures of the wife. Two weeks, tops."

"Then?"

Beth Freeman leaned forward onto Hugh Ransford's desk, smiled in a vague and ethereal way, and spoke the hard reality in a soft tone.

"Then? Then you can fire his ass."

※

THE FIVE O'CLOCK NEWS WAS UNDER WAY. WILL SAT ALONE AT HIS DESK, STARING at the one truly personal effect he owned in the office: a photo of Cheryl, riding hard in a mountain-bike race in Vail two years ago. Two years? Was that it? So long, so short, he couldn't judge time anymore.

He stared, and he smiled.

I do miss you, he thought. I do, more than you'll ever know.

The picture didn't answer him. His heart did not fill with joy or sadness or loss or anything.

Nothing. There was nothing beyond the silence of the atrium and the quiet mutter of Zorro filling in for Roger Flynn on one of the monitors in the background.

The phone rang.

Without looking away, without breaking his mood, Will reached over and picked up the receiver. As soon as he put it to his ear, he froze.

There was a long pause. Finally, in a quiet and almost trembling voice, Will whispered, "Sports—Ross."

There was another long pause. Finally Will heard a voice that sent a cold knife deep into his heart, generating the first strong feelings he had had in six weeks.

The voice was quiet. Assured. And deadly.

"Hello, Clarice," it said with a chuckle.

"I'm back."

CHAPTER TWO

INTO THE MAZE

R AYMOND WHITESIDE WALKED BRISKLY DOWN THE GOVERNMENT-
designed and -engineered halls of the Denver Police Department,
trying to stay one step ahead of his day. He had four cases working
this afternoon, including a weekend doozy of a head found floating in a pond
after a late-summer downpour. No body was attached, just a floating head
getting in the way of an impromptu fishing trip for two neighborhood boys.

Given the reaction of the one who had really found it, reeling in what he
first thought was a basketball, Whiteside doubted the boy would ever consider fish a primary source of protein in future diets. Top that off with two
domestics and a police chase and shooting, with half the annual department
bullet budget now lodged in a 1982 Cavalier and a LoDo wall as well as the
guy who had jacked the car after a night of binge drinking, and Whiteside
knew he'd be here late again tonight. So much for thoughts of dinner and a
movie, or even a good laugh as the local TV reporters mangled the stories on
each of his cases in their late reports.

Twenty-five feet ahead, Paul Timmons stuck his head into the hallway
and scanned quickly in both directions. Whiteside recognized the look and
considered turning on his heel, making tracks in a new direction, but there
was only one direction to go—back—unless he wanted to duck into somebody else's office. He paused, sighed, stutter-stepped, and kept walking forward. Seeing Whiteside, Timmons straightened up and gestured.

"You've got a call on 62."

"Any idea who it is," Whiteside asked, "or do I get to guess?"

"It's a voice from your past," Timmons answered with a tired smile.
"That's all I'm going to say." He turned back into the Homicide office to

continue *his* day finding the remaining seven-eighths of the body left behind by whoever had turned a human head into a fishing bobber.

Whiteside entered the office and walked to his desk, calling across the room to Timmons, "Any luck yet?"

"Naw," Timmons replied. "Dental records aren't in, Missing Persons hasn't called back, and Forensics hasn't even identified the sex. But the body can't be far. These things tend to travel together."

Whiteside snorted a gallows laugh that loosened something in his sinuses. He wiped his nostril with the back of his right index finger and answered the phone with his left hand, punching the line at the same time.

"Detectives. Whiteside."

The voice on the other end was agitated, but Raymond Whiteside recognized it immediately.

Ross.

"Ray. Hi. This is, uh, Will Ross. We haven't talked in a few weeks, and I, well, I still have your card—and I—hell. Whiteside, he called."

"Who called?"

"He called. The bomber. The killer. The little asshole that killed my wife."

Raymond Whiteside took a moment, cleared his mind of everything currently taking up space, and pondered the remaining thought. He sat down, took a pen, pulled a yellow legal pad toward him, and began to take notes in a large, loopy hand.

"Are you sure, Mr. Ross?"

"Yeah, I'm sure," Will said with a tone of harsh exasperation. The police drove him crazy, leading him through the simplest questions with the patronizing style of Regis Philbin, though until now he hadn't counted Raymond Whiteside among those using that style.

"It could have been somebody just screwing around, Mr. Ross."

"No, it was him. I have no doubt at all. Same voice. Same tone. Same threats. He's still here. He's still in town. It was him."

"Did you get a chance to record him? Or get a caller ID on the number?"

Will rubbed his eyes and gritted his teeth. "No, I didn't, Ray, seeing as how your guys took out all the equipment during the funeral six weeks ago—then sent me a bill for the stuff they couldn't find."

"I'm sorry about that, Mr. Ross. So you didn't get anything on him this time?"

"No, Ray, sorry, just my ear," Will snapped, trying to keep his temper. He paused, then added, "You'll be happy to know he's still got the same fucking sense of humor."

Whiteside was thrown for a moment by the edge in Will's voice. The last few times he had spoken with Will, some two and a half weeks before on a follow-up call, it had been like talking to Rip Van Winkle ten minutes after he awoke from his twenty-year nap. He had been a man in a serious state of shock: exhausted, uncaring. Now he was brittle, on some sort of manic high, ready to leap through the phone and throttle Whiteside with the news.

"Are you there, Ray?"

"Yes, Mr. Ross. Yes, I am. I'm just surprised. ..."

"You're surprised, shit! Two weeks ago you're telling me this guy has gone to ground. He's either run away to East Timor because Chuck Green is belittling him in the *Denver Post* or he's lying low until you guys give it up. Odd, you've never told me he's as good as caught. Is he as good as caught, Ray?"

"What time was the call, Mr. Ross?"

"Two-sixteen. I marked it down."

"What did he say, Mr. Ross? Exactly?"

Will sighed.

"He did this Hannibal Lecter thing, with 'Hello, Clarice,' and then he said, 'I'm back.'"

"Then ..."

"Then nothin'. He draws out the 'I'm back' like the kid in *Poltergeist*, then hangs up. That's it. The line was quiet for a second, then he hung up. End of call, end of story."

Whiteside tapped dots around the few fresh notes with the tip of his pen. "You're sure it was him?"

"Yes, I'm sure," Will barked. "The little fucker is playing with me again, Ray."

"All right, Mr. Ross, all right."

"Hey, why the hell are you so unconvinced that he'd call me back and start this shit all over again? Didn't you ever think he might have unfinished business with me?"

"Look, Mr. Ross—let me just say I'm surprised—if he did come back— let's say he did—that he made direct contact with you. We've got an FBI pro- file of the bomber that says he's gone. He's done his work and moved on. He loves the attention but hates the condemnation. If he is still in town and does reappear, then you will no longer be the target."

"You're sure?"

"They're sure. And they've been doing this for a long time."

"Bullshit," Will said, sharply.

"Now, Mr. Ross," Whiteside said calmly.

"No, Bullshit. Capital B Bullshit. They're guessing and you're hoping, Ray. You're hoping this guy wandered off to Baltimore and is calmly blowing up people in somebody else's backyard. Well, fuck that. He's still here. He doesn't give a rat's ass about the *condemnation*, and he's looking to fuck up my life a little bit more."

"I understand how upset you are, Mr. Ross. We'll come out to the sta- tion and put the recorder and caller ID back on your line. You still have them at home?"

"I still have them at home."

Ross was starting to calm down. Good. Whiteside began to ease him away from the truth of the matter.

"Very good, Will, very good."

"Okay, so what do we do?"

"Well, I'll be very honest with you: we're back to square one. I'm sorry. I'll send out an officer to check the phones at the station—see if we can get a fix on the number he called from, which as you remember never really worked the first time. That phone system out there, well—and he's clever enough to use pay phones or random dead-end lines—but still, we can try. We'll see what we can do. Do you feel threatened, Mr. Ross?"

"What?"

"Do you feel threatened by the call? Do you want us to put protection on you and your house?"

"Well, yes. No … I don't know. Yes, for Christ's sake. This guy has tried it once. He'll try it again, sure as shit."

"You're afraid he'll come after you again?"

"Well, yeah," Will answered angrily. "He's still got some bug up his ass about me. But whenever he comes after me, he kills everybody else. He's a lousy shot who never hits his target."

"The target being ..."

"The target being me."

"Okay. This is what I'll do. We'll increase uniforms in your neighborhood for the next few nights to keep an eye on your house. We'll check the phone records at the station. We'll reactivate the case. ..." Whiteside froze. Shit. Too much, too far.

"What do you mean, reactivate the case?" Will asked.

Whiteside cursed silently. He put down his pen and stood in front of the desk, making a small pacing loop in his nervousness.

"I didn't mean that, Will—so much has been going on lately that we've had to pull some of the investigating officers off your wife's case and put them on other things. This call will just help us get them back—that's all, Will—that's all."

"Okay, okay, Detective. I understand. Just know that he called. I'll stay in touch."

Whiteside struggled to recover from his blunder.

"What if I come out to the station, Will? What if I come out and we can talk about this. ..."

"No. No. That's okay, Detective. My statement would be just what I've told you already. Two-sixteen. Phone call. No more than thirty seconds. That's it."

"I could still come out, Will."

"No, I'm busy, you're busy, and it would probably be a waste of time. You've got it all, we'll just, well, we'll just keep an eye on the situation and try not to get blown up, okay?"

"I've got it, Will. I've got it." There was a long pause. "Look, we're going to find him, Will. I promise you that. We're going to find him and nail the bastard."

"Right. Good. Thanks, Detective. I appreciate it."

"Stay in touch, Will. Okay? Promise? Stay in touch."

"You got it." Will hung up.

Whiteside stared at the floor, put the receiver down, and collapsed into his chair with a groan that made Timmons look up from the coroner's report on the disembodied head.

"What you got?"

"Oh, man, I just royally screwed up with the husband of a murder victim."

"How's that?"

"Essentially, I just let Will Ross know that his wife's murder investigation has slipped to the back burner and is quietly simmering until something new pops up."

"So?" Timmons asked with a quiet laugh. "Somebody ought to let him know the realities of big-city life."

"I suppose," Whiteside answered. "But Ross says he got a call today from the killer."

"Really?" Timmons said, surprised.

Whiteside chewed his lip in thought. "Yes—no—maybe. Dunno. We'll send somebody to check. That phone system out there is so screwed up, though, you'd never know who called in, or from where. They keep meticulous records for calls out so no employee screws the company, but calls coming in are a different story."

"So just tell him, 'Sorry, bud. A random call isn't enough. We need the guy to make a move before we can nail him.'"

"In other words, we need the guy to kill you or your kid or your dog or the rest of your goddamned family before we can do anything."

"Well, Jesus, Ray. That's the way it goes sometimes. The bad guy disappeared. He set up a few major devices that didn't go off and a simple secondary that did. Then he disappears, what, six weeks, two months ago? Not a word? Not a peep? Not a single Black Cat tossed in a dumpster? There are only so many leads you can follow, man. Only so many things you can do if the bad guy isn't moving around and making mistakes. This one isn't. This one went underground. This one pulled a disappearing act."

"I know."

"Even with cases like that kid in Boulder, you can't keep the heat on forever. Especially when nobody—including the bad guy—cooperates."

"I know."

Timmons was quiet for a long moment as if pondering whether to proceed down the path that had been laid out in his mind but never traversed beyond a boldfaced headline in a supermarket tabloid.

"Besides," Timmons said, almost under his breath, "what do you know about this one, Ray? What do you think about this guy?"

Whiteside rubbed his eyes one last time and looked at his partner.

"What do you mean?"

"What do you think? What's the basic rule of thumb in a case like this?"

"I don't follow."

"Police 101: Follow the Money or Follow the Family."

"I'm not sure about that, Paul."

"Well, with a disappearing act like this," Timmons stood and began to walk the room, pondering the case in the air before him, "is the guy gone and gone for good? Sure seems that way. Been awfully quiet. The case gets slow. The case gets quiet. Too quiet for the husband's good. No more attention. No more headlines. Then, suddenly, the husband is saying, 'Oh, no, Mr. Bill, he's back!'"

Whiteside smiled at Timmons's falsetto.

"You gotta wonder, Ray. You gotta wonder."

"Wonder what, Paul?"

"Oh, come on. You gotta wonder if it's the husband. I'm just saying." Timmons raised his hands in defense of his position. "I'm just saying. We've got too many missing pieces that the husband fits into."

Whiteside shook his head slowly, then stopped and stared out the window into a very hot and bone-dry Denver day.

"I know," he said finally. "I've thought the same thing. But remember, I was there in Breckenridge. I saw him."

"Yeah. You saw him (a) find the bomb in the planter, and (b) find the bomb in his satellite phone. Convenient. If a bomber with any skill at all set two bombs, what are the chances that the target, without the slightest idea what to look for, would find them both in, what, ten minutes' time?"

"What about the secondary on the porch? What about the bomb that killed his wife?"

"Did anybody see it planted? How many people are going to notice a small ball on a porch, Ray? Could have been there all day."

"He says ..."

"He says, Ray, *he says*—but who knows? Who knows? He lays low for six weeks, things get quiet, then suddenly he calls you back and starts making noises again. He killed the wife. Got away with it. Pretty clean. Maybe he wants to kill the kid now."

"Oh, Jesus, Paul, stop."

"Why not? Why the hell not, Ray? It fits. It makes sense. It even fits the FBI profile. Timing. Attitude. Targets. Opportunity. Guy in need of attention. Nice fit, there, Ray. Ex-athlete with nothing to live for ... hey?"

"No, Paul, no ... you watch too much TV."

"Possibilities, Ray. That's what this job is all about."

Timmons gathered up the photos of the pond where the floating head had been found and tapped them on his desk, then shoved them into a manila folder. He slid the packet into yet another folder, which went into a larger, olive-colored sleeve. He tapped the entire assemblage on the desk again, started to walk toward the door, then stopped at Whiteside's desk.

"Possibilities, Ray. That's all this job is. Possibilities. It may be full of shit, but you've still got to think it through."

Timmons turned and walked out the door.

Raymond Whiteside turned toward the window, turned back, bent his chair back, then forward, and leaned heavily on the top of his standard government-issue, industrial-steel desk. He drummed the top of his legal pad, directly over the notes he had made during the phone call, thinking about Will Ross and phone threats and cold cases and bombs and unspeakable possibilities. Quiet searches of the Ross house, ostensibly looking for other devices, had turned up nothing even remotely resembling bomb-making equipment or knowledge. Nothing in Will Ross himself, his life or his personality, seemed to indicate the necessary knowledge, training, or intent. Still, Whiteside knew such surface impressions meant nothing. He looked back at the small reminder of the month before in the upper left-hand corner of the desktop calendar, then turned, opened his right top drawer, and pulled out a photograph, a snapshot of a young woman in her prime riding a mountain bike across a treacherous piece of Colorado real estate.

She had fallen off his radar in the past few weeks, that was true, but now she had returned. Timmons may have been right, he thought, Timmons may have been full of shit, but his rant had reminded Whiteside of an important thought.

It was not for her husband, her mother, or her child that Raymond Whiteside decided in that moment to find Cheryl Crane's killer. It was for her. It was for the soul and memory of Cheryl Crane. The victim was eventually forgotten in this sort of thing, by the police, by the public—even by the family, sometimes—just as he had forgotten in the crush of new demands and crimes and murders and bureaucratic hurdles.

Whiteside carefully placed the photo in the edge of a frame on his desk. He stared at her face, alive with determination and excitement about the course, the road ahead.

"I'll find him," he said aloud to the picture. "I'll find him, Cheryl. You can count on me." He paused for a moment and stared at the picture. His focus drew him in close to her. "No matter where it leads."

Raymond Whiteside picked up the phone and called down to Records.

"I need everything we've got on the Cheryl Crane Ross killing—last month."

"Need it before tomorrow morning?"

"Need it tonight. Checking it out."

"Not before 6."

"I'll come down."

He hung up the phone and continued to stare at the picture.

"I'll find him, Cheryl. I'll run him to ground, and I will make—him—pay."

Standing quietly at the door, Timmons had watched the drama unfold over the past few moments, transforming his partner into a man possessed. He loved watching Whiteside catch the bit in his teeth. This was going to be fun. The reason Paul Timmons had gotten into police work in the first place.

Timmons smiled and called out, "Hundred bucks says the husband did it."

Raymond Whiteside sat silently at his desk staring at a small photo.

There were no takers.

*

WILL STARED AT THE PHONE FOR A LONG TIME, STILL REELING EMOTIONALLY from the first call, still stunned by the realization of the second, the realization that the case had cooled, that the investigation had stopped, that the officers and detectives had moved on to other cases, other murders, robberies, rapes and assaults, the stuff of daily living in the modern American city.

He felt as if somebody had just slapped him with a punching bag. When Whiteside had referred to reactivating the case, Will had realized with a sharp tug at the front of his brain that Whiteside had been calling him "Mr. Ross" during the entire call up to that moment. Not "Will," though they had been on a first-name basis in the earlier days of the investigation.

Suddenly, very clearly, Will had understood where his case and the death of his wife stood on the priority list for the Denver Police Department.

Way—down.

Will felt himself fill with the cold reality of what faced him. He was alone, frankly, in caring, something he hadn't had much time to do in the past few weeks. The sudden return of feeling tightened his chest and shortened his breathing. He had given it over to them to care about Cheryl, about the killer, about the danger still lurking in anything found anywhere by anyone.

Now it was his turn again.

Will had simply been trying to feel, something, anything, himself. His own emotions had beaten him up and left him for dead by the side of the road. He had lost his wife, in a heartbeat, because of his own foolishness and stupidity. He had allowed a nut job to get in close, to make threats that nobody, including himself, had taken seriously, and then to kill off the one person in his life who truly mattered.

Will had allowed it. He had allowed it to happen. It was almost as if he had helped. And now he was allowing the police to walk away from the investigation and give the killer a free shot at whatever Will had left in his life. What was he to them? To the killer, a target. Shit, Will didn't have the slightest idea why. To the police—what was he to the police? Bait? Dangle him out there and see if the killer bites again and blows him up? Or Rose, or the dogs, Rex and Shoe? The house?

What else was there? What else was there? The realization hit him like a cold bucket of water in the face.

Elena. Oh, God. Elena.

The baby. He leaned down and held his forehead with his right hand. He hadn't even included the baby in his thoughts. Jesus God Almighty. What kind of father was he? What kind of man? He had been pushing her away since the very first day. What? In blame? In sorrow? In shock?

There was no excuse. No goddamned excuse. What kind of human being had he allowed himself to become? Who had died on his front porch? Who had died in the emergency room of Denver Health Medical?

Who had died, really? Cheryl or him?

Cheryl or Will?

Or both?

Get busy living or get busy dying. Get busy dying. He was already dead. He took a breath. Then another. It rattled in his chest. The breath hurt. He took another. And another. He felt like a man rising from the depths of a cold lake, fighting to reach the surface before his lungs burst. They burned and his eyes watered and he knew he couldn't make it. He couldn't make the surface. Not this time, unless he kicked one more time, one more, and reached for …

The phone rang. Will jumped.

He paused for a moment, almost fearful, before picking it up.

"Sports," he said quietly, "Ross."

"Will—hey, this is Bruce in the newsroom. If you feel up to it, why don't you wander over here? We've got an interview with some sculptor we'd like you to do this afternoon … if you feel like it. Do you feel like it?"

Will shook his head.

"Yeah," he gasped, grabbing his eyes and wiping away the tears. "Sure. What's this got to do with sports?"

"It's that two-million-dollar horse sculpture they've got for the new stadium. We're finally getting a shot at the guy who did it. Channel 4 had it tied up for months. Real simple. A little sound and a few pretty pictures for the Five. Sure you want it, man? We can give it …"

"No. That's fine. I'm on my way."

Will hung up the phone and gasped for breath, hard and fast, feeling each breath fill his lungs, then push itself out to make room for the next. Rise to the surface. Up to the light.

He didn't know what else to do. He pushed himself away from the desk and stood. Checked the heavy redness of his eyes in Roger Flynn's mirror, then picked up a pad and pen as he walked out the door of the sports office and across the empty atrium toward the newsroom.

Will stared straight ahead but saw nothing.

Nothing at all. Nothing around. Nothing behind.

Nothing coming at him, straight on, dead silent, right for the middle of his forehead.

WILDERNESS

The photographer was talking. Will looked at him, unseeing, unhearing, his face adorned with the look of a man who was feigning interest poorly, then turned forward and stared out the windshield, his face frozen in an empty smile.

Will was sliding through the dream again. Wherever he turned, he could see her on the edge of his vision, just beyond the periphery.

When he looked, full on, she was gone.

The car moved down 13th with a snap, snap, snap of hot tires against burning pavement, toward an interview with someone he didn't know, on a subject he didn't care about, filled with questions he hadn't thought of and couldn't seem to consider.

There, she was there again, just outside the corner of his eye.

"Are you there?"

"Is it you?"

Nothing. There was nothing.

I need you, Cheryl.

I need you.

Where are you?

CHAPTER THREE

SPINNING

ROSE CANGLIOSI WALKED FROM THE KITCHEN TO THE DINING ROOM, scrubbing her hands dry with a dishcloth. Dinner was done. Once again, her son-in-law hadn't eaten anything. He now stared at the TV set in the corner of the living room, tipping a bottle of Leinenkugel to his lips every few moments, his child asleep in the bassinet beside him.

"Hey," she called out in a sharper tone than she intended, her frustration at long last getting the best of her, "why don't you wake your daughter up and feed her? It's about time to feed her."

"Hmm? What?"

"Why don't you feed your daughter? It's about time to feed her."

Will looked into the bassinet. Elena was sleeping soundly.

"She's asleep." He turned back to the TV, a show about deadly shark attacks around the world that used a lot of thrashing water video and red-tinted backgrounds to heighten the suspense.

Rose flipped the towel over her shoulder, walked to the back of the couch, picked up the remote control, and turned off the TV. In the sudden silence, Will continued to stare at the screen as if nothing had happened.

"So wake her up. Either you do it now, or I'll be doing it in the middle of the night, and it's about time this child slept through the night and you actually had a hand in raising her."

It was a difficult statement for Rose to make, this declaration of abandonment of her one and only grandchild. She knew in her heart that she would walk to hell's door itself for anything this child could ever want or need. There was nothing this child would ever require in her life that wouldn't suddenly appear next to her right hand, courtesy of Rose Cangliosi, Rose's brother, and her friends.

The word was out: the girl already had twenty-five stepparents, most with lengthy and colorful criminal records of one sort or another.

Will sat silently for a moment, then turned toward Rose, his eyes red and rheumy. She was unsure whether that was from the beer, the lack of sleep, or the continuing heartache she knew he felt because she felt it as well.

"Can't you … ?"

"No, frankly, I can't," she said sharply. "I can't. I've been with her all day. I need a break," she lied. "I need a walk. I've made you dinner, I've cleaned the dishes, and I need to step out for just a moment to get my head on straight."

"All right. You can feed her when …"

"Nope. She needs to be fed now, and you are the likely candidate. A vote of the people. You win."

She dropped her voice to a gentler tone.

"Will, it's fine. I know what you're feeling. You're thinking you might break her. You're thinking you might hurt her. You and …" she paused a moment, took a deep breath to move the name aside, then continued, "you never got to share the joy of bringing her home, of passing her off, of being a part of something. A family. Well, the family now is you and her. You two. I'm just visiting. I'll go home eventually" (fat chance of that, she thought) "and you two will be relying on each other. Come on, Will. It's time to be a father."

Will could feel his face flush with shame, with anger, with acceptance. Yes, he had been a crappy dad; there was no argument with that. Elena was like a stranger to him, had been since the day she was born. Even stroking her in the Pediatric ICU at Children's Hospital, he had felt a distance, a dread, and a horrible thought that he couldn't shake in his madness over Cheryl's death.

"Why," he had thought, "why couldn't it have been you?"

So small, so frail, so perfect she was, but burdened with that thought and faced with a father who couldn't leave the shame behind, the shame of a moment, a thought, a statement to no one but himself.

Rose was wrong, Will knew, but he couldn't seem to reach across the gulf that had opened in that moment the day after Cheryl's death to forgive himself or allow Elena into his world—a place where she could never be safe.

Rose paused for a moment as Will stared off into space. Then she stepped to the bassinet and gently lifted the baby, rubbing her back to wake her up. Elena struggled for a moment but didn't cry, as if she were ready to wake and waiting only for the gentle touch of her grandmother to do it.

She stared at Rose with huge brown eyes, gurgled, then did her loose-necked, bouncy-headed-dog-in-the-back-window impression as she looked around the room. Her eyes stopped at Will and opened wider while her mouth wiggled into the rough approximation of a smile.

Will smiled back but didn't reach out for her. That didn't matter to Rose. She walked around the bassinet, stopped in front of Will, and placed the baby in his arms, carefully arranging her so her head was supported and she was properly aligned for feeding. She stood up and admired her handiwork. Father and daughter went well together.

"Be right back."

Will felt as if he was holding a piece of museum-grade china from the fifth century B.C. One breath and she would crack and fall to pieces in his lap. She stared at him, wiggled, and opened her mouth. Will shifted his weight, caught himself, and then slowly shifted again. Don't break, don't break, don't break, he begged.

She didn't.

Rose came back with the bottle and put it in Will's hand. It was warm to the touch. Will held it as if it might explode.

"I'm not sure if she's going to like this all that much. The doctor and I switched her over to a soy formula because she was really gassy and uncomfortable with the milk-based foods. Weren't you? Huh?" She leaned over and clucked Elena under the chin. "You were able to clear out a whole room, weren't you there, cutie?"

Elena focused her attention on Rose, then rolled her head back to face Will. Rose was her shining star, to be sure, but this one held dinner.

Rose stood, walked over to the closet, and pulled out a light jacket, one of Cheryl's old Haven windbreakers.

"I'm going for a walk. Should be about an hour. That should be enough time for you to get to know your daughter's feeding habits, which I have to say are impressive, and for you to get to know her just a bit. Support her head, yeah, like that, but don't worry. She's not going to break, Will. Honest."

"I don't know …"

"I don't care, Will. It's your baby. Get to know her. You don't do this now, my friend, you will hate her in about fifteen years and you will hate yourself in about twenty-one when she steps out the door for the last time."

"All because I didn't feed her tonight?"

Rose smiled.

"Yes. All because you didn't feed her tonight."

She turned and walked to the front door.

"So feed her, burp her, hold her—and save your soul."

She opened the door, stepped outside, called out, "Back in an hour," pulled the door closed behind her, and smiled again.

This was a good thing.

And she knew she'd be gone for only twenty minutes.

✸

WILL STARED AT THE ROUND FACE FOR A MOMENT, THE EYES GAZING UP AT HIM expectantly, the mouth straining to reach the nipple he held in his right hand.

"Hi," he said quietly. "Don't blame me as a teenager if I screw this up, okay?"

Elena didn't answer, her eyes locked on the food-delivery device in Will's hand. At this moment she didn't care who was feeding her, just that she was going to be fed.

Will gently lowered the bottle to Elena's mouth. The nipple went in, was sucked on hungrily, slid over to one side, and popped out, drizzling a stream of formula down the baby's cheek and onto Will's pant leg.

"Christ, swell," he muttered, then caught himself, realizing that he would have to start watching his language or Mrs. Boykin in kindergarten would get an earful five years down the road.

He readjusted as Elena watched him carefully. He slid the nipple back into her mouth, and she clamped her lips down, refusing to let it move a centimeter. There was a few seconds' pause as both sides juggled the bottle-nipple-mouth stalemate before Elena began to suck hungrily at the formula.

Will opened his eyes wide.

This kid could eat.

She was a Ross.

✺

BETH FREEMAN WAITED OUTSIDE THE BUNGALOW UNTIL THE OLD WOMAN TURNED the corner and disappeared up the street toward Colorado. It took the woman a good five minutes to do so because she kept stopping and looking back at the house as if there might be some loud noise or intangible signal calling her back. There wasn't. After a time, she walked northwest and disappeared.

Beth waited another moment, sure the woman would appear again at the corner to check on the house. She didn't. Beth took a breath, tugged her white silk shirt down taut over her breasts, pulled the aluminum pan from the King Soopers bag, and walked to the front door.

She paused at the door, considered again what she was going to say, and then knocked gently.

There was a pause; then she heard a muffled "Just a second" from inside. She looked down the street to see if there was any sign of the old woman returning. There wasn't. She turned back to the door, took a deep breath, and smiled.

The door rattled and opened. Will Ross stood in the doorway with a baby, her face riding a white cloth diaper, cradled over his shoulder.

Will stood for a moment, recognizing Beth but unsure who she was or where he had seen her. She was hoping for that.

"Hi, Will, how are you? I'm Beth Freeman from work."

"Work?"

"Yes, TV6?"

Will stared for a moment, his mind frantically recalling the day, the people he had met and remet at the station. Unless it was Zorro, Roger Flynn, Shirley at the front door, or Barbara Gooden, Will wasn't sure he'd recognize many people there.

He gave up.

"Yeah, hi, hi—how are you?" They stared through the screen for another moment before Will added, "Oh, sorry, sorry—come on in."

He unlocked and pushed open the screen. Beth stepped into the living room, exaggerating her smile to overcome the reaction to a room that smelled overwhelmingly of baby.

"Hi. We only met today, I realize, I'm new in Denver, but I just wanted to stop by and say 'hi' and ask if there was anything you might need—and drop this off."

She pushed the aluminum pan of store-made lasagna forward, more to simply get rid of it than as an offering, and stood shyly, expectantly.

"Oh, uh, gee. Well, thank you," Will mumbled, suddenly realizing that some action, any action, was called for on his part. "I uh … oh."

He tried to take the pan while holding Elena, realized that the aluminum was too flimsy to support a one-handed grab, tried to reach around Elena but felt her start to slip, then pretty much gave up.

"Let me put her down for a minute."

"Okay, I'm sorry," Beth said softly.

"No, no. No problem. I'm just not much of a baby juggler yet." He stepped over to the bassinet and began to pull Elena away from his shoulder. She started to cry. He pulled her back to his shoulder, and she stopped.

"Damn. Uh … here, uh. Can you bring that into the kitchen?"

This wasn't working the way Beth Freeman had hoped. She needed more time. She couldn't just drop off dinner, then leave. She needed a connection. She needed a touch. And then she knew.

"Do you mind? Could I take the baby?"

Will stopped for a moment.

"Uh, yeah, sure, I guess. Sure."

"Then you can take the lasagna into the kitchen and, well, since it's late, put it in the fridge. I'm a little late for dinner tonight."

She laughed.

Will smiled.

"Yeah, yeah, that makes sense."

His eyes drifted down to the pan of lasagna, which Beth held carefully just below her breasts. Will couldn't help looking at one without looking at the others. Beth took a deep breath.

"Well, let's see," Will said, pulling his eyes away and glancing around the room. "Why don't you put the pan there." He nodded toward the coffee table. "Then we'll do the pass-off."

"Okay," she said with a soft smile, stepping over to the table and bending slowly over it, accentuating her bottom. She rose up and smiled. Will had been watching that too.

"Okay, my turn with the beautiful baby—a girl, right?"

"Yeah, yes … her name is Elena."

"Elena. That's beautiful. Italian, isn't it?" She stretched out her arms to take the baby.

"Um, yeah, maybe. Her mother chose that name." He paused for a moment, then slowly pulled Elena off his shoulder, turned her clumsily, and handed her over to Beth, not releasing his grip until he was sure the woman had her securely.

"You didn't have a choice in the matter?"

"Well, sure, but I liked the name."

With great effort, Beth Freeman slowly pulled the baby to her shoulder. Elena didn't make a sound.

"I've got her. Why don't you get that into the fridge?"

Will watched for a moment to make sure Elena was safe in Beth's grip.

"Yeah, why don't I?"

He scooped up the lasagna tray, still warm on the bottom, and hustled it into the kitchen. "This is really nice of you," he called back over his shoulder.

"It's the least I could do," she called back, bouncing Elena, who was starting to wriggle, on her shoulder. "Stop moving, kid," Beth hissed, "or I'll bounce you off the wall and call it modern art."

Elena stopped wriggling.

Beth smiled. It worked for adults. It worked for kids. Attitude. There was nothing like it.

She could hear Will clinking and clanking in the kitchen, moving things around in the refrigerator to make room for the pan.

"Doing okay in there?"

"Yeah, yeah … there. I think I've got it. Damn."

More clinking and rearranging. Then she heard the soft thump of the door closing and Will saying, "Yesssss."

Beth looked quickly at the clock with the cracked face over the mantelpiece. She had been inside less than five minutes. Five minutes more and she'd have to be out the door and on her way to stay on schedule. The last thing in the world she wanted was to have the old lady find her here.

Will came out of the kitchen.

"So, uh, Beth. How long have you been at the station?"

"Oh, only a few weeks. I came in with Hugh. He hired me away from our old station. It's one of those things where I work well with him. I guess I make him look good—and what news manager doesn't want that?"

"I dunno about news all that much, but that's the way it is in cycling. Here," he said, reaching for Elena, "let me take her back."

"That's okay. Can I hold her for another second?" Beth cooed at Elena. "She's just the sweetest ..." Her tone dropped so quickly it took Will by surprise. "You were a professional athlete once, right?"

"Uh, yeah. A cyclist. I rode in Europe for a couple of years."

"Europe. Oh," she nodded, "I'd love to hear about that someday."

"Oh, I'm sure ... here, let me take her ..." Will said, reaching out for the baby.

"No, please, I'm enjoying this." She pulled Elena away from her shoulder and held her eight inches from her face. "And we're getting along famousl—"

The formula was not there one moment and there, full force, the next. It arced out of Elena in a torrent, touching Beth's chin, then cascading down the front of her custom-made white silk shirt, forever tinting it a light soy beige.

The word *shit* leaped into Beth Freeman's mouth but was held there by sheer force of will. This was not the time to blow; this was the time to play the game. Keep the ball in play. Win his trust. Don't rage at his baby for destroying a $235 shirt.

"Oh, my God, oh, my God," Will stammered, snatching Elena away from Beth, who stood stock-still in the middle of the floor with a shocked look on her face.

"Oh, I am sorry. I am so sorry, Beth. Oh, my God." He quickly carried Elena to her bassinet and laid her down, turning her to the side in case anything more wanted to appear. There wasn't a drop on her. It was all on Beth.

"Let me get you a towel," Will called over his shoulder as he raced into the kitchen.

"I'm fine, I'm fine," Beth forced herself to say. "I'm okay." She looked over to the bassinet with hatred in her eyes. She started. She could swear the baby, this newborn, lying helpless on her side, was giving it right back to her. Beth snapped her eyes away and then looked back. The baby's eyes were closed. Christ, let your imagination go, kid, she warned herself. It's going to kill you someday. She looked up and forced a smile as Will came running back.

"And would you look? Elena has drifted off. I guess she had something she had to get rid of."

Without thinking, Will took a wet washcloth and began to wipe up the puke, starting at Beth's beltline and running his hand up under her left breast.

"Oh, my," she sighed.

Will stopped, stared at her face, then at his hand, and jumped back as if electrified.

"Oh, Jesus! I am sorry … I didn't think … I didn't …"

Beth smiled and took the washcloth from his hand. "Don't worry. That's fine. I didn't think about it either until you jumped back. Don't worry." She wiped up what she could, the lukewarm, wet cloth making her shirt transparent. She handed the washcloth back to Will, stretching toward him to highlight the shirt and what lay within, then said quietly, "May I have the towel now, please?"

Will stared at her, still dumbstruck, for a split second, shook his head, and woke.

"Sure, you bet. Here it is."

"Thanks." She began to pat her chest dry.

"I am," Will muttered, "so very sorry. Can I at least pay for your shirt?"

"What? This old thing?" Beth asked, pulling the fabric away from her belly, then dropping it back down. "No, Will. This was on sale, and believe me, there is no harm or foul in being anointed by a newborn. Elena and I now have a bond."

"I'm sorry."

"Forget it." She looked at the clock over the mantelpiece. Time was up. She had to leave before the old lady returned.

"I've got to run, Will. I just wanted to stop by. …"

Will nodded. "Yeah, well, thanks. Thanks for stopping. Thanks for thinking. Thanks for the food."

"It was my pleasure. Will you be at work tomorrow?"

Will had to think for a moment. Yes, yes, he would be back at work tomorrow. He had survived one day. He could survive another. "Yeah. I'll be in about noon."

"Great. I'll see you there. Maybe we can have lunch someday."

"That'd be nice." He nodded.

She smiled and walked toward the door.

"You take care—and you—" she looked at Elena, "you learn to keep your dinner down."

Elena slept on and ignored her. Will smiled.

"Thanks. And sorry about this."

Beth took a deep sigh, again accentuating her white bra through the now translucent fabric. "These things happen, and I will survive." She reached out and took Will's hand, giving it a gentle squeeze. "Good-night."

Will felt a blast of electricity shoot through him for the second time that evening.

"Good-night. Thank you again for stopping."

"My pleasure."

She walked out the door and down the steps, all the while thinking, Keep watching. Keep watching my walk. Keep watching my ass. Now I'll turn and show you my boobs again. Keep watching.

She turned from the waist and gave Will a backward glance. He was still watching. Almost surprised at having been caught, Will waved again and closed the door.

"Got him," she whispered.

She walked over to the car door, unlocking the Bimmer with the remote. The car beeped and lit up the calfskin interior. She opened the door, paused, looked back at the house, didn't see anyone, quickly scanned the empty street, then peeled off the sodden shirt, stuffed it into the empty King Soopers bag, and slipped behind the wheel, daring Denver onlookers to spring to attention at the woman driving the Bimmer in a lacy white brassiere. Who knew? Maybe she would even catch a mention in tomorrow's *Denver Post*. "Seen driving shirtless ..." Christ. Oh, well. Any press is good press when you're making a name.

She started the car, turned on the lights, gave a backward glance, sat up straight for maximum effect, and pulled into the street.

"Fucking kids," she muttered and disappeared into the night.

✸

ROSE CANGLIOSI STEPPED OUT FROM BEHIND AN ANCIENT SILVER MAPLE AND watched the lights of the BMW convertible turn toward Colorado.

"That's right," she whispered, "drive back to your little Cherry Creek condo, *puttana*. Keep your meat hooks out of my family."

Rose looked at the house, then down the street, then back to the house.

"Out of my family."

She made a sign with the fingers of her right hand and pushed them off toward the end of the street, then walked through the front door. She called, "I'm home." The baby stirred in her bassinet, rising, unfocused, to the sound. Will walked out of the kitchen, a fresh Leinenkugel in his hand.

"Hi. Nice walk?"

"Yes, in fact, it was. Who, uh, who was your guest?"

"Oh, that was Beth ... Beth something-or-other from work. She dropped by with a pan of lasagna. It's in the fridge."

"How nice. What did she want?"

Will took a slug from the chilled brown bottle. "I dunno. Just being nice, I guess. She's new in Denver."

"New to you?"

"Well, yeah," Will said, stammering, as if caught somehow by the protocol police, "new to me. New to the station. I guess looking for some friend or connection."

"Well," Rose sighed, "that's just what I'd go for—the jolly widower who just buried his wife and can't keep his head out of a beer bottle."

Will brought the conversation to an end. "Stop it, Rose."

She nodded. "How did Elena eat?"

"Great," Will said with relief. "Downed it. Then threw it up all over Beth when I took the food she brought into the kitchen."

"Really?" She glanced down at Elena, still struggling in the bassinet toward the sound of her voice. She reached down, picked up the baby, and rubbed her back.

"Good girl," she whispered. She cradled Elena, then moved the baby up to her shoulder, rocking her gently.

"Why don't you sit and enjoy your beer, dear? Watch the news. Elena and I will clean up the kitchen."

"Sure, if that's okay," Will answered.

"Certainly. Just relax. You've had a big day." She smiled darkly. Will decided to cut his losses and sit down, flipping on the set just as Frightening Freddy March declared no end to the heat wave at the end of the preshow tease. He wasn't sure how he had set her off, but something had, and he was sure he was at the center of Hurricane Rose.

Rose Cangliosi and her granddaughter watched the headlines for a moment, then walked quietly into the kitchen. Rose cleaned the counter, the baby over her shoulder. She set the coffee pot for the next morning, the baby in the same position. She emptied the sink of dirty dishes and filled the dishwasher, the child never moving from her. She glanced over the kitchen, saw no other dishes needing to be cleaned, and pushed the buttons to start the washer. It roared to life, shaking the tiny kitchen with the pulsing power of the water jets.

Rose smiled sweetly. Just enough noise. Just enough.

She opened the refrigerator door, rebalanced Elena on her shoulder, the baby's head and neck supported by her own, and swept up the lasagna, the aluminum pan perching precariously in her right hand. She walked to the kitchen door, balanced the pan against the window, unlocked and opened the door, pushed open the screen door with her knee, walked to the side of the garage, balanced the aluminum pan again, this time on top of the plastic lid of the garbage can, then, in one swift motion, grabbed the handle, pulled the lid, flipped it over, and dumped Beth's culinary gift into the rancid depths.

Gone forever. She quietly replaced the lid.

Rose smiled as she gently patted Elena's back.

"You and now me," she whispered. "No one should ever cross the women of this family."

Rose Cangliosi and her granddaughter turned back toward the house, walked up the short flight of wooden steps, and locked themselves in for the night.

Safe.

And together.

CHAPTER FOUR

THE MAZE

WILL WANDERED THROUGH THE STATION ATRIUM, ODDLY QUIET FOR A Tuesday afternoon, cut across a planter, and stepped into the sports office. He pushed the envelope of feeling, giving his tone a sprightlier edge than he felt at the moment.

"Hey, how you doin', Z?" He paused and looked at Clyde Zoromski, whose eyes were red from heavy drinking, lack of sleep, or both. "Worse than me, I'd say."

"Funny. Jesus, what's with you? Are you on some kind of manic swing? Yesterday I was convinced you were going to kill yourself; today you're Bubblin' Brown Sugar. I can't keep up. I'm old."

"What are you doing here?"

"Some early '60s Chicago Cub dropped over in a hotel lobby yesterday, and Herr News Director, who grew up in Winnetka or some goddamned suburb with a stupid-assed name, decides that we've got to do obituaries for the guy starting at 5 A.M. So I get a call at 2:30, hit the air at 5, and spend the past eight and a half hours talking about some reserve second baseman I've never heard of and the Denver audience has never heard of and none of the other stations have ever heard of—so they're not doing fucking stories— and I'm becoming the poster boy for all those baseball card stat nerds like Billy Crystal played in that stupid-assed cowboy movie."

"I liked that movie."

"I did too," Zorro answered with a yawn, "I just don't like it twelve hours after they got me up for no good goddamned reason." He yawned again, the thing taking on the appearance of the black hole of Calcutta, the smell, as he exhaled, an overpowering mixture of coffee, stale doughnuts, and cigarettes.

Will nodded and turned to his desk. Zorro stared at him for a moment, shaking the sleep out of his eyes.

"So what's with you? If I didn't know any better, I'd say you got laid last night."

"No. No. It was just a good night. I fed Elena and got my mother-in-law out of the house for a few minutes … she took a walk."

"Well, that's a start. Now you've just got to get her to keep doing her little walks, each and every day, until she takes that last little walk down the concourse at DIA for her flight home."

Will shook his head. "Not that easy. I'm not sure she'll ever go without Elena. And I'm not sure I really want her to go … permanently."

"You will," Zorro whispered, turning back to his keyboard. "You will."

Will sat at his desk and tapped a pencil on the Formica top as he stared out the window. Despite the water that was being poured on it daily, the station lawn was browning. Some of the leaves were starting to turn, not from a change of seasons so much as the dry oven they lived in daily. Better to give it up for now and come back to life next spring in the hope of water. He stared out at a wall, one hundred feet away, the living room of a loft in a new condo complex springing up across the street. They were like weeds in Denver—every place that was green or old or abandoned became housing or shopping or dining or gasoline.

"Beth stopped by last night," he finally said quietly, letting the statement drift out into the room.

Zorro didn't turn from his computer. For a moment Will thought he might be asleep. "Beth who?" he eventually asked.

"New kid in the newsroom? News director's friend? Beth … something or other?"

There was a pause as the sporadic bits of information filed into Zorro's sleep-deprived brain. He sat stock-still for a moment, then turned slowly to face Will.

"You wouldn't be talking about Beth Freeman, would you?"

Will thought for a minute. Freeman. That sounded right.

"Yeah." He smiled.

"Jesus H. Christ, Ross, what the fuck do you think you're doing?"

Will looked puzzled.

"Hey, man—I don't know all the stages of grief, but I'm guessing that stupidity is one of them on your list. What did she do? Bat her eyes, flash her tits, or what?"

"Zorro, I haven't got the slightest idea what you're talking about."

Zorro stared at Will for a moment, his mouth working as if to say something, something harsh from the way it was skittering around. He stood, crossed to the door, and closed it. He walked back and sat down, staring at his hands, then glanced up at Will.

Will looked at the door, then back at Zorro.

"What's the problem here, man? What's going on?"

"Just tell me, from the start, what happened last night. Everything. Then, like Sybil the Soothsayer, I will explain it all to you."

Will stared at him for a moment, nodded, and began the story. About halfway through, about the time that Elena was launching dinner toward Beth Freeman's chest, the doorknob rattled, then a fist pounded on the door.

"Goddamn it, Zorro, let me in."

Roger Flynn had returned.

"Hey, asshole, I'm having a private moment in here that you wouldn't understand since it deals with humanity. Why the fuck don't you go to the newsroom for five minutes and watch the new interns to see how this business is supposed to work?"

"*Zorro!*"

"*Fuck off and die, Flynn. The door will be open in five minutes!*"

Flynn banged his fist on the door one final time and stomped off.

"So, finish up—the baby has puked, the shirt is toast, and Beth is flashing her high beams at you. So what's next?"

Will quickly explained the rest, right up through discovering the lasagna in the bottom of the trash can this morning.

"Did you say anything to your mother-in-law about that?"

"Naw."

"Good man. You never introduce store-bought pasta into an Italian household. You'll get the evil eye."

"You're not Italian."

"Wife number three was."

"Ah." Will nodded with understanding. "So, what do you make of my evening, doctor?"

"Look, I haven't worked with her, I've just … heard: Beth Freeman is a walking cluster bomb—destroying everyone and everything that crosses her path. She'd sell her grandmother to white slavers to get a tip on her next story. She hasn't been nice to anyone."

"She was nice to me."

"Jesus, Will—it's easy to be nice to Barney the Dinosaur—especially when he's got a broken wing."

"He doesn't have wings."

"Okay, flippers, feet, those little fucking stupid hands, I dunno. The point is, man," he lowered his voice to a conspiratorial whisper, "you cannot—*cannot*—trust this dame. Not as far as you can throw Cleveland. She uses people like Kleenex, then tosses them in the trash—grinds them with her heel first, too, from what I've heard. And she'll use anything to get what she wants—she can be a sexpot, a bullyboy, an avenging angel, *your best friend*. Get my drift?"

"Yeah, but …"

"No 'yeah, buts,'" Zorro wailed. "She was at your house for a reason last night. She was dressed the way she was for a reason last night. She held the baby for a reason last night. She let you dry her treasure chest with a towel for a reason last night. There was a purpose to everything."

"Like what?" Will asked.

"Jesus, I don't know. But you cannot—*cannot*—trust her."

"I dunno, she was …"

Zorro sighed heavily and stood up, walking toward the door. He stopped, put a hand on Will's shoulder, and patted it once. "Look, I know you've been through a lot, pal. You don't know it, but you're grabbing at any emotional life belt that floats by. Be that as it may, don't let yourself be used. Not by her, not by this place. Keep it in mind. You've got to play the game, but take it from somebody who knows: play it smart. Use your head, not your heart. Your heart will fuck you up every goddamned time."

Without another word, he turned, unlocked and opened the door, calmly walked back to his desk, sat down, and began quietly tapping away at the computer, Will staring at him the entire time.

"How do you know so much about her?"

Clyde Zoromski sighed.

"It's not the first time she's worked in Denver."

Will sat back, his eyebrows arching in a look of mild surprise. Before he could compose himself and ask about her first time in town, Roger Flynn arrived at the door with Burt Young, the head of station operations, in tow. Keys in hand, Young looked disgusted at having been bothered once again by Roger Flynn.

"Door's open, Roger," Young said flatly.

"It wasn't," Flynn steamed.

"Was the door open, Clyde?" Young asked.

"What? Oh, hi, Roger, when'd you get back?"

The three stared at each other for a long, uncomfortable second. Will thought about crawling under his desk and building a basement.

Zorro broke the angry silence.

"Well, don't stand out there in the cold and rain, Roger," he burbled. "Come on into the house and warm yourself by the fire."

"So, what happened?"

Hugh Ransford leaned back in his full-brushed calfskin office chair, twisted toward the window, pondered an obnoxiously wonderful view of the mountains, soon to be swallowed up by a promised six-story assortment of lofts two blocks away, and waited for the answer he wanted to hear.

Beth Freeman, he knew, always had wonderful stories to tell him about insight and access, touching souls, and the easy manipulation of human beings. Her stories here were even better than the ones that found their way to the air, and those were annual award winners. Local, national, major, and minor, the stories won everything, including viewers. Beth Freeman was a prize on air, but even better one on one in a closed-door meeting.

"Oh, I don't know, Hugh," Beth said demurely. "It was a special night. I don't know if I want to ruin it with wanton exhibition."

"Oh, please ..."

"All right," she said quickly, jumping up from her chair to lean on his desk. "Damn it, I hate it when you toy with me."

"Toying is what I do best. I went to King Soopers and bought a tray of their lasagna. Took the labels off and covered it with aluminum foil to make it look homemade. Okay? Dropped by and waited for the old lady who lives with Willie Boy to take off. Hoped she would. Timed it perfectly. Needed him alone."

"What did you wear?"

"Liz Claiborne slacks. The black numbers that hug my hips?"

"Make your butt look like an inverted heart?"

"Ah, you know the ones. You've been looking. And my Garibaldi silk shirt—for which, incidentally, you owe me 250 dollars."

"Why?"

"I'll get to that. In other words, boss of bosses, I was looking good."

"Great."

"Knocked on the door. Made contact. Stretched, bent, twisted. You know the riff. Commiserated. Gave him the food. Met the baby. Held the baby. Got puked on by the baby. ..."

"Thus the 250 bucks. Any chance to clean it?"

"None." She smiled. "I looked into his eyes. He looked into mine, when he wasn't examining my chest. We talked. We touched. We made first, tentative, very sweet contact. He's one messed-up kid, even though he'll never admit it. Should be easy. Any word on Jeremy yet?"

"He can't get off to do the freelance shooting," Ransford leaned over his desk, squinting through the lower third of his glasses at his desk calendar, "until Monday of next week. He'll be here next ..." he stared at the calendar, "Monday night."

"Let's aim the interview for a Wednesday dinner shoot. That might be tight. We'll have to figure out a place. Edit last part of the week in the back room, where nobody can butt in ... then start airing, what—a week from Sunday if all goes well?" Beth said, reading the calendar upside down. "That should give me plenty of time for the setup and to dig up pictures."

"We've still got some on video from when she died."

"Yeah, but people will want to see the baby now—the baby will make this series. The baby is the key. I'll get him to bring her along."

"How?"

"Don't worry. Jesus, Hugh, you worry too much. This is going to be great. This is going to be wonderful. This is going to be warm and fuzzy and tender as all hell. It is a people story from the very depths of the soul. 'Stepping Beyond Tragedy.' Good title. Keep that in mind. People love this stuff. Courage. Heartbreak. Life. Death. Babies. I just have to find a place to shoot it. Talk, play with the baby, videotape quietly—not the kind of restaurants I usually frequent—but we'll find a place."

"He'll never know?"

"Not 'til it airs. And then he can't do anything about it. While we're cutting and promoting, can't you get him out of town for a few days? Send him on the road with the Broncos or something?"

"Road trips aren't that long," Ransford explained. "And if I tried to stretch one to fit, Barbara Gooden would notice and have a cow." He tapped his pen on the corner of his calendar, searching the squares for an answer. The obvious one rose up underneath the piles of blue dots he had placed upon it.

"Ride to the Sky. Ride to the Sky."

"What are you babbling about?"

Hugh Ransford leaned forward, excited with the thought of what he had found. "No, this is it. This will work. We'll have to hold for another week on airing, but we can do this. …"

"What?"

"Every fall, soon after Labor Day, the *Colorado Times*—third-place newspaper, barely alive—sponsors an end-of-season ride through the mountains. Real barn burner, according to their press handouts. One thousand riders. Lots of peaks. Hundred miles a day for, what, four days? We commit to cover the story, have Will leave town the day after your interview, ride the course. Live in the mountains. Do preview stories, then ride the race. He's gone, out of our hair. We promote simply and subtly so nobody calls him freaking about what he's done. We shoot, cut, and get it on the air without any interference. He's out of the loop."

Beth Freeman sat back and smoothed the jacket of her imported Italian suit. She nodded as she thought about the idea, rolling a pencil back and forth between the tips of her thumb and index finger. In the few seconds she had, she pondered the possibilities, the ways this scheme could go all wrong. Caught shooting, caught cutting, caught promoting: all were unavoidable dangers. Secrets were difficult, if not impossible, to keep in this business. But, oh, the joy if one got kept, if in the end you got away with the secret and unveiled the story in just the way you hoped. There was nothing better in the world—not food, not wine, not sex. Such a story, such a moment on the air, was worth all the hassles. It was worth all the dangers. It was worth the difficulty of just plain keeping your mouth shut when all you wanted to do was shout from the top of the D&F Tower downtown that goddamn it, this was your story, your idea, and those thick-headed boobs in the audience were going to lap it up like so much indescribable eye candy.

Finally she stopped. "That's good, Hugh, that's really, really good." She leaned forward. "Logistics?"

"I'll get the desk on it right away."

"Tell him too, so he can get mentally set for it. When does it start?"

"Late next week. Like Thursday or something," Ransford said, looking over his desk for confirmation from a discarded press release.

"Okay." Beth started snapping her fingers with each bullet point she made, Ransford taking notes. "First," snap, "let's find a place to shoot. Comfortable. Good ambient lighting. Lots of places to hide a camera. Good place to talk." She stopped and looked at Ransford, then pointed at him with a fresh point. "Doesn't mind kids." He nodded and made the note.

"You really want the kid there? She could break the atmosphere, the thread of your interview," Ransford warned.

Freeman thought for a moment and nodded. "Good thought. Let me think on that. We might want to get the baby on her own."

"How?"

"Somehow. I haven't gotten that far yet." Beth Freeman smiled. Some of the best parts of this were in making it up as you went along. "Second," snap, back to the list, "make sure he knows of his assignment today or first thing tomorrow so he can start making plans. Don't spring this on him."

"Done," Ransford muttered, another note taken.

"Third," snap, "make sure he leaves late Thursday for this thing. I don't want him to be all rushed and uncomfortable about going out on Tuesday night. I need him relaxed, and I may need another night for follow-up questions."

"Okay," Ransford said, another note made.

"Four. Let Jeremy know that he's my shooter and taking my orders. I don't want that little son of a bitch causing problems again like that shit with the congressional intern. He takes my orders. He doesn't go his own way."

"Right."

"And he keeps his mouth shut the entire time he's in Denver."

"Easily done."

"Don't count on it," Beth Freeman said.

There was silence in the room for a moment, Ransford looking over the list. Finally he broke the silence.

"Anything else?"

Beth Freeman was quiet for a moment, staring out the window at the soon-to-disappear glory of the Colorado Rocky Mountains.

"Yeah," she whispered. "Is there any way you can get rid of Clyde Zoromski?"

"What, the sports guy?"

"Yeah."

"Why, has he been bothering you?"

"No," she said. She continued to look out the window, staring deeply past the Front Range into the depths of the mountains beyond. "No, no reason."

Ransford stared at her.

"He's just a voice from my past, and I want that voice to shut the hell up. That's all," she said lightly before turning, opening the door, and stepping back into a newsroom filled with people who hated her guts, and for whom she returned the favor.

❈

ZORRO WAS WAITING FOR HIS OBIT PACKAGE TO COME OUT OF EDITING AND, while waiting, snored peacefully at his desk, his feet propped up next to his computer monitor, his chin tucked deeply into his chest, his breathing slow and regular, injecting everyone else in the office with a vicious form of sleep venom.

"Oh, man," Art Jackson whispered, "I can't do this. I've got to get out of here. You want some coffee?"

Will shook his head.

"I don't think coffee would help. Do you know anybody with some Benzedrine in the newsroom?"

"I'll check." Jackson walked out.

Will turned back to his computer screen and began the effort of focusing again on the words. He was anchoring the Five tonight, courtesy of Roger Flynn taking the evening off and Barbara Gooden appearing at the sports office door.

"Haven't had time to see you or chat since you've been back," she had said.

"No fault, no foul," Will said with a smile.

"You doin' okay?"

"I'm doing fine," Will assured her.

"Look, Zorro is going home early. ..."

"Late, really," Will replied with a laugh.

"He earned his hours today," she said with a nod. Barbara paused. "Have you ever heard of this baseball player?"

"I've heard of him, but I haven't heard of him enough to get me up at 2:30 in the morning to report on it."

"Neither have I. Neither has my husband, and he's a sports fan." She was silent for a moment, then said, "Look, you can say no if you want, but since we need an anchor in there today, would you be willing to handle the Five and Ten for us?"

Will stared at her for a moment.

"You can say no," she assured him again.

There was a moment of panic in the back of his mind, the "Can I do this?" primal scream, followed by a quick examination of his very full schedule for the evening: go home, drink beer, watch Australian Rules football on some obscure cable channel, listen to mother-in-law tell him to hold the baby, drink beer, drink beer. Pass out.

He would be missing a lot, but ...

"Sure, happy to," Will said with a smile.

And so here he was, gathering sports shorts from around the league to fill four minutes in the 5 P.M. newscast. Four minutes that the producer would trim to three and three-quarters, then three and a half, then three minutes before he actually hit the air.

The sports producer was arranging ideas and gathering video and scores, the sports editor was catching the time codes and cutting the pictures, and Will was writing one piece after another of deathless prose that would somehow do justice to the athletic pursuits of the day. As the stories got trimmed, the prose would tighten, Will knew, to the point that he was reciting nothing more than headlines in order to get all the stories and sports in. College football, the NFL, Major League Baseball, and the NBA were all busy, and despite the heat, pro hockey was already up and running and would be until it was hot again next June. Plenty to talk about, not enough time to talk about it.

Soccer would go. Cycling would go. Any notion of women's sports would go. There were no rules to what he was doing, but there was a reality. The big four were always first. The big four were always there.

He looked at the hockey script and trimmed it again. No use taking the chance that his time would be cut again and he'd have to wing the script. Bad idea all the way around. He had to have the words in front of him. Will wasn't about to trust his ad-libbing abilities to get him through the video. He had to see the words. It wasn't as smooth or as easygoing as Zorro, wasn't as tight and tough and punchy as Flynn, but it was the best he could do.

He knew he was still amateur night when it came to any of this. Even Art Jackson, the new guy, had more experience, more time in the chair, than Will. His chest began to hurt again. He paused for a moment, rubbing the spot hard with the heel of his hand, which didn't help, then went back to typing.

He couldn't get the thought out of his head. Why him? Why not Art? Zorro would tell him to suck it up and take the chair with a smile because he was next in line, next in the rotation, the pecking order, the hierarchy of the sports office, but Will still didn't see it. Will still didn't want it. Will was just doing it.

And he was starting to wonder if just doing it was enough.

✳

"I STILL SAY ART."

Barbara Gooden looked out Hugh Ransford's window, her old office window, and shook her head.

"No. It's Will. This is good all the way around. It's good for him to get back on the air. It's good for the audience to see him. It's good for the staff to see him back. It's the best thing."

"I don't want my newscasts to be therapy. I'm here to win."

"Your newscasts," she said sarcastically, "will be fine. It's one night, and I'll bet you once the word gets out after the Five, we'll have an audience spike at the Ten. People will want to see him. See how he's doing. See that he's surviving."

Ransford laughed. "Didn't expect that from you."

Barbara Gooden turned on her heel with a snap, her eyes boring into Ransford's. "I'm not doing this for some goddamned audience spike, Hugh. I'm doing this for Will, and I'm doing this for us. He needs to get back on the bike. We need a fourth. We can't spend the next six months letting him hang around the office writing ten-second voice-overs about the play of the day. He needs to get up and running for his own good, and we need him there."

"I only ..."

"I don't give a shit, Ransford. I really don't give a shit. Don't think you know me, and don't think you know my newsroom."

There was more to say, but as they looked at each other over the tenuous professional truce they had formed, neither wanted to say anything to push the war of words.

"It's Will," Barbara said finally. She turned and walked out of his office, which still felt like her office, toward her office, which felt like no one's office at all.

Hugh Ransford leaned back in his chair for a moment, staring at the door she had just walked through, waiting for her scent to dissipate. He found it interesting that she had said "my newsroom" rather than "the newsroom" or "your newsroom." It was, in effect, still hers. They were her anchors, her reporters, and her hires on the desk and photo staff. It would take him close to two years to put his own imprint on the place, drive out her mistakes, and replace them with his own people.

People loyal to him.

Beth was just a first step. Maybe Jeremy would be a second. He'd make a good chief photographer. Then he could control that staff. Maybe bring Ann Gray in to run the assignment desk. She'd have that thing humming.

Ransford's thoughts began to wander back to the problem at hand. Will Ross. Will Ross as complicated by Barbara Gooden. Will Ross as complicated by Barbara Gooden's soft heart or guilty conscience, he didn't know which. He had heard stories about her in the wake of Ross's wife's death. Barbara hadn't called. Hadn't warned him. Something. Now she felt bad enough to make him a TV star in the hope of cleansing her own soul.

Not on my time, Ransford thought. Not with my career. Not with *my* newsroom.

There was no way to get around tonight. That he knew, but maybe there was a way to get around all of this in the future. And that way was with Beth and her story idea and getting Ross the hell out of Dodge for a week.

❋

IT TOOK WILL THREE STORIES TO FIND A RHYTHM IN THE SPORTSCAST, AND GIVEN the possibility of late-summer, desperately needed thunderstorms, that meant he found the rhythm when he was halfway finished. He realized suddenly that the scripts he had written only vaguely followed the video that had been cut by the sports editor and that he was far better off trying to wing it, ad-libbing with the pictures as they rolled across the monitor embedded in the desk before him. He had practiced his scripts enough that he knew the action and the people dancing through the video. Well, he didn't know them, but he could guess, and as the sportscast progressed, he knew he was guessing right. It lacked style and substance, but it was smooth, and it moved the station right along to the next commercial.

Will finished the last story and turned on the three-shot to Tom and Martine. He was done. He had done it. He had survived.

Tom Blakely looked at Will for a split second, then asked, "What do you think CU's chances are against Mizzou this weekend? Old grads like me want to know."

Will stared at him for what seemed an eternity. What the hell was this old fart talking about? Will didn't know. Shit, Will wouldn't even have known who CU was playing if it hadn't been in one of the scripts the producer had cut out of the show at 4:30. Now Tom was asking Will, on live TV, to analyze and pontificate about something he knew absolutely nothing about at the very best of times, and certainly not after having been out of the loop for, Jesus, God knew how long it had been.

Will opened his mouth.

Words came out.

"Tom, the Buffs have very quietly been building up their defensive line. They're going to be able to stop Missouri on the ground. It's going to be tight because that's only half the game, and Colorado hasn't exploded yet in offense. But that's coming. Let's just hope it's coming this weekend."

Will smiled. Tom laughed.

"Let's hope so, Will."

Tom Blakely turned into the two-shot with Martine and read a promo for the next segment. Elliott Green appeared live on the screen from a downtown theater dressed as the Beast from a road-show production of *Disney's Beauty and the Beast*.

"Let me entertain you with a 'roaring' good time in Denver tonight. I'm Elliott Green live from Theater Alley at the Buell with an *exclusive* story about the newest Beastie Boy. Me!"

The camera cut to Frightening Freddy March in TV6 Storm Central, who didn't say a word but simply stared at the monitor screen in the desk in front of him, amazed by what he had just seen. He finally mumbled, "Heat continues, more to come," then snorted a derisive laugh.

The camera cut again to Tom and Martine, both sitting stunned at the anchor desk in the studio. Martine finally said, "Back in a minute."

The tally light on Camera Two went dark. As soon as it did, Martine muttered, "I have no doubt that story is exclusive."

Tom nodded.

"Who else would be stupid enough to do it?"

After which the technical engineer who had been training on the audio board finally found the controls to dampen their microphones, thus sparing the city of Denver the rest of their conversation.

◈

WILL TOOK THE LONG WAY AROUND ON THE WAY BACK TO THE SPORTS OFFICE. Rather than cutting through the back of the building and coming up past the commercial production offices, he walked up toward the newsroom, then cut across the back of the atrium, past the line drawings of Tom and Martine and Frightening Freddy and Roger Flynn. The atrium was silent, the building empty. Five o'clock comes and everybody goes. Except two. Two he noticed out of the corner of his eye, standing quietly, inconspicuously, near the men's room. Odd place to hang around, Will thought.

He turned his head back and kept moving toward the door of the sports office. A voice rang out across the atrium, echoing off the walls.

"Will! Will Ross!"

"Yeah?" Will turned and squinted as if that might help him recognize the faces across the room. Wait. One he recognized, it was Ray Whiteside, the guy who had defused the bomb in Breckenridge. His contact with Denver Police. The other he had seen but didn't know.

"Oh, hi," Will said, stepping down to the atrium floor. As he walked across, he extended his hand about five feet before he should have. The damned lobby was so big that he had to take four extra steps, looking like an elephant with an erection, before he reached Whiteside.

"Hello, Will."

"Hello, Ray. How are you?"

"Good, Will, good," Whiteside answered smoothly.

Too smoothly. Will's antennae leaped up.

"This is Paul Timmons," Whiteside said, motioning toward his partner. "He's working on the investigation."

"Great. That's great. Nice to meet you." Will shook Timmons's hand, amazed at how cold it felt, as if there was no circulation in the hand at all, no blood flow, no feeling. Will had to concentrate so as not to wipe off the feeling on his pant leg. He looked at Whiteside and changed the subject.

"Anything new?" Will asked. "Have you got anything on this guy?"

"Not really," Whiteside answered. "We've got a crew coming out here tomorrow to reinstall all the ID equipment and trace lines on your phone. The problem we had before, though, was that this phone system is so screwed up we don't know what good it will be."

"Still be nice to have it there."

"I agree. I agree, Will."

They stood there for a second staring at one another before Will finally said, "Why, uh, don't we go into the sports office for a while? We can sit there, talk if you want."

"Sure, Will, that sounds great."

The other detective nodded but didn't say a word. Will scrunched his mouth, nodded, turned, and began to lead the way back to the sports office.

He began to make small talk.

"I asked about the phone system," Will said over his shoulder. "When they were putting up this state-of-the-art building, they left the phone system to one of their engineers, who did all the wiring and connections. The thing worked like a charm, and everybody was thrilled with it—especially since they saved a ton of money …"

"Of course," the officer whose name Will had forgotten said.

"… but they forgot it was *his* system. There were no blueprints. Schematics. It was all up in the guy's head. So they couldn't fire him. And came the day he dropped over into his soup in the lunchroom, they were screwed."

"That's a pisser," No Name said.

"Sounds like City Hall to me," Whiteside muttered with a smile.

Will nodded. Something was wrong here.

The three walked into the sports office. Art Jackson was busily typing away at his keyboard in the corner. The last of his things had been moved from Will's desk. He swung out on his rolling office chair and adjusted the audio on one of the monitors.

"Hi, guys, come on in."

"Oh, sorry, Art. I didn't know you'd be in here. These guys want to chat for a minute."

"No problem," Jackson said with a smile. "I've got to run across to the newsroom for a bit. Let me just save out here. ..." He maneuvered the mouse and clicked on a few windows. The monitor changed to a wallpaper of warships silhouetted in a brilliant orange sunrise.

"I'm gone. Ten minutes enough?"

"Ten minutes is plenty," Ray Whiteside said with a completely insincere smile.

Will felt the hair on the back of his neck rise.

Jackson left. No Name closed the door. Whiteside turned to Will.

"Will, I know you got the feeling today that we had given up on the case. On Cheryl's death."

"Cheryl's murder," Will corrected.

"Right. Right." Whiteside nodded. "But I'm here to assure you that that isn't the case. We haven't given up. Some investigators, yes, have been reassigned, but for the most part, no, we haven't given up. Still, every now and then, an investigation or the people involved need a jump-start: a clue, a suspect, a statement, street gossip—a reason to get going again. Understand?" Will nodded. "Maybe today you were my reason. I heard the disappointment in your voice today. That got me going again. I thank you for that. But now I can say, yes, we are going. We are doing. We are ready to chase this one down to the end. You with me on this?"

Will sat back, a stunned look on his face. "Well, yeah, of course I am," he countered. "Why would you think otherwise? It's all I think about. It haunts me. For Christ's sake, I want to find him too, and wring his fucking little neck."

No Name leaned forward.

"That's why we'd like you to come downtown with us for just a few minutes."

"Huh?"

Whiteside jumped in.

"We just want to chat for a minute about the case. Go over the details once more. That's all. I spent most of last night and today going over the case file. There are some gaps. I'm just wondering if we can fill them in."

"Can't we do that here? Ask me your questions."

"Well, we could," the second officer said, "but everything we need is back at headquarters."

"It's only a few blocks; why don't you go get it?" Will asked, his suspicions rising.

"Hmm. Naw. Too much stuff. It just works better if you come along with us."

"I'll bet it works better."

"There's nothing to this, Will; I just want to go over what you remember and how you saw it. When this guy called. What you heard from him. The threats he made. What did he look like … you saw him, right?"

Will didn't take his eyes off … Timmerman. That was it. No, Timmons. "Yes, but no. I was outside. Sitting down. He stood with his head just to the side of the sun. I couldn't make out his face. I was blinded."

Timmons nodded. "Even from two feet away?"

"Yeah. Even from two feet away," Will snapped, staring the guy down.

"Paul, please," Whiteside cautioned. "Look, Will, I just want to chat at our office. Nothing to it. Just information. I want to go over everything again so we can start fresh. You want to nail this bastard, right?"

Will continued to stare at Timmons. "Yeah. Right."

"Then give us the chance to start fresh here. Go over the old, find the new. That's all there is to it."

"Do I need a lawyer?"

"I dunno. Do you need a lawyer?" Timmons smiled. Some joke.

"Ray?"

"No, Will, you don't need a lawyer. This is just information. I need this. You and I have been through a lot together on this case. I need to refresh everything. Everything. And that starts with you. I'm going to—we're going to—nail this guy. Okay?"

He put out his hand. Will began to reach for it, stopped, cast a glance toward Timmons, who sat smiling at Zorro's desk, then continued the move until he shook Whiteside's hand.

"Okay. I'll do it."

"Great, let's go."

The three stood as one, turning toward the door just as Art Jackson walked back into the room.

"Sorry. You guys done?"

"Yes, room's all yours again," Timmons said with a grin.

"Thanks." Art looked at Will. "You off somewhere?"

"Yeah," Will nodded. "I'm going to chat with these guys for a while … how long do you think it will be?"

"An hour," Whiteside answered. "Two at the most."

"Hmm." Will turned back to Art. "Just to be safe, I'm on the Ten—can you start writing and producing it for me? Just so I don't fall behind? I'm not too fast on …"

"No explanations necessary. Happy to help out." Jackson looked past Will toward the two officers. "Take your time, fellas."

A bell went off in Will's head again. Of course take your time. The longer Will was gone, the more chance little Art had of doing the Ten. Zorro was right. You had to watch your back every goddamned second in this business.

Face time. Getting the mug on air. That was the name of the game.

Will shook his head. Stop it. This was about something important. That—that was nothing more than TV. And TV was always there tomorrow, with yesterday forgotten.

"Let's go," Timmons said with a shit-eating grin.

"After you, Will," Whiteside added.

The three walked off, Will in the middle. For some strange reason, Will felt like he was under arrest.

Art Jackson watched the three of them walk around the atrium toward the front door of the station.

"Bye, boys," he whispered. "Have fun storming the castle."

Jackson turned back into his office, picked up the phone, and dialed the extension for the 10 P.M. producer.

"Janet, hi, Art Jackson. Hey, uh, Will Ross has just been carted off by the cops for some reason—so I'll be doing the Ten tonight? Okay? Check with Hugh, make sure that's okay."

Without waiting for an answer, he hung up the phone.

Score one for the kid.

He smiled.

CHAPTER FIVE

AVENGING ANGELS

IT WAS ONLY ABOUT SIX BLOCKS TO THE STATION HOUSE. WILL SAT IN THE backseat of the unmarked police car, a car that screamed *Police!* at the top of its nonexistent lungs, and didn't say a word for the entire ride. Instead he moved to the middle of the backseat and stole glances out toward the passersby, who stole looks back in at him, wondering who he was and what crime he had committed to get himself hauled in on a beautiful September night. Maybe they weren't thinking that, but he was. He felt like a goddamned crook.

He couldn't seem to get a handle on what was happening here. His mind was racing, but it was all a jumble of fear and hope and emotion. It was fear at being what—accused? He hadn't done anything. It was a hope that maybe, just maybe, they had really gotten the message to try harder. And then there was the emotion, the racing, peaking, dropping, roller-coaster of emotion, well, hell, everything he did now was based on pure emotion. His head hadn't been involved in a decision for nearly two months. He was not thinking at all, acting blindly, unable to engage his brain before putting his life into gear.

Fight or flight? No, even more primitive than that. He was burrowing. Hiding out inside himself, deep in his cave, waiting for someone to come get him and tell him everything was going to be okay. Someone to save him.

But that person would never come because the only possible savior was dead. She had died because of him and left him with nothing. His failure, his fault. Will knew it to be true.

He was adrift, alone, lost in the maze and at the police station.

THE ROOM WAS INDUSTRIAL CINDER BLOCK, PAINTED WITH A LIGHT-GREEN, easy-to-clean epoxy-based paint. Will knew this stuff. Bad fumes when you were putting it on, but it was easy to clean and lasted forever. There was a dirty yellow bulletin board screwed into the wall directly behind his chair. There was nothing on it, not a Police Athletic League notice, not a wanted poster, nothing. On the opposite wall was a dark pane of mirrored glass, slightly recessed into the wall. Will stared at it for a moment, ran his hand through his hair, and stopped. He stared directly at the glass, then ran his hand through his hair again. He acted as if he were pulling a gray hair. He turned his head to one side and saw it again. A shadow. Not from him but something behind the glass. One-way glass. He was being watched from another room. Even the hair he had just plucked stood up on end.

The door opened, and Whiteside walked in, Timmons directly behind him carrying a tape recorder. Will watched Timmons put the recorder in the middle of the table and push the buttons to record. Will looked at Whiteside.

"Do I need a lawyer?"

Timmons repeated his comment from the station.

"Do you need one?"

Whiteside shook his head. "This is just information, Will. Nothing more than that. I just need to get everything clear one more time so we can move forward again. Do you think you need a lawyer for that? We can get you one."

Whiteside sat on the opposite side of the table, perhaps forty-five degrees to one side of Will. Timmons sat on the other side. Whoever behind the glass, for Will saw the shadow again out of the corner of his eye, had a clear view of the suspect.

Suspect? Shit. No. No. Couldn't be. No, don't do this, Will, he thought; you're thinking with your heart, not your head. They're trying to help. They're going to nail this fucker, but only with your help. Let them ask. Maybe you've got the key.

Maybe. Maybe. Maybe.

❀

AT 8:05 P.M., ROSE CANGLIOSI CALLED THE TV6 NEWS DESK.

She hadn't heard from her son-in-law all evening, and she was determined not only to get her walk for the evening but to keep up her schedule of introducing her granddaughter to the child's father.

"TV6 News, this is Jan."

"Hello, is Will Ross there?"

"I'll check. May I ask who's calling?"

"Just tell him Rose. I'm his mother-in-law."

The title didn't seem to carry any weight with the incredibly young-sounding voice on the other end of the phone.

"I'll check. Hold, please."

Rose held through three replays of the TV6 News Phone Message telling her that Tom and Martine, Fred March, and Roger Flynn would bring her all the day's news, weather, and sports just the way she wanted it, each and every day at 5 and 10. By the time someone returned to the line, she had the message memorized.

And this someone was a different voice.

"TV6 News, this is Bruce."

"Oh, hello, Bruce."

"May I help you?"

"Yes. I'm Rose Cangliosi. I'm holding for Will Ross."

"I'm sorry, Will's not here."

"Oh, but Jan said he was. ..."

"I'm sorry, ma'am, Jan is an intern who took your call, then wandered off to worm her way into the business without bothering to tell anybody about you. ... But, as I said, Will isn't here."

"Well, as I told *Jan*, I'm his mother-in-law and I'm just trying to track him down and see what his schedule is for the night."

"Well, like I told you, ma'am, Will isn't here right now."

She talked slowly and carefully, as if doing so would make the voice on the other end of the phone realize who she was, what she wanted to know, and that she was deadly serious about it.

"I'm—his—mother-in-law. Do you know where Will is?"

"No, ma'am, I just know he's not here." He held the phone away from his mouth. "Does anybody know where Will Ross is?" he shouted to the newsroom. "Nope, nobody knows," he said back into the phone, long before anyone could possibly have answered him.

Rose sighed heavily into the phone. She shifted Elena slightly in her left arm.

"Would you connect me with the sports office, please?"

"Sure. Hang on."

The line clicked and went silent. Then there was a hum, a ring, and a voice at the other end of the line.

"Sports, Jackson."

"Hello, I'm looking for Will Ross."

"He's not here tonight."

Rose sighed.

"Would you have any idea where he is?"

"Well, all I can tell you is that the police carted him downtown about ninety minutes ago."

"What?"

Art Jackson smiled. He was enjoying tonight.

"Amazin', ain't it? About 6:30 two cops hauled Will off to Denver Police headquarters. Said they wanted to talk to him."

"Talk to him about what?" Rose asked, loosening the grip on Elena that had tightened over the past few moments.

"I guess about his wife. You know his wife was murdered, right?"

"Yes, I do," Rose said darkly, the ache returning to her chest.

"Yeah, well, I guess they wanted to talk to him about it. Didn't look none too happy."

"Who?"

"Any of them. Can I leave Will a message?"

There was a click, and the line was dead. Art Jackson slowly hung up the phone and wondered for a second whom he had been talking with. After all, should he be slinging office gossip with just anybody?

He smiled.

Sure. Why not? At that moment, the inspiration struck him.

He picked up the phone and dialed the voice mail of the gossip columnist for the *Denver Post*.

❂

Rose Cangliosi hung up the phone and stared at it for a long moment.

Then she picked it up, dialed a number she knew by heart, waited for the second tone, and dialed a second number. Then she waited for the answer.

"Yes?"

"Home. Call."

"Ten minutes."

"Now."

There was a pause, and the line went dead. Rose hung up the phone and stared at it, willing it to ring with the return call and the answer to her sudden prayer.

❁

In Detroit, the FBI wiretap specialist shook his head. The call was too quick. All he could say was that it had originated from out of state.

"Don't worry," the agent in charge said. "He'll walk to the phone booth at the corner and make his return call. Old Cans is a creature of habit. Old habits."

"And some new ones if he's tied up with the Russian mob."

"His name on a list is one thing. Catching him in the act is another."

The door of the bungalow opened and an aging, rotund man, moving far more easily than one would expect for a man of his age and size, stepped out the door and walked quickly down the street toward the pay-phone booth.

"Gotcha, you fat bastard," the agent said, watching through binoculars as the man passed the phone booth and turned the corner. As he did, the man pulled a cellular phone out of his left pocket while lifting his right arm up and back toward the federal officer's vantage point.

The agent watched as the middle finger on the right hand was lifted in his direction just as the subject vanished around the corner.

"So, what's up?"

"Will's in trouble. The police have taken him downtown for questioning."

"Has he got a lawyer?"

"Not that I know of."

"He hasn't asked for help."

"He won't. He's too screwed up to ask for dinner."

"He's got to ask."

"He won't, I'm telling you. So I am. Help him."

There was a long pause on the other end of the line.

"Done." The line clicked and went dead.

Rose hung up the phone and carried Elena, now sleeping, into the living room. She sat slowly down on the couch and gently rocked her grand-daughter, waiting patiently for her son-in-law to return home.

THE GROUND WAS FAMILIAR.

Will had covered the same thoughts, the same memories, the same facts, such as they were, hundreds of times before, if not thousands. He had told them to Whiteside and other police officers, federal explosives experts, FBI agents, and all sorts of other shadowy people in dark suits.

Where were you? What happened? Did you get a look at him? Are you sure? Think back. Can you see him? What can you tell us? What was he wearing? How did he know your satellite phone number? How did he get your satellite phone? Did you know he had planted a bomb in your satellite phone?

Back and forth, forth and back, scattershot and to the point, dumb as a stump and right on the mark, the questions kept coming. Asked and repeated and skipped, then asked again in a slightly different way. The answers never changed, but both officers, Timmons especially, looked as if they expected those answers to change at any minute, giving them the joy of slapping the cuffs on Will.

As Whiteside asked another question, Will dropped his head and closed his eyes. Stay focused, he thought, stay on target. Stay on target. Get yourself a lawyer. Get yourself a lawyer. You're too tired to do this. You haven't slept worth a damn in six weeks. You can't keep up. Get yourself a lawyer.

"Maybe … maybe I need," Will mumbled.

"… a lawyer?" Timmons answered, finishing the thought. "Well, you know, Ross, maybe you do. Maybe you do."

"Timmons," Whiteside warned.

The other detective shook Whiteside away.

"No, Ray. I'm beginning to think maybe this guy does need a lawyer."

"I've told you what happened," Will said, his voice cracking with exhaustion. "I don't know what else it is you want."

Timmons leaned in close. "I'll tell you what I want, buddy boy. I want the truth. I want to know if you ever stopped hating your wife. I want to know how you figured all this. How you created a red herring out of whole cloth that got you the life you have now?"

"What are you talking about?"

"Bomb goes off at the station. Oops. Will Ross gets that job. Will Ross goes out of town—he gets chased through the mountains by a bomber—oops. They all miss him. But Will Ross seems to know where all the bombs are—the tree. The vase. The phone. The ball on the front step. Oops, sorry, buddy boy. No more wife to worry about. You said you tried to stop her," he said sarcastically. "Did you?"

Timmons poked Will in the chest.

"Did you really?" He poked again. "Trying isn't doing, if you know what I mean."

Will felt his face grow hot. The rage that boiled up inside him was outrageous. He hadn't felt anything even close to this emotional level in six weeks. If ever. It was as if the emptiness inside him had suddenly been filled with molten lava.

"You son of a …"

Without another word he launched himself across the table at Timmons, kicking out with his feet. One of them caught Whiteside in the left ear and knocked him out of his chair. Timmons blocked Will's hands from his neck, but Will had thrown himself out of the chair so quickly and violently that Timmons could not stop the other man's shoulder and chest from ramming into his sternum, driving him backward onto the floor. Timmons had the wind knocked out of him.

"You fucker! You motherfucker!" Will screamed, out of his mind, out of his head, as if he was out of his body. "I'll fucking kill you!" he ranted, grabbing Timmons around the throat. He felt himself squeeze as Timmons gasped underneath him. "I'll fucking kill you!"

From the right, Will's eye caught a moment of a dark shape before his head exploded in multicolored lights and his ears filled with the sound of a John Denver LP scratching back and forth under a phonograph needle. He fell to one side of Timmons and felt his right cheek start to expand. He looked back with bleary eyes and saw Whiteside standing over him, panting, holding a chair like a club.

The door opened. Will looked up to see a fastidious man standing in the doorway holding a briefcase.

"Oh, my. This is interesting. Is this Interrogation 2?"

He went ahead without waiting for an answer.

"Right. My name, detectives, is Felix Ramirez, and you had better have a good goddamned explanation for why you're beating my client with a chair."

"Your client?" Timmons wheezed.

"My client."

"Your client?" Will muttered with surprise.

Ramirez pressed his toe lightly into Will's side, telling him without telling him to be quiet. "Gentlemen, the rubber hose went out a long time ago, even here in the Wild West. You will release my client to me at this time, you will hand over that tape, as whatever statements it contains were obtained under false pretenses, and you will give me whatever information you have that ties my client to any crime. If you do not accede to my demands at this time, each and all of them, you will appear in Courtroom Two at 9 A.M. tomorrow to answer charges of police brutality that will find their way onto the 10 o'clock news tonight. With your names and pictures attached. All six TV news stations. Do I make myself clear?"

"He's dirty," Timmons spat.

"Back it up or back off, Detective. By the way, given the looks of this room and you three, I'd suggest you each get yourself a good lawyer." He looked down at Will. "You've got one. But you," he eyed Timmons. "You want a card? My nephew is good. Just out of law school, but very sharp."

"Go fuck yourself."

"Maybe later," the lawyer continued without pause, "but right now my client and I are leaving. Any further questions, call my office in the morning." He reached down with his right hand and helped Will to his feet. He made no move to help Timmons, who writhed himself up into a sitting position against the green concrete wall. Ramirez leaned over the table and pulled out the tape.

"You can't take that."

"Stop me—and prepare to explain yourself in Courtroom Two tomorrow morning at nine. Besides, the steno in the next room already has a transcription. I checked while you were in here beating the crap out of my client."

"Take it."

"Thank you."

Ramirez opened the door.

"One last thing, detectives—don't you dare talk to my client in any way, shape, or form again without going through me. Try it and …"

"Yes, I know," Whiteside muttered, holding up a hand. "Courtroom Two, 9 A.M."

"Thank you, gentlemen. Come along, Mr. Ross."

Will didn't know what to say as he began to pull the door closed. He felt alive. Thrilled. Fresh blood rushed to his brain, replacing the stuff that had been pooling around his medulla oblongata. Every nerve ending was jangling wildly. The accusation and the fight that followed had stirred him in a way nothing had in so very, very long. It couldn't be over. Not already. He clung to the emotions, the feelings, as if they were a life ring in a vast, empty ocean. He had to say something. He had to get in one last word. He had to have his say.

He looked back into the room, where Whiteside sat slumped down into a chair and Timmons continued to wheeze against the wall, and said, quite simply, "Night." He closed the door behind him.

The room was silent except for Timmons's labored breathing.

Whiteside looked over at Timmons with disdain. "I wish he had broken your goddamned neck, Paul."

The speaker in the room crackled before a voice filled with amusement said, "You boys need any help in there?"

❧

IT HAD RAINED SINCE WILL'S LAST CAR RIDE. THIS TIME HE WAS IN THE FRONT seat. He rolled down the window to feel the last few drops of moisture on his face, his lips, his eyes. He reveled in the fresh air and the sound of the tires swooshing toward Park Hill and home.

The lawyer hadn't said anything since they had left the police station other than "Buckle up."

Will had, and for a time had enjoyed the comfort of the silence, the sounds and feelings of the night. Now he wanted answers.

As he turned to Felix Ramirez, the lawyer answered the unasked question.

"I got a call about forty-five minutes ago asking me to stop by Denver Police headquarters and look in on you."

"Who knew? Who sent you?"

"That's between you and them."

"But how ..."

"Just a friend of the family. Why don't you leave it at that?"

"But ..."

"Leave it at that, Mr. Ross. Enough questions. Some answers, now. I've got to listen to the tape, of course, but what did they ask you?"

Will, thought back for a moment, trying to clear his head of the cool mist that covered the street, and said, "First they just asked me what happened. Same thing they had asked me any number of times in the past. But then Timmons, the wheezy guy on the floor, started accusing me, me," Will could feel the pressure begin to rise in his ears, "of setting it all up. Of killing Cheryl. He wouldn't let up. Whiteside tried to stop him. ..."

"How?"

"Told him to stop."

Ramirez nodded. "Good cop, bad cop. Go on."

"Well, he kept pushing it, and I went over the table at him."

"Did they touch you first?"

"No. Well, Timmons poked me, and I went ballistic."

"He poked you?"

"Poked me." Will held up his right index finger. "With his finger."

"Well, we might have self-defense. Frankly, Mr. Ross, I'm amazed they let you go and that I got out of there with the tape. Physically assaulting a police officer is a heavy-duty felony. You must have really thrown them. Good thing I showed up and got you out of there before they got themselves together."

"Good thing. Say, how did …"

"Look, here's your house. What time do you go in to work tomorrow?"

"About 1."

"Come to my office at 11. Here's the address. Don't be late; I'm squeezing you in as it is. Whatever you do, don't talk to anybody. If a police officer even looks at you cross-eyed, I want to hear about it. Okay?"

"Yeah, all right." Will nodded dumbly.

"Here you go. See you tomorrow."

"Thanks." Will held out his hand. Felix Ramirez shook it lightly. "I appreciate your help."

"Well, just know who is there to help and who is there to hurt you. Good-night."

Will stepped out of the car and closed the door behind him. Ramirez pulled the Jaguar XJS into the neat suburban street and dropped away into the night. Will stood on the curb for a moment until the lights of the Jag disappeared in the darkness.

"Who was that masked man?" he muttered before turning to his front door and the child, held by the mother-in-law, who waited for him.

◉

THERE HAD BEEN LITTLE OR NOTHING SAID THAT NIGHT. WILL WAS SO EXHAUSTED from his adventures in crime-solving that he simply gave both Rose and Elena a hug before stomping upstairs and collapsing in his bed. For the first time in months, he slept straight through. The forty-five-minute wake-up call was absent. He didn't even think of it until his second cup of coffee the next morning.

Will sighed and rubbed his eyes. He'd have to relive all this with Rose, who was starting to move upstairs. He could hear Elena fuss. Will followed Rose's steps as she moved down the hall toward the nursery.

Yeah, he'd have to tell Rose, but that would require at least one more cup of coffee and time with the newspapers.

Speaking of which … he got up from the kitchen table and shuffled to the front door. He picked up the key off the table and unlocked the deadbolt. He fiddled with the doorknob lock for a moment, then yanked the sticky door open.

He jumped.

Two men stood on his front porch.

One short and fat.

One tall and lean.

And they had murder in their eyes.

"I have one question," the fat one said.

"We want one answer," said the skinny one.

CHAPTER SIX

THE
BREAKFAST CLUB

OLVERIO CANGLIOSI STARED AT THE COFFEE CUP IN HIS HANDS, ROLLING the mug back and forth in his palms, warming his hands while collecting his thoughts. His sister-in-law, Rose, sat at the kitchen table to his right, her brother, Stanley Szyclinski, his partner in crime and lifelong friend, sat to his left, and Will Ross, no relation that he could figure out this early in the morning, his reason for being in Denver on this steamy day, sat directly across from him, looking scared, tired, and woefully embarrassed.

Ollie went right for the main point.

"Do you want our help?"

There was only a momentary pause.

"Yes, I want your help," Will said hollowly.

"Why didn't you call us before?" Ollie looked down at his cup, waiting for the answer.

Stanley picked up the conversation. "We were hurting just as much as you were. Maybe more. We just wanted to be asked."

Will shook his head. He didn't have an answer, certainly not an answer that made a lick of sense after last night.

"I don't know. I wanted to let the police handle it. They knew what they were doing. They were here. They helped. They told me. They said they'd get him."

Stanley snorted.

"Well, they did. I believed them. And it's not like they didn't try, for Christ's sake."

"Don't curse," Olverio said quietly.

Will opened his mouth to protest, then shut it without saying another word.

"The police can only go so far in most cases. They need rats, and they need mistakes. People dropping dimes on their boyfriends or neighbors or small-timers who keep bragging or spending big or leaving a trail like a mole in a backyard."

"They know what they're doing."

"Yeah, that's why they hauled you in and turned the thumbscrews on you last night." Stanley chuckled.

"Who sprang you?"

"Ramirez. Felix? Yeah, Felix Ramirez. Very good. Didn't take any shit from anybody."

"Don't curse," Olverio whispered.

"Sorry," Will answered.

Olverio tapped his fingers on the table for a moment, lost in thought.

"Would he be Anna's son?"

"Maybe," Stanley answered, "maybe."

"Hm. Don't know him. Don't know him." He looked up at Will. "You're talking to him today, right?"

Will nodded.

"Then ask him about himself. I'd like to know. Don't really want him to know about us."

"He said he was a family friend," Will said. "You know, *family*, Don Corleone stuff."

"Jesus, you've got a hell of an imagination." Stanley chortled.

"Don't curse."

"Oh, stop, Ollie."

"No, you stop. I won't have that kind of talk around me. Especially at my sister's table."

"No, *my* sister's table," Stanley answered sarcastically. "*Your* sister-in-law's table." He turned to Rose. "Does my talk bother you?"

Rose looked up from her coffee, her face worn and tired from the past six weeks, and smiled.

"I grew up with that talk at my table. Daddy did it. You did it. So it doesn't bother me. But what kind of host would I be if I allowed it to go on when it bothers a guest? And Olverio is a guest. So watch your mouth, Stanley."

Olverio smiled triumphantly.

"Etiquette doesn't mean shit to me," Stanley mumbled, sotto voce.

Ollie ignored him. "When do you meet with Ramirez?"

"Eleven. I've got his address," Will started patting the front of his T-shirt, as if the card was hiding there, "somewhere."

Stanley waved him off. "Don't worry about it. Keep the appointment. Don't say anything about us being in town."

"If you need us, Rose will have our number."

Will sat back.

"You're not staying here?"

Olverio smiled.

"No, that's not a good idea."

"Not a good idea," Stanley repeated, shaking his head.

"I don't understand."

"Well, how do I put this?" Ollie asked rhetorically. "We have some people who are interested in us."

"Interested," Stanley added.

"Interested?" Will asked.

"Yes, interested."

"How?"

"That's nothing to concern yourself with," Ollie said with a smile. "But with that in mind, I think it's a good idea for us to stay away. Find our own accommodations, keep in touch—well—quietly. Rose?"

"I understand," Rose whispered.

"If you need us, call Rose. Use some kind of one-word code. She'll know how to get in touch with us."

"How?" Will asked.

"Believe me, it's better if you don't know," Ollie replied.

"Better," agreed Stanley.

Olverio looked at his watch, then pushed the chair back from the kitchen table. There was a long, deep screech as it moved across the polished wooden floor. He stood and looked at Will.

"We'll be close, Will. Don't worry."

"Doing what?"

"Making, how shall I put it? Discreet inquiries." Olverio smiled darkly.

"Discreet," Stanley said, rising from the table to tower over the other three.

Will smiled back without sincerity.

"You know," Will said, "the police are thinking I did it."

Stanley nodded. Olverio answered, "We know."

"I didn't do it. I wouldn't. I couldn't."

"We know that too, Will," Olverio said.

Rose reached over and put her hand on top of Will's, giving it a squeeze.

"But the police seemed so sure last night," Will said as the fear of being falsely accused began to knot his stomach again.

"I know, Will. I know. But they're just fishing. They haven't gotten even a nibble yet, so they're madly casting their line out in the water to see if and where the fish might be biting."

"Fishing," Stanley said quietly, nodding in agreement.

"Don't worry, Will. They won't find anything. They'll move on and fish somewhere else. They'll know what we know."

Will felt the tears begin to build behind his eyes.

"And what do you know?"

"We know," Olverio said, leaning forward and putting both hands softly on the kitchen table, "that you had nothing to do with this. That you tried to do everything in your power to save Cheryl."

The bubble of emotion that he had fought so hard, so long ago, was back, struggling to break from his chest, race up his throat, and burst free in tears and rage. He struggled with his breathing, calming himself, pushing it all back down again. He took a deep breath, and another.

Rose squeezed his hand, watching his face carefully.

"So," Will struggled to say, "how do you know? How do you know I did everything?" He took another deep breath. "How do you know?"

"Because, Will," Olverio said, turning his head slightly, his voice barely above a whisper, "if we thought for a second that you did anything less than everything ..."

"Everything," Stanley said.

"... you'd already be dead."

Will nodded. He understood.

"That's a comforting thought, boys."

Rose squeezed his hand again and smiled at him.

Will gave a rough approximation of a smile and continued to nod, even though, in his head, he wondered if he might, indeed, be already dead.

CHAPTER SEVEN

"HAVE I GOT A RIDE FOR YOU ..."

I T WAS WILL'S SECOND MEETING OF THE DAY.

The first, with the man Will now assumed to be his lawyer, had been a memory exercise. Remember what happened last night. Everything that was said by the police, to the police, with the police.

"But you have the tape," Will had said.

"Yes, I do," Felix Ramirez had answered. "Now tell me everything that is not on this tape."

So Will had. After a final reminder not to get into strange police cars in the future without at the very least calling Felix first, Will moved on to the television station and his second meeting.

This one, with Hugh Ransford, was, to put it mildly, ridiculous. Ransford was waving his arms and striding around the office as if he had just realized he had won the lottery. He was way too excited about an idea that wasn't all that exciting, especially to Will. Will would ride and report on what was, essentially, a four-day excursion through the Colorado mountains.

Stay with the people, Ransford was saying, report on the people, don't ride ahead, don't blow them out, stay with the people each day, ride the tough sections with them, get to know them, let them get to know you—it will be great promotion for you and the station. By the end of it, these people will love you.

Will smiled and nodded, then took a deep breath and rubbed his eyes with the tips of his fingers. God, had it come to this already? A few years ago he was winning Paris-Roubaix. Now he was leading some used-car dealer on vacation up and over Trail Ridge Road. It was like some old movie star doing a guest spot on *The Love Boat* to prove to the audience that he was still alive. Take a cruise with Fred Astaire! Dance with the man himself!

Will started to smile, thinking about Fred Astaire on a cruise. His smile broadened. Fred Astaire was dead, but he could still pull them in. *Fred Astaire— On Roller Skates!*

Ransford took the smile as a sign that he was winning Will over.

"You see, Will, this accomplishes a couple of things for us. First, it gets you out of the station," there was a strange pause, almost a hiccup, "and out with the viewers: the sports viewers, active people, perfect demographic, to meet and greet and ride. They get to meet you, they get to know you, they will come to like you, just like everyone else has around here."

Will blinked. He didn't know that anybody in the station liked him, except maybe Zorro. And that was only because Will was an unambitious son of a bitch who didn't want Zorro's job. He didn't really know anybody else, aside from a couple of photogs and Barbara Gooden.

Will nodded. Ransford continued, "You'll ride every day with a new group of people. Maybe have them with you at 5 P.M. for a live shot. Surrounding you. You and your new friends, know what I mean?" He was thinking out loud, giving Will the strange sensation that Ransford was making this up as he went along. "We'll hit you at 5 and 10 every day. Two live shots, with a package of the day's ride. When do you think you'd be done every day? We could do it late in the Five, I suppose, if we had a fast cutter. Do you think you could write something quickly at the end of the day?"

Will had no idea. He nodded anyway.

Ransford smiled. "Great. Great. This is going to be great for the station, this is going to be great for you, this is going to be great for our relationship with the newspaper. All the way around, this is a positive for us." Ransford paused as if he were juggling thoughts: *Five Ideas at Once!*

Will smiled again.

"You'd be up next week. Riding almost a hundred miles a day. Can you be ready? Will there be a problem keeping up?"

Will blinked again. That was a good question. He hadn't even been near his bike since the day after Cheryl died. He had ridden almost daily until that moment, but that moment had been six weeks ago. He hadn't done a thing to exercise or stretch or build his lung capacity or even break in his butt for the saddle.

The only thing he had ridden was a couch. The only thing he had shifted was a remote. The only thing he had negotiated was a *Brady Bunch* marathon on *Nick at Night*. Oh, shit. Mr. Paris-Roubaix might just wind up blowing chunks over the guard rail on Berthoud Pass while being comforted by a formerly chubby housewife from Arvada who had gotten a new bike for Christmas and found it to be a marvelous escape from the man who had given it to her.

Will grimaced.

"Problem, Will?"

"Hmm?" Will left his reverie and actually looked at Hugh Ransford for a second before shaking his head. "No, no problem. I'll be there. Sounds good. Let's do it."

"Great. I'll send a field producer up there with you. Maybe a photographer who knows how to field produce. We'll have the satellite truck. That will just leap ahead every day. Meet you at the next overnight. How's that sound?"

Will had no idea. He nodded. "Sounds great." His head continued to bob. "When does this start?"

"Next Thursday. You'll leave from Boulder, right in the middle of town, Thursday morning at 9 A.M. Can you do it for me?"

Will stared at Ransford. What an odd question, he thought. "Can you do it *for me?*" Sure, I can do it for you, but why would I? What was the point in personalizing an assignment? Did it make it more compelling? Did it make it more important to complete it? What the hell was this guy talking about? It was a job. Then Will nodded. He understood. It was a job that this guy was taking personally. You screw this up, boyo, and you screw up your relationship with me, and you screw up any kind of future you might have across the atrium in that little sports office.

It was a realization that made Will wonder: Given the knife edge the staff seemed to be riding with this guy right now, was there really any way to do it right? Was there any way Will could succeed with this assignment, or would he fall short no matter what he did or how he did it or how many awards the coverage might carry off? Maybe he was screwed with Ransford no matter what. Maybe he was already in the cannon and they were just waiting for the right time to light the fuse. Maybe Art Jackson was already having Will's chair steam-cleaned.

Maybe Will was starting to get as bad as Zorro.

Will smiled and scratched his head, doing his best Will Rogers impersonation. He stood, took a step toward Ransford's desk, and put out his hand. Ransford paused for a second, then reached out and took it.

"Don't worry, boss," Will said. "We'll get it done for you. Top-notch. A-number-one."

Ransford nodded and smiled. "Good, Will. Good. I appreciate it. I think this can really help establish you and make a mark with the audience we're trying to capture."

"Good excuse to get me out of the building too," Will said with a smile his eyes didn't match.

Ransford blanched and almost yanked his hand out of Will's. He caught himself quickly, but there had been a split second when he thought, "Good God, this guy knows," before he realized that Will was talking about himself rather than about Ransford and the overall plan.

"Wish I could go with you," Ransford said, laughing, "but they don't let old fat men on bicycles."

"Wish that was true," Will said, dropping his hand. "That would get me out of this."

Ransford laughed too loudly. "No way, José. You're stuck, and so am I. Let's just make the best of it."

"We will. I will. Thanks."

Will nodded and turned toward the door to the newsroom. He opened it, stepped through, and nearly ran headlong into Beth Freeman.

"Oh, hello," she said with a smile. "You've just been where I've got to go."

"Yeah, fresh assignment." He didn't know what else to say. Zorro had said to be careful, but it wasn't easy. She was wearing a lavender scoop-necked shirt that hinted at the top of her cleavage, with a gold necklace that drooped just a touch in the center, drawing his eye right there. Will fought the temptation. She reached over and touched his arm, sending a small electric shock through his entire body.

He very nearly jumped.

"Are you going to be around later today?"

"Me? Yes. All day. Somewhere. Here."

Christ. He sounded like a Neanderthal.

"Let me give you a call later. Would that be all right? Take a few minutes to chat? What do you think?"

"That, uh, that would be great."

She squeezed his forearm. The electricity ran through him again, gathering at a certain point where he wished it wouldn't gather. Not here. Not now. Not in the middle of a crowded newsroom that had stopped in its tracks to watch Beth Freeman actually deign to talk to someone on staff.

"I shouldn't be long with him." She cocked her head toward Hugh Ransford's office. "I'll give you a call then."

"Great. Great."

She smiled, gave him a weird kind of wink, squeezed his arm lightly again, and then glided toward the door to Ransford's office. Will stood stock-still in the newsroom, staring straight ahead. Slowly the newsroom staff around him turned back to whatever it was they had been doing before the Bitch on Wheels had actually made human contact.

Will stayed where he was, not moving a muscle, living inside his head for the moment, trying to mentally command his erection to leave him in peace.

❋

It had been a quiet afternoon.

Roger Flynn was back, which meant he was anchoring all the shows. Art Jackson was live at Broncos camp. Will wondered if he should have demanded that story, but the upcoming ride through the mountains, for which he knew he wasn't ready, had set up shop in the back of his mind. Better to focus on that, he thought, then wander around demanding face time. Zorro would have a fit, Will knew, but that couldn't be helped.

Will finished writing a series of voice-over scripts for Roger Flynn to follow as he ad-libbed his way through the game video, then handed them over to the sports producer and turned off his computer.

There was no assignment. No more help was needed or wanted. No live, no package, no story at all to do tonight.

Will stared at the wall for a moment, then glanced up toward the clock. Four fifty-five. He hadn't even been inside the station for five hours, and he was already thinking of sneaking out. Some employee.

Sneaking out and what? Sneaking out and drinking? Sneaking out and watching *Diff'rent Strokes*? How about sneaking out and riding? Riding? Jesus, he didn't know if he could balance on the bike anymore.

The phone rang. He answered it without thinking.

"Sports. Ross."

There was a pause, and Will felt dread build in his chest.

"Hi."

Will paused and let out a sigh of relief. "It's you."

"That's nice. No one has been that grateful to hear my voice in a long time," Beth said.

"No, it's ... well ..."

"What?"

"Nothing." Will felt his face flush.

"Are you busy tonight?" she asked.

Will was quiet for a moment, thinking about his plans: the ride, a drink, and an evening with Gary Coleman once again using the same one-liners he had used for the entire run of the series to create gales of electronic laughter on the TV set.

"After about 8, no, I'm free," Will heard himself say.

"That's great. I'm off at 8:30. You want to meet at 9? Have a drink? Chat? I understand if you don't want to. ..."

She actually sounded hurt.

"No, no, no," Will burbled. "No, I'd, uh, love to. Love to. I have to ride tonight, that's all. Ransford just assigned me to some bike tour, and I figure I'd better get in shape fast so I don't embarrass him. Or me, for that matter."

"I don't think you could ever do that," she whispered.

"Oh, believe me, I could. I do on a regular basis."

She laughed. "Well, you want to ride. I have to work. Let's just meet at 9—say at Frisco's?"

"That would be great. I'll look forward to it."

"Good," she said quietly. "I'll see you at 9."

"Nine. You've got it."

"Bye." She hung up the phone.

Will held the receiver at his ear for a long second, then hung up. He immediately dove under his desk, digging frantically for a phone book.

He had absolutely no idea what or where Frisco's was, but he wasn't about to miss it.

He could hear Zorro's warning in the back of his head, but he was like a moth—the flame was just too damned enticing.

❁

"WELL?"

"Nine o'clock. Frisco's."

"Why Frisco's?" Ransford asked.

"Quiet. Intimate. Lots of privacy in the booths."

"Good, good."

"And I know the owner. He'll let me bring a camera in next week, once Jeremy is set to go."

"How do you know?"

Beth Freeman smiled sweetly.

"Because if he doesn't, I'll drop a dime on him with the Health Department and they'll shut him quicker than shit through a goose."

"Would it get that far?" Hugh Ransford asked with a touch of trepidation in his voice.

"No. No. Don't worry, Hugh. You've got to remember, I've been here before. I've got a lot of contacts. People know me. They know my work. They'll help me any way they can."

"Because of your sweet nature and warm personality, right?"

"Yes," she laughed.

"But most of all because they want to be on TV."

WILDERNESS

It was a familiar place, filled with familiar smells.

He stared at the bike for a long moment, like a man returning to an intricate job he had done all his life after a very long vacation. What did he do? How did he do it? What was the order?

There was dust in the garage. That would have to be first.

He took a clean shop rag and slowly ran it along the top tube. The dust peeled away in a cloud, curling in circles as it floated through the late-afternoon sunlight toward the floor.

He moved up to the seat, then across the rest of the diamond, pulling the rag in such a way that the ribbons of dust fell away from the chain and the gearing. He rubbed at the spot of mud that may have come from France years before. He wasn't sure how it got there, and it certainly wasn't going anywhere now.

He ran his thumb along the top of the front tire and pushed down. Soggy. What did he expect after six weeks? He pulled down the pump and put it on the front tire. The gauge said 10. He wanted 110. He began pumping.

He remembered the days when other people worried about things like this for him, and he smiled. The movie star back to doing her own laundry. The champion dusting his own trophies. As he pumped, he noticed how the sunlight was catching the electric blue-and-yellow frame of the mountain bike. It sparkled. The dust hadn't settled there. The dust never would. That was hers.

You'd think the dust would coat the bike by now, seeing how it had been hanging there from the ceiling, against the wall, ignored, even longer than his, but maybe, he thought, shaking his head, it was clean because it was hanging rather than leaning against a work bench.

"Is it you?"

"Are you ... "

He felt the pressure begin to build deep inside his chest. He took a deep breath and pushed it away. The dust dancing in the sunbeam swirled in little cyclones down and away, disappearing into the corners, ready to attach itself to something else in the garage.

Will ran his thumb over the rear tire. It had held its pressure.

Not all of it, certainly, but close enough for government work.

He picked up his helmet and gloves and walked gingerly toward the garage door and an evening ride.

CHAPTER EIGHT

RIDING THE KNIFE EDGE

FOR THE FIRST MILE, WILL WAS SURE HE HAD DRESSED TOO WARMLY. WITHIN a few blocks he was sweating, the late-day sun of early autumn still too direct for long sleeves and layers. He had begun to wonder if he should pull over and take a few seconds to strip down to a T-shirt when the sun moved behind a taller building and he felt the chill congeal the beads of sweat on his forehead. Suddenly he wondered if he was dressed warmly enough.

Too long away. Too long away.

"Yeah, yeah," he mumbled, "it's just like riding a bike."

Except when you thought of the way he had once ridden a bike, and how far and how long and with what determination and energy, you realized he should be riding far better than he was riding this one now.

The Beast had become an unfamiliar creature. The seat seemed too high. The pedals felt out of line. The front wheel rolled thickly and felt mushy. The whole ride was a mess. He was amazed, as he played with shifts and adjustments and balance, that he didn't roll out into traffic and finally get the lead story on the Ten. He thought back to Tomas Delgado, so long ago, who had been able to look at him and adjust a bike, even hanging out of a car at thirty miles an hour, until it was perfect in look, tone, and feel.

The wheels would hum.

This was a drunk singing Abba tunes at the top of its lungs.

The seat dug into his ass, rubbing on a seam in the riding shorts he had never noticed before but that now felt like a hawser running down his crack. He stood up on the pedals and rolled along, pulling at a cheek in order to get the thing out of there. It must have been quite a show for the lady in the red Mustang who honked twice and then passed with a wave.

"Sorry, lady," Will called after her. It hadn't been a come-on, it had been derriere distress.

He settled back onto the seat and tried to find whatever spot might be comfortable. It was embarrassing. How many hundreds of rides, how many thousands of kilometers had he ridden? How many hours had he spent in the saddle? Now, six weeks off the bike and the first thoughts of giving up, turning around, and heading for the comforting safety of the refrigerator light lay a mere mile and a half away from the house. That state of mind used to live about thirty-five kilometers out, which meant that when it hit, he still had a solid thirty-five to go before he was home and safe and warm and off the goddamned bike.

Traffic wasn't helping. Will spent as much time worrying about being clipped by a passing pickup mirror than he did about his ankling. He slipped up on a sidewalk ramp, drifted to the right, and found himself on a bike path heading southeast out of the city. A few people walked their dogs along the path, and a few dogs left small piles of steaming personality to remember them by, but for the most part, he had the path to himself. It ran along a stream, then up into a park, then across a main drag, then along the stream again. He kept coming to bike path intersections where offshoots went toward neighborhoods. He had no idea where he was going.

He just turned on what appeared to be the main drag and kept going.

Nice and easy.

Nice and easy.

❦

THE GLORY OF RIDING IS LOSING YOURSELF, LEAVING CARE AND TROUBLE AND JOBS AND heartache on the road somewhere behind you. They'll find you on the way back and climb up on your shoulders again, push their way back into your life and consciousness, but for those precious few moments they disappear, left behind in a chaotic pile, and all that seems important are the road and the circles and the hum of the tires and the click click click click click of the metronome that begins to set itself inside your mind. The gears shift as if by magic, the world comes alive in a burst of Maxfield Parrish colors along the edges of the tunnel of the road directly before you. An invisible hand pushes you along. Deep in your rational mind, you're convinced it is the wind, pushing and guiding and helping you up the grade. You also know, deep within your pocket of fear, that as soon as you make the turn toward home that same hand will place itself directly in your face, no matter what direction you ride, and make you work for your rest and comfort. And the metronome in your head continues to grow louder, more insistent: click click click click clickclickclickclick.

And you ride, to who knows where, carried on a wave of joy.

❁

WILL COULD HEAR THE MADNESS OF THE TRAFFIC OFF IN THE DISTANCE, VAGUELY SMELL the cloud of rush-hour exhaust, but he was in a sanctuary of sorts after negotiating a series of turns and tunnels and underpasses that had brought him here to Cherry Creek State Park. The deeper he went, the quieter the ride became and the less the impact of the petrochemical cloud on his VO$_2$ Max.

Will sat up on the bike and let gravity pull him along for a moment. The last hill had brought home a harsh reminder of the basic concept of wind. He had none. He was at VO$_2$ Min. It had taken him years to get into shape but only six weeks to get completely out. He remembered his first sprint on a bike, when he had overextended himself, stopped, gotten off, and stood breathing deeply for a few seconds before suddenly doubling over and barfing up a lung.

The last hill hadn't been all that steep, but it had been long, the kind of low-slung, false-summit climb that always made him nuts: "Oh, you're at the top, no, you're not, now you are, no, you're not, yes, no, goddamn it, where's the crest?"

Will glanced back over his shoulder. It wasn't all that long. It wasn't all that steep. It didn't have all that many false summits. His imagination and rubbery legs had concocted the entire fantasy in his head.

He laughed.

This is going to be great, he thought—some appliance repairman from Aurora was going to send out his Christmas cards this year with a picture of Will struggling over a mountain pass, the greeting reading, "Happy Holidays! Look Who I Beat over Berthoud!"

Will pushed the thought out of his mind, hunched over the headset, and began to drive his legs in their calculated rhythm again.

Click, click, click, click …

❉

THE HAIRPIN TURN CAME UP QUICKLY ON HIS RIGHT. HIS RIGHT LEG ROSE TO THE TOP of the stroke, and he dropped into the high-speed turn that Davis Phinney had drilled into him earlier that year. It was a balls-to-the-wall approach to riding that Will had never been able to master. Self-preservation was ingrained too deeply within him. But now, in a strange way, he realized that he didn't care. If he caught some gravel and lost the edge, sliding sideways, peeling away the top layers of Spandex and skin, at least he'd feel something. He'd have something to talk about with Zorro tomorrow. He'd have his red badge of courage.

He might even get some coos of sympathy tonight from Beth.

The dam road was closed to traffic, so he negotiated the barriers and rode it anyway.

Catch me if you can.

Will dug down deep into the bike as the wind grew cold and began to shift again. Tailwind out. Headwind back. It never changed. It never would.

The road swept away in an easy curve before him. To his left, I-225 was a parking lot. To his right, the state park was deserted, the last rays of the sun peeking through the mountain valleys, shimmering over the reservoir surface. It was a strange dichotomy.

Click, click, click, click …

Civilization rose up again at the eastern edge of the reservoir. Parker Road, one of the most congested pieces of concrete in the city, was the outer edge of his ride. Will turned sharply back onto a sidewalk, picked his way through the gravel tossed up by cars and construction and street sweepers, picked up the bike path again, and zipped back down the hill that had very nearly killed him on the way up.

Denver was in a bowl. Riding out would always be a pain; riding in, no matter how the wind hit you, was always easier. He shot down the path, set up the 90 degree turn, and took it fast, cutting in just before the barricade at the spill-way. He tore through the neighborhoods, the parks, the golf course, under highways, past an impromptu landfill, along the creek, past the mall, which was not a mall, he was constantly reminded, but a shopping destination, along University and up past City Park, right past the zoo and the museum, across Colorado with the light, how did that happen, and back into the neighborhood.

He cut right and left, never slackening his pace, until he came to his street and he came to his alley and he came to his home. He rolled up the gravel drive and onto the grass of the sideyard.

The air still held some warmth, but there was a bite in the air. Fall was on its way, sometime. Sometime soon. The mountains would be far more unforgiving. He'd have to remember to put some thought into what he packed for each day—each evening—on the road.

He popped his right foot from the pedal and swung it over the bike, his butt relieved that the reintroduction to the leather seat was finished, at least for tonight. He balanced himself, snapped his left foot free, and leaned the bike against the outside corner of the garage before he sank into a crouch, leaned back, and rolled himself out onto the grass.

Will stared up at the sky, the darkening blue still illuminated by a few streaks of light that were finding their way through the peaks forty miles to the west. A few of the brighter stars were making an appearance. Jupiter made its presence known in the south. A few random stars peeked out, and Will stared at them for a time, creating his own constellation, like a boy finding patterns in the stucco ceiling of his bedroom.

A face here, a figure there, a ship, a plane, a gun, a bomb, a person.

Cheryl.

He took a deep breath and rolled up into a sitting position, purposefully looking away from the sky, directly at the ground, refusing to look up again.

He felt shame.

He rose, moved the bike into the garage, and then walked inside to try to wash it off.

❀

Will looked at his watch: 9:15.

Five more minutes, that was all he was going to wait. There was fashionably late and there was rude, and this was getting rude. Then again, he had to think, after that five minutes, would there be another five, and another, and another? After all, it was clear that Beth had thought ahead and was likely on her way. The maître d' had been expecting Will. There was a booth in the back, prepared just for them. Will had followed a waiter through the tony, high-end restaurant, through the oak bar, and into a short hallway with sheltered booths on both sides.

You couldn't push the definition of *intimate* much further.

Will looked at his watch: 9:20. Five more minutes.

He looked up and she was there, smiling, at least her lips were, in a pastel turquoise V-neck sweater that hugged her chest like Glad Wrap hugged tomatoes on a hot day. Will glanced, then forced his eyes up to her face again, horrified by the thought that if he looked at his watch now, it would likely say 9:25.

Had it been a glance or a stare? He smiled, hoping she hadn't noticed. She smiled back. This time her eyes were bright. She had, he thought, goddamn it.

"Hi," she said, sliding into the seat across from him. "I got caught at the station a few minutes longer than I expected. I'm sorry."

"That's okay. It happens."

"Well, I wouldn't have been surprised if you had gone."

"No, never even crossed my mind. Besides, the guy at the podium out front would have probably blocked my way. I ate all his breadsticks."

Beth laughed lightly, but the smile shot from her eyes. John, the maître d', had been told specifically to not let Will leave, that she was on her way, and that under no circumstances should Will be allowed out the front door.

The waiter appeared as if summoned by Samantha.

"Would you like a drink?" he asked Will.

Will nodded at Beth, who smiled and turned her face up to the waiter. She sat with her arms crossed under her breasts, which, given the sweater, gave her an amazing amount of cleavage. Will looked and turned away, embarrassed. The waiter was looking. Will glanced to his right. A gentleman two booths down on the other side of the narrow hall was looking. Will wouldn't have been surprised to see the chef glancing out the window of the kitchen.

"Jameson and water, please."

She sat back, breaking the spell. The one she needed to be looking wasn't.

Will glanced at her and smiled, then said to the waiter, "I'll have the same."

"Very good." He disappeared, quickly and quietly.

"This is a nice place," Will said, rolling his eyes in a cursory glance around.

"It is. It's always been one of my favorites, no matter what it's been. It's been a jazz club and a steak joint and Frisco's. I like it best as Frisco's."

"I didn't realize that you had been in Denver before. When were you here?"

"I was here for five years a few years back," she said, warming to her own story. "I was an intern at Channel 4, then got a reporter's gig at a regional cable news operation, small-time stuff, weekends, mornings, read the headlines, be your own photographer with a little home video camera, worst job the world had to offer ..."

"Sounds dead-end."

"It could have been, I suppose, but I had *ambition.* ..." She emphasized the word in a way that was meant to be comical but came across as the unvarnished truth. "I developed some stories on my own time, tried to sell them to the news director, who wasn't interested in anything that might make people stop and actually watch, then started shopping them and me around town. Barbara Gooden snapped them up at TV6, and I got on there."

The waiter arrived and put the two drinks in front of them. Will smiled and said thanks. Beth nodded. Will took a long pull on the Jameson. Beth let hers sit.

"Didn't the cable place try to keep you?" Will asked.

"No. They knew they were a doorway operation. A place people like me could make tapes and jump into the biz. That's what I did. Besides, I think the guy in charge was just happy to get rid of me."

"That's great. It's great that Barbara took a look and gave you a chance."

"I had connections. My tape mysteriously appeared on her desk one day."

"Zorro keeps telling me that's the way the business really works."

"Really, he does?"

"Yeah. Not what you know but who you know, that sort of thing. You're only as good as your last story. 'What did you do for me today?'"

"He's just full of pithy insights, isn't he?"

"Yeah, if you can get past the curmudgeon in him. And the fact that he doesn't trust anybody as far as he can throw Cleveland."

It was a guaranteed laugh line—at the very least a smile. Beth didn't react at all. Will felt his face flush and the first traces of flop sweat bead on his forehead.

Beth realized she was losing him. She smiled and drew him back toward the conversation.

"Enough about me. Let's talk about you," she said.

In his mind, Will completed the joke: "What do *you* think of *me?*" He pushed the thought away as rude and unfair. After all, she was here, she had reached out, she was smiling. Everybody else seemed to turn away, race away from the walking bummer. He'll bring me down, I'll catch it.

Not Beth. She was there. She was smiling. She was interested in him.

And she smelled good.

She smelled young and fresh and exciting. There was an aura about her. The rest of his world smelled like garlic and olive oil and the sour scent of used diapers hanging in the air and sticking to his teeth.

Will's hands cupped the glass of Jameson. He stared down at the glass and watched his left hand pull away to rest beside the glass on the table. He watched as her right hand moved effortlessly across the table and touched him. She rested her hand there. For a split second, Will considered yanking the hand away as if shocked. There was a flinch, but he left it there. He stared at it for another few seconds. It was a different, unusual, electric feeling that he hadn't felt in a very, very long time.

"What are you thinking?" she asked softly.

He smiled and pulled his hand away, moving it to his lap, away and safe and covering his erection.

"I don't know what I'm thinking. My brain has been like Jack Benny's old Maxwell lately."

She smiled and shook her head.

Shit, Will thought, dated reference, lost on younger conquests. He muddled ahead. "It's all rattletrap thoughts and ideas and emotions all bouncing around like peas in a dried gourd." There, that reference might work. She nodded. Okay. That one she understood. "I'm sad and I'm scared and I'm lonely and I'm lost, and then I get this shot of euphoria, then that disappears, and I'm drinking too much, and I can't sleep more than forty-five minutes at a time, and when I do sleep I have these dreams that there's a little guy in my head building walls with bricks and mortar and I can't figure out what the hell he's up to. ..."

"Do you dream about your wife?" Beth asked quietly.

Will paused for a long moment, ashamed of what he had to say if he was going to tell the truth.

He took a deep breath, then brought his hand up from his lap and took a deep pull of the Irish whiskey and water. He put the glass down softly and stared at the cubes. The surface of the drink was now well below the top of the ice. The icy warmth coated his throat, then exploded in a wave across the sides of his stomach.

He looked at her. His eyes were edged in red.

Will took another breath and just said it.

"No. No, I don't," he said. His lip began to quiver. He sucked it in and bit it, pushing the thought, the emotion, back down. Beth reached across the table and took his hand again. She smiled with as much sympathy as she could muster, all the while beating herself up just behind her eyes.

Goddamn it, she thought. Save it for next week! Save it for the fucking interview!

She squeezed his hand.

And changed the subject.

※

IT WAS NEARLY 11:30. AFTER A ROUGH START, THE CONVERSATION HAD DRIFTED INTO safer areas, free of most emotional tiger traps. When had Will started riding? How did he decide to turn pro? Why don't Americans give a rat's ass about cycling except when Lance wins another Tour? Will, what, when, where, and why.

They talked about trips. They joked about family.

She had grown up in small-town Wyoming. He had grown up in Michigan.

It was small talk that only grazed the surface of a life but somehow built trust. Will opened up a bit as the evening progressed, but certainly not as much as he had at the beginning. It was an embarrassment for him, it was an emotional stop sign for her. Whenever he came close, she pushed him away.

Not here. Not now.

The bill came and Will paid for three drinks, two for him, one for her, his empty, hers still full.

He noticed it, but it didn't sink in too deeply, too many other thoughts and feelings and worries were crowding in, from excitement to grief to embarrassment to release to shame. He was feeling good, which, perhaps, was the most shameful feeling of all.

They stepped out into the cool Colorado night. Beth hugged herself tightly.

"This sweater seemed perfect—three hours ago."

"Always does around here." Will laughed. "Ten minutes and the weather changes to an entirely different season."

"You've got that right," she said, smiling. "I should have paid more attention to Fred March at 5."

"Well, I watch him, but I can never be sure. Is he being Mr. March, the Merchant of Truth, or is he being Frightening Freddie?"

She laughed.

"I can't keep up." He smiled and opened his arms in a sign of surrender.

In that second, she leaned forward impulsively and kissed him lightly on the lips. Will froze. They stared at each other silently for a long moment, unsure of what they felt and what should happen next.

"Sorry," she whispered.

Without hesitation, Will leaned forward and kissed her lightly, brushing her lips with his, sending a lightning pulse through his entire body. He pulled his head away and looked at her again.

Beth leaned forward and buried her head in the crook of his neck and shoulder, hugging him tightly, fusing her body to his.

"I enjoyed this," she whispered. "I'd like to do it again—if you would."

Will paused, his mind too many channels all tuned in at once, a ragged jumble of thoughts and words and emotions, all screaming to be heard.

"I would," was all he answered.

She hugged him again and backed slowly away from his embrace.

"You're a good man, Will Ross. A delicious man," she said quietly. "Don't ever forget that."

Will stood silently. He smiled with embarrassment.

"Good-night," she whispered. She reached out, squeezed his hand, turned, and walked quickly into the night.

Will stood stock-still, afraid to move, determined not to break the mood. She turned a distant corner and was gone.

Still, he stood.

"Delicious," he whispered. "She said I was delicious."

With a laugh, he shook his head, turned, and strolled easily back to his car, his step light, his mood lighter, his mind and memories, for the moment, anyway, left on the street behind him.

❋

THE TWO MEN WATCHED WILL WALK OFF.

"What did you get?" Timmons asked.

"Whole roll, thirty-six," said the police photographer. "Exit, chat, kiss—both of them—and both leaving. Him standing and watching her go."

"Good. When can you have them for me?"

"First thing in the morning they'll be on your desk. You know that Whiteside is going to have a cow, don't you?"

"Yeah, maybe," Timmons said. "But I've been telling him this guy is dirty. It's time he saw what Will Ross is doing while the body's still warm."

"I dunno—seemed pretty innocent."

"Just get me the pictures. The pictures will make my point."

The photographer held up his hands in surrender.

"Hey—you've got 'em."

❋

"WHAT DO YOU WANT TO DO ABOUT THAT?"

"Which?"

"Either."

"I don't know. I don't know."

"Doesn't look good."

"Which?"

"Either."

"Never does, does it?"

Stan and Ollie watched the police officers return to their car. They waited a minute until they were sure Will was no longer being followed, then turned and walked silently back toward the Tattered Cover parking garage.

WILDERNESS

"Yyy-yyyyy-aaaHHH!"

Will screamed, pushing himself frantically away from the bed. For a split second, he didn't know where he was, so he stood, shaking, breathing hard, by the side of the bed, staring at where he had been sleeping. Only seconds before, he had been so comfortable, so lost in the night, so soundly asleep.

He concentrated on where he was standing.

He looked around and came slowly to consciousness.

Bed. Home. Nightmare.

He looked at the clock. He looked at the door. The hallway was dark. Silent.

He had screamed, and Elena hadn't heard him. Rose hadn't heard him either. When Elena sniffled in her crib, Rose was up and moving. When he screamed at the top of his lungs, or at least thought he did, not a soul in the house stirred.

As his breathing returned to normal, he wasn't quite sure anymore.

He was in his house. He was in his room. He was beside his bed. But had he screamed? And if he had, why had he screamed? And why had he leaped out of bed? The dream?

Remember the dream: What was it?

Nothing. Nothing he could recall.

Will looked at the clock. One forty-eight. He had closed his eyes at 1. Forty-five minutes again, give or take. What the hell was that?

He rubbed his hip through his Hanes.

Damn.

He looked down at his right side.

What the hell was that? Bug bite?

He'd have to call Orkin in the morning. He took a deep breath and circled the bed, stood in the doorway, and looked down the dark hall. The door to Rose's room was open, dark, and silent. The same for Elena's room.

He had screamed. No one had heard. And now he had a wicked bite on his hip. What the hell was going on in this house?

CHAPTER NINE

FAMILY MATTERS

FRIDAY PASSED QUIETLY, WITH ONE OR TWO EXCEPTIONS.

First, Will was scared out of his wits to find Stan and Ollie quietly drinking coffee in his kitchen at 5:30, the only giveaway being the green light on the base of the coffee pot, which usually glowed red with the timer until 6 A.M.

He walked into the kitchen, stared at the green light for a second, then heard Stan say very quietly, "Good morning, Will."

He didn't shout, which later surprised him, but he did jump for the ceiling, swallowing the sudden shock and fear, which, as his heart rate returned to normal, made him want to throw up.

They merely wanted to chat about the digging they had been doing and the sources for the explosive RDX that they had been running down and the possibilities of who might be Peter the Great. And there was something else, something Stan kept running up to with an *um*, an *uh*, and a clearing of the throat that he never did ask, maybe because each time he ran up to it, Ollie was right there kicking him in the shins.

It never occurred to Will that they had followed him the night before. After all, he had been discreet, and the meeting with Beth had been innocent. A few stolen kisses between friends after a soulful conversation was nothing to get cranked about, and if Will, who was possibly the most easily cranked human being in North America, wasn't cranked about it anymore, despite a late-night erotic dream and an early morning tent pole, then it certainly wasn't that big a deal. It was just two friends talking, which was why sitting in the darkness of his kitchen sipping coffee with two former mob enforcers who Will had never believed to be all that former made Will snort.

"Something funny?"

"No," Will answered to the shadow in the darkness, wondering how Ollie could have seen the smile from across the table if Will couldn't see him. Hell, Will couldn't see his own coffee cup, let alone anyone or anything else at the table.

"Can I turn on a light?"

"No," came a simultaneous whispered answer.

"Even if I keep missing my mouth and pouring coffee down the front of my shirt?"

"It'll wash," said the short, round shadow.

"It'll wash," said the tall, thin one.

"Coffee's not that easy, boys. It leaves marks."

"It'll wash," came the answer, sharper now, ragged with lack of sleep.

"Yeah, okay." Will went back to drinking his coffee by Braille.

"You hear from the police yesterday?" Stanley asked.

Will shook his head, realized Stanley probably couldn't see it, despite the fact that the sky was beginning to change from deep black to slate gray, and said, "No, not a peep. I'm thinking Felix scared them off."

"They don't scare easy."

"Well, I didn't hear from them. I didn't see them. They weren't tailing me, so I'm guessing Felix scared them off. Maybe they're actually tracking down the guy who really did this."

Stanley nodded. In the half light, Will made out a silhouette moving its head up and down.

"Maybe," the shadow said.

"Where'd you go last night?" the other shadow asked.

Will froze for just a moment, then relaxed and answered. What was he worried about? He hadn't done anything wrong. He hadn't run off with her. They had just talked. And kissed. But mainly talked. It wasn't even a kiss, really, was it? It was a peck. A peck wasn't a kiss like rubbing your nose wasn't picking it.

He was still debating the idea when his mouth answered, quite without his knowledge, "Frisco's. In Cherry Creek. I just went out with a friend from work for a few drinks and to chat."

"Male friend from work? One of the sports guys?" Stanley asked.

Will paused.

"Nope. Female friend."

"What's she do?"

"She's an investigative reporter named Beth Freeman, if you want to do any checking."

"What did you talk about?"

"Work. The newsroom. How tough it's been. The baby. You."

"Us?" Stanley shot up straight.

"Naw, just shitting you, Stanley. Just like you're shitting me right here and now. What is this all about, guys? Do you want a blow-by-blow account of the evening, or is this just small talk?"

Ollie raised his hands in a gesture of surrender.

"Just want to keep an eye on things, Will, watch for anything unusual. Just keepin' track."

The anger began to boil in Will again. Jesus, he was tired of being pushed around.

"Well, then, you should know that she kissed me when we left." He pointed at his lips. "Right there. And you know what? I so enjoyed the sensation of a woman actually doing that to me that I jumped forward and kissed her back. Do I feel guilty? Do I feel ashamed?"

Will waited for an answer. None came. Both men stared at him, as did Rose Cangliosi from the doorway.

Will glanced over at her, then back to the two uncles sitting at the table.

"Yes. Goddamn it, yes, I did. I felt guilty as hell. *But I liked it!*"

"Easy, Will," said Stanley.

"Don't curse," said Ollie.

"Screw you, Ollie," Will snapped. "I've got the police treating me like I tried to kill my wife, I've got you two asking me when I took a dump today and what did it look like, I've got a woman at work who Zorro tells me to steer clear of, which I would, except every time I turn around she's there, smelling real good—I've got a boss who wants to send me out of town for some two-bit bike tour that I don't want to ride—am in no shape to ride—and I'm living with my mother-in-law, who my daughter thinks is the sun and the moon and the stars all rolled into one."

He looked down at Rex and Shoe, sleeping by the doorway.

"At least my dogs still like me."

At that, Shoe lifted his head, wagged his tail, put his head back down, and farted.

"Will," Stanley said in a calming tone, "there's nothing to get upset about. We understood …" He caught himself, pulling the statement up short.

"Understood what?" Will asked, suddenly suspicious.

"Nothing, Will," Ollie said, shooting Stanley a glance.

The sun rose with Will's realization.

"Oh, my God. You two followed me last night. Didn't you? Didn't you?" He turned on Rose. "Did you know about this? Did you suggest it? Follow him so he doesn't do anything I wouldn't like?"

Tears welled up in Rose's eyes.

"I had nothing to do …"

Will turned back to the uncles, sitting silently at the table, hands warmed by mugs of coffee.

"You sonsabitches. You followed me, didn't you?"

Neither said a word.

"Well, thanks for all the faith. Thanks for all the freedom. Great way to start a day." Will took one more slug of coffee, then walked to the stairs to start getting ready—five or six hours early—for work.

He turned to his mother-in-law.

"Rose, I'm sorry if I've angered or upset you. But for the love of God, I'm just trying to get through the day. And as I try to get through the goddamned day …"

"Don't curse."

"Fuck you, Ollie. Why don't you just take a bullet and put it in my goddamned brain, huh? Then everybody would be happy. Christ. I'm just trying, Rose, and I'm doing the best I can, and I *know* it's not good enough. Not for you, not for Elena, and sure as shit not for Cheryl. And as I try to get through the day, Rose, I'm going to make mistakes. I'm going to make mistakes with you and with Elena and with my job and with women I meet at work or in bars or wherever—because I am an emotional goddamned mess. I've got so many walls built inside my head, it looks like a goddamned maze. I don't know what I'm thinking or what I'm feeling or what is right anymore. On top of that, the cops and these two screwups think I killed Cheryl. And I can't abide that one goddamned bit. Do you, Rose? Do you think I killed her?"

He was shouting now.

Rose stared at him, her eyes red rimmed but hard. "I …"

"*No* would have been sufficient, Rose. *No* would have done the trick. Thank you all for your care and concern. Now, if you would please, each and every one of you, get the fuck out of my house."

He turned and marched upstairs, hitting each step with a slightly harder stomp than the one before until the frame of the house rattled with each step.

Rose took a deep breath and then sniffed up the tears. She turned to Stanley. "Did you follow him?"

"No. We followed the cops who were following him."

"Why didn't you tell him that?"

"Never got a chance," Stanley said. "He takes up all the air in the room."

Ollie shook his head.

"It's better for him to be a bit paranoid right now. One cop has an idea about Will, and he's going to make his point no matter what he has to do to make it. I'd rather Will was looking around and saw them while he's looking for us."

"He's more afraid of us than the cops, I think," said Stanley.

Rose nodded, crossed the kitchen to the coffee pot, and poured herself a cup. She turned, sat down, and looked intently at her brother and brother-in-law.

"Okay. What's this about a kiss? Who, what, where?"

Olverio Cangliosi sighed.

THE OTHER EXCEPTION, WHICH WOULD HAVE BEEN FAR MORE TELLING, ESPECIALLY if Will had been paying the slightest bit of attention, came that afternoon, following a long morning of staring at the walls of an empty sports office and pulling down wire copy about the Japanese baseball World Series. It wasn't really the Japanese World Series but the Japan Series, which at least was more honest than Major League Baseball calling its final series the World Series.

The air conditioning in the office was an off-and-on affair, and today it was off again. The room grew stifling, and Will felt his eyelids grow heavy. Ten-pound weights headed south, along with his chin, balanced on his chest, creating a double chin that made him look like Jabba the Hutt's younger, thinner brother.

"Yo, Will!"

Will felt something poke his shoulder once, then twice. He struggled toward consciousness in the thick air.

"Yeah, what? What? Oh, hi, Z. How you doing?"

Clyde Zoromski stared at Will for a long moment, then poked him again.

"You dead or alive?"

"Not sure. How's it look from out there?" Will asked.

"Dead, sure as shit. But that said, our fearless leader wants to see you in his office."

"Which fearless leader?"

"The only one I know—short, dumpy guy with a beard? Looks like he should be smoking a pipe, teaching freshman English, and banging the co-eds? That one?"

For a second, all Will could picture was Barbara Gooden standing in the front of a lecture hall with a tweedy jacket and a beard. Then he remembered Hugh Ransford, the man who was forcing him back onto a bicycle whether he wanted to go or not. Hugh Ransford. Will plugged in a face. It fit. He nodded.

"Right." He sighed, slapped his hands down on his knees in the hopes of waking at least a portion of himself, then stood, wobbling dangerously in the close air before he walked drunkenly toward the door.

"Be careful, man," Zorro whispered. "Ransford's the kind who doesn't go for a reporter having a liquid lunch."

"I'm not drunk. It's this damned office. I'm suffocating."

"I'll fix that. Yeah, and watch out for the Dragon Lady. She's in there with him."

"Who, Barbara?" Once again the image of her wearing a beard leaped into his mind.

"No. The *other* Dragon Lady—Beth. You remember her?"

"Hey, man, she's not so bad."

Zorro chuckled darkly. "Don't count on it, man. Don't count on it."

He opened his desk drawer, pulled out a short screwdriver, and jammed it into the thermostat. There was a buzz, a snap, a click, and a puff of blue smoke, followed by a hiss and a blower that kicked on in the middle of the ceiling.

"See?" Zorro said with a look of Cheshire cat satisfaction. "Nothing to it. By the time you get back, this place will feel like a meat locker."

"Don't know if I want that," Will said, slowly reviving in the cool of the atrium. He began the long walk across to the newsroom.

"Yeah, well, once I stick that thing in there, there's not a whole lot I can do about temperature control," Zorro called after him.

Will smiled and walked toward the newsroom double doors. The atrium was cool enough to bring him at least partially back to life. He blinked his eyes continually along the way, one last wake-up trick, then pushed his way through the doors and turned right toward Ransford's office. The door was open, and Ransford was letting somebody have it. There was no way you could stand anywhere in the newsroom and not be a part of the dressing-down.

"How long now? How long? And you have yet to turn a halfway decent story—let alone a series."

Will heard a word of argument from whoever was getting reamed before Ransford launched into it again.

"I brought you in because you begged. You begged that you could make the stories happen."

Will stepped over to the wall and tried to sink in but couldn't. He tried to block his hearing but couldn't do that either.

"You haven't turned in a single idea that's been worth a damn. ..."

Will looked down the newsroom as Zorro walked in, a bit flushed from hurrying across the atrium to hear the battle. He had gotten the call from a friend on the assignment desk, and for some reason this was one Clyde wanted to be a part of. He sidled up to Will.

"Has he killed her yet?"

"Killed who?"

"I'm told he's got Beth Freeman in there. I want to be on hand when she gets the axe."

Will was genuinely shocked. "You really want that to happen?"

"Sure, why not? Fills an afternoon." He chortled. "Besides, couldn't happen to a nicer person."

Will was about to say something, defend Beth, when Ransford's voice dropped to a tone of dismissal and she walked out of his office. Her face was flushed. She glanced at the looks of smug satisfaction on the faces in the newsroom. They were happy to see her taken down a peg or two.

Will stepped away from the wall and walked toward her as she left Ransford's office. Without pause or embarrassment he took her hand.

She glanced at their hands, then gratefully up into his eyes.

"You okay?"

She nodded. "Yeah. Thanks. That makes it easier."

"I don't know if that shit ever gets easy," he said.

She squeezed his hand. "Thanks," she whispered.

Without looking back, Will walked toward Ransford, standing in his door, watching the tableau before him.

"Will, come on in," he said, stepping aside. Will crossed into the office, and Ransford began to close the door behind him. As he did, he glanced one last time into the newsroom, catching Beth's eye. There was no smile, no frown, no reaction at all; they simply caught each other's eye.

Which, to Zorro, was like hanging a historical tapestry with every step of a great battle woven into it on the wall of a castle. It all became clear. He knew what was going on.

Beth turned away from Ransford's door and saw Zorro staring at her. She started, then quickly regained her composure.

"Hello, Z," she said.

"Hullo, Beth," Zorro said lazily.

She turned and began to walk away.

Quietly, almost under his breath, Zorro called after her, "Keep your hooks out of the kid, Beth."

She paused, then looked back at him. "I'm sure I don't know what you mean."

"Ah, but you do, my dear, you do. And I know what *you* mean, which in some ways is even worse."

Zorro pushed himself off the wall and sauntered over to her.

"The only thing I can't figure out, at least now, is what you might get out of him."

"There's nothing I want. He's been kind to me. The only person in this god-damned newsroom who has ..."

"That's because he's the only person in this goddamned newsroom who doesn't see through you like a new windshield."

"Stop it, Z—get in my way and you'll be out of here like you were shot from a cannon."

"Ah, the Puffed Rice routine. You've got that kind of clout? Interesting. But— no problem. It might even be a blessing. Still, you're thinking you can fuck that kid up, or just fuck him, or get something out of him. What could that be? Money? Trip to Europe to meet his old cycling buddies? What? Instant family?"

She smiled and leaned forward conspiratorially.

"I suggest," she whispered, "that you back away from me and never talk with me again. Otherwise, I'll accuse you of harassment or worse. Understand? And as for hooks and Will, you fuck this up for me, Clyde, and there won't be a place in this world where you'll be able to find a job—even shoveling camel shit in Outer Mongolia. Got it?"

She turned on her heel and marched away toward her cubicle. Zorro watched her go, her hips still pneumatic under the sheer fabric of her skirt. Damn. Dangerous combination: great looks and an evil mind. Not just ambitious, not just driven, but filled with the Daffy Duck view of existence: it's not enough that I succeed, my brother must fail. Zorro shook his head and walked back out the double doors toward the atrium and the coffee machine.

This was one to ponder—what, when, where, why—and Will.

❦

WILL SAT AND SMILED AT RANSFORD, WHO SMILED BACK WITH THE LOOK OF A MAN who had just been through an unpleasant task.

"You okay?" Will asked.

Ransford shook his head slightly as if surprised by Will's question. No one on his staff had ever asked him that before. It seemed so simple, but it was simply something staff reporters didn't ask management. The question usually was, "You alive?" followed by a poke with a sharp stick before the bonfire and the party began.

"Yeah. Yes, Will, I'm fine. Thank you for asking. How are you? Are you getting some riding time in? You said you were going to have to build up ... what, miles?"

"Yeah," Will nodded. "Miles, wind—butt. Toughest part is getting used to that leather seat all over again."

"Well, I suppose the station could spring for one of those padded ones if you want it."

"Naw. Get used to leather and there's nothing like it. It breathes, it's smooth, it's soft, in its own, nonpadded little way. No thanks, I'll stick with what I've got."

"Well, it's your ass," Ransford said with a laugh. "I just wanted to touch base with you and make sure you were set. You know the route … Boulder, Estes, Grand Lake, Breckenridge, then over Hoosier Pass and a long damned ride back into Denver. Are you set for that?"

"Well, let me tell you," Will said, shifting uncomfortably in his chair, "I've ridden for a lot of years, but I've never been ready for any of it. Sometimes it works, sometimes it doesn't. It all depends on what Our Lady of the Road Bike has to say about it."

"Let's hope she thinks kindly of you and gets you to your live-shot locations on time."

"How many shots?"

"Five a day. Six a.m., noon, 4, 5, and 10. You don't have to put much together; we'll have somebody shooting video for you. All you'll have to do is tell them what you're going to talk about, and they'll edit to fit. Otherwise, just talk."

"Who's my shooter?"

"Tony Carver, to start. He'll travel with you at least through Friday night. You worked with him last summer, right? At that bike race?"

Will nodded. "Yes, *that* race." He shut the thoughts of that race and its aftermath out of his head. The images didn't want to go. Carver, he knew, he could work with. Good guy. Solid shooter. Willing to sit down for a beer after the Ten.

"Carver will be fine. He'll work."

"Good. I'd like you to set up for a Wednesday live shot, 5 and 10, just to promote what you're going to be doing. Maybe do a package on the route. I've got Carver out today shooting some Estes Park, Trail Ridge, and Breckenridge video, so you'll be able to work with that. Graphics is doing an animated map for you too."

"Good." Will nodded. This guy had it covered.

"So for you, the biggest job next week is to ride your bike, get in shape, and make it look easy. The *Colorado Times* is thrilled we've signed on, and even more so that you're going to ride. They're getting one of their best fields in years."

Will laughed.

"I hate to think what these people are signing up to see."

"You're a European pro. People love that shit. Look how much they spend to smoke cigars with John Elway."

Will was surprised.

"Really?"

"Oh, yeah," Ransford said, sticking out his hand, indicating that the meeting was over, "big money. Guys like you are a draw."

"Well, this draw had better get some pedal time, then."

"Like that T-shirt I saw: 'Shut up and ride your bike.'"

"That's it, boss. That's it exactly."

Will stood and shook Ransford's hand, then turned and opened the door leading back into the newsroom. For a split second he wondered why the door had been open during Beth's dressing-down but closed for his quiet meeting about a community bike ride. Then the thought was pushed away by a blast of his own ego.

"Sure, people want to ride with me. It's just like hanging with John Elway."

❧

THE MAN WHO CALLED HIMSELF PETER THE GREAT WOVE THE PICKUP TRUCK IN and out of traffic, his anger building with each slowdown. He was late, and he had a lot on his mind.

The fury rose with each delay, then subsided with each new forty feet of pavement gained.

Still, it wasn't the traffic that caused him the most concern. It was the fact that one of his suppliers for RDX was pulling the plug on him. There were people asking, he had said.

"Asking about what?" Peter had demanded.

"Asking about who might have blown up that TV sports guy's wife."

"But was it the cops?" Peter asked

"No," came the answer, "not the cops. Two guys who looked funny but weren't—at all."

"Who were they?"

"Don't know, but they looked like they were willing to kill me to find out."

"What did you say?"

"Jack shit, pal. Jack shit. But they're looking. And I wouldn't want to be that guy when they find him."

Peter laughed. "Me neither. Can I get the stuff? I need more."

"Give me two weeks. Three. These guys meant business."

Even with the air conditioning on full, Peter the Great wiped the sweat off his upper lip. He should never have closed up shop and lain low. He should have kept playing the game. Should have pushed his advantage. Now someone was trying to get the advantage on him.

Now he had to get it back again. Bring the ball back into his court.

He pulled to another stop and sat up straight in the bucket seat. The idea emerged, fully formed.

He knew what he had to do.

First, move his gear. The house was too hot.

Second, make a statement to Will Ross and the police and the two funny guys who weren't funny at all.

Make a statement.

And make that statement loud and clear.

CHAPTER TEN
DÉJÀ VU
ALL OVER AGAIN

WILL GATHERED UP HIS THINGS IN THE SPORTS OFFICE AND PREPARED TO head for the door and home and a few days of hard training for the ride to come. The ride to come was a pip, that was for damned sure. Boulder to Estes meant back roads or heavy traffic; there were no two ways around it. Estes to Grand Lake meant Trail Ridge Road, the highest paved road in the United States, if not the world. Grand Lake to Breckenridge meant Berthoud Pass, which meant an endless climb and a hairy descent through construction, in traffic, and Breckenridge to Denver meant Hoosier Pass from the back side, then a long slog through South Park.

He had to build up some legs, or that office manager from Arvada was going to blow him off the side of the road in Fairplay and tell the story for the rest of his life.

"And there he was, wheezing and puking by the side of the road, Mr. Big Ass Paree-Roubaix himself!"

Will wasn't about to let that happen.

Zorro sat sullenly in front of his computer. He wasn't typing. He was staring. He was at war, but with himself.

Finally he turned to Will.

"Look, I'm real big on life lessons, you know what I mean?"

Will turned and smiled.

"I haven't the slightest idea."

Zorro sighed. "This is serious, Will. When I see people heading in the wrong direction, I usually let them go because one, I'm not their father; two, it's usually none of my damned business; and three, I don't really give a good god-damn what happens to other people. Okay?"

Will nodded. "Okay."

"But you, I like. And you are one fucked-up young man right now."

"Well, thank you for that …"

"Goddamn it, Will, listen to me. This is not a game. Something is up. Rans-ford is setting you up for something. So is Beth Freeman. I don't know what it is, but I'm sure as shit going to find out."

"Aw, come on, Z. Ransford was just laying out the bike tour stories for next week, and Beth—shit, she told me last night that she wasn't getting the sto-ries she wanted here … Ransford wasn't happy."

"You talked with her?"

"Yeah."

"How?"

"How do you mean, how?"

"Like 'let's go out and have a drink' talked with her?"

"Yeah."

"Where? Wait, don't tell me: Frisco's, right?"

A sudden chill ran up Will's spine. He felt defensive.

"Yeah, Frisco's. What the fuck is it to you?"

Zorro put up his hands in mock surrender. He was not smiling. "Okay, Will, okay. You win. I'm just saying," he said each word slowly and distinctly, as if that would somehow get past Will's defenses and make the point, "something is up. I don't know what it is. That little drama you saw with Beth and Rans-ford was bullshit. I'm thinking it was for your benefit. …"

Will started to protest. Clyde Zoromski held a hand up.

"Your benefit, Will. Don't ask me why. After you and Beth talked and you started walking into the office, she and Ransford gave each other a look that …"

"That what?" Will demanded angrily.

"That I don't fucking know! It didn't fit, Will. It just didn't fit."

Will sighed and shook his head. "So, what—this is a hunch?"

"No, it's a memory, Will. It's a goddamned memory."

"Which wife? Number three, number two?"

"Number four, if you must know—just hear me out—then tell me to fuck off,

I don't care. I've done my bit, and you've got to deal with your choices. You're a big boy. That's fine. *But*—something is not right. The cheese stinks in Denmark, or whatever the saying is—so just be aware, okay? Just be aware."

Will was about to say something, thought better of it, then simply nodded. "Fine. Okay. I'll be aware of Ransford, but I don't …"

"You don't have to know anything. Just don't trust those bastards. They're setting you up for something."

"Okay! Okay, I'll keep my eyes open."

Will put the last of his things in the oversized *VeloNews* messenger bag and slung it over his shoulder.

Zorro shook his head.

"You hate my guts now, and that's fair. But don't let them use you as a dupe. Or a dope. Or a pawn. The only thing we really have in this business is our ability to think for ourselves. Beyond the managers, beyond the producers, beyond the people telling us every day who we are and what our stories should be and what makes us people. That's it. Don't let them take the power of independent thought away from you."

"Don't worry. I won't let him," Will said, walking toward the door. "You in next week?"

"I'm off Monday and Tuesday."

"I'll see you Wednesday, then, before I leave. Have a good weekend."

"Where are you off to?" Art Jackson said as he squeezed past Will in the doorway.

"Training," Will muttered.

"Excuse me. Well, Mr. Zoromski. Cheery as ever, I see."

"You would be too, pus-head, if you had to fly to seven high school football games tonight in a helicopter that was old when Sikorsky was young."

"Hey, I'll do it."

"I bet you would. Sorry. I'll manage."

"Training?" Art turned back to Will. "What kind of training?"

"Getting ready for that station ride next week."

"Ah, don't want some housewife passing you on Berthoud, right?"

"No."

"Must be nice. Just riding a bike for work."

Will sighed. He thought about what he was going to have to ride today—Lookout Mountain at the very least. Maybe twice.

"I'll be happy to trade with you."

"He'll never trade with you, Will," Zorro said. "It would mean less face time for our little friend."

"Hey—I make no apologies," Art said. "I'm going to be big someday."

"Your ego already is."

Jackson shot Zorro a look, then smiled. "Like I said, no apologies."

"While you two play *The Bickersons*, I'm losing sunlight. See you on Monday."

"Remember what I said, Will," Zorro said softly.

"Yeah, remember what he said, Will," Art mimicked.

Zorro smiled sarcastically, and Will noticed him flip Art the finger along his pant leg.

"Bye, boys." Will turned and walked down the hall, happy to be leaving, ready to get to the release of the bike.

Zorro sat quietly for a moment, thinking about the conversation he'd had with Will before Art Jackson's unfortunate arrival. Something wasn't quite right. Will hadn't gotten the point about something. Beth. That was it. Everything Will had said he'd be careful about had to do with Ransford, not Beth Freeman. Ransford was a dupe, Freeman was the key, and Will was blind to it all. But what else could he do? If Will wouldn't see it, then Will would just have to learn for himself.

"Fuck," he said under his breath.

"No, thank you," Art answered quickly.

※

AT THE FRONT DOOR, A YOUNG MAN IN BLUE JEANS AND A WORK SHIRT, SPORTING A blond ponytail, stood just beyond Shirley's domain, looking back and forth across the atrium.

Will stopped. "Can I help you?"

"Yeah, I'm looking for Hugh Ransford's office. I've got an appointment with him."

Without thinking, Will pointed at the double doors.

"Right through there and then a hard right. Can't miss his office."

"Thanks."

"Does he know you're here?"

"Yeah," he nodded back toward Shirley, "she announced me."

"Great."

Just then Ransford poked his head out the newsroom double doors.

"Jeremy, good to see you. Come on in."

"Take care, man." The fellow nodded to Will.

"You too," Will answered. He walked out the door and promptly forgot the world inside.

It was time to ride.

꽃

"WHAT ARE YOU GOING TO DO WITH HIM?" BETH FREEMAN HISSED INTO THE PHONE in her cubicle.

"Who?" Hugh Ransford said defensively.

"Who? You know very well who," she barked before lowering her voice again. "Zorro. Z. Clyde Zoromski. Weekend sports anchor. That one."

"Beth, I've told you before, there's not a whole lot I can do about him. Gooden's got me on a tight leash for hires and fires."

"Well, you'd better do something," she said, cutting him off, "because that asshole knows me well enough to know that something is up. And if he tips it to Will Ross, we're up shit crick without a paddle."

"Okay, okay. I understand. I'll keep him running all weekend. You won't have to worry about him getting a chance to see or talk to Will, let alone spill anything."

She sighed.

"Okay. Thanks. Dear God, just don't let him screw this one up. Not this one. Not when I'm so goddamned close."

"You know, Beth, there are very few prayers of intervention that include the word *goddamned*."

"Thanks. By the way, when you're done with the paperwork on Jeremy, send him over to me. I want to take him to Frisco's tonight so he can start laying out the shoot."

"Done. He's got about ten more minutes of stuff to do, then I'll send him over."

"Great. See ya …"

"Beth, wait a second. What's the big deal with Zoromski anyway? You've been pissin' and moanin' about him since the day you walked in … what's the deal?"

"The deal, the deal. Well, Hugh, it's like this …"

There was a long pause.

"Yes?"

"Clyde Zoromski is just about the only human being I ever let get close to me, and …"

"And what?"

"He's using that knowledge against me."

"Fair enough. I'll get him out of your way."

Ransford hung up. Beth Freeman slowly put down her receiver and turned to look out the newsroom window.

"He's using it against me," she whispered to herself. "Ex-husbands have a way of doing that."

CHAPTER ELEVEN

TRAINING DAZE

THERE COMES A MOMENT, USUALLY IN THE MIDDLE OF A RIDE, WHEN THE body takes over for the mind, when the pain goes away, when the effort pushes itself, even in a horrific climb, past the point of caring to an alpha state, a state of grace, the center of the rider's very being, a place where the bike becomes an extension of the self and the ride simply exists as a moment in the universe. The anguish disappears and the soul carries the bike forward toward the summit, the finish, the feed station in the distance, the next turn in a series of never-ending turns.

Will wasn't anywhere close yet.

❧

"JEEEEEEE-ZZZZZZUUUUUZZZZZZ."

The first climb up the Golden side of Lookout Mountain was bad, just plain bad, with its endless parade of short switchbacks, each new turn arriving and throwing off his rhythm just as he was finding the pace to deal with the climb. And on each turn, it seemed, he not only met a dead animal, forcing him to break his line and sweep out to the side, but a minivan going up or a school bus heading down, a back-and-forth pilgrimage to the grave of Buffalo Bill Cody, who wanted to be buried near his ranch in Nebraska but who had the bad luck to die in Denver and got snatched and planted at the top of Lookout under a couple of tons of concrete by the landmark-minded publisher of the *Denver Post*.

Another pumpkin-yellow school bus roared by in low gear, the driver wrestling with the wheel, the brakes screaming in fear for their very pads. The kids had the windows down and were yelling at Will. He couldn't make out what they were saying. He could make out what appeared to be a half-empty can of Coke that went sailing past his forehead, dotting his sunglasses with drops of secret-formula cola syrup.

He made a final turn and realized he was at the top, a short stretch of asphalt that hardly seemed worth the trouble. He followed what appeared to be a service road past the visitors' center, which sat in the shadow of a forest of TV and radio towers that irradiated Bill's bones and encouraged residents who had moved to the mountain long after the towers had arrived to now protest their existence, much like the people who move into subdivisions near airports.

Will could swear that the heavy filling in his left lower molar was picking up Detroit Tigers baseball.

Not paying much attention, Will suddenly found himself on the back side of Lookout, riding down through gentler switchbacks, through the residential areas, the road looking out to the southwest and the growing late-day traffic on I-70. The foothills commuters were heading home, and the folks taking off for a weekend in the mountains were making the best of the lighter traffic. The interstate would be a parking lot in an hour, then worse about 3:30 on Sunday afternoon.

The turn came up and caught Will by surprise, spooking him out of his ponderings. He dropped from the outside to the in, never touching the brakes, kicking up his knee, and found just the right lean to the bike. It was unconscious. It was natural.

It was just like riding a bike.

"Ha!" Will screamed. "Ha! Hot damn. Hot damn. You bet. All right."

Anyone who wasn't sitting inside his head at the moment, anyone who was watching from a distance, would have thought him nuts, just plain dog-nuts crazy, the kind of guy who would spend his golden years talking to a brick in Civic Center Park, convinced it was a pigeon.

But Will realized that just for a second, a split second, he had found it again. He had rediscovered himself.

He was a professional rider. In the primal recesses of his brain, past the beer-swilling couch potato who now sat on the surface, he still had the touch. The years of training were buried but not dead. Not by a long shot.

The road fell away at a gentle angle toward the frontage road of I-70. Will picked it up, turned east, and rode in a great loop, down 70 to Morrison Road, down Morrison to Sixth, down Sixth to the place where he had parked his car, which he passed, much as he wanted to stop, and continued on, back up toward the buses and the switchbacks and the pile of dust that once was Buffalo Bill Cody.

This time the riding was easier, if only because this time he knew, deep down, that somewhere beyond the thin, soft layer that had added itself to his legs, his arms, his gut, he still had it.

There was still the question of finding it, working it, bringing it fully to the fore, but now he knew it was there, somewhere.

Halfway up Lookout Mountain, Will Ross found his state of grace.

❀

"Hi."

The voice on the phone was cool and warm at the same time. Will's eyebrows peaked, and he felt a smile cross his face.

"Hi back," he said. "How are you?"

"I'm good. I'm good," Beth said. "I, uh, just wanted to call and thank you."

"For what?"

"Well, after Ransford kicked me six ways to Sunday, you were the only one in that newsroom to actually give me a hand. I appreciate that."

"No problem."

"I'll bet Mr. Zoromski gave you an earful back in the sports office."

Will shook his head. "No. Don't worry about that. He seemed bothered by Ransford for some reason. Not you."

"Really?"

Will thought back, his mind capturing only selective memories of the afternoon. "Yeah, really."

"We still on for next week?"

"You bet. You still busy this weekend?"

There was a long pause before Beth Freeman said, "Yes, I think I am—but who knows, we might be able to find some time somewhere. Breakfast, maybe?"

"That would be good. I know a little place in Littleton that's really nice. Ever heard of the Iris?"

"No, but I'll take your word for it, Will. Give you a call in the morning?"

"Sounds good. I'm planning a ride about 10 or so—call me before that if you're interested."

"I will. Take care."

"You too. Sleep well."

"Thanks, I appreciate it. 'Night."

"Good-night."

She softly hung up the phone and stared at it for a long moment, a gentle smile playing across her lips. She picked up the phone and punched in a new number.

"Hello?"

"Hugh, Beth. Forget what I said this afternoon. He's still on the hook."

"Who?"

"Will."

"Ah. Good. Now you can enjoy your weekend, and you can leave me alone to enjoy mine."

"Now I can get to work."

"That's what I like to hear from my employees."

She hung up the phone and turned to Jeremy, her freelance photographer. "Let's go. I want you to see the location and map out two cameras—wide and tight on the table."

"What about your reaction shots?"

"We can pick those up later after everyone has gone."

"That's dishonest."

"Shit, man, that's TV. Where the hell have you been?"

"Who was that, Will?"

"A friend from work, Rose. Just a friend from work."

Will bounded up the stairs past Rose and Elena, toward his bedroom and the master bathroom. After a third liter of water, he needed some serious magazine time, followed, perhaps, by a beer and an old movie to round out the day's workout.

Rose Cangliosi watched him go, then waited until the door to the bathroom closed behind him.

She bounced Elena on her shoulder.

"*Puttana*, I tell you, Elena. That woman is a *puttana*."

She stood on the stairs for a moment, thought about what she should do, nodded to herself and the baby, walked downstairs, picked up the phone, and called her brother.

If Rose Cangliosi was going to meddle in the life of her son-in-law, she was going to do it right.

And she was going to know, even for her own benefit, what in the name of God this woman was doing.

Elena cooed in her ear.

Rose took that as a sign from all the women who had lived in her family before her and all that were yet to come.

CHAPTER TWELVE
REFINING THE RIDE

IN THE END, BETH HADN'T CALLED, WHICH, IN A WAY, WAS JUST FINE WITH WILL. He rose lightly off the seat, flexing his knees and adjusting slightly to hit the railroad tracks dead on.

He wasn't climbing today, he was just riding. Just getting in seat time and miles. North from the house, through the worst that Monaco had to offer, he cut across to unknown roads that led him into unknown parts of the city: small subdivisions that gave way to warehouses, warehouses that gave way to refineries and grain elevators, in the midst of which he passed a high school that seemed to be in the middle of nowhere. The placement was odd, and he thought about it for a time as he rode mindlessly away from the city into the endless stretches of the northeast plains.

In the end, Beth hadn't called, which, in a way, was fine with Will.

It had gotten him on the bike earlier, as he was pushed out the door by his mother-in-law, Elena locked perpetually on her shoulder like a conjoined twin. He already had a good twenty-five miles under his belt at a solid pace, so there was something to be said for the ride.

But, in the end, it remained. Beth hadn't called.

And if it was indeed just fine with Will, he wondered why he kept wondering why she hadn't called.

He puffed a coffee-tainted breath from deep inside his gut, bent over the headset, and picked up the pace again, interval training toward the next refinery and its cloud of petrochemical stew.

❁

"HELLO, IS WILL THERE?"

"No, I'm sorry, he's not. Could I take a message, please?"

"Oh, I'm sorry. I told him I was going to call this morning."

"Well, he waited for a call, then got disgusted and went for a training ride. May I take a message?"

"No, that's fine."

"May I tell him who called?"

"He'll know."

"Oh. I didn't know he was a mind reader. May-I-tell-him-who-called?"

"Yes. All right. Tell him Beth called."

"Any last name?"

"Just Beth."

"Beth Beth?"

"Just Beth. Beth Freeman."

"Beth Freeman. Now, that wasn't so difficult, was it, dear?"

"Thank you."

"No, thank you."

"Good-bye."

"Good-bye."

"Bitch."

"Bitch."

❁

THE REFINERIES WERE LEFT BEHIND IN THE VALLEY, AND FARMS ROSE UP TO GREET WILL the deeper he rode into the Colorado plain. There were cattle and corn and summer wheat and low-lying green fields that someone had obviously spent a good deal of time cultivating but that Will wouldn't recognize until the mystery green was properly washed, packaged, and displayed at his neighborhood King Soopers.

It was backroads America.

And he was free.

He rose up out of the seat, shifted gears, gritted his teeth, and rode toward a point that not even he could see in the distance.

CHAPTER THIRTEEN
WEEKEND WARRIORS

WHITESIDE DIDN'T WANT TO BE AT THE COP SHOP ON A SATURDAY AFTER-noon. He had plans with his family. Being there was keeping him away from the people he wanted to be with, the places he wanted to be, and the things he wanted to be doing—like—cleaning out his gutters.

Walking into a mostly empty room at 2:30 on a Saturday, the building filled with the quiet only Saturday can bring, was vaguely disturbing. Timmons had insisted. But then, Timmons hadn't shown up. Five more minutes. That was all Ray Whiteside was going to give the asshole before he was down the hall, in his car, on his way south toward home.

He sat down at his desk and waved at Ackerman, passing the door with a sheaf of papers, looking disgusted for having pulled the short straw. In that passing glance, Whiteside recognized the look of a man who had pulled the on-call and desperately wanted to be hit with a three-hour attack of food poisoning so he could pass the duty off to somebody else. That somebody else was now enjoying a Saturday afternoon in the backyard with a beer and a portable TV set balanced on his belly. The yard was mowed, the gutters cleaned, the minutiae of home ownership dealt with for another week—unless, of course, there was a cold snap and the leaves that hung precariously over the pristine lawn decided to let go and cover the ground with a blanket of fresh raking material.

Whiteside smiled as he spun the chair back to his desk and saw the manila envelope. There was a case number in the corner that Whiteside recognized but couldn't place for a second. Just under the number was a sticky note with a message in heavy black marker: "Thought you might find these interesting. Timmons."

The note made Ray Whiteside realize that he had been set up, that Timmons wasn't coming in, and that if he opened the envelope, he'd probably be stuck here, in a room that smelled of stale coffee and tired people, for the rest of the afternoon. But by now he had placed the case number, and his curiosity was getting the better of him.

He reached for the envelope, paused, then undid the brass clasp on the back and emptied the photos onto his desk. He realized at once that he wasn't the first person to see these and handle them. They had fingerprints across them and marks with a grease pencil on the back denoting time and date, location, and subjects.

And the subjects would have been interesting, especially to anyone Timmons was trying to convince of the righteousness of his accusations.

The first picture showed Will Ross leaving Frisco's in Cherry Creek North with an unidentified woman. Young, good-looking. Whiteside didn't recognize her at first. The next, marked No. 8 but second in the pile Whiteside was holding—the seven between the two must have been more walking shots—showed Will Ross and the unidentified woman standing close and looking at each other under a streetlight. The final *s* in *Frisco's* could be seen behind Will's back. The two were obviously talking. Will had a smile on his face. The woman had her left hand on Will's biceps. The next series of six pictures gave a split-second account of what happened next. The woman began leaning in and kissed Will. The kiss held for two frames. Will had not reacted backward. Whiteside felt his heart sink a bit.

The next photo, after the woman had leaned back, showed Will with a look of surprise on his face, clearly there, even in the darkness, registered forever on the grainy, high-speed film stock.

The next photo was a stare-down between Will and the woman, but the next series of eight showed Will, clearly making the move, leaning forward and kissing the woman full on the lips, the kiss holding for four frames. Instinctively, Whiteside leaned forward and turned the picture of Cheryl he had propped on his desk away from the black-and-whites.

Damn that little son of a bitch, he thought, not sure if he was thinking of Will or Timmons or both.

His instincts told him that this evidence was circumstantial, that there could be a perfectly innocent explanation for it, but he knew Timmons was determined to make his point. A six-week widower on the town, kissing a good-looking young woman on a dark street in Cherry Creek North after dinner and drinks at a quiet bar known for its intimate setting and its popularity among the not-quite-faithful crowd.

Whiteside leaned his head back and sighed.

He moved to the next pictures. As the two broke apart, the woman held Will's hand and let her growing distance drag her fingers out of his. That struck Whiteside as odd, almost dramatic, but still photos couldn't tell much of a story. There was context to be considered. And there was no context here, just images.

Damning images, that was for sure, but this was nothing more than a pile of separate images on paper, telling a story that might or might not be real.

The final three shots showed Will standing alone in the frame, staring off into the distance, obviously watching her go—or was he? Once again, the context was missing, even though it seemed obvious.

On the final photo Timmons—it had to be Timmons—had taken a grease pencil and circled a shadow just below Will's belt. Whiteside paused for a moment, then leaned in close, searching for whatever it was Timmons had seen in the grain of the photo. He still couldn't see it, but he realized suddenly what Timmons thought he was indicating. The irregularity on the film could have been a shadow caused by a turn of the subject away from a light source. It could have been a flaw on the film caused by the lack of light and the high-speed 1000 ASA film. Or it could have been an erection carried by a man who, Timmons was convinced, had just carried out a romantic rendezvous with his new squeeze.

Could be, Whiteside thought, could be. Could be a lot of things.

He tossed the pictures onto his desk and let them spread across the desk calendar. The woman's face poked out from under the pile. He stared at it. He knew her. He knew he knew her, but he couldn't get past the question to the answer.

A sheet poking out from under the final picture in the set cleared up the mystery. Timmons wrote:

Thought you might be interested in our boy's nocturnal activities with BETH FREEMAN, reporter at TV6. She did the 55 story that told the city it was okay to drive 65 because we wouldn't ticket before that—which means that everybody is driving 75 now. I suppose we should thank her because the city is getting rich off speeders. I'm sure this means we'll get a raise.

Six weeks.

Shouldn't he still be in mourning?

Doing pretty good for a grief strickened daddy.
See you Monday.
Timmons.

Whiteside sat back and read the letter again, then tossed it on top of the pictures. Circumstantial. That's all it was. Circumstantial. No context. It was a dangerous foundation on which to build a case. Any kind of case in any kind of setting.

Circumstance.

Context.

But Timmons was making his point, which was certainly more than Whiteside could do at the moment.

❋

THE CREATURE WAS ELEGANT IN ITS SIMPLICITY: TWO WIRES AND THE IGNITER FOR A model-rocket engine.

All you needed was a power source and a stable explosive moved quickly to instability by ignition.

And Peter the Great knew where he could find both.

Wasn't it wonderful what you could learn from the movies?

❋

"SO—WHAT'S HIS NAME AGAIN?"

"I'm telling you, all I know is that his name is Pete. Peter."

"Where do you meet him?"

"I don't. It's all by phone and note and drop."

"Drop where?"

"Sometimes Alamo Placita Park. Sometimes City Park. Sometimes Washington Park. I leave a bag, walk away, he picks it up, leaves a bag."

"How do you get paid?"

"How do you get paid?"

"*AAAAAaarrrrrr*—you're breakin' my fucking arm!"

"Don't curse, or I'll break the thing off. How do you get paid?"

"It's in the bag he leaves!"

"You trust him?"

"Got to. It's the only way to do business … aaaaaarrrr … Jesus!"

"Lighten up," the round one said.

"Why?" the skinny one asked.

"Because Randy here is our friend. He's going to tell us everything we want to know, and then he's going to disappear from Denver and Colorado because if he doesn't, we'll make him disappear from life. Do you think he understands that?"

"I'm not sure. I'll ask: Do you understand that?"

"I understand. I understand," Randy whimpered. "Just tell me how far away I've got to go and how fast you want me to run."

"Oh, a long way. But first, before you run, we want you to do us a little favor—think you can handle that?"

"Sure. Sure. Sure. What?"

"We want you to wait. Just wait until he calls you, then let us know. He's been asking for a new shipment, right?"

"He's low. He's low on RDX. Ow, Jesus."

"Don't curse."

"Okay, so when he asks for a new shipment. Whatever it is, firecrackers to an atom bomb. Think you can do that?"

"I can do that. I can do that."

"Then it's so long, Colorado, right?"

"Right."

The fat man nodded. "Let him go."

"Can I break his arm?"

"No, no, please!"

The fat man thought about it for a moment. "No, just let him go." He produced a card with a phone number on it. No name appeared, just a number. "Day or night, you hear from your friend with the penchant for all things explosive, you call me, okay?"

"Okay," Randy said briskly, nodding his head quickly for emphasis.

"Fine. You're a good boy." The round man patted his shoulder. "You're going to make it out of this alive."

The thin man shook his head. "I dunno. I don't trust him."

"Oh, come, now. We can trust Randy, can't we?"

"Yes. Yes. You can trust me. You can trust me," Randy said frantically.

"Yes, I know we can. I want you to get rid of all of your stock too."

"What? Do you know how hard it was to get …"

"I want you to get rid of all of your stock," the man said flatly.

Randy nodded.

"You bet. I'm thinking I should get out of the business for a while."

"Forever."

"Forever."

The skinny man looked at Randy hard for a moment, then said quietly, the threat in his voice completely unveiled, "You see, my friend, this is personal. You are dealing with two men who have a personal stake in this and will kill anyone—anyone—who stands in their way of getting to the son of a bitch who killed a friend of ours. Do you understand?"

The frightened man nodded frantically.

"Don't give us away. Or we'll be back. Don't save any of your stock, or we'll be back. Give us a call when you hear from your client, you know the one, or we'll be back."

"How can you be sure it's him?"

"Gut feeling. It's never missed yet. He is the one who likes it all: RDX, plastique, nitro—right?"

"Peter."

"Peter."

"Peter."

Stan and Ollie nodded. The young man between them stood, his shirt covered with sweat. The crotch of his pants was wet from a weak bladder.

"I'll call. I'll call."

Ollie patted Randy gently on the shoulder.

"You do that. We'll be waiting."

The two turned to the back of the house and started to leave. Randy watched them go. He heard the back door open and then the screen. He sighed and began to relax.

It was time to run. He'd give it half an hour, add ninety minutes to that, and he'd be gone.

Stanley suddenly reappeared in the doorway.

"By the way. You run and we'll find you. Simple as that. And you will die in a way that I wouldn't want to wish on my worst enemy." He motioned over his shoulder in the direction Ollie had taken. "Once I get started, he won't help you in any way, shape, or form. You understand?"

"I understand."

Stanley turned and left. The door in the rear of the kitchen closed behind him. Randy Disson's bladder let go again.

❋

WILL STRETCHED OUT ON THE GREEN OF HIS BACK LAWN, CAREFULLY CHECKING THE GRASS for any surprises left behind by Rex or Shoe. They both used another corner of the yard as their usual elephant-dung burial ground, but there were always surprises.

He stretched up and looked at the late-September-afternoon Colorado sky. It was gorgeous. A gorgeous day.

He knew that meant nothing. By tomorrow morning, the temperature could drop 70 degrees, Trail Ridge Road could be snowed shut, and winter could be upon them like Spandex on a lady in Walmart.

But now, at this moment, it was gorgeous. God's gift to him: this day, this moment, this feeling of accomplishment.

He had made the ride. He had pushed himself. He had done seventy-five miles and he felt good—tired but good.

He let his eyes drift over the single cloud that wandered slowly through the shocking blue of the sky, his mind wandering with it through the shapes he saw: a duck, a rabbit, no, a reaching hand.

A warm breeze began to kick up. Will could see the top branches of the ash tree begin to bend back and forth. It felt good now. It would have been a bitch on the road.

He smiled at his luck, his changing luck, it seemed, and looked back up toward the reaching hand. It was still a hand, thinner now, as the wind at altitude stretched it out, soon to reform it into some other image.

Will stared at it until it disappeared, shredded into streaks of water vapor.

But in that last second, the last second that it looked like a hand, a thin, almost skeletal hand, Will could swear that it had been reaching for him.

He shuddered.

The breeze was growing cooler in the shade.

That's what it was. The breeze was growing cooler. He had lain down without cooling down, and now he was feeling the chill.

He sat up, stood up, and hobbled on quickly tightening muscles toward the back door. He'd stretch on the living room rug rather than outside.

Will looked above him one last time as he stepped through the door.

There wasn't a cloud in the sky.

CHAPTER FOURTEEN

THE ZEN
OF THE BICYCLE

IT FELT LIKE A MOMENT OUT OF "RHAPSODY IN BLUE," WITH THE ROAD RISING up and carrying him without effort toward the horizon. Somehow, the pace was back within him. It was still an effort to ride, a question of just having the endurance, the strength to come off the bench and outwit, outlast, outride the competition, but there was a certain liquid smoothness to it now, a feeling he hadn't had in close to twenty-five years, not since he had ridden on a cast-iron bike for no other reason than to just plain ride.

It was becoming fun again now. It had been exhilarating then.

At nine years old, he had wanted to know everything about a bike: what made it work, what made it move, why putting the seat so low that he could comfortably get his feet on the ground was making him slower than Greg Greenburg, his next-door neighbor, who was riding a brand-new Schwinn with plastic streamers coming from the plastic handlebar grips. All Will could do was take strips of rawhide and wind them around the handlebars for a grip. How was he supposed to know that he was on the right track because leather was the professional grip of choice, and that Greenburg, for all his streamers, would wind up as a fat accountant with three wives, two alimonies, and an above-ground pool that exploded one night, flooding three neighboring yards and leading to a huge, soggy lawsuit?

In discovering everything he had ever wanted to know about bicycles, Will had torn apart his brother's bike, not his own, spreading bearings and screws and chain rings all over the garage floor. In order to have a bike again after his was given to his brother, he had to learn how to put one back together.

It took most of the summer, but he did it. Then his brother took back the newly retooled bike and returned the cast-iron minibike, now in a pitiful state of disrepair. Slowly Will began to rebuild it, piece by piece, bearing by bearing, one final BB continually skittering away across the garage floor to become a toy for the cat.

To learn all that he could, on a bet, he rode Terry Bingham's bike as fast as he could down a hill and tried to jump the irrigation ditch beside the road. He didn't make it. Later that same day, riding home on the back of his sister's bike, he stuck his bare toes into the spokes in an attempt to make that Jack of Hearts motorcycle sound.

His scream was more like a siren.

It wasn't the smartest thing in the world to do, but he learned. One week and a painfully bruised foot later, his cast-iron bike was repaired and restored and he was on the road again. It was another chance to learn—bikes may not fly, bikes can bite back, but, joy of joys, bikes go fast. Despite small rims and weird gears and short legs and a frame that weighed as much as a '59 Buick, bikes do, indeed, go fast.

And that year, as late summer turned to fall on the back roads of West Michigan, as the leaves changed in their canopies from green to brilliant golds and reds and electric yellows, he rode as fast as he could, as far as he could, just to feel the wind whip across his buzz-cut scalp and to feel the joy of riding a bike.

Riding a bike.

Today, on the back roads of Colorado, somewhere between Elizabeth and Castle Rock, dodging speeding traffic, the joy was with him again. There was no push, there was no shove, there was no need to catch up or break away or pace or draft or solo, there was only the need to ride, to pedal, to move forward smoothly.

It was a need from deep inside: to ride to somewhere, to get there sometime, to simply do it so that the final strokes ended with a smile as the bike went back on the rack in the garage, with the hope that the bike would never gather dust again.

Not as much, certainly.

As he rode, Will came to a realization about the week ahead. His ego just didn't care anymore about making sure no one ever beat him. If the appliance salesman from Fort Collins beat him down the mountain, so be it. Same for the doctor, lawyer, Indian chief, housewife, hairdresser, TV reporter, produce manager, and various other professionals, craftsmen, or pedaling-fool human beings who might see it as a badge of honor to smoke a guy who once rode Le Tour.

Rode it poorly but rode the thing, nonetheless.

To leave the winner of Paris-Roubaix in the dust.

Could happen. Could be. So what?

Will thought back to a book he had read on a transatlantic flight one summer, Mark Twain's *Life on the Mississippi*. Twain complained that once he had learned the details of the river as a steamboat pilot, the Mississippi lost its mystery and beauty—ripples became snags, and snags became danger. The same was true for riding. In driving himself to go pro, Will had lost the magic of the road. He had trained himself beyond the glory of the pedal stroke. A gentle turn through majestic hills had become nothing more than a series of angles and speeds to analyze and overcome rather than a death-defying lunge into the unknown with the wind screaming in his ears, his eyes glistening with tears, his muscles electric with the sheer joy of just doing it.

There had been times he had thought he could never get it back, never again feel the joy, always just feel the job of riding.

And yet now, riding alone, setting his own pace and not caring one whit when he got there or how, Will Ross felt something he hadn't felt in a decade on a bike.

He felt alive.

Alive.

Will rose out of the seat, planted a smile on his face, and rode hard toward the next turn, the next death-defying lunge into the unknown.

❋

THE BALL WAS STILL IN PLAY, A KEY CONCEPT IN THIS BUSINESS. KEEP THE BALL IN play because you never know when the other guy will trip or falter or fall away.

He just needed a little help, that was all.

And a little help was what he was going to get—two bits of help, as a matter of fact.

One was simple: two wires, the igniter for a rocket motor, and a broken taillight.

The second, oh, the second was a work of art: a tiny charge, designed not to kill but to maim, perhaps not even physically, though the plastic shards would certainly cause some scarring. The mental anguish, in the home, in the heart, would be deep and exceedingly wrenching, especially for a new father who seemed to ignore his child.

He reached into the locked case and removed the last of his Semtex, the final piece of his plastique.

Damn. He hadn't had much to begin with, but it had been his favorite. The RDX was too messy. It went everywhere. The nitro, well, the nitro was like playing Russian roulette with a fully loaded gun. No, the Semtex and the C4 were his favorites, safe to handle, easy to use, spectacular results. No doubt, he needed more.

He'd find a phone and call today.

He rolled it into a ball about the size of a worn pencil eraser in his fingers, then fitted it with a tiny wire charge attached to a watch battery. The contact detonator, however, was the prize, the masterpiece of his own design: a stiff copper pendulum that when shaken lightly would not make contact. The harder it was shaken, however, the greater the chance the pendulum would eventually swing to either pole and make the final contact.

A plastic bead rolled freely in the case to make a noise.

The final contact, however, would make the greatest noise.

Genius.

He smiled wide as he touched glue to the edges of the rounded plastic lid, about the size of a blown-out half dollar, and carefully fitted it to the bottom half covering the device. Let it sit for a day so the glue could set, then he'd reattach the ribbon.

Peter the Great sat back in his chair and smiled at his handiwork. Two small masterpieces: one simple, one complex, the simple idea deadlier than the difficult. The incongruity made him smile.

As did the thought that he needed to get back in the game.

The ball was in play, the ball was in his court, and he was about to fire it back. Kill shot.

No need to thank me anymore, Will Ross.

Now comes the time to damn me—and, while damning me, raise me to the top of my game.

✿

ROSE CANGLIOSI WATCHED HER GRANDDAUGHTER STRETCH OUT ON THE BLANKET IN front of the television set.

Elena was almost two months old now and reaching and grasping and lifting her head as if to search the room for sounds and people.

"Elena," Rose called softly, and the baby immediately began to search the air around her for the voice, for her love, for her grandmother. Then, just as quickly, she began to search the room blindly for something else Rose could not see.

Rex and Shoe sat silently by the wall, staring at the baby, starting and growling darkly at any sound on the street, any child's shout in the yard, any creak in the timbers of the house.

Occasionally one, or both of the dogs would walk over to the blanket, sniff Elena's head and lick her, then resume its post, its eternal guard. Rose knew. They had failed their mistress; they were not about to fail her child.

It was a thought that made her smile. She felt exactly the same way.

She watched Elena move and thrash and try to gain control of the muscles in her arms and legs and neck. She cooed and smiled and accidentally flopped herself over onto her back. Elena stared at the ceiling in shock for a moment, then barked in an odd sort of laugh, which threw Rose into hysterics.

As she laughed, she watched her granddaughter with tears growing in her eyes for what was and what could have been and how she should be sharing this moment with Cheryl.

The baby clutched the air above her.

Rose smiled through her tears.

Elena was ready for a rattle.

CHANCE ENCOUNTER

R ANDY DISSON STARED AT THE CLOCK: 2 A.M.

The two men, the fat one and the skinny one, had said, "Call any-time, day or night," but this was just too late, too damned late for just about anybody, and these were two guys that even Randy Disson, for all his firepower and surface bravado, didn't want to piss off.

He looked at the newly stolen Nokia and sighed.

"Look," he said aloud to himself and the darkened storage shed, "do you want them pissed at you for calling or for not calling?"

That clinched it. Better safe than sorry. Especially with these two who scared him even more than the constant threat from the cops, the Fibbis, and the ATF. He sighed, looked at the card on his workbench, and dialed the number.

It rang twice.

"Yeah," the voice answered distantly.

"This is … this is …" Randy couldn't bring himself to say his name.

"I know who it is. What have you got?"

"He called. He's out of plastique. He wants Sem or C."

There was a pause on the other end of the line. "When and where?"

"City Park. West end. The bus stop near the blocked entrance. East side of the street. Seven-thirty A.M."

"That's rush hour."

"He likes noise and crowds."

"What's the cover?"

"Huh?"

There was a sigh. "How do you make the pass without being caught?"

"Bus stop. Identical briefcases. Black plastic Samsonite. He puts one down and walks into the park. I come up, put mine down, pick up his, and leave. He comes back and picks his up. One minute tops."

"You ever seen him?"

"His back. From a distance. The fewer who know …"

"Yeah. I know. Seven-thirty. Be there. We will."

"Oh, I'll, I'll be there."

"Don't screw it up, and don't let on that we're there."

"I won't. I won't."

"Just remember, Randy," Ollie said, quietly philosophical, "life is too damned short. Isn't it?"

"It is. It is."

"And we don't want to make it any shorter."

The line went dead. Randy Disson clicked off, took the phone into the kitchen, and put it on a plate in the microwave, setting the timer for ten minutes. He'd steal another one this afternoon.

If he was still around to do it.

The timer set, the microwave humming and occasionally sparking, Randy Disson calmly walked into his bathroom and threw up.

❦

STANLEY ANSWERED ON THE FIRST RING.

"Yeah?"

"We're on. Seven-thirty is the drop."

"What time do you want to leave?" Stanley asked, scratching his hair into a peak.

"Five-thirty. I want to scope. I want to watch. I want to be ready and out of sight."

"Okay. Five-thirty. Can I go back to sleep now?"

"I don't give a crap what you do, Stanley. Be in the lobby at 5:30."

"Don't curse, Ollie. It doesn't suit you."

"*Crap* is not cursing, Stan, *crap* is just *crap*, and I …"

Stanley smiled as he hung up the phone, turned over, and went immediately back to sleep.

Directly above on the next floor, Olverio Cangliosi hung up the phone, then stared at the wall for a long moment. He lit a cigarette and blew a stream of smoke, colored blue in the darkness, toward the ceiling. He thought of the old line: "Sure, I can give up smoking. I've done it a thousand times."

Well, when this one was finished, it would be for good. Once and for all.

He took another drag, held the smoke deep in his lungs for a long moment, then blew it out through his nose.

Five-thirty couldn't come soon enough for him.

❂

WILL WAS AWAKE AND BUMPING INTO THINGS AT 7 A.M., DEEP IN A PITIFUL SEARCH for his first cup of coffee. The phone rang. He stared at it for a good, solid three rings, hoping Rose would answer it, but she had been up any number of times with the baby during the night, so it fell to him.

"Yello?" he mumbled.

"Will, good morning!"

Will shot awake.

"Well, hi. Good morning, Beth. How are you?"

"Great. Sorry we didn't get in touch this weekend."

"Well, so am I," Will said with a smile. "I was hoping you'd call."

There was a pause on the other end of the line.

"Will, I did call. Didn't you get the messages?"

Immediately, Will felt his mood change from light to darkly angry. Rose. Goddamn it, Rose.

"How many times did you call, Beth?"

"At least four," she lied. "Left a message each and every time."

"Well, I'm sorry. I didn't get them."

"I'm not surprised."

"Sorry. I'm very sorry. How can I make it up to you?"

"Hmmm," she said playfully. "How about Frisco's—tonight. Eight o'clock?"

"That sounds great. Dinner?"

"Maybe. I'd just like to talk again," she said. "I enjoyed that. A lot."

Will smiled. "So did I. So did I."

"So," she said happily, "8 at Frisco's. And bring your daughter. Bring Elena."

Will paused, mentally crabbing about cramping his style, then chuckled. "Really? After you two got along so well the first time you met?"

"She's a part of you. I want to get to know her better."

Will thought about it, silent for a moment, then said, "Sure. Okay. Why not? We both deserve a night out."

Somewhere in the dark recesses of his mind, he recalled that babies were a chick magnet.

"Good. Frisco's at 8."

"And, uh, Beth? I apologize for your messages not getting through. It will never happen again. I promise you."

"That's okay, Will. At least I finally got to you."

She smiled at the statement. She smiled at the thought.

"See you tonight."

"See you at work. And then tonight."

"Okay. Bye-bye, now," Will said. He paused for a second and hung up the phone, cursing himself for saying "bye-bye." How old was he now, and he was still saying "bye-bye?" Jesus. As he muttered to himself, Rose Cangliosi walked into the kitchen, directly into his mood, Elena on her shoulder.

"Who was that?"

"That," Will said, with an edge of steel in his voice, "was the woman who called here four times over the weekend and left messages that you didn't bother to pass on to me."

"You only had one call, Will, and she didn't want to leave a message," Rose said defensively.

Will sighed heavily, the anger growing inside him, the emotions running unchecked but barely held back by his twenty-year love of and respect for the woman in front of him.

He fought the feelings down and said as calmly as he could, "Right, Rose. Look. I'm not besmirching Cheryl's memory—I love her. Love. Loved. Will love. Forever. I'm just trying to get on with my life. Do you understand that?

That I need to do that? Do you have a problem with that?"

"Will, I …"

Will held up a hand. "Stop. Stop now. I'm going out tonight. Tonight. And I'm taking Elena with me."

"Elena?"

"Yes. A friend wants to meet her. And you know what, Rose? I want this friend to meet her and like her and want to hold her on occasion, and Jesus Christ, you know what?" The floodgates of emotion burst open and Will began to prattle, his mouth running at full tilt, his brain nowhere near being engaged. "Maybe she'll enjoy holding Elena, and later on, maybe she'll want to hold me a bit! Understand? Maybe she'll want to hold me! God! Can you believe it! Will Ross getting held. Kissed. Dare I say it? Will Ross getting laid! Wouldn't that be a shocker?"

Without hesitation, Rose slapped Will, hard, across the face.

They stared at each other silently for a long time.

After a full minute of shocked silence, Will spoke quietly.

"Fine. I apologize. I deserved that, Rose. But I'm also telling you—I'm gonna get busy livin' because I'm sick of sitting on my ass and dying. I had a great weekend on the bike. I'm beginning to feel human again. Slowly. And Beth Freeman, that is her name, by the way, Rose, not *puttana*—you see, I know, I've heard you—Beth Freeman is making me feel that way. I am …" he nodded at Elena, " … we are going out tonight. Together. To see Beth. To talk with another human being who isn't related by marriage or blood to us. Got that?"

"Got it," Rose said quietly, holding her rage in check, her desire to grab Will by the lapels and shake him until his head rattled. Didn't he know what was going on? Didn't he know that this bitch, this *putta* … this Beth was up to something? Oliver could see it, Stanley could, she could, hell, even Elena could. But Will, Will was thinking with his … with his penis. She calmed herself slowly, as if she felt a warm hand on her shoulder. She took several deep breaths and said again, "Fine, Will. I've got it. I understand."

"Good." Will turned to walk upstairs, then stopped and turned back to Rose.

"And don't trying one of those things where you and Elena go to the mall and 'oooh, just lost track of time.' She's going with me. Understand?"

"I understand."

Will nodded once, sharply, as if that finished the conversation, then turned and stomped off toward the shower.

Rose waited until she could hear him clumping around upstairs, then whispered to Elena, "You will be my eyes and ears tonight, sweetheart. Watch out for your father. He is in a very dangerous place right now. Will you do that for your nana?"

Elena searched the air around Rose's head for the sound of her voice and finally found her eyes. They locked. Elena wiggled her mouth.

Rose cried and held her tight.

❋

AT 7:20, TIMMONS READ THE LOOSE-LEAF REPORT THAT CLARK HAD HAND-DELIVERED to his desk. There wasn't much to it, but it still made interesting reading. Only three phone calls over the weekend: one from a relative in Detroit, the two old ladies talking for hours, one from Beth Freeman, short and sweet, Timmons could see, a real catfight, and another old-lady call from Detroit, short and sweet.

Then he saw, turning up the sheet for this morning, an early call from Beth Freeman to Will Ross setting up a meeting tonight at Frisco's. Clark had circled the time in heavy red marker. Timmons looked up at the clock.

Twenty minutes ago. Fresh coffee.

He read through the handwritten transcript once, quickly, then again, carefully.

Timmons sat back and smiled. Fascinating, isn't it, Mr. Ross? That was what media pull could get you. Frisco's was closed on Mondays.

Ray Whiteside walked in, a curled copy of the *Rocky Mountain News* under his arm.

"Ray—hey, good morning!" Timmons said with a grin.

"What's got you so happy?" Whiteside grumbled.

"Just a notion. Just a notion."

"And just what," Whiteside asked, "would your just a notion be?"

"I have a notion," Timmons said, "that we'll both find it really interesting to be at Frisco's tonight."

Whiteside dropped the paper on his desk in front of the picture of Cheryl Crane and stared at Timmons. His teeth were clenched as he pondered what road Timmons was leading him down and where they were going to wind up.

He sighed.

"Okay, what have you got?"

❀

THERE WAS A BITING CHILL IN THE AUTUMN AIR UNTIL THE SUN CAME UP. THEN the heat rose quickly.

Stanley bounced quietly back and forth, trying to warm himself and shake down the two cups of coffee he had drunk the hour before. They were starting to make themselves known in his bladder. At 7:25, he stepped out from his position on the back side of 21st and walked down York toward the bus stop on the opposite side of the street from City Park. The downtown bus. The one that would have people actually riding it at this time of the day.

In the distance, half a block ahead, he could see Randy Disson standing at the uptown bus stop, alone, a black plastic Samsonite case beside his leg. There was no one else on Disson's side of the street. The park behind him was empty. Disson looked at his watch, then looked south down York for the bus.

Stanley looked at his watch, looked north for the bus, then glanced back toward the row of houses and buildings on the west side of the street, wondering where Oliver was set up and what kind of view he had of the situation.

He looked back across York.

Disson was not alone.

A young man in khakis, white shirt, red tie, black sports coat, sunglasses, and hat had stepped out of the park and stood behind Disson. Stanley tried not to stare. It had happened so quickly that he hadn't noticed the bag going down. He didn't know which of the black plastic briefcases held the plastique and which held the money.

He glanced up the street. His bus was coming. Damn! He wanted to stare blindly like the people beside him and catch the pass, but the bus was going to block it. It was all falling apart around him. He dug in his pocket for a handful of change, hoping it was enough for the fare.

The two men stood in front of him, about thirty feet away, both silently staring straight ahead. The bus pulled in front of Stanley. He bullied his way to the front of the line and poured all the change he had into the collector.

It rattled so that he never heard the driver offer him a transfer. Stanley moved quickly down the aisle and found a seat on the street side of the bus.

Disson was alone. One briefcase next to his leg. He picked it up, turned south, and began to walk away.

Frantically, Stanley shot his look back toward the north and east, searching for the bag man. He broke his search into quadrants and picked up the khaki pants crossing the park to the north as the bus started to pull away.

He watched the walking man disappear in the trees.

He had to find Ollie.

He got off at the next stop to a chorus of grumbles from the people he had pushed out of the way in order to get on first a mere two blocks before.

❄

"What is this?"

"It's just some notes."

"Is this a tap?"

"Naw," Timmons said sarcastically, shaking his head, "I'd say it's just overheard conversations."

"Overheard how?" Whiteside asked.

"Don't know. Just happens sometimes."

"You're walking a thin line here, Paul. You know this is inadmissible. It's illegal."

"What? Who said I was admitting anything? Information is power, Ray. You know that." Timmons crossed over and sat on the top of his desk, balancing his feet on his swivel chair. "At least I'm getting somewhere. What have you got?"

"I've got nothing, but I'm thinking Randy Disson. It's not much, but it's a start."

"Who the fuck is Randy Disson?"

"Jesus, man, don't use that word. It's too goddamned early. That's an afternoon word. After the day is already ruined."

"Oh, excuse me, Miss Manners. Who, pray tell," he whined, "is Randy Disson?"

"Randy Disson is a dealer. A dealer with a big mouth."

"Drugs?"

"Maybe. But he's a real fan of things that go boom. We had him on the hook when Cheryl Crane bought it."

"How big boom?"

"Big enough," Whiteside said.

"Do you think he had any contact with Willie boy?"

Whiteside sat back and made a sour face at Timmons.

"What boy would that be, Paul? You've had a bug up your ass for days about Will Ross, and you've been sniffing around him like a bloodhound," he tossed the legal pad transcript at Timmons, "and getting nowhere—except that he's eyeballing some dame at work. Jesus. He's doing less than you are with the blond in the Second District. Are you going to whack Sue so you can more easily date your *schnootzie?*"

"Stop it. This is a possibility."

"Come off it, Paul. Anything's a possibility, but this is so thin, it's absolutely anorexic. I've seen better chances at a carnival."

"What do you want to do then, just let him walk?"

Ray Whiteside sat back in his chair and sighed, his eye catching the framed photo of Cheryl Crane that sat on his desk. He hadn't forgotten the promise.

"No. I'm not going to let anybody walk, Paul. But Will Ross isn't going anywhere. He's got a job and family here, and if he did run, he's known. He's a celeb. He'd stand out like Abe Lincoln at a jockeys' convention."

Timmons laughed.

"Laugh all you want, pal. I'm going to take my time and do this right. I'm going to nail the son of a bitch."

He stood up and slipped on his sports coat.

"I'm going to nail the son of a bitch—whoever it is—and tear him a new asshole."

"Isn't it a little early for that kind of talk?" Paul Timmons said.

"Come on. I'm thinking to start by rattling Randy Disson."

Timmons smiled and grabbed his jacket. He loved working with Whiteside because he loved working like this: taking two halves of the same idea and running them up against each other until all the parts began to fit.

This was police work.

Right and wrong and right again, until the puzzle was solved.

Timmons followed Whiteside down the hall toward the elevator. Ray had the bit in his teeth, he thought. The race was on.

Will Ross was toast.

❀

Ollie was sitting at the bus stop as Stanley ran back up to it, wheezing.

"What ... did ... you ... where ... ?" Stanley grunted.

"I was over there, up, working on that gas meter."

Stanley looked over at an ancient mansion with an outdoor stairway leading to a second-floor apartment. Fifteen feet off the ground was a gas meter.

"What did you use for tools?"

"A stick. Nobody noticed."

"What did you see?

"I saw you get blocked and miss it all, then piss off a bunch of people when you took cuts onto the bus."

"Did you see him? Did you see the guy? Did you see our guy?"

"I saw him."

"Did you notice anything about him?"

Ollie looked at Stanley for a moment, then recited a list of obvious facts: "Khaki pants, black jacket, briefcase, hat, sunglasses, fast mover. He was in the park and gone before I got across the street. Which is what you were supposed to be doing. We might not get a chance like this again, Stanley."

"Yeah, yeah, yeah," Stan nodded, with just a bit of shame in his voice. "But Ollie," he added, searching his mind for something he knew was there but couldn't quite find, "what did you *notice* about this guy?"

"What do you mean?" Ollie asked, looking toward the park as if the target would suddenly reappear, wave his arms, and ask them to follow him at a discreet distance.

"Well, shit," Stanley said, staring toward the park, toward the trees where he had last seen the khaki man, then looked down at the street, as if the answer might be there, then back up to the park, then the sky, then down. He put his palms over his eyes and tried to reimagine the face, pulling off the hat, pulling off the sunglasses. See him, Stanley told himself, *see him*, goddamn it.

Ollie stared at his friend for a long moment, wondering if he was stroking out in the middle of a Denver sidewalk, then finally put his hand on Stanley's shoulder.

"Good God, Stan. What is it?"

Stanley pulled his hands away from his face.

"Remember the guy, Ollie. Remember the guy. See his face."

"Okay." Ollie nodded.

"No, see it. *See* it."

"O-kay," Ollie said with a final nod. "So *what?*"

"The what is," Stanley said distantly, "the what is—that I've seen him before."

❋

RANDY DISSON WAS MOVING TOO QUICKLY TO NOTICE MUCH OF ANYTHING. HE WAS worried about the drop. He was always worried about the drop. He was worried about the money he carried home. He was always worried about the money he carried home. He was worried about the police. He was always worried about the police.

But more than anything else, he was worried about the two men. The fat man and the skinny man. He had seen the skinny man across the street, just before the drop. The bus had come and blocked the view, but he had still known that the skinny man was there. And if the skinny man was there, the fat man was there too somewhere, out of sight but watching, watching very closely.

The pass was made, bass-ackward to the usual scenario, just because Randy Disson was so nervous that for the first time, he had actually turned and faced his best customer. The man had looked at Randy and smiled a 150-watt, unforgettable grin.

That unnerved Randy as well.

Randy saw, and in that split second, he knew.

He turned back to the street, counted to ten, picked up the bag at his feet, and walked as quickly as he could toward the corner and his car and home.

The drive home was a masterpiece of mind over machine, his hands shaking on the wheel, his will forcing the car to drive in a straight line to the small home in the comfortable South Side neighborhood.

Here, in his storage room, a back room of the house, northwest corner, the windows forever shuttered, he put the case nervously on the workbench, snapped on the single high-intensity light, and wiped his upper lip. Damn. He knew. It was not a good thing to know clients. It made them nervous. No telling what they'd do if they were nervous, since there was no telling what he'd do if the police started to squeeze him for information.

Your client's or your life, Randy? Your clients or your life?

Well, officer, here are my clients. Have a nice day.

Still, what bothered Randy most about the moment, the glance, the shock of recognition, was that Peter hadn't seemed to mind. He didn't look nervous. Not at all, which, if Randy had been thinking clearly, should have made him all the more nervous.

In point of fact, however, he was still too uptight from the entire morning, a morning that had started with a call at 12:05, to be too nervous about anything other than what was currently in his mind's eye. He was tired. He was nervous. He wasn't thinking clearly.

And that was why, when he should have been most cautious, a trait for which he was known and respected in the dark corner of the business world in which he lived, he reached without thinking for the black plastic briefcase, snapped the locks to the side, and lifted the lid.

In doing so, he pulled a separator from between two clear plastic containers. They were arranged in such a way that, even lying flat in the case, their contents began to flow into each other immediately, mixing furiously.

Randy Disson recognized the containers and the fluids they held at once. Beautiful. Hypergolics. Separated, they were safe. Mix them, and they ignited spontaneously, with spectacular results.

Devastating results.

As the room was engulfed in a pressurized ball of flame, Randy Disson's last thought was a simple word of praise: Ingenious.

The smile was burned from his lips.

※

THE UNMARKED BUT IMMEDIATELY IDENTIFIABLE POLICE CAR WAS HIT WITH THE blast wave as it turned the corner onto Randy Disson's South Side street. Whiteside floored the Ford, racing toward the house, with Timmons already on the radio calling in for immediate fire, police, and paramedic backup.

The flames had shot out the windows of the house and then straight up, scorching the homes on either side, setting fire to their roofs. Not a window within a block was unbroken. Neighbors were running out of homes up and down the block, half dressed, bloodied from flying glass, breakfast eggs on their chins, dragging sleeping children, desperate for information and safety.

Dogs barked with both sound and fury.

The scene was a madhouse.

Ray Whiteside stood by the car and just stared at the burning house. There was nothing to do. Whoever was inside was gone. Ten minutes, he thought, ten minutes might have made a difference. Ten minutes might have saved both Randy Disson and the case.

Now he was back to square one. Worse. He was at go, and it wasn't his turn.

He kicked the ground and said, "Shit."

Timmons hurried up beside him and shook him hard.

"Ray, if this guy was dealing explosives we've got to clear the area—*now!*"

Whiteside, through the thickness of his anger and disappointment, realized what Timmons was saying, nodded, plucked his badge from his belt, held it up, and started forcing people back.

Timmons worked the other side of the street. Small pops came from inside the house, one bang, a sound like a machine gun going off, then the roof collapsed in on itself.

Ray Whiteside ignored the sounds and the danger of flying debris and just kept moving the residents of the neighborhood back, away from the blast, one house at a time.

WILDERNESS

Will stood in the bathroom staring into the mirror, deep in conversation with himself and anyone else who might be listening.

"Cheryl, I know I have upset your mother, and I am sorry," he said to the man on the other side of the glass. The man said the same words back to him. "I'm trying, I'm trying, love, but I just can't seem to do anything right. Anything right according to her. I'm working too much, I'm not paying enough attention to Elena, I'm not honoring your memory. ..."

The words trailed off. Will suddenly wondered if that was right. Was he, in fact, not honoring Cheryl's memory? Was there a period of mourning that he was somehow ignoring, that was proving to the world that he hadn't loved her to begin with, that it was purely a physical thing? He bent his head down and rubbed his forehead madly with the palms of his hands. In his mind's eye, he could see an old white-haired bricklayer, in a flannel shirt and tattered coveralls, furiously building red brick walls inside his head. To protect him? To keep him safe?

Was he trying to keep something in? Or trying to keep something out?

"What, Cheryl? What is it? What am I supposed to feel right now?"

The mirror didn't give an answer.

"Cheryl, love, give me a sign. Am I doing this wrong? Am I ignoring Elena? Am I rushing? Why can't I see Beth? Is that wrong? Am I wrong in what I'm thinking abou—"

There was a whump *outside the window, and the bottles in the medicine cabinet rattled. Will turned and looked outside. There was nothing to be seen. Nothing at all.*

Will sighed.

He turned back to the mirror.

"Any sign, Cheryl. Anything at all," he begged.

The room was silent, for both himself and the haggard man on the other side of the mirror.

CHAPTER SIXTEEN

I SEE BAD
NEWS ARISIN'

W ILL RODE TO THE STATION TO CHECK MAIL AND GRAB SOME QUICK
saddle time. It was an easy ride, all loose pedaling and city streets,
a quick burst followed by a stop sign or traffic light.

No matter how he timed himself, he seemed to hit each and every one.

In the end, it wasn't a problem. He was not even considering this a stretch
ride. This was city commuting. He could have blown the signs and blown the
lights and listened to the drivers blow their horns, but he was in no hurry. He
would beat the traffic and ride this afternoon out Morrison Road to catch some
light climbs in the foothills before riding home and showering really thoroughly
for his evening out.

His evening out.

Just the thought of it brought a smile to his face.

Will rode the final few blocks to the station with a stupid grin on his face that
made more than one driver wonder if he was retarded.

"They should really watch those people more carefully," said the rising
young attorney.

His rising young attorney wife looked up from her copy of the *Wall Street
Journal* and nodded.

"Yes, dear," she said in a bored whisper, noticing Will's crotch as he stood over
the top tube at the stoplight, "but at least he's wearing a helmet."

The object of their attention waited for the change, set his right foot, and ped-
aled off toward TV6 and his mailbox.

He loved mail. It was like new surprises every day.

He loved TV6 now too.

For many of the same reasons.

❀

THE ATRIUM WAS QUIET, BUT, EVEN NOW, AT 10:35, HE COULD HEAR SHOUTS AND panic coming from the newsroom as people threw information across the room at the top of their lungs, then raced, leaden-footed, across the raised computer floor to deliver it in person three seconds later.

Will shook his head.

Obviously, someone on the assignment desk had been bored and prayed, once more, to the gods of spot news, always a dangerous act.

Be careful what you wish for, for you'll get more than you bargained for.

Stopping for a moment in the center of the atrium, Will considered walking over to the newsroom to see what was up. He turned back to the sports office and decided it was best to hide out there.

Even in his inexperience, on days like this, especially early in the game, when the information was coming in faster than it could be processed and then sent out to the audience raw and blind and with any luck right, Will knew that he would at best be invisible, at worst be in the way.

The same was true for Elliott Green, the entertainment reporter. People said that during the recent tragic events in New York, he'd wander through the newsroom, holding his glasses at arm's length, pretending to be the invisible man. He was off the air for nearly two weeks. No one, it seemed, wanted to hear what part of her body Madonna was pondering while they were still searching for corpses.

The sports office was dark and cold. The air conditioner was blasting, giving the room the feeling of a tomb. Will shuddered as if a cold hand had run up his back.

He hadn't come within fifty-five beats of breaking a sweat on the ride in, but the chill in the air made him shiver as if he were soaked. He flipped on the lights and manhandled the thermostat, hoping it still worked after Zorro's screwdriver surgery.

There was a hiss. No heat, but the air conditioning stopped. That was something.

Will opened the door wide, hoping to heat the office or cool the atrium. Either one was a step in the right direction.

He hit the power strip on the floor that controlled the bank of television sets and booted his computer while they came on. Turning back to them, he saw that each channel, with the exception of ESPN and Fox Sports, carried the image of a small house on fire, the flames reaching out to engulf other houses around it. Channels 4, 7, 9, 31, and 2 all carried the story live, each getting the image from a slightly different angle. TV6 was there as well and closest in, the camera low as if the photog were crawling in on combat patrol.

Will leaned in toward the wall of images. The mail could wait. E-mail could wait. The afternoon ride could wait. This was, at its most basic level, compelling television, the images that grab and transfix without conscious effort. Denver firefighters were working the fire from a distance, doing what they could to protect what was left of the homes on either side, pumping water from a cannon into the flaming mass in the center of the screen.

Two firefighters ran past wearing what appeared to be flak jackets. As Will wondered what or why, there was a smattering of what sounded like small-arms fire, the sounds picked up by the shotgun microphone on the TV6 camera, low and close to the action. The picture shuddered for a moment as if the photog had ducked his head during the sound.

Seconds later came a small explosion, and Fast Eddie Slezak, the noon anchorman, came on the air, voice over the live video, to explain that TV6 was showing live coverage of a major house fire burning out of control on the South Side of town. There was silence for a moment as Slezak clearly let the natural sound from the scene, firemen shouting orders and warnings, the roar of the water cannon, the snap of what sounded like occasional gunfire, take over the drama from his commentary.

It was a smart move. Nothing he could say could match what was coming from the scene, a mix of rain and fire and sound and fury.

Madness, brought live and uncut into the comfort of your very own living room.

"Denver Fire is moving very cautiously in the area, you can see some firefighters, especially those going in close, wearing bulletproof vests. We still don't have any official reason for this, but obviously, given what we're hearing from some of our cameras on the scene, the owner of the house owned a large stash of ammunition that is going off in the fire. *Caution* is the watchword here for the firefighters. They're doing what they can to protect houses in the vicinity. The homes on either side seem to be complete losses, but those farther down the street appear to be in fairly good shape. Police have evacuated a two-block radius from the fire. We're still waiting for official word.

"Maybe this is it. Let's go live to Terry Elliott, live at the fire and police command post in …"

Terry Elliott jumped her cue. She had the information first, and by god, she wasn't going to let the reporters from the other stations beat her on the air with it.

"Eddie, I've just finished talking with the Denver Fire commander on scene, and he says that the problem they're having in fighting this blaze, and the reason they've asked Denver Police to evacuate the area, is that the home is filled not only with ammunition but with volatile chemicals and possible explosives."

The live shot cut away to tape with the Fire Department spokesman: "The problem we're having in fighting this blaze, and the reason we've asked Denver Police to evacuate the area, is that the home is filled not only with ammunition but with volatile chemicals and possible explosives."

The tape ended with the spokesman's jaw flapping soundlessly. There was more to what he had to say, but the audience wasn't going to hear it. The scene cut back to Terry Elliott.

"Homeowners are obviously frightened by the threat to their property right now, but they're also concerned that this house was filled—according to police—with such dangerous material and had been for quite some time."

The live shot disappeared, replaced by a man who had obviously left his home in a hurry, wearing a dress shirt, hiking shorts, and bedroom slippers.

"Well, I can't believe," the man said, shouting as if the stress of the situation had destroyed his internal volume control, "that this guy filled his house, a neighborhood house, with so much dangerous material. Christ! It's been like that for quite some time too. That's what the police are saying, anyway. I'm worried about losing my house, sure, but having that kind of crap so close—man, that's frightening."

Terry Elliott came back live.

"We're going to stay on the scene as long as it takes …" There was an explosion in the distance, and Terry Elliott flinched. As she did, the camera shook just a bit as the photog ducked as well.

"Good God! We don't know what's happening. …"

The shot cut away from her to the ground-level camera, which was on its side. The photographer had obviously let go as he ducked to safety during the explosion. Was he there? Was he hurt? The camera slowly righted itself, and Will felt a wave of relief pass over him. He liked the photo staff here. He didn't want to see anyone get hurt.

Will stared at the scene. Where there had once been a burning house, there was now one wall and a portion of a brick chimney. Firefighters had retreated, but now the water cannon charged in again, trying to keep the fire from spreading to yet another house down the street.

This was a mess. And it was going to continue for a long time.

Fast Eddie was calling, live, on air, for Terry Elliott, asking her what had happened, what information did she have? The camera cut to location, but there was no Terry to be found.

The camera slowly panned down to find Terry Elliott stretched out flat on the ground, desperately trying to dig herself into the dirt. She would have gotten lower, but the buttons on her Liz Claiborne suit got in the way.

Mercifully, the camera panned back up and moved right across the scene as fire and police officials began to rise back up from behind trucks and cars to see what was happening. Will sat up and leaned forward.

In the background, he could make out Ray Whiteside and Timmons, that asshole who had given him the third degree the other day.

What the hell were *they* doing there?

@

BETWEEN OPENING MAIL, WATCHING THE LIVE COVERAGE, AND GOING OVER THE LIVE-shot schedule for the Ride to the Sky, Will watched the rest of the morning and early afternoon slip away.

The live-shot schedule was not to be believed. He was not only going to have to rise and shine for the 5 A.M. show but then catch 6 and noon, ride like a bastard, hit the Four, catch something in the Five, and then have a presence in the Ten. The sports producer said he was lucky they didn't have the 6:30 P.M. newscast any longer because sure as shit he'd be live in that too.

Frankly, the producer said, he was surprised that the station was giving any ride this much coverage. Dawn to dusk just wasn't in the usual game plan, unless, of course, it somehow involved the Broncos.

"New news director, new ways of fucking things up."

Will nodded. He had no idea how he was going to cover that much distance and make that many hits.

"Must be wanting to give you some serious face time, Will."

Will shrugged outwardly, but inside the thought gave him a bit of a thrill. Face time. More face time. He felt like a fifth wheel here, behind Flynn and Zorro and Art. He didn't feel that he was going to be around much longer at all.

He hadn't been around much to begin with, and that had been under a different administration. How many managers want to hang on to their predecessors' mistakes?

Face time?

Maybe things weren't so bleak.

They wrapped up their meeting, and Will looked back at the bank of TV monitors. All the stations had returned to regular programming with periodic updates on the fire, evacuation, and explosions. Shortly after 11:30, things had finally been brought under control. Now, at 1:30, HazMat units were taking charge of the site while Denver Fire began its investigation.

Some morning.

Will sat back for a moment, wondering if there was anything else to do. According to what Ransford had told him, the only thing he needed to concern himself with this week was riding. Getting into shape.

And so he would.

Art Jackson walked in. He'd cover the field reporting, such as it was, for Roger Flynn's sports segments at 5 and 10.

Jackson was aglow with spot-news fever.

"Can you believe this? Can you believe this shit? Man! I've never seen anything like this. Jesus H. Christ! Did you see that house go up? Man, I wish we'd been on the thing live when it did. Hi, Will, how you doing? God, when the camera started shaking and Terry Elliott dug a tunnel to China, man, that was great fucking TV. I'll bet you money, man, that I don't even get on the air today. What do you bet? What do you bet that we do so much on this—especially at 5—that they cut Flynn to two, two and a half minutes? What do you say? Wanna bet?"

"Naw, I ..."

"I wouldn't take it either. I wouldn't take it either. Sucker's bet. Damn. Do you know who the photog was who crawled up to the side of the house across the street? Man, I wonder if he was rolling tape when the house went up? Do you think he was?—shit, he had to be, or Ransford will have his nuts in a vase. Did I say vase? I meant vise. Shit. This is too much. Too goddamned much."

"Yeah, I …"

"When you leaving town, Will? Wednesday? Don't you start in Boulder?"

"Thursday morning. Civic Center Park."

"I hear they've changed it to Boulder because of traffic problems. Hey, thirty less miles. Hey, at least you'll get a free night at the Boulderado. Shit. Can you believe this shit? I've got to see what's happening in the newsroom. I love this shit. News. Real news. With explosions and everything …"

His voice trailed off as he hustled himself across the atrium toward the newsroom. It had been calming itself after a busy morning. There was only so long that they could keep up such a level of excitement. Now Art would throw himself into the room and stir things up all over again.

Will shook his head and turned off his computer.

It was time to ride.

As he stood at his desk, Zorro walked in, bleary eyed, unshaven. He wore a brightly colored Hawaiian shirt that looked as if it had been slept in by an angry herd of Asian elephants.

"I need to talk to you."

"Isn't this your day off, Z?"

"Yeah, it is," he said, struggling with the words and rubbing the stubble on his face. "Yeah, this is my day off, and I don't mind telling you that I've been spending last night and this morning drinking heavily, trying to decide what to do about you and your little buddy Beth."

Will raised both hands in mock surrender.

"How about you do nothing? There's nothing to be done. There's nothing you can do. There's nothing you can say right now."

"Goddamn it, Will, there's something going on. This stinks."

"So do you, my friend. Why don't you just hustle on home—keeping to the side streets—and get some rest."

"Will, you don't understand. …"

"I do understand, Zorro. I do. Thank you. I appreciate your concern. But right now, I've gotta ride and you've gotta get some sleep."

"Will ..."

"Take it easy, man, I've gotta go."

Before Clyde Zoromski could say another word, Will scooped up his helmet and gloves and padded in stocking feet toward the back door of the station, where he had left the Beast and his shoes parked safely inside.

First Rose, now Zorro.

Christ.

Wasn't anyone going to let him get laid?

CHAPTER SEVENTEEN

THE SWEETEST LITTLE FLOWER

WILL ROSS WAS NERVOUS AS A CAT.

He used up all the hot water showering for the evening. He stood before his steamed-up mirror, shaving carefully, putting on just the right amount of sweet smell, not too much, but enough that you knew it was there, all in preparation.

He took his time, trying to make everything right. For what, he didn't know. He just had a feeling, a sense, a longing, a need. He checked his nose for blackheads. He checked his ears for stray hairs. He brushed his hair carefully, then dressed in a pair of khakis and a button-down shirt, light yellow, before slipping on a blue sports coat. He completed the outfit with half socks and loafers.

Lookin' good, he thought as he stood and stared in the mirror. Lookin' good. He looked at the clock. Seven twenty-five. Best get Elena ready.

He took a deep breath and walked down the short hallway toward the stairs. The last thing in the world he wanted to do was face Rose right now and try to crowbar Elena off her shoulder, but the baby was a part of this tonight, whether Rose wanted it or not.

He stepped off the landing at the base of the stairs and was surprised to see Rose sitting on the couch, Elena next to her at an odd, floppy, baby sort of angle. Elena was dressed in a new jumper with breakaway legs for easy diaper changes. She was washed, brushed, and clean. As Will walked over, he realized that she smelled sweet as well.

"She's been fed, so don't jostle her for a while or you might be seeing it again," Rose said, never looking away from the TV set and some new detective program. "She had a great nap this afternoon and a mighty poo about twenty minutes ago, which makes me think she's done for a while, so you shouldn't have many bad surprises."

"Thanks, Rose."

"You're welcome. I'll be here if you need me—you won't, but I'll be here."

"Thanks."

"Don't forget the diaper bag."

"I thought you said ..."

"Oh, Will," she sighed, "you *always* take the bag. It's like your support car. There are tools, supplies, fresh diapers, wipes. Take the bag. You *always* take the bag."

He nodded.

"Thanks again, Rose."

She was silent for a long moment, then finally said, "Don't mention it," as much to get rid of him as to answer him. Will turned and walked into the kitchen. Seven-thirty. He had fifteen minutes before he was scheduled to leave. He sat at the kitchen table and stared at the clock, willing it to move forward faster.

❁

BETH FREEMAN WAS NERVOUS AS A CAT.

She had spent the last hour checking herself as well: shower, makeup, hair, outfit, a silk blouse with just a hint of a shimmer. Teeth, breath, perfume. She looked carefully in the mirror, scanning for any flaws, saw none, then shot out of the house and back to Frisco's for a final check on Jeremy's setup.

Three digital cameras, smaller than the professional norm but still capable of solid results at short range, were set up in the room. Two replaced security cameras high on the wall, giving wide shots of the table from two different angles. One was in a housing, hidden among a random pile of junk at a serving station, to pick up Beth's reaction shots. She had thought that wasn't necessary, but Jeremy had insisted. No reaction shot was as good as the one that happened naturally, he argued. Waiting until after the interview and bobbing your head up and down was simply bobbing your head up and down. It wasn't real. She finally agreed. The reaction camera was a tad wide, not just a head shot but a head-and-shoulders shot, cutting her off just under her breasts. As long as she remembered her spot, there wouldn't be any problem. She could even hold the baby in the crook of her right arm and have her in the shot as well. Because of the angle, it had to be her right arm, and it had to be tight.

Beth nodded. She could do it.

The fourth camera, the key camera, was the capper. Jeremy had essentially set up a duck blind in the end booth, a masterwork of plants, black scrim, and cut glass that looked like a work of art in progress as created by a mad designer. Behind the scrim, he controlled the three remote cameras, the audio, discreetly hidden at the table, and the main shot, the key camera on Beth's interview and the baby.

"I gotta pee."

"Well, pee quick," Beth snapped, "then get in there. And remember—you're in there for the duration. No sneezing, no pagers, no cell phones, no camera alarms, no nothing. You hear me?"

"I hear you. Jesus, Beth, we've done this before. ..."

"And you've fucked up in the past."

"Thank you for reminding me."

"It can't happen tonight, Jeremy," Beth said slowly. "It can't happen tonight. We're going to get one shot at this, and he can't suspect a thing."

"He won't. Don't worry. I've used the blind before. If he asks, just say there's a water leak behind it and the manager wanted to hide it away with modern art."

"Just pee. And get back there."

"Jawohl, mein herr." He walked off, wondering if one more award was worth the level of bullshit he had to take working with this bitch. Christ. Money and prizes couldn't wash off the scummy feeling he got when she nailed somebody who didn't deserved to get nailed.

He thought again about the money.

Hey, it paid the bills. He hurried to the john and peed, squeezing out the last few drops, knowing it would be at least a few hours before he got another chance.

Seven-fifty.

He hurried back, checked the remote cameras one last time, did a quick audio check, and wiggled into his blind. He didn't have monitors on the remote cameras. He just had on/off switches. Jeremy put that control close by, checked his power supply on the main camera, did one final white balance on a card

Beth held where Will's head would be, listened in his headphone to her whisper at the table. Audio check. He was ready.

He was always ready. He was the best. Slimy as shit, but simply the best.

He cleared his throat.

"I can hear you."

"Last time."

"Better be."

The owner hurried in. "He's coming down the street."

"Thank you, Paul. Let him in, then, after we're seated, lock the door. We don't want any company. Keep the music very low and in the next room. I want atmosphere, not audio problems."

"No problem, Beth."

"Thank you, Paul. I'll remember this."

Paul Sanibel nodded and turned, his smile frozen on his face, wondering for the umpteenth time how the hell he had allowed her to talk him into this charade.

Beth walked back into the private dining area, took one last, quick look at Jeremy's very subtle lighting plot, then slid into her seat.

"You ready?"

"Yeah, yeah. I'm ready. Quiet as a mouse."

"Better be one fucking silent mouse."

Jeremy chuckled to himself. What the hell was that supposed to mean?

He settled himself in, put the cameras on standby, and waited for the signal to start.

He waited for the ducks.

The sitting ducks.

❁

PAUL TIMMONS WAS NERVOUS AS A CAT.

Part of that came from simple exhaustion. He had been working the blast and fire at Randy Disson's house all day long, he and Ray Whiteside finally leaving the site at 4:30, two hours after the last of the ammunition blasts, one hour and change after the fire commander on scene declared everything under control and ready for investigators.

The site where the house had stood this morning was little more than a pit tonight, a pit filled with enough water to make it look like a rubble-filled indoor swimming pool. This was going to be a mess.

The homes on either side had each lost windows, facing walls, and part of their roofs.

Timmons went home for a few hours, took a fifteen-minute nap, showered, scrubbing as much of the day off him as possible, made contact with the still photographer, and was in place in the parking structure across the street from Frisco's by 7:15. He watched Beth Freeman arrive, dressed to kill, and the owner unlock the front door to let her into the restaurant. An animated conversation between the two followed just inside the glass.

If he had had the day, he would have gotten a microphone in there somehow. Now he just had a shotgun microphone for their good-byes and the photos. The photos, though, weren't selling Ray Whiteside, and Whiteside was the one he needed to sell on his theory. *Will Ross. In the Study. With the Exploding Tennis Ball.*

Whiteside wasn't biting. Yet.

Ray was determined on this one, Timmons could see that, but he was stuck on the trail of the explosives. Timmons knew that it was money and sex that drove people, not the joy of watching things blow up.

Timmons had to pee.

He patted the photographer on the shoulder to let him know he was leaving for a moment, crossed over to a corner of the garage, and relieved himself against the wheel of a silver BMW.

This was the money part.

Not only was his bladder now empty, but he felt good as well.

❀

STANLEY SZYCLINSKI WAS NERVOUS AS A PUP.

"You're pacing like a cat," Olverio said quietly.

"I hate cats."

"What the devil is your problem?"

Stanley paused for a moment, gathering his thoughts, then began to pace back and forth again in the short alley between the buildings on Milwaukee.

"This stinks, Ol, it stinks to high heaven. You've got a locked restaurant, some kid going in and out all day, you've got cops with a telephoto in the parking lot one hundred feet away, a dame dressed to get something on, our one contact with the bad guy blowing himself up, and our grandniece being carried into the middle of the situation by a daddy who is thinking with his dick. This stinks, Ollie."

Olverio Cangliosi nodded. Stanley was right, no doubt, but there was something else grinding at him.

"What? If you don't stop pacing, I'm going to sap you right here and toss your body in a dumpster for pickup."

"Oh, it's just … shit. Ollie, I tell you—I know the guy."

"Which guy?"

"The guy in the park. I know the son of a bitch, and it's driving me cra—"

"Shhh. Will."

They both unnecessarily crouched down as they watched Will carry Elena and a huge diaper bag toward the front door of the restaurant.

It was 8 o'clock.

❁

"Hello, sweetheart," Beth cooed.

For a split second, Will thought she was talking to him, but then he realized from the tone of her voice that she was talking to Elena.

Elena didn't react. Beth reached out a hand to Will. He shuffled the diaper bag and took her hand in his left, giving it a squeeze.

"Nice to see you," he said.

"Nice to see you too," she whispered. "Come on."

She turned and led the way to the back. Table lights and candles were on, but the bar and front dining room were deserted.

"Is this place closed?" Will asked.

"Tonight—it's a private party." She smiled over her shoulder, pulling his hand gently toward the table. She took a deep breath and listened intently as she passed the camera location. Jeremy was as good as his word. He was silent. He was invisible. He simply wasn't there.

Beth let go of Will's hand and slid into her seat, hitting her mark perfectly.

She knew, instinctively, that she was right on the money. She could sense the camera framing.

Will pushed the diaper bag into the booth, up against the wall, and slid into his side, Elena wriggling with discomfort as he tried to get her into position with him. He realized he should have brought the car seat carrier in with him. He could have planted her in there rather than hold her all night. Shit. Maybe he could run back out.

"Here, give her to me," Beth said. Will half stood and passed the baby over. Elena fussed for a moment, then calmed down, watching Beth with anxious, untrusting eyes.

Beth was surprised by the look. "She's suspicious," she thought. "She knows something's up." Then she caught herself and pushed the ridiculous notion out of her head. As soon as Will was settled, she handed the baby back to him, then discreetly wiped her hands on the leather seat beside her.

Will smiled, cradling Elena in his left arm.

Perfect for the camera, Beth thought.

"Nice to see you," Will said, kicking himself mentally for saying the exact same thing he had said only moments before.

"Nice to see you too," Beth said politely. "Do you want a drink?"

"I dunno, the baby …"

"One? Wine?"

"Wine would be nice."

Beth glanced toward the end of the room. Will heard a shuffling behind him, and a waiter with a bottle of merlot appeared beside the table. He showed the label to Will, who nodded as if he knew what he was agreeing to, and spun the bottle toward Beth, who nodded without taking her eyes off Will.

She smiled.

Behind her eyes, she thought, "Christ, I hope to hell Jeremy isn't wasting tape on this …"

❧

"So, how did you meet?" Beth said softly.

Elena slept soundly in Will's arms. She hadn't fussed at all since returning from Beth's embrace. Will smiled and looked past Beth's eyes into the distance of memory. He drifted off to a good place, where for the first time in a long time he felt warm and safe.

"We met in Paris. Four years ago? Yeah. You can count it by months. This makes what—forty-five. Forty-five months since we met. Met again, anyway."

"Met again?" she offered, drawing him out.

"Yeah. You see, when I first got into riding, I rode with her brother. My best friend. He was killed during a race. Drunk driver ran a barricade. He was killed. I was hurt. I kind of … well, ran away from it all."

"How old were you?"

"I dunno. Maybe fifteen."

"You sound ashamed. You shouldn't be. You were just a kid."

"I was. I am. I wasted a lot of time before I got back into the game. Met Cheryl again. She was a soigneur—a masseuse, a manager, a gofer—for Haven, a pro cycling team in Europe. We met when I was hired by them."

"Love at first sight?"

"Ha, no. No, no, no. Matter of fact, I don't think Cheryl could stand me at first. Certainly didn't think I could make it. I'll tell you, I didn't even know who she was at first. She had changed her name to ride in Europe."

"Really?"

"Yeah. Cheryl Crane."

Beth made a mental note of the name.

"How did you fall in love?"

"Over the spring, through the Spring Classics, the one-day races through northern Europe. By the time we hit the Tour we were pretty much an item."

"How did you ask her to marry you?"

Will chuckled.

"We were in Vail, and I had just watched her smoke a bigmouth male team-mate on a downhill—double slalom—course. Jesus," he said wistfully, "she was good. So smooth. So calm. No nerves at all when she was riding."

Will grew quiet.

"It was beautiful to watch," he whispered. "God, the way she moved …" The pain began to rise up in his heart, to beat back the walls in his mind.

He pushed it all away again, waiting a second to make sure it was gone. He glanced down at Elena, then back up to Beth, who looked at him with a warm smile.

"You miss her."

Will paused for a moment. That was not the question she was supposed to ask. They were supposed to be talking about other things. Not the past. The future. Their future. Their immediate future. A future in the sack, if possible. The past rose up to intrude. Will sighed and let it back into the conversation.

"Yes, I do," he said finally, simply. "The thing is, if I think about her too much, if I remember her too well, if I'm just not careful, then I know I'm going to collapse. In a heap. I haven't. I haven't collapsed since the hospital and the moment I found out that Cheryl had died and," he looked at Elena, "she had lived."

"Does that make you resent the baby?"

"What? No. No, not at all," Will said defensively, looking quickly at Elena to make sure she hadn't heard his moment of denial. She opened her eyes, yawned, gave a half smile, and fell back asleep.

"She's, uh, special, something special to me. Always will be."

The pressure grew in Will's chest again. He knew he was lying. If Elena was so special, why had he spent so much time pushing her away? What was he afraid of? Why wouldn't he let her get close?

The tears began to well in his eyes again. He pushed them back. Once again. For the umpteenth time. If he wasn't careful, they were going to get out when he least expected or wanted it.

◎

SILENT IN HIS BLIND, JEREMY PEERED INTO THE VIEWFINDER AND SLOWLY MOVED IN toward Will's face.

Beautiful. Beautiful.

The moments of silence were even more impressive than the conversation. The looks between man and baby were startling.

This story was cutting itself in his head as he rolled. Jeremy wondered where he'd put his next award.

THE CONVERSATION WENT ON, BETH PROBING, GENTLY PROBING, WITH QUESTIONS about Cheryl and Elena, family and friends, their relationship, his feelings about the baby, being a single father, the bomber, the investigation. She would probe deeply, then back off, playing Will like a professional might play a fish: a tug, some play, a tug, some play. He responded perfectly as she reeled him toward the gaff.

Will, for his part, had been hoping for a romantic evening, not memories of his dead wife. He wanted something emotional for him, right now, tonight. He wanted something to lift his heart rather than dredge his soul, stirring up the pain once again.

He kept trying to turn the conversation to her, them, now, tonight, and Beth would respond. Within moments, however, the conversation would move back to him. And Cheryl. And Elena.

Them. Not him.

Not—us.

Shit.

WILL LOOKED AT HIS WATCH. 11:30.

"I'd better get her home," he said, nodding toward Elena.

"She's a beautiful girl. Does she look like your wife?"

"Yeah, I think so. Rose, that's Cheryl's mom, thinks she got the best of both of us."

"Maybe she did. That would be nice."

Will shook his head.

"No, I'm not sure there's much to the best of me. I hope she got her mother's good stuff and she just uses me for filling in gaps."

"You sell yourself short, Will Ross."

"I dunno about that."

"I do."

She reached over and squeezed his hand. Will felt a gentle electric shock run up his arm and something—different.

"Thank you, Beth. I appreciate just, well, getting to talk."

She nodded. "Oh, Will, just know I'm here for you always. Thank you for coming here. For bringing Elena. For talking. You opened up to me like few people ever have before."

"You make it sound like an interview."

She blushed a hot red and smiled. "Sorry. The curse of the business. Every time I chat with someone it comes out sounding like the third degree."

Will shook his head.

"Not so much. Sorry I said it." He looked over his shoulder. "Where's the waiter? I'd like to pay. I've got to get Elena home."

"Don't worry about it. This was, as I said, a private party—of two." She nodded at Elena. "Three. This one's on me. You can buy dinner this weekend."

Will smiled, then frowned.

"Shit. I'm out of town with that bike tour all weekend long."

"Aw, darn," Beth said as sincerely as she could. "I'm sorry. Next week, then."

"Next week."

They slid out of the booth, Will reaching back and slinging the diaper bag over his shoulder. He hadn't needed this after all. Rose was simply loading him down with "dad" stuff in order to scare the new lady away.

He smiled.

"What?"

"Oh, nothing. Just a nice evening, that's all."

Elena slept, packed tightly on his shoulder, her hot breath on his neck, warming it with a steady rhythm.

Beth took Will's hand and led him through the empty restaurant to the front door. The owner stood by, stepped up, unlocked and opened the door for them. The three walked out, the door locking behind them.

"Nice night," Beth said.

"Mmm-hhh," Will agreed. "Not many more left. Especially in the high country. I've got some hard riding and cold sleeping over the next few days."

She smiled.

"Maybe this will help keep you warm." She leaned into him and kissed him passionately, her tongue surprising him by the leap into his mouth. In seconds, he was kissing her back. In seconds more, Elena was wriggling like a bluegill on a hook.

They parted. Elena settled back into her position on her father's shoulder. Beth could swear she saw a smile on her face.

"We'll get back to that when you return," she whispered. "Maybe alone next time."

Will nodded. "That would be nice."

"I've got to go," she said. "I've got an early morning tomorrow logging tapes and writing."

"Will I see you at the station?"

"Probably not. Don't come looking for me. I'll come looking for you. How about that?"

"Fair enough."

"I'll see you, then." She leaned forward and kissed him quickly, almost too quickly, and walked briskly away down the sidewalk. She waved as she turned the corner and was gone.

Will stood for a moment in the courtyard of the restaurant. He looked back inside. The lights were off in front, but there was some movement in the back. He looked back to the corner where he had last seen Beth and wondered why it had all seemed so—well, so quick at the end.

So long and thanks for all the fish, that kind of thing.

Bing, bang, boom. Gone.

Damn.

He turned his head toward Elena.

"Let's get you home, kiddo. Your grandmother is either having a cow or sending out search parties."

As they walked back to the car, Will heard a distant sound of trumpets, then smelled something that must have been born in hell itself.

He looked at his daughter with disgust.

"Oh, how could a sweet little thing like you create something so incredibly foul?"

He shook his head to clear his nostrils, suddenly glad he had brought along the diaper bag.

"Did you get the kiss?"

"Both. Hot and hotter."

"Good deal. I want those on my desk by 7 A.M."

"Yeah, and people want ice water in hell."

"Seven."

"Whatever. You'll have 'em."

Stanley walked back up to Ollie, shaking his head.

"What's the problem now—did you lose her too?"

"No, I didn't," Stanley answered sarcastically. "Where's Will and the baby?"

"On their way home. Will stopped for a minute and changed her out of the hatchback and then left. Made a U-ie and headed up toward Sixth."

Stanley continued to look back toward the corner, then the restaurant, puzzled.

"What is with you?" Ollie asked impatiently.

"Well, just this: damnedest thing. So she scratches Will's tonsils there," he said, pointing at the restaurant door, "then she hustles her ass down to the corner there. ..." He pointed again. "Then she waves," he gave a little wave, "hustles, almost runs, down to the alley behind the office building on the corner, jogs down the alley, looking between buildings to make sure ..."

"Make sure what?"

"I dunno. Make sure Will wasn't seeing her, I guess," Stanley said sheepishly.

"Then what?"

"Well, this is the weird shit."

"Don't curse," Ollie said quickly.

"Yeah, yeah. But it *is* weird shit, Ollie. She runs down the alley to the back of the restaurant, knocks on the door, it pops open, and she jumps in."

"Maybe she forgot her purse."

"No, she had it over her shoulder."

"Maybe she forgot something. Who opened the door?"

"Don't know. Wasn't the guy at the door or the waiter we saw wandering around."

"Cook?"

"Wasn't dressed like one."

"What was he dressed like?"

"Jeans. Dark shirt. Baseball cap turned backward."

"What team?"

"ARRI."

"Never heard of them."

"Me either."

"Anything else?"

"No, it just said A-R-R-I."

"Curiouser and curiouser."

"What now?"

"You go around to the back. I'll stay here. Let's wait until she comes out."

Stanley nodded and disappeared. As he crossed the street, he forgot the police photographer with the telephoto lens in the parking structure who was busy taking a low-light, high-speed, black-and-white photo of a thin man running across the street, three-quarter face.

✳

THIRTY MINUTES LATER, THE BACK DOOR OF THE RESTAURANT OPENED ON THE ALLEY. The man in the jeans and black shirt stepped out, looked around carefully, and walked quickly to a Jeep Cherokee rental parked in one of the restaurant management spaces. He backed up and drove it to just beyond the back door.

As he turned off the engine and stepped out of the car, the back door of Frisco's opened again and Beth Freeman stepped out, carrying the first of many loads of camera gear.

The man in the jeans and black shirt opened the back of the Jeep and began to load it as Stanley moved quietly out of the alley, around the corner, and back to where Olverio Cangliosi was keeping vigil.

This he had to see.

WILDERNESS

The house was silent in the darkness.
Will stared at the ceiling and thought of the evening.
Not the entire evening, just the end.
Not the entire end, just the kiss.
The kiss. That kiss that was something akin to jumping into a swimming
pool with a 220 line attached to your nether region.
That kiss.
"Are you there?"
"Is it you?"
"Do you know?"
He felt himself grow hard.
He felt himself grow ashamed.
He thought of baseball.
And wished that he smoked cigarettes.

CHAPTER EIGHTEEN

PUTTIN' ON
THE MOVES

W
HO'S THIS GUY?" WHITESIDE ASKED, HOLDING UP THE LAST
picture in the stack, newly delivered to Paul Timmons's desk.
It was 9:45.

Timmons brushed it away, pulling Whiteside's attention back to the sheaf of
pictures that focused on the kiss. The kisses. The rather passionate kisses.

"Look at that. Look at that. Any deeper and they'd have to go to medical
school. There's motive."

"It's thin, Paul. You can't place him at the scene. You can't place him with the
materials."

"Eh ... eh!" Paul Timmons barked and jumped away, pointing. He stepped
quickly over to his own desk, opened a file cabinet, and pulled out a manila
folder. ROSS was written in block letters in the corner. He opened it and began
to read from his notes.

"Few years back, he's nothing. Less than nothing. Going belly-up in Europe.
Broke. Drunk. Hopeless."

"Yeah, okay, I get it." Whiteside leaned back to listen.

"The team is Haven Pharmaceuticals. They pick him up after—after—a
bomb blows up the world champion. Stuck it in his toaster. *Boom!* They found
the guy in a cupboard."

"I'm listening."

"So. Will gets the call. He's back in the game. Now one of the mechanics is
working late. Accidentally triggers something under Will's bike seat. *Boom!*"

"But it was under Will's bike seat. Maybe he was the target."

"Maybe that's where he stored it. Better than having the stuff found on you."

"But how much? You can't hide much under a seat. And even if that's where you hid it—in plain sight—you wouldn't put a trigger with it."

"Maybe the mechanic knew something. Found something. Somewhere." Timmons's argument fell off.

"Wait, though, Ray, there's still a good finish. One other guy, head of the company, dies when his car mysteriously blows up—just after Will tells him to get stuffed, he's leaving."

"What do the French police say?"

"Who the fuck cares what they think? They were probably drunk. He was close. There is opportunity. He has been near the stuff. There's the source."

"How did he get it here?"

"I dunno. Randy Disson. Maybe he knew Randy Disson. But the point is, Ray, he's been involved in this sort of thing before."

Timmons threw out his fingers to make his points.

"One. A bomb goes. He gets a job. Two. A bomb goes, he's lost a wife and is free to cat." He took the two fingers and pounded them onto the stack of pictures of Will and Beth. "Three. He's still low on the totem pole at TV6. Could any of the guys above him be a threat?"

"Well, he could blow up Roger Flynn and the town would probably make him a hero, the way that asshole talks about the Broncos like he knows something."

"I'm not joking, Ray. I'm not joking. Christ. I've just talked my way into a brainstorm. You watch, Ray, you watch. Flynn and that other guy, that weekend guy, the Lone Ranger, the Cisco Kid, whatever they call him, some damned nickname. Maybe even that young kid they've got—Jack—Art Jackson." He pulled the name out of the air. "They're next on the list. Mark my words. They're next in line."

Timmons flipped the file on Will Ross shut, triumphantly. He knew he had made an impression.

Whiteside nodded, trying to digest everything Timmons had just thrown at him. It was still thin, but it was no longer anorexic. Bombs had been in Ross's past, his recent past, even though the tie to the Denver bombs was tenuous at best.

But even he had to admit—there was a link. And Timmons was hitting the point hard. Whiteside glanced at the picture of Cheryl on his desk and nodded. Timmons was hitting the point. The newly single father, the newly widowed husband, never had shown all that much emotion over the past two months. A few crocodile tears at the hospital, but stoic at the funeral, and since? Little contact, but nothing seen.

He looked down at the pictures.

And what kind of man starts catting seven weeks after his wife dies? He had read enough true crime stories to tell you.

The husband who doesn't care.

Raymond Whiteside tapped his pencil on the side of the desk. He nodded. Timmons smiled.

"Okay. You've made your point. Keep watching. Keep digging this vein. I'll keep looking into Disson and the explosives. See if there is a connection. Also, very quietly, get somebody out to TV6 to keep an eye on those guys in the sports department. Watch their cars, watch their houses, strange packages, that sort of thing."

"All three?"

Whiteside considered the possibilities. He shook his head.

"Watch Flynn. But keep an eye out for anything strange with the other two. But keep an eye on Flynn."

"It's a start. I'd say watch all three."

"You can keep an eye on all three while they're at work. Follow Flynn."

"You've got it."

"And," Whiteside called as Timmons had already turned away to set up the surveillance, "find out who this guy is." He tossed the single picture of Stanley toward Paul Timmons, who picked it up and stared at it.

"I'll look into it, but Chuck nailed it because he said the guy was hanging around Cherry Creek last night. Kept seeing him. Maybe a shop owner."

"Find out."

"Maybe a customer."

"Find out."

"Maybe somebody walking from the neighborhood."

"*Find out.*"

Timmons nodded. "Right."

He turned to walk away and set up the surveillance at TV6.

Maybe a guy who couldn't find a parking spot, he thought as he walked out the door.

"Just find out," Whiteside called out after him.

✳

"WHERE'S WILL?" THE NEW FOCUS OF A POLICE INVESTIGATION ASKED.

Rose bounced Elena on her knee to a new and surprising chorus of giggles.

"Oh, God, this is heaven. What? Oh, he's riding. He's got that four-day mountain trip starting tomorrow. Well, it starts on Thursday, but he leaves for it tomorrow afternoon."

Stanley nodded.

"I don't like it. Bad stuff always happens when he rides that bike."

Olverio Cangliosi was silent in the corner.

"What's wrong with you?" Stanley asked.

Olverio looked up silently. He was rising up from a pit of deep thought. It took him a while.

"Well," he said finally, quietly, "do you realize that we've lost our one contact? Our one direct link to this asshole?"

"I thought you said don't curse."

"Don't screw with me, Stanley. This is serious. We've lost our one link. He was blown up right after a delivery. I'll bet you money that whatever it was that got Disson was in that briefcase we saw."

"Ruined a good briefcase."

"Stanley, Jesus. Follow the point, will you? This guy is starting to move again. He's starting to sweep up after himself. I don't like it."

"Who do you think he'll sweep up next?"

"I wouldn't be surprised at all—if it was Will."

He turned to Rose and the baby.

"Or—her."

Rose pulled Elena close, protectively.

"This one likes to hurt."

✳

BETH FREEMAN WAS AGLOW. SHE WAS TINGLING WITH EXCITEMENT, THE ALMOST orgasmic anticipation of a solid story well told in pictures and words. Just logging the interview with Jeremy, the story wrote itself. There were at least two stories here, Will's past with the wife, Cheryl, and Will's future with the baby, Ellen. No, Elena. Beth smiled. The second half was the killer. She hadn't noticed it while she and Will were talking last night, but Jeremy had. He had the eye. He saw the whole picture. He focused on the baby, and the baby lit up the screen. She was darkly gorgeous, with huge brown eyes that leaped off the monitor and touched even Beth's heart.

There was her image. There was her title.

"In the Eyes of a Child," she muttered.

"What?" Jeremy asked over his shoulder, shuttling the digital images back and forth.

"Nothing," Beth smiled, "just writing."

Beth Freeman felt electric.

This was writing itself.

"In the eyes of a child, you find the pain of the past. In the eyes of a child, you find the hope of a future—alone, without the courageous heart of a mother. A mother who gave her life to protect … no … who gave her life so her child could live."

It was writing itself.

She wondered where she'd put the Emmys, Peabodys, and Columbia Journalism Awards.

There was a knock on the door.

"Get the fuck out of here," she shouted. The footsteps moved away from the door.

She couldn't take her eyes off the baby.

Will didn't enter into it at all.

✳

PETER THE GREAT QUIETLY LOADED THE LAST OF THE MATERIAL INTO HIS PICKUP TRUCK.

He liked working at home, he liked having the material handy, but the whole Randy Disson business was making him squirrelly. He didn't know why. Just a feeling. A gut feeling. Never let anyone get too close for too long.

He slammed the tailgate of the truck shut, a little too hard, perhaps, for what he carried inside, and slid into the front seat.

As he pulled away from the house, he went over the move, why it was necessary, and what remained in the house. Only two pieces, both for use tomorrow, both unobtrusive, both easily mistaken for something quiet and common.

And then he thought about Randy Disson and how he had known that Randy Disson had to die.

Randy Disson was not above flopping over and showing his belly to save his own ass. The last few calls had convinced him of that. Randy Disson was beginning to turn. Maybe to the cops, maybe to somebody else, but he was beginning to turn.

And Disson had noticed him. Disson had known. So it was right to give him a surprise. The last of the hypergolics had been rather spectacular.

Quite a show.

But only a prelude to what would begin tomorrow night.

Only two pieces remained inside, both for tomorrow.

✹

OBLIVIOUS TO IT ALL, WILL RODE THROUGH THE FARMLAND OF EASTERN ADAMS County, noting the farms and the houses and the long, rolling stretches of land stripped of their crops as autumn, true autumn, came sliding in, soon, he hoped, to prepare the soil for next spring.

The air was hot but clean, and Will rode with a smile.

The ride seemed endless, as endless as the land. He read the names of farmers as he rode past: Miller, Smith, Kenyon, Monica, Jackson, Williams, Steinholt, all solid American farming names.

And he rode.

Click click click click click click click clickclickclickclickclick …

He rose up out of the seat and drove himself harder than he had in months. Deep inside, he felt alive again, for no reason that he could fathom.

He rode toward the horizon and whatever future awaited him.

Clickclickclickclickclickclickclickclick.

CHAPTER NINETEEN
SEPARATION ANXIETY

D O YOU HAVE EVERYTHING, WILL?"

"I haven't had any complaints yet."

Rose stared at Will for a moment before shaking her head and returning to her coffee.

"What I meant was," Will began to explain before Rose held up a hand.

"You don't have to explain. It was a yolk."

"I guess not much of one."

"No. Not much of one. Let's see, how can I put this: Are you packed?"

Will thought about the heavy leather travel bag and nodded. "Yeah, I think so. I'm sure I forgot something important, like underwear, but it's only four days."

"Have you got all your riding gear?"

He thought of the heavy canvas duffel sitting in the living room next to the door. This one he mentally unpacked at the table. "Five days' riding gear. Short- and long-sleeved ..."

"You're going to need the long sleeves in the mountains. The nights have been frigid up there. Winter's coming."

"I know. Got 'em. Helmet. Gloves. Unguent."

"What's *unguent?*"

"I'm not really sure," Will said. "I use it for saddle sores, and I just liked the word." He waved his hand through the air and said dramatically, "*Un*-guent."

He smiled at Rose. "I've got it all."

She smiled back. "It's nice to see you smile. Was it your, uh, date, Monday night?" she asked carefully. Her eyes turned down to her coffee cup.

Will sat quietly for a moment, not sure how to deal with the question and certainly not sure how to answer it. He decided on honesty—dangerous but practical.

"I'm not sure, Rose. Could be. It was nice to have a woman—a woman I wasn't related to—to talk to, to listen. To nod and say, 'Everything's gonna be all right.'"

Rose nodded with tense understanding.

"What about her?" she asked cautiously, as if her words were walking through a minefield. "What about the, uh, future?"

"Well, Rose, it has been nice. Nice to think that somebody could like me. Might want me. I don't think you have to worry. I dunno what it is, but one day Beth is my best friend in the whole world, and then the next, she's telling me to get the hell out of her life."

"She told you that?"

"She was editing. Didn't want to be bothered."

"That doesn't sound right."

Will chuckled at the suddenness of her opinion. "No, I guess not. I dunno. I'll talk to her about it sometime. It's nice. It's not special, Rose. It's just nice."

Rose nodded again, seeming somehow relieved. Will smiled at her reaction and continued, "But the truth be told, Rose—I think I'm happy just because, over the past week, I've gotten back on the bike. Do you believe that?"

Rose relaxed. She smiled sadly and nodded.

"You forget, Will, I had a whole family who felt that way."

"Yeah." He reached over and squeezed her hand. "You know, Rose, I keep forgetting how much the bike means to me. I get away from it. Nobody forces me to ride, and by God, I don't. I sit on my ass. I start riding again, for one reason or another, and all of a sudden my life starts working better. I can think. I can move. I don't get as angry at, well, everybody. It's all there: two wheels, frame, and saddle. I guess that's all I need.

"It's a part of me."

Rose leaned forward and cradled her coffee cup in her hands.

"You're missing a step, Will."

"Like what?"

"Like life," she said.

"Don't worry," he said with a confident smile. "I've got it under control. Got it under control."

Like hell, she thought.

The phone rang. The sudden sound made them both jump in the silence of the kitchen. Elena began to cry in the next room. Shoe and Rex both anxiously clacked into the kitchen as if to say, "Don't you hear her? She's in distress. Why don't you come? *Now?*"

Rose stood and answered the phone, then turned to Will. "It's for you. Fellow from the station. Art?"

Will nodded. Right, right. He had mentioned something to Ransford yesterday about where he was going to leave a car. Rose brought the cordless handset to him, then immediately walked out of the kitchen to soothe Elena.

She called after the dogs as she went. "Come along, you two, I'll make her better. You'll see."

Will smiled. Rex and Shoe were like guardian angels.

"Hello?"

"Hi, Will, Art Jackson."

"Jesus, Art, you sound awfully damned perky for this time of the morning."

"Yeah, well, what can I say? Life is good. I heard you talking yesterday, then Ransford asked me to give you a call. You want a ride in today? You can haul your gear in my truck."

"Yeah, that would be great, but this is your day off, isn't it? You don't have to do this."

"No problem. I've got a Sunday feature I want to work on, so this will just force me in to do it."

"You're sure?"

"I'm sure. I've gotta go a bit early. Is 11:30 okay?"

"Yeah, that sounds good. I've got to make sure everything is in place, then get up to Boulder for the first live shot tonight. Eleven-thirty is good."

"See you then, pal."

"See you then. Thanks, Art."

Will turned off the phone and paused, then turned toward the living room. Through the kitchen arch he could see Rex and Shoe and Rose and Elena, the two dogs bouncing in circles happily as Elena cooed and laughed at the patter of googly sounds emanating from her grandmother. After all this house had lost, it was a wonderful scene.

Suddenly Will didn't want to go. It was as if a cold hand had run down his back. Suddenly he didn't want to leave, he didn't want to ride. This was what he had done two months ago: packed up and headed for Boulder to start a race into the mountains of Colorado. Look what had happened then. Something about Art's phone call had reminded him of that departure, that mistake.

He didn't want to go.

After all he had said about riding and the bike and thinking and life, he wanted to stay here to protect these four and everything he had left in his life.

More than anything.

❈

WILL CONTINUED TO MENTALLY INVENTORY HIS BAGS AT 11:30, SURE SOMETHING vital was missing. The suitcase he wasn't worried about. He would be wearing street clothes for only a few hours a night. He could always repeat a shirt if he needed to. The riding gear was the question.

Something was missing, and it was nagging at him, as if someone was standing behind him—hitting him on the back of the head.

A pickup truck pulled up out front. He was out of worrying time. Art Jackson stepped out and began to walk up the sidewalk. The dogs barked wildly. Will shushed them and opened the door for Art.

"Come on in. Any problems finding the place?"

"Not a one, Will. Not a one. How you doing?"

"Great, Art. Thanks for the ride."

"This your daughter?"

"Yeah, either that or somebody is leaving babies in living rooms around the city." Rose came down the steps and looked over the banister.

"Do you have all your riding gear, Will?"

"Yes, Rose," he whined. "I've got everything. Rose Cangliosi, my mother-in-law, this is Art Jackson, ace young sports reporter. He'll be driving me to work today."

Rose smiled. "Nice to meet you. Thank you for giving Will a ride. I don't like to drive in this city."

"Oh, where are you from?"

"Detroit," she said flatly, and walked back up the stairs.

"Cute."

"Ain't she, though?" Will said.

Art crouched down beside Elena's blanket. "Hi, sweetheart. How are you?" He reached out a hand, as if he was meeting a dog for the first time, to see what Elena would do.

"She's not going to bite you."

"Hey, I was an only child. Never had babies around."

As he stretched out his hand toward the baby, Shoe growled. Will fwapped him on the back of the head. "Relax. She's fine."

Elena leaned away.

"I guess she's growing up," Will said. "She's never been standoffish before. Do you hit the terrible twos at two months?"

"I don't know," Art smiled. "Maybe she's already entering those nasty teenage years."

"Thank you," Will said sarcastically. "I'm thrilled to hear that."

"You ready to go?"

"Yeah, let me get the bike. I'll roll it around front."

Art stayed crouched near the baby. "I'll get your bags and carry them out."

"I can do that."

"No problem, don't worry about it. I've got them."

"Well, thanks. I appreciate it. Come on, guys," Will said to the dogs. Neither moved. They stared protectively at Elena.

"See how well trained they are? I'll just be a minute."

"Take your time," Art said as Will walked away through the back of the house.

He looked at the dogs.

"Okay. You two just remain calm."

Slowly, Art Jackson reached into his pocket. Watching the dogs intently, he carefully moved toward the baby as if to stroke her.

Rex gave a small "woof." Neither dog took its eyes off Art Jackson as he stayed close to Elena. He slowly leaned away from the baby, rose, then backed toward the screen door and carefully picked up Will's bags.

Without taking his eyes off the dogs, he elbowed open the screen and stepped out onto the concrete landing.

The screen door slapped shut behind him.

"Have a nice day," he whispered to the dogs.

Rex and Shoe began to pace.

✸

TONY CARVER HAD BEEN ASSIGNED TO THE WEDNESDAY LIVE SHOTS FROM THE Boulderado Hotel in Boulder, Colorado, just a block or so from the west end of the Pearl Street Mall. Between shots, he and Will wandered to the mall for dinner, then browsed a small mystery book store.

As they walked back to the hotel and the live truck, Tony Carver waved a mystery novel in Will's face.

"You know what I love about these things?"

"There's always a skull on the cover?"

"No, no. Shit, no. They always get the bad guy. It's like a rule. They always get the bad guy. They don't do that in real life."

"They don't? Tom Blakely says every night that they caught some other guy who did the deed. I mean—that's our regular lead story. Criminal caught." Will paused. "Or—car wrecked. We're good at that one too, especially if we've got pictures."

"I think the cops are as surprised as anybody else. But even those—somebody made a mistake, somebody dropped a dime, the bad guy was talking to mouthy buddies, the cops picked up on it—stuff like that."

"So it wasn't ace detective work?"

"I don't think there are ace detectives." Carver held up the book. "Except here. The rest is luck. Look at JonBenet."

"That's only one case, Tony. There are tons. They do okay."

"Sure they do. That's why I read these," he said, waving the book at Will again. "They give me faith."

Will peered at the title in the gathering darkness. He knew this character.

"Somehow, Tony, I never took you for the kind of guy who read tea-cozy mysteries featuring little old ladies who live in New England towns with the highest murder rates in the country, who then solve said murders thanks to nothing more than their astute knowledge of the exotic poisons of South America."

"What the hell are you talking about?" He turned the cover toward him. "Aw, shit, I picked up the wrong book. Where's my *Sniper Kill?*" He turned and looked around on the ground as if it might be following him on tiny paper legs.

"Crap. I'll have to go back."

"She was closing up."

He looked at the book.

"Oh, well, it's something."

Will reached for the book and flipped it open to the last page.

"And rest assured, she catches the bad guy in a mere 247 pages."

He handed the book back to Tony Carver, who took it with a grin and good-naturedly flipped Will off.

✳

THE MAIN TARGET WAS TOO OBVIOUS, THAT HE KNEW. THE BRAND-NEW MERCEDES convertible was sitting near the door, under a pool of light, in direct view of the newsroom windows. He pondered it for a moment, wondering how he could pull it off, as it would make his life, everyone's life, so much easier, then, realizing it was next to impossible for now, he steeled himself, made the decision, and moved on to the secondary target.

Roger Flynn would live another day.

Clyde Zoromski, on the other hand …

"Sorry, you old, fat bastard," he whispered to himself. "It is time to meet your maker."

He crept up in the darkness behind the old Chevy, located the gas cap, opened it, then waited. He could hear traffic in the distance, but here, next to the fence that led into the alley, there was nothing. He took the small drill with the hole saw and went through the brake-light housing. It gave him just enough room to wiggle a finger in, detach the light, and connect the leads. He ran the wires to the gas tank and fed the igniter into the hole, just enough to get it well into the fumes. He closed the access door on top of the wires, both to hold them in place and to make everything less obvious, threw the gas cap into the weeds, and slipped out of the parking lot.

He took one last look at the security cameras. They hadn't moved. Unless you were parked in one or two spots in the middle of the lot, they were a false assurance of safety.

He smiled.

This was too easy.

"So, WILL," TOM BLAKELY ASKED THE CAMERA, "THAT ROUTE YOU JUST DESCRIBED.
Four days. Four hundred fifty miles. Uncertain weather. Trail Ridge Road. How
do you think you'll hold up?"

Will stood in a box next to the anchorman, one in Denver, the other in
Boulder, thirty miles away, and answered as if it really meant something more
than just chitchat, filling the prescribed time though the story was already told.

"Most of the climbing, Tom, is steady climbing. Berthoud will be tough,
that's day two," Will paused, "or three." He laughed. "I guess it's bothering me
more than I thought because for the life of me I can't remember what day
Berthoud's on. But—that aside—"

The voice in his ear said, "Wrap."

Will tripped over his next few words, trying to gather his thoughts.

"But Trail Ridge. Trail Ridge—that will be the climb that kills. Highest
paved road in North America. Or something like that."

"Hard wrap," the disembodied voice called into his ear.

"Well, good luck on that, Will, we'll be looking for your stories."

"Thanks, Tom, we'll see you tomorrow," Will replied.

He held steady, freezing the smile on his face and staring at the camera until
Tony said, "Clear."

He held the pose for another few seconds just to make sure, then relaxed
and pulled the wireless microphone transmitter from his back pocket. He made
sure he had turned it off before he said anything.

"That oughta hold the little bastards for another week."

"You know, that's an urban legend. The guy never said that."

"Said what?"

"The radio guy," Tony said. "The radio guy who supposedly said that on an
open microphone."

"Oh, I didn't know that. I just heard it somewhere."

"Urban legend. Like alligators in the sewers."

Will carefully wrapped the microphone cable around the transmitter and
handed it to Tony. He looked around for something else to break down and
pack away, but Tony waved him off.

"Don't worry about this stuff. I've got it. Why don't you go in and get some sleep? You've got a big day tomorrow. And the next day and the next day and the next day and the ..."

Will held up his hand.

"Yeah. So do you, though. I thought you were coming along."

"Was," Tony replied, clearly miffed, "but Ransford told me today that he can't afford to send all his shooters out of town this weekend for some God-knows reason, so he hired a freelancer to shoot this for you this weekend."

"Really? They do that often?"

"No, they don't. That's the pisser. The little son of a bitch has been hiding out in the back of the station all week with Beth Freeman, working on some big project."

"With Beth?"

"Yeah, the original Bitch on Wheels. They've been hunkered down in the one edit room with no windows where you can lock the doors. Sort of the 'secret shit' room."

"What's the story?"

"Don't know. Nobody knows. But word from Traffic is that it airs this week-end. First thing they did was cut the promos for the goddamned thing. They start running tomorrow. Hope they've got a story to go with it."

"Yeah. Hope so." Will nodded and shook Tony's hand. "Gonna miss you, man, like working with you."

"Same," Tony said. "We'll do it again. Don't worry." He hitched the last of the gear up and threw the tripod over his shoulder. "Have a good ride."

"Thanks, I will." Will walked toward the hotel entrance and tossed his notes into a trash bin on the street. As he climbed the steps toward his room, he thought about what Tony had told him. He wondered about Beth. He wondered about the story. That would explain where she had been the past few days. He wondered what the story was—she hadn't said anything the other night. He wondered about this photographer whom he didn't know and hadn't worked with before. He wondered in general about the wisdom of going on this ride, leaving Cheryl alone.

He caught himself. No. Not Cheryl. He had already done that. He had already left her alone. This was Rose and Elena. He didn't want to take this ride, but his feet kept carrying him toward his hotel room and his bike and tomorrow's start.

It was as if he had no will of his own. As if he was driven by fate.

He was like a freshly smashed grasshopper—his legs kept moving, even though his spirit had fled.

He opened the door to his room and went in to hide from himself once again.

✦

"ROGER, I KNOW THIS WILL COME AS A SHOCK TO YOU, BUT THEY'RE IN THE BREAK before your segment. You might want to get your ass out to the set."

Clyde Zoromski pointed at the clock, then out the door, then at the clock, then out the door, one-two-one-two-one-two, until Roger Flynn got the hint, realized he was late, snatched up his coat, and raced out the door.

"I want that score from LA, asshole. Call it into the booth as soon as you've got it."

"Right, Rog. You got it."

Zorro waited for a moment until he heard Flynn turn the corner on the other side of the atrium, heading for the studio, then shut down his computer, turned off his desk light, picked up a sheaf of papers, threw them in the trash, and walked to the door.

"Get it yourself, asshole," he whispered, smiling, before heading across the atrium toward the employees' exit and the parking lot. "Just enough time to get home for some *Simpsons* and about forty drinks before bedtime."

As he walked to his car, he realized that the weather was starting to change. The nights had a decided edge to them. He didn't envy Will, riding in the mountains. The mornings were going to be bitter, and who knew? At this time of the year, Trail Ridge could get snow at any moment, no matter what was happening downtown.

As usual, he rubbed his thumb along the rust spot next to the antenna, more out of habit than hope of chipping it off, then walked around the car, unlocked the door, and slipped behind the wheel.

Zorro sighed. He used to drive nice cars. Now all his ex-wives drove nice cars and he drove this—a hunk of junk sure to fall apart at any second, just when he least expected it.

He fiddled with the keys and worked one into the ignition. He pumped the gas twice and turned the key. The car cranked twice, caught, then lifted into the air.

For a split second, Clyde Zoromski experienced the same feeling as when the station helicopter took off.

That was just before he heard himself scream.

CHAPTER TWENTY

STARTING LINE

ILL ZIPPED THE HEAVY LEATHER SUITCASE CLOSED, THEN PICKED IT UP off the bed and dropped it on the floor with a dull *thwap*. He took one more tour around the room and checked the bathroom. Shit. He had left his toothbrush and a minitube of Crest next to the lavatory.

He picked those up and, with increased paranoia, looked around again, walking out to check the closet before finally giving up and deciding he had it all. He unzipped the top of the bag and stuffed the brush and toothpaste inside, zipping it closed.

As he stood hunched over the bag and the edge of the bed, he noticed a dull, sparkly residue on the bedspread as if someone had wiped bits of a sparkler on the comforter. He wiped his hand across it, and it came away waxy and covered with gray specks.

"Great. I'll get charged for that one, that's for damned sure."

He wiped his fingers across the other palm, the slick grittiness vaguely reminding him of something, something he didn't have time to ponder. He brushed the bedspread as well as he could, hoping the cleaning crew wouldn't notice—at least until the next occupant—washed his hands, and called down to the front desk for a bellman. He took one last look around the room and finally relaxed.

He had everything. There was a knock at the door. Will opened it and handed his bag to the bellman. The bellman then held the door for Will as he maneuvered the Beast out the door and into the hall.

Will looked back into the room. At this angle, he could see the stain on the bedspread clearly. Shit. That was gonna cost him.

He let the door close behind him, and the bellman led him downstairs toward the front desk, checkout, a morning live shot, breakfast, and the start of the Ride.

Christ on a Colnago, he didn't want to do any of this.

❋

PAUL TIMMONS STOOD IN THE PARKING LOT OF TV6 AND STARED AT THE BLACKENED outlines of Clyde Zoromski's ancient Chevrolet, both where it had left the ground and where it had landed.

Ray Whiteside walked up silently behind him.

"What do you have, Paul?"

Timmons jumped and spun, his nerves alert, seemingly ready to draw his weapon and start popping away at anything or anyone.

"Jesus, hang on," Whiteside muttered. "It's just me."

"Sorry. Sorry, Ray," Timmons apologized. "I've been with this one all night. No matter where you are in the night, dawn is a long way away."

"Don't I know it. What have you got?"

Timmons blinked hard, trying to clear the fog from his eyes and the crust from the corners of his eyelids. He reached into his back pocket and pulled out a notebook, flipped it open, and read clumsily from it.

"Our man is Clyde Zoromski, forty-two, weekend sports anchor here at TV6. He was the owner of the car and the only occupant at the time of the explosion. According to witnesses, he was doing some producing for Roger Flynn's 10 o'clock sports report last night. He left the station at approximately 10:25 P.M. A few moments later, those same witnesses noticed a fiery explosion in the parking lot and called Denver Fire."

"Hard not to notice. Where were these witnesses?"

Timmons looked at his notes again. "One intern, one assignment editor just inside those windows. They say he walked out that door, which is pretty well lit, then into one of the darker areas of the parking lot. Then, boom."

"Anything on the security cameras?"

"We're checking, but this corner of the lot is not under surveillance." Timmons pointed up to the cameras on the tops of the light poles. "The motors that pan those puppies around have burned out."

"Okay. So, old car blows up—why were we called?"

"At first they thought old car, mechanical failure, gas-tank leak, bottom of the tank corroded, but then, come over here …"

Timmons and Whiteside walked to the back of the burned-out Chevy. Timmons pointed down at the left rear light.

"It's melted some, but you can still see where somebody cut a neat little hole in the plastic, then wired up the light to …" he drew his finger across the wires "… to this."

"It's a smaller wire."

"Nope. Fire investigator says it's an igniter for a model rocket engine. Put some juice to it and it burns real hot for a few seconds."

"Where did it burn?"

"Real hot in the gas tank."

"Well, that'd do it."

"It pretty much did. They figured our friend was back at work and called us. I was in the barrel last night, and I got the page."

"Aw, gee, Paul. You're always the lucky one," Whiteside said sarcastically.

"Ain't I, though?"

"Is this, uh, Zoromski dead?"

Timmons shook his head.

"No, but he won't be wearing any wool shirts for a while. Paramedics on the scene said his back looked like a roasted wienie. He also burned his hand getting out of the car, second-degree burns, I think, and he broke his leg because he was still three feet off the ground when he jumped."

"Lucky man," Ray Whiteside said, staring at the blackened shell of the car.

"Very lucky," Timmons replied. "He came within a few seconds of being a crispy critter."

"Where is he?"

"Denver Health Medical. ICU. They're going to transfer him to University Burn Center."

"Has he been awake?"

"Just long enough to tell a nurse to 'fuck off' and say a name."

"Who?"

"You'll never guess—our old friend: Will Ross."

Ray Whiteside stared for a second, then finally said under his breath, "You've got to be shitting me."

Paul Timmons smiled triumphantly.

※

"Hey, you must be Jeremy."

"Yeah, Jeremy Paxton. You must be Will Ross."

"Yeah. How'd you know?"

"You're dressed for a ride and you've got an IFB sticking out of your ear. I just assumed."

"Good call. Who's running the live truck?"

"Me. I've got the satellite truck for the mountain shots. They were going to send me with the microwave, but they had spot news in Denver, so Ransford has blown your live shot this morning. They'll rerun your package from yesterday if they've got time."

"What spot news?"

"Car fire. Nothing big," Jeremy lied as instructed, "but they've got pictures. So you know how that goes."

"If it bleeds, it leads?"

"Definitely."

"All right. By the way, which satellite truck do you have?"

Jeremy shook his head. "I dunno. Number Two, I think."

"Ah, Challenger. The engineers call it that because it's always blowing up."

"Riiight. Well, I'll shoot the start and some of the ride, then just hopscotch you all the way into Estes Park today. Then we can cut a little package for tonight's Five."

"I don't know if I'd drive that thing through Left Hand Canyon."

"I'll be fine. I've gotta shoot and cut anyway, so I don't have much choice."

"Lotta work for you."

"Hey, that's the way it goes." Jeremy Paxton smiled. It was creepy as hell. Will shuddered involuntarily.

"Hey," Will said, changing the subject, "you've been working with Beth Freeman all week."

Jeremy was silent for a moment, then said, "Yeah."

"So, how's she doing? Didn't get a chance to see her Tuesday or Wednesday. Just wondered how she was."

"She's fine," Jeremy chirped, realizing he was on safe ground. "She's happy. Her editing went very well. She's got an award winner."

"Good," Will replied. "That's nice to know. What are you two working on?"

"Oh, well, that," Jeremy muttered. "That's, uh, that's a secret. It's one of Beth's special projects, and I learned from working with her at her old station— that's where I worked with her—you don't—you just don't talk about her work. Freaks her out. She's convinced that, uh, the competition will find out. Real paranoid about it. Need-to-know basis."

"And I'm not …"

"Need-to-know." Jeremy gave that smile again. Will couldn't remember when he had ever seen anything so insincere.

"Yeah, well, I understand that," Will lied. Truth be told, he didn't understand much of anything in this business. "So, how are things back at the ranch?"

"The what?"

"The station. I assume you got the truck at the station garage this morning. How are things at the station this morning?"

Jeremy Paxton smiled again, quickly remembering what a pain it had been to get past the police tape and the smell of burned rubber and asphalt to get to the garage and get the truck out and on the road. It was only through Hugh Ransford's intervention that he had gotten out of there at all.

"Not a thing," Jeremy said, the smell of toasted asphalt still in his nostrils, "quiet as a mouse back at the old ranch."

"Good. You wanna catch some breakfast?"

Jeremy nodded. "You buying?"

Will eyeballed him carefully, then finally said, "Sure."

They walked to the small breakfast restaurant at the Boulderado, sat down, and Will spent the next forty-five minutes learning how magnificent and professional a shooter Jeremy Paxton was and how, if he was indeed hired at TV6 News, they'd finally have an awards horse on board who would start raking in prizes like leaves on a November Sunday.

Will groaned.

It was going to be a long damned weekend.

CHAPTER TWENTY-ONE
CLIMBING

EARLIER THIS SUMMER HE HAD RIDDEN SOUTH OUT OF BOULDER TOWARD the mountains, through Wondervu, Black Hawk, Idaho Springs, Georgetown, and Fairplay, on to Breckenridge and tragedy.

Now he rode west, toward Ward, heading for Estes Park, Trail Ridge, Grand Lake, and beyond. The first stage was only fifty miles or so, a long but lovely climb to Estes Park along the Peak-to-Peak Highway. At least, that was what he had been told. He had never ridden the Peak-to-Peak himself. The warning he had given Jeremy about the satellite truck, though, had been based on personal experience, a hellish grade leading into a spot on the map called Ward that he had ridden once when he first arrived in Denver and vowed never to ride again—a little place called Left Hand Canyon.

And here he was again, riding a road that took you nowhere in a way that could only be described as hell on wheels at a very stiff angle. It was Sisyphus time again, but instead of a rock, he'd soon be pushing a bike up a mountain, on a grade that seemed only a few degrees off 90, riding to a turn that would only take him up another road and another and another and another until he crossed over the top of the Rocky Mountains, which, when you did it, especially on Trail Ridge, seemed like the top of the world.

The first few miles out of Boulder had been bump and grind with traffic on Highway 36, the riders bunched on the flats, but that had passed quickly as they turned left en masse into Left Hand Canyon. Will had started in the front of the crowd but had now fallen about fifty riders back.

He was merely riding. They were working. The racers were yet to come.

The climbing began almost immediately, with at least ten riders, two groups of four men each and two women riding as a team, powering past Will, some doing it quietly, some crowing their power and expertise. There were moments, some immediately following each other, when Will's pride forced him up and out of the seat as if to chase those passing, especially the guy at the end of the second pace line, wearing a purple Masi jersey, who screamed, "Some champion" as he and his group ground past. Will recognized the feeling as the same he got on a two-lane highway when someone passed in a rush and he felt the accelerator start to move toward the floor, unconsciously, imperceptibly.

He needn't have worried.

The seven miles or so up to Ward were beautiful to look at but a bitch to ride, with a short shoulder, crumbling granite on the side that tossed bits, chunks, and honest-to-God boulders into the road, and the pitch from hell. The closer they approached Ward and the turn onto the Peak-to-Peak Highway, the more the angle grew. It rose to the point that Will could have sworn some of the riders who had passed him were in fact riding backward.

He glanced ahead.

Some riders knew the road. They were above him and working it well. Others, well, they didn't know the road. They hadn't trained at altitude. They hadn't been prepared for this. They were flatlanders. And they were rolling road kill.

Will leaned in over the headset but stayed in the seat, grinding away, playing with the gears, trying to find something that worked and kept him moving forward. The road grew steeper, steep enough that Will began to wonder who the hell had built this road and for what possible reason. This wasn't a climb, this was a crawl, with a few people in scattered clumps gathered by the side of the road yakking up everything from breakfast to the coffee cake they had had at Aunt Edna's funeral four years ago.

There was a certain satisfaction for Will, especially as he passed the bigmouth in the Masi jersey lying on his back and puking straight up into the air. The smell was horrific but the joy deep and wonderful.

It made Will realize that there was, indeed, a God.

Will stood and dug in, pushing himself up a climb that in many ways was bringing him to a stop as well. Alpe d'Huez might be longer, but the sheer pitch on this climb was the worst he had ever seen. The thought of what road engineer had approved this grade kept wandering through his head, along with the thought of where he'd find Jeremy on the side of the road with a burned-out satellite truck.

A mile or so, that was all this was, Will told himself, but it was a never-ending grind. A few feet forward, a few feet up. The ratios of forward motion to climb were growing equal. Will glanced up off the front tire in search of the next turn. It wasn't far, but it seemed straight above him, a ride that would take forever.

He had done this before, with Cheryl beside him, and they had both agreed: this was their version of hell, so maybe it was time to become good people and maybe go to church in order to have a shot at a heaven of flatlands and tailwinds.

Will smiled at the memory. It was a mistake. It opened the door, and more flooded into his mind, clutching at his heart and setting free the pain. He focused on the road and forced the door shut again.

"Stay away. Stay away from it," he wheezed. "Focus on the road. Focus on the road."

Click—click—click—click—click—shit.

He felt as if he was moving straight up now. But at least he was still moving. He passed steadily through a pace line that had roared past him earlier. He did not ride beside it, he rode through it, right through it, the four team members all over the road, desperately in search of a line that would get them up into Ward.

Will felt the first stirrings of dehydration. Bonk wasn't a worry. He had eaten well at breakfast and it was staying put, but he needed water soon or he'd be pushing the Beast up to the turn.

He looked up toward the next turn.

"This would be a good fucking place for a ladder!" he screamed.

Nobody heard him, and it didn't make a damned bit of difference, but it did make him feel better.

It seemed to take him forever to make each turn. He did, one after another, only to meet homemade speed bumps in the middle of the road, piles of tar cobbled together for some unknown reason. Like anybody could race up this road. Will slid wide but realized in doing so that he was sliding toward a nonexistent shoulder and eternity. He clipped the edge of the speed bump and cut back into the middle of his lane.

This was hell.

Deep inside, Will began to feel his own lack of preparation for the ride and this climb in particular. At the peak of his form he could have done this, found the sweet spot, jumped into it, then ridden like hell in some half-dazed alpha state, but he was nowhere near the peak of his form. He had been riding Lookout Mountain, but that was only for the past week, and it certainly was nothing in pitch compared to this—it would be easier to ride Paris-Roubaix in the wet season on a tricycle with a flat front tire.

He kept adding to the image—worn bearings, one gear, fat man on his back—until he reached the next turn, not a switchback, just a turn. He didn't have the speed to lean through it, so he just cranked the handlebars over, made the turn, and continued the climb.

How the hell did he get himself stuck in this?

Click—click—click—click.

How the hell did he let Ransford talk him into this?

Click—click—click—click—click.

I'd like to see Ransford ride this goddamned thing.

Click—click—click—click.

I wonder how Beth is doing.

Click—click—click—click.

I'd like to see her ride this thing.

Click—click—click—click.

I'd like to see her ride this—naked.

Clickclickclickclickclickclickclickclick.

The road flattened out without warning, still uphill but ridable, and Will found himself on the run up to Ward, a few buildings, a few cars, a few people staring, another few glaring, one right turn, and onto the Peak-to-Peak Highway.

Thank you, Jesus.

I'll never be bad again.

He emptied a water bottle, swishing the last bit around in his mouth before he swallowed. It caught just behind his Adam's apple on a chunk of something nasty. He hawked it up and blew it sideways, the glob landing somewhere between his bike and the sidewalk, between him and an ancient woman in a flowered dress who gave him a look that would have frozen Arnold and Sly in their tracks.

Will smiled and waved.

"Ah, yes. Making friends and winning viewers wherever I go," he muttered.

He took a deep breath, rose out of the seat, and left Ward behind him as quickly as his little legs could carry him.

✦

TIMMONS WANDERED INTO THE OFFICE, BLEARY EYED, THE SHOWER AND A CHANGE of clothes having done nothing to help either his mood or his exhaustion.

"God, I hate this middle-of-the-night shit."

"Crime doesn't take the night off," Ray Whiteside intoned in a stentorian voice. He poked one finger majestically into the air.

"Yeah, I'll give you one finger," Timmons said, slumping down into his chair, dropping his head back, and closing his eyes.

"Don't do that. Don't do that," Whiteside warned. "You'll wake up in two hours, feel like shit, and be in an even worse mood."

"Yeah, I know, but forty-five minutes of sleep just ain't enough for a growing boy. What have we got?"

"Chuckles is bringing the photos up this morning, so we can take another look at the scene."

"I'm telling you, pick up Ross. The vic is spouting his name. We've got motive and opportunity."

"Ross was out of town last night."

"Yeah, but he and Zoromski were at the station at the same time yesterday afternoon. Coulda set it then."

"Paul, I know you've got a hard-on for Will Ross, but I don't think even he has the balls to drill a hole and set a bomb in broad daylight."

"Maybe, maybe not. He's not the smartest card in the deck."

Whiteside chuckled at the mangled image.

"People at the station say he and Zoromski were friends."

"Hey, I always make friends with the criminal element before I shoot them."

"Yeah, maybe, but think of this: Are you in any shape to deal with Felix Ramirez this morning?"

Timmons was quiet for a long moment, then shook his head.

"Thank you, no. That little weasel can keep away from me today." He paused, then asked, "You think Ross is a runner?"

Whiteside shook his head.

"Naw. Like I said. He's too well known. No underground connections. That sort doesn't disappear well. He won't run. Got the kid, anyway."

Timmons shrugged.

"Maybe, maybe not."

An ancient police photographer shuffled in the door, his overhanging belly obscuring all but the tip of his shield hanging on his belt. He carried a manila envelope and tossed it on Whiteside's desk.

"Lovely to see you this morning, Chuckles." Timmons laughed through closed eyes.

"Fuck you, Paulie boy."

"What do you have for us, Chuck?"

"I got your shots this morning and," turning back to Timmons, "one of yours from the other night. I made notes and marked up a few interesting things I saw."

"Thanks for your help," Whiteside said. "Why one of Paul's from the other night?"

"Didn't want to waste another envelope, seeing as how they were all coming to the same place. Besides, I was just wondering, Wonder Cop," he said to Timmons, "where the hell you dug up Mr. Beans."

"Who?"

"Christ, you don't know who you've got here, do you? Mr. Beans. A.k.a. Stanley Szyclinski. Old-time hit man out of Detroit."

"*What?*" Timmons and Whiteside were both up and out of their chairs.

"Aw, shit. Fucking amateur night around here nowadays. Stanley Szyclinski. Mr. Beans, Stan the Man. The Tap Dancer? You guys don't know shit, do you?"

"No, I guess I don't," Whiteside said in a rush. "Explain it to me."

Chuck Vernon smiled a Cheshire grin and sat on the edge of a desk.

"He and his partner, fat guy named Olverio Cang—Cangliosi—Old Cans, that's it—were the deadliest twosome in Motown in the '60s. They took on everybody. The cops, the gangs, the feds, Jesus, they weren't afraid of anybody."

"What happened?"

"Time. Old age. I dunno. Disappeared, oh, ten, fifteen years ago. I heard the feds still kept an eye on them, but I've got some pals in Detroit who say they've been quiet. Retired. Dropped off the face of the earth to live on their investments."

"Their ill-gotten gains," Timmons muttered.

"Yeah, which you and me both wish we had," the photographer countered.

"What's he doing here?"

"I dunno. Guess he's interested in the same stuff you are."

Whiteside looked at the photo of Stanley Szyclinski taken on Monday night in Cherry Creek across the street from Frisco's. Why would he have been there? And what interest would he have in Will Ross?

"You think Will Ross is connected?" Whiteside asked.

Timmons shook his head.

"You mean mobbed up?"

"Maybe."

"I wouldn't know," Timmons answered. He pulled his feet off the desk and leaned forward. He stood up, rubbing his eyes.

"Might be a new path to examine."

Raymond Whiteside tapped his pencil on the side of the desk while he stared at the photo of Cheryl Crane.

"A new path," he whispered. "Let's take it, shall we, Paul?"

He stood up and slipped on his sports coat, picking up the picture of Stanley Szyclinski as he did. "Let's start looking at connections here."

"I'm suddenly wide awake and right with you."

The two walked out of the office with an air of purpose, leaving Chuck Vernon alone in the room staring after them, listening to their footsteps disappear down the hallway.

"Well, that makes me just goddamned glad I busted my ass to do these other pictures for you, assholes," he called after them.

❖

JUST OUTSIDE WARD, WILL PASSED THE SATELLITE TRUCK, STOPPED BY THE EDGE of the road. Jeremy Paxton sat next to one of the rear wheels, smoking a cigarette. His eyes were as big as dinner plates.

Will smiled.

"Are we having fun yet?"

Jeremy didn't have the energy to flip Will off. He had used it all wrestling the satellite truck up the grade to Ward, coming perilously close to the shoulder at least twice, then finding himself unable to get over a six-inch homemade speed bump without backing up twenty feet, gunning the engine, and rattling equipment in the back.

He just didn't have the energy. He sucked on the cigarette. At altitude, it was giving him one hell of a buzz.

He flicked the butt toward Will's receding form.

"Maybe I'll just bump your ass off the fucking road," he wheezed.

CHUCK VERNON STOOD IN THE SILENT OFFICE AND LOOKED DOWN AT THIS morning's crime-scene prints spread out before him, each covered with his grease-pencil marks and arrows and circles pointing out interesting bits of wreckage, like the Chevy hubcap perched on a second-floor windowsill in the distant background.

And the face he had circled on the edge of the parking lot.

Chuck Vernon squinted at it, just to make sure. His eyes were going, but his memory was just fine. It had been twelve or fifteen years, easily, but there was no mistaking that angelic face. He hadn't changed a bit, and recurring tragedy hadn't marked the features.

Petey was back in town.

CHAPTER TWENTY-TWO
OH, BY THE WAY ...

WILL ARRIVED IN ESTES PARK AT 12:30, WAS CHECKED IN TO HIS hotel by 1, and had showered and gotten back out to the finish by 1:30, when the largest group of riders came trundling past the line. Will applauded and cheered them on. The wall outside Ward had done any number of them in. He wondered how many would even get out of bed the next morning to take on Trail Ridge Road.

Though the calendar said fall and the air had an autumn scent, the sun and heat of the afternoon said it was still summer. No hard frost yet, which meant it was still regular summer, not Indian summer. He looked around. Even the aspens had yet to change.

He wondered if it was global warming or if God would get to changing the seasons as soon as he finished changing the oil in his car. And what kind of car would that be, Mr. Ross? Oh, well, Phil, I'd say a classic T-Bird from the '50s. It's not as if he's got a family to haul around, and being all-power-ful, he can have just about any car he wants, now, can't he?

Will smiled at his blasphemy, then wondered if he'd be hit by lightning crossing Trail Ridge Road sometime the next morning. He looked up at the sky, said a quick "sorry," and went back to applauding the riders.

Jeremy Paxton had recovered his energy, if not his mood, and was busy shooting the groups coming in; he had also stopped along the Peak-to-Peak Highway to gather beauty shots for the package.

"Did you get the ride into Ward?" Will asked.

"Fuck you," Jeremy answered.

Will nodded. Nice working with the pros, he thought.

The package itself was a simple affair, taking a grand total of ten minutes to write. Here's where we started, here's where we finished, and here is the guy in the purple Masi shirt heaving his guts in somebody's front yard.

Good times.

A few beauty shots, a little music to cover the sounds of retching and cursing, cut, paste—done.

Three in the afternoon and the story was cut, fed, and ready for the Five. With that in mind, Will stretched out under a tree in the mountain sunshine and immediately fell asleep.

❧

THE FIVE HAD ITS SHARE OF HITCHES.

Jeremy went up on the bird some ten minutes before the shot, fed the package, and then made sure the video and audio live feeds were solid. He wandered over to Will.

"You set?"

"Yeah," Will answered, "ready to go. Don't have IFB, though. I can't hear the station in my ear."

"You'll get it. I don't have you plugged in yet."

"Well, what if it doesn't work?"

"It'll work. Don't worry. My old station we didn't turn the IFB on until the last minute. Reporters said it got in the way of their thought processes."

"Hm. I've always had it early here. It helps me get in the rhythm of the show."

"Let's try it my way now ... we'll turn you on early at Ten. Then tell me which one you like better." Jeremy nodded as if he had just heard a cue in his ear, turned, and jogged back to the satellite truck, maybe forty feet away. A few seconds later Tom Blakely popped into Will's ear, loud and distorted.

"Will Ross in Estes Park ... Will?"

Will frantically grabbed for the volume control on the box hooked to his hip and turned the IFB down. He could hear Tom asking for him: "Will, can you hear me?"

Will scrambled to say, "Yeah, Tom, right here," then to remember the lead-in to his package. He couldn't hear anything in his right ear, the one with the earpiece.

Will fumbled a few words, then found his stride, his copy, and his roll cue. The package started. Immediately the producer was in Will's ear: "Hey, tell whoever is running your truck to turn on the goddamned IFB and listen to me before we're halfway through the shot! Okay?"

Will held up his hands in agreement and surrender. "Yeah, you bet."

The mic key in Denver was still open.

"Jesus! Where did we find these assholes?"

There was a snap, followed by the sound of the package. Will heard the out-cue and started talking.

"That was today. That wall in front of Ward was a treat, I can tell you that. Tomorrow we head for Grand Lake, up and over Trail Ridge Road. We'll have more on that part of the Ride to the Sky tonight at 10. Tom?"

"Thank you, Will Ross, live in Estes Par—"

The IFB went dead. Jeremy Paxton was walking back from the truck.

"Did you hear any of that?"

"Any of what?"

"Any of the producer screaming at us not to cut the IFB so close next time."

"Hey, no problem," Jeremy said. "They always overreact. I'm just getting it done."

❖

Hugh Ransford turned away from the set and picked up the phone, punching in the number for the newsroom pager.

"Beth Freeman, please see Hugh. Beth Freeman, please see Hugh."

Fast Eddie Slezak sat at his desk and started the riff he always did when Ransford used the paging system.

"I see Hugh, do Hugh see me?"

"Shut the fuck up, Slezak," Beth Freeman said as she rushed past the desk.

"Nice going, Eddie," somebody whispered. "You woke the dragon."

Beth marched quickly across to Ransford's office. She hadn't liked the tone in his voice.

"What's up?"

"Get in here and close the door," Ransford snapped. "Are you sure you're done with this interview?"

"Yes, I'm sure I'm done," she answered defensively.

"Okay." He nodded, tapping a pencil on the table.

"What—is—the—problem?" she asked.

He paused for a second, then stared at her with an angry look in his eyes.

"I just don't know if it was a good idea to send Jeremy up there with Will Ross. First, I've got the union on my ass for handing a truck and equipment over to a freelancer who hasn't been here ten minutes; then, I've got a producer screaming at me because he's not turning on the talent's IFB until the last damned second. Ross looked like he was some kind of zombie out there."

"That was Will's fault for not being ready. You know Jeremy and I never turned on the microphones until the last second at the old place."

"That was so you could diss the rest of the staff and they couldn't hear you. This wasn't the microphone. This was the IFB. Will couldn't hear the station in his ear until they were already in the live shot. He panicked. He blew it. It looked like shit, and he's blaming Jeremy—which means that I'm getting blamed for sending Jeremy, which means I'm blaming you for insisting that I send Jeremy along as soon as he was done with your package."

"I still think it should be two parts. I've got plenty of great material for two parts."

"I don't have room for two parts, and don't change the subject."

Beth took a deep breath and decided to tell the truth. It was an odd decision for her.

"Look, I told Jeremy to handle it that way. To cut Will off before and after the shots so he couldn't hear the promos. He hears the promo—'Beth Freeman reports "In the Eyes of a Child"'—and he realizes whose eyes we're showing on air, how long do you think before he's charging down the mountainside to rip both you and me a new asshole?"

Ransford looked out the window, silent for a long moment. "Good point," he finally said, "but you could have told me what instructions you were giving to your henchman."

"I never discuss my instructions or my henchmen," she said, laughing.

Ransford nodded, seething inside from being kept out of the loop, the latest machinations by this—this *employee*.

"I want to know what else you told him."

Beth shrugged. "Sure. I told Jeremy to keep him from listening to the IFB. To keep him away from a TV set if he could. Don't let him see Thursday's paper because of the print ad. So far Jeremy's been clumsy, but Willie Boy hasn't seen anything and hasn't started shrieking."

"Maybe."

"You know, Hugh, the story is in the can. There's nothing he can do about it."

"I've told you before. He goes to Barbara Gooden before the fact and she'll pull it on ethics alone, no matter how good the story is. If we get it on the air, I go to Andy and just apologize for trying to do an award-winning story without one of the subjects knowing about it. Good journalism, Andy, that's what it was, good, solid, emotional journalism."

"I don't like sneaking around."

Ransford laughed. "You love sneaking around. You're a weasel. You love sneaking around and digging through the trash of people's lives and show-ing the world what you found—knowing that the worse off they are, the better you look."

"Then why do you keep hiring me if I'm such a goddamned weasel?"

"Because, my dear," Ransford said flatly, "you're the best damned weasel I ever met. And weasels make this business run."

She stood up, knowing that he was resigned to what she had told Jeremy to do and that the interview was over.

"Squeak, squeak," she said as she walked toward the door.

"Beth," Ransford called after her as he turned and looked out the window once more, clasping his hands in front of him, "what's the latest on Zorro?"

The question stopped her in her tracks and froze the smile on her face.

"Who the fuck cares, Hugh?"

She marched out of his office and across the newsroom, her mouth frozen in a straight line, her face bright red from rage.

✦

ABOUT 9:15, WILL CALLED BILL ROYAL, AN ENGINEER AND UNION STEWARD who regularly ran the satellite trucks, and asked him directly, "What switch do I flip to give myself IFB, and will the union grieve me?"

"Yeah, I saw you at 5. That was cute. They put goddamned amateurs on those trucks and wonder why the newscast looks like something out of *Bowling for Dollars*. Yeah, the union will grieve you, but I wouldn't worry about that, we've gotta catch you first, and I never talked to you. Even if they do catch you, you'll just get a slap on the wrist. As for the button—which truck is it?"

"Challenger."

"Oh, Christ! He drove that up Left Hand Canyon? Amazed he's still alive. Let's see. Sat Two, so the switch for you is the little back button, dead center on the audio panel, right under the sign that says, 'Talent IFB One or Two.' Switch 'em both on to be sure."

"You sure?" Will asked.

"No," Royal said, "I just make this shit up to amuse myself. Hey, did you hear about …"

"Thanks, Bill. Gotta run, Bill. The little asshole's on his way up."

Will hit the red button on the cell phone, and the connection died.

"Who you talking to?" Jeremy asked.

"Just called home to leave a message for my mother-in-law. She wasn't home. She must be out showing the baby to all her new friends."

"Ah, okay. No problem with that."

"No problem with what?"

"Nothing. Just no problem." Jeremy smiled insincerely again and walked off toward the truck.

"What the hell?" Will whispered.

✦

JUST BEFORE THE TEN, WILL WALKED OVER TO THE SATELLITE TRUCK, LOOKED around for Jeremy, climbed inside, and looked over the audio panel. There were the two buttons, Talent IFB One and Two. Will pushed both down.

The red lights glowed in a dead giveaway. A roll of black duct tape was stuffed under the operator's chair. Will tore off two small squares and taped over the lights. Perfect. As long as nobody looked closely at all, perfect.

He slid out of the truck and tried to look nonchalant as he walked back to the live location. He plugged into the wireless IFB box on his back pocket and listened to the return from the satellite. As Jeremy approached, Will kept tapping his ear as if to indicate that he didn't hear anything.

"You gonna turn this on?"

"Yeah, in a minute."

It was the end of a movie, some half-wit comic romance starring two young actors he had never heard of before and would likely never hear of again. Will smiled to himself. He was in charge. He was in control of his own destiny.

Like Rose had any idea what he was capable of emotionally.

He smiled, caught himself, then tapped his ear again just as an announcer said, "Beth Freeman Reports: The Tragedy and Hope of Starting a New Life—and Restoring Your Own. 'Through the Eyes of a Child,' Sunday only on TV6 News at 10."

Hmm, Will thought. Wonder what that was. Must be her big project.

He heard the theme music come up, followed by the preshow headlines: "A Denver Favorite Clings to Life."

"Police Investigate—Was It a Bomb?"

"One more day of nice—then Martha, get out the moccasins in the mountains."

Will smiled. Frightening Freddie March was in full bloom.

"And in sports ..." Will smiled again. Ah, the smooth tones of Roger Flynn, so solid when he wasn't being a jerk. "... the Rockies are in the stretch, and the Broncos have to dig themselves out. TV6 News is next."

The sound died to silence. Whoever was running the audio board had cut this commercial break out of the satellite feed. There was a tease at the end of the first segment and then the live shot itself after weather.

The silence seemed to last forever.

"I don't have IFB," Will lied.

"Don't worry. I'll get it for you in plenty of time."

"Like the Five?"

"Screw you. You'll have it."

Will nodded.

The opening theme began, and Tom and Martine began to narrate over video of what sounded like a fire. Sirens, noise, chaos.

"A TV6 News employee hangs on to life …"

Will's eyebrows shot up at the mention of the station.

"And police investigators say … this was no accident."

A cold hand ran down Will's spine.

"Oh, shit," he whispered.

"What?" Jeremy looked up from the camera and stepped over to readjust Will's backlight.

"Nothing. I, uh, think I just forgot something at, um, home."

"Okay."

Will concentrated on what he heard and tried to appear blasé as the story continued.

"Clyde Zoromski, our weekend sports anchor, better known to all of us as 'Zorro,' clings to life tonight after what police describe as a sophisticated explosive device detonated in his car late last night. Karen Hudson has the story."

The package began. Will listened for any kind of new information, any information that might help him understand what had happened or how Zorro was, but realized after a time that Hudson knew no more than Blakely. She said the exact same things he had but said them with pictures and sound bites. Hudson closed her package, and Tom began to speak again.

"Clyde Zoromski is now in the burn unit at University Hospital, receiving the very best of care. Zorro—we're praying for you."

Will stood staring at the ground. The newscast moved on to other stories. Jeremy Paxton left the camera and ran to the truck. There was a snap in his ear, and the audio went dead. Then it popped back on.

Jeremy ran back to the location.

"Did you?"

"Did I what?"

"Did you mess with the switches in the truck?"

"I can't. I'm not under the union master contract. You think I want to be grieved?" Will paused for a moment, then decided to embellish the story. "There were some kids climbing in there a while ago. I chased them away."

Paxton stared at him for a moment, then bent down to his camera.

Will smiled at his lie. "Aren't you proud of me, Jer?"

"Don't call me *Jer*," Paxton snapped.

"Ooo, gee, sorry." Will smiled.

There was a live tease at the end of the first segment of the news to promote Will's story after weather. Will heard the music and quickly considered what he had to say.

First came Blakely.

"When we return, the latest on our top story—a bomb in the TV6 parking lot."

Jesus, Will thought. Now it was officially a bomb. And what did they have that was new that they didn't have six and a half minutes ago?

Martine stepped in.

"The mayor looks to shorten lines while improving security at DIA."

Jeremy pointed at Will just as he heard the word *"Go"* from a producer in his ear.

"I'm Will Ross, live from Estes Park. The first day of Ride to the Sky is history, and so am I if the news director doesn't call me in the next five minutes."

He stood silently and smiled for the camera.

There was silence in his ear. He had caught everybody off guard. The pause continued until he heard Fred March tease the weather for tomorrow.

"When winter comes, it'll come on fast—that's next."

Paxton had run back to the truck, and the earpiece return from the station died in his ear. Silence reigned for ten seconds until the phone rang.

Will gave his cell two rings, then slowly picked it up and pushed the green button.

"Hell-o?" he said sweetly.

Ransford didn't let him finish the greeting before the screaming began. "What the fuck was that all about? I have never—ever—seen anyone do a live shot like that and use it as a message board. What kind of amateur are you?"

"Only the best kind, Hugh. The gifted kind."

"What the hell do you want, and it better be goddamned important."

"It is, my friend. Are you ready?"

"Am I ready for what?" Ransford asked.

"Are you ready for this? *Look, you two-bit son of a bitch! If you ever try to cut me out of the loop again, I will jump down your throat so fast and so far I'll be able to tie my shoes through your asshole! Do you understand me? I've got Silent Joe out here with me keeping the IFB off so that I can't hear about Zorro. What the hell is that! What are you trying to keep from me? That my friend is hurt? Is he dead? Dying? You think I won't cover your goddamned bike ride if I hear this stuff? Well, you know what? I won't! I won't. And if you try to cut me out one more time, I'll be out of this race like a cannon shot, on the road, in your office, and jumping up and down on your goddamned face! You understand? I'll give you a Brooklyn face dance. understand? I'll stomp your ass. You hear me?*"

For a moment Ransford wanted to leap through the phone and grab Will by the throat, fighting him out of sheer pride, but before Will had finished, Ransford realized something. Will knew he had been cut off, but he thought it was for all the wrong reasons. He thought it was because of Zorro. Ransford knew it was because of the interview promos. Beth had pulled it off. She had created subtle ads that made no sense without the pictures. Will, listening in seventy miles away, may have heard the promo but was still in the dark. Perhaps they could run one past him even if he was listening.

Ransford took a deep breath, settled his anger, and agreed with Will.

"Will, I'm sorry. I hear you, and I apologize. I just knew that you and Z were very close. And because you were, that you would want to rush right down here and do whatever you could for him. Thing is—there's nothing you can do. He's stable. Still out of it. But we will keep right on it for you. It was a mistake on my part. Don't blame Jeremy. I told him to keep your IFB shut down until the last moment. And he did.

"My call. Wrong one. Can you forgive me and keep riding?"

Will was silent for a long moment, then finally said quietly, "Don't ever fucking do anything like that to me again. Never."

"Never, Will. Stay on the road. The package today looked great. I think after tonight we'll get into the swing of it, and the live shots will go fine as well. As for Z, well, I don't think they're even letting him have visitors out-side immediate family until Monday, and you'll be back by then. He's sta-ble now. Okay?"

Will sighed. "Okay."

"Good. Good. Just do your best and ride. The time will move quickly. I apologize again. I guess I misunderstood my job—and the depth of your friendship."

"Okay, Hugh. Thanks for listening. Sorry I popped."

"No problem, Will," Ransford said. "It's all a part of the business. I'll call you right away if anything changes, and if it does and he gets worse, we'll get you down here in a heartbeat."

Jeremy gave Will a cue for one minute to live.

"Take care, Hugh. Gotta play TV. I'll talk to you later. Thanks again."

"No problem. Do well."

Will turned off the cell phone and stuffed it in his pocket. He turned to the camera, rearranged his thoughts, waited for his cue from Roger Flynn, and started talking. It went smoothly for once.

BACK AT THE STATION, HUGH RANSFORD HUNG UP THE PHONE AND STARED INTO the darkness outside the building.

"You can put money on what I'm going to say right now," Ransford hissed aloud to himself. "That asshole is back on Monday. By Tuesday, there's not going to be a trace of him at this station."

IN A SPECIAL BED, TUCKED INTO A FAR CORNER OF THE BURN UNIT AT UNIVERSITY Hospital, partially hidden in shadows from the muted lights that dotted the room, Clyde Zoromski moaned once and opened his right eye. Without thinking, he started to move, and the pain shot down his right side from just behind his ear to the middle of his butt. It was as if a thousand cats were all clawing him at once.

The scream caught in his throat, and he settled back as quickly and as gently as he could. When he opened his right eye again, how much later he didn't know, there was a lovely young woman standing beside him. A nurse? Maybe, but she wasn't dressed like a nurse.

She reached out to him and he flinched, realizing without knowing it that the pain of her touch would be severe.

"Shhh, shhh," she whispered. "Don't worry, Zorro. You're going to be fine. You're going to be just fine."

He shuddered with anticipation of the pain as her hand moved close, then relaxed and fell into a deep sleep at the moment of her touch. A cooling wave rushed over him, lifted him, and carried Clyde Zoromski off to a better place, a place without pain, a place without fear, a place where he could rest.

Zorro slept soundly in the darkened room.

The darkened, empty room.

CHAPTER TWENTY-THREE
RIDE TO THE SKY

THE FIRST THING WILL DID THAT MORNING WAS CALL THE STATION TO check on Zorro's condition.

Bruce Mason on the morning desk had just checked and been told that Zorro had spent a very comfortable night, surprising in a burn patient with such severe injuries.

"How severe, Bruce?"

"Well, they haven't checked him this morning, I guess, but they were saying he had second- and third-degree burns yesterday when they took him in. I guess the right side of his back looked like a newspaper after it had been burned."

"Oh, Jesus." Will gagged.

"Sorry, man. You wanted to hear it."

"I saw a picture of the car. How the hell did he survive that?"

"Can you believe it? The son of a bitch jumped out of the car. Didn't think he could move that fast. He was about three feet in the air. Jumped, fell, broke his leg, and crawled away. He would have been toast otherwise."

"Yeah, literally."

Hanging up, he called home. No one answered.

Will took a moment and convinced himself that all was well, that Rose had simply gone to church and taken the baby with her, that Stan and Ollie were watching over them, protecting them, keeping them safe.

So why wasn't he convinced? He checked the phone. It was fully charged. He just hoped he could catch a cell on the top of Trail Ridge Road.

❧

THE FBI REPORT WAS STREWN ALL OVER RAYMOND WHITESIDE'S DESK. HE pushed the sheets of fax paper and photos this way and then that, trying to make sense of the information that reached back more than forty years.

"Okay, so what do we have again?" he asked.

Paul Timmons stood up, walked to the desk, and started pointing at pictures to make his point.

"We have: Stanley Szyclinski, reputed mob hit man from Detroit. He is the brother of Rose Szyclinski and the reputed business partner of one Olverio Cangliosi, better known as Old Cans, another reputed hit man out of Detroit. Cangliosi is the brother of Reynaldo, at least that's what I think this says," he said, squinting at the smeared government fax, "Cangliosi, who married Rose Szyclinski. They had two children, Raymond and Cheryl, both deceased. Cheryl is the dead wife of one William Edward Ross, formerly of Kalamazoo, Michigan, Eindhoven, which is someplace in Europe, don't ask me where, and Senlis, France, which is someplace in Frog-Land, don't ask me where either. In Europe, Mr. Ross was connected to a series of violent crimes against persons of a personal nature, some involving explosives. A nice tidy package."

"So, why is he here?"

"*They* are here," Timmons said, "to keep an eye on Mr. Ross, I figure. Maybe to whack him for doing in their niece."

"That doesn't wash, Paul," Whiteside argued. "If Ross did it, wouldn't he be dead already?"

"Maybe he's conned them too."

"I don't know." Whiteside shook his head. "If they thought there was even a chance, I've gotta figure they'd whack him in a heartbeat."

"Maybe, maybe not."

"Jesus, Paul, you're stretching to make a point here."

"Look. The day Ross leaves town, the next guy on the ladder in the TV sports department goes boom. We've established that they were at the station during the same period of time."

"Broad daylight," Whiteside countered. "Setting a bomb in broad daylight isn't easy."

"Doesn't matter. Just follow me. They're there, same time. Plants bomb. Leaves town. Bomb goes boom! He's in Boulder! Ross has alibi."

"You're still thin, Paul."

"And you're still defending him, Ray. I don't get why."

Whiteside stared at Timmons for a long moment, then finally said, "Because you didn't see him that night. You didn't see him in that emergency room. You didn't see the light go out of his eyes."

"Well, he hasn't been all that broken up since, scraping that dame's tonsils this week."

"You don't get it, Paul. I'm going along with you, but I won't jump until you convince me, and you haven't so far. You're taking two and two and making eight. It's all circumstantial."

Timmons nodded.

"Okay. Okay. I'll buy that. But at least let's go talk to his relatives?"

"All right. That I'll buy."

The two left the office and drove to the home of Will Ross in Park Hill. Parking in front, they realized that the house seemed unusually quiet. Walking through the yard, they realized that the house seemed too quiet.

After ringing and looking inside, they realized no one was home.

Ray Whiteside stood silently at a corner of the house, scratching the back of his ear as he considered the situation.

"Where's Ross now?"

"From what the morning news said, he's on his way to Grand Lake."

Whiteside nodded.

"Time to chat with him again."

Timmons smiled. "Should we call his lawyer?"

Whiteside shook his head. "Screw the lawyer. This is merely a chat."

They walked quickly back to the car and headed down to the office to sign out before the two-hour drive to Grand Lake.

❧

THE CLIMBING STARTED AS SOON AS THE RIDE LEFT ESTES PARK. THEY WERE starting at 65 degrees at eight thousand feet, riding up to the top of the

Continental Divide on Trail Ridge Road, crossing the imaginary boundary at twelve thousand feet and probably 30 degrees cooler with a chance of snow.

According to Frightening Freddie March, there was always a chance of snow on Trail Ridge. Winter, spring, autumn, or the Fourth of July, there was a chance of snow on Trail Ridge Road. March had also said that he was surprised that the road was even still open this late in the season. It might be 70 in Denver, but it was in the 30s and 20s up there. The Ride was late this year, but so far the weather had cooperated, and Trail Ridge remained open.

Will rode past the eastern entrance to Rocky Mountain National Park, waving at the ranger in the booth as he did. He got a smile and a wave in return.

He heard a muffled, "Have fun, it was snowing this morning," as he passed.

Great, he thought. At least he had stuffed a newspaper into his fanny pack for the top of the Divide. Old habits died hard, as did memories of riding the Alps without any insulation at all.

He shifted, rose up out of the seat, and began pedaling up to speed, setting his own pace, his own internal metronome for the ride and the climb to come.

❊

WILL WAS AMAZED BY HOW NARROW THE ROAD LEADING UP TO THE DIVIDE WAS and how tight the turns were all along the way. There were some passing lanes but not many. That being the case, he wondered how in hell anybody could drive an RV up the mountainside without winding up, suddenly surprised, back at the bottom.

He thought about Jeremy Paxton in the satellite truck and smiled.

"Have a nice day, asshole," he wheezed.

It was then that he noticed he was sucking a lot of air and not getting much in the way of oxygen. The four-thousand-foot climb was a grind, and the altitude was thinning the air to the point of nonexistence. Added to that was the fact that it was dry, and getting drier at altitude. There was no way he had enough water on the bike or in his fanny pack to carry him cleanly over the top.

He looked back, hoping to see a support van driving the route. He saw it, but it was fighting its way through the mass of riders trying to handle the climb and doing so using every available part of the road.

He'd have to conserve his water as well as he could. It would be a while before he got any more.

❋

CHUCK VERNON STUCK HIS HEAD IN THE OFFICE DOOR.

"Hey, boys, where you off to?"

"We're off to the mountains to chat with a friend," Paul Timmons said with a smile.

"Well, take those pictures I gave you. There's something in there that might make some fun reading."

"What's that?"

"Little Petey is back in town."

"Who?"

"Little Petey. Just read, Timmons. You can read, can't you?"

Chuck Vernon smiled and disappeared down the hall. Timmons picked up the file, on which Vernon had scrawled "Read This" in red grease pencil, then tossed it into his briefcase.

Ray Whiteside walked back in, wiping his hands on a white paper towel.

"You ready?"

"You bet."

"Let's went."

❋

WILL REACHED DOWN AND MASSAGED HIS RIGHT CALF ONCE EACH STROKE.

Stroke, squeeze, stroke, squeeze. It didn't help. The old, familiar ache remained, digging into him and threatening to retear the muscle from the Achilles to the back of the knee. He had done it in France, on the slope of Mt. Ventoux, carrying the brother of a dead friend to safety from—from whom? The angel of death? The angel of death wears a brown tweed suit?

He shook his head. Madman, that was what he was, a madman.

The leg cramped, hard. He sat up on the bike and yelped. Reaching down, he massaged the calf, kneading it like a log of stiff bread dough. It wasn't responding.

Jesus, he thought, I'm too old for this shit. Midthirties and I'm too old for this shit.

He looked back down the run up to Trail Ridge Road and saw a few hundred of the riders from the *Colorado Times*' Ride to the Sky strung out behind him. He looked up. A few were above him, including two senior citizens on a tandem.

Damn. Maybe he was just whining. *They* weren't too old for this shit; maybe *he* wasn't too old for this shit. He was just too out of shape for this shit.

He gave the calf another squeeze and dug down, standing up on the pedals to give his ass a break and to stretch both legs a little differently. He looked out over the guard rail as he made another turn on yet another switchback and saw nothing more than valleys, peaks, and a sea of green, lodgepole pines that had so far beaten off attacks by pine beetles.

Colorado took his breath away, every day and in every way.

Then again, maybe that was the altitude.

He was climbing higher. The air was getting thinner and colder and, worst of all, drier. Will felt it on his skin, as if a vacuum cleaner were sucking out whatever moisture was there, leaving his hands ready to crack and split. A gallon of lotion wouldn't save his thumbs tomorrow morning, especially if the cold came in and hung in overnight. He felt it in his nose, his eyes, and his lungs. Each breath was getting sharper, harder, carrying more of an edge, a burn, a bite. He had to keep hydrating, but before he reached for his last bottle, he glanced back again. No van anywhere on the road below. Drink it now, he thought, and you'll be fine for thirty minutes, but beyond that, nothing is certain. Nothing for sure. He had to make the summit visitor center in that time and hope it was open.

The crowds were thick below. Even if Will could have seen the van, it was likely it couldn't have made it up to him, given the great clot of riders blocking the road like corks in a hose.

Mmm. Hose. Water. Hmm. Water good.

Will shook his head, trying to stop the Homer Simpson imitation rattling around in his head.

In the sun he was warm, even sweating. The differences in temperature from the plains to Estes seemed greater than from Estes to the Divide. Drop into the shade, however, or come around a switchback into an open valley, and it was a whole new story.

The shade was cold, the wind bitter and biting, the valleys between the granite peaks acting like gigantic chimney flues, directing the air into a cold blast that pushed him back down toward Estes Park. When the shade and the wind combined, the combination was bone-chilling, driving right through jersey, skin, muscle, and bone, only to repeat the process as it leaped out on the other side. The higher he rode along the ridge, the more consistently cold and dry the air became.

Will realized that he had relaxed on the saddle and was simply churning out mileage, one after another after another after another, inch-foot-yard-mile. He came over a short rise and discovered that he was very nearly at the top, rising to the grade over the Divide. Twelve thousand feet, the highest paved road in North America. Come on in, he said to himself, it's thirty degrees cooler inside.

Will shivered. Even in the sun, chilled by the wind, it was simply too cold to be riding this road on this day in this month. The proof was in the distance: building clouds that simply screamed *snow* and *winter* and the kind of cold that made wood stoves move home to mama. They grew quickly. They came in fast, the big, white, puffy kind with a dark purple edge that liked to dump a lot of snow in the mountains. The kind of snow that closed this road in a hurry.

They were late this year. But they were early enough to catch him. As cold as it was, it looked like snow by morning. And glory be almighty—he'd be riding in it.

He cursed his luck and laughed.

Will reached into his fanny pack and pulled out two chunks of the *Denver Post*, brought along specifically for this problem. Wadding them up and stuffing them into his jersey, he built up a layer of insulation between the chill on his jersey and the permafrost now coating his chest hair.

The sweat had cooled quickly as the sun jumped behind a cloud, and his muscles were beginning to tighten up.

The front section went first, page by page. Husted and headlines, foreign news and whatever it was the Broncos were doing, all jammed under his shirt. He then took the entertainment section and peeled back the cover page. He was about to stuff it under his jersey when Elena's eyes caught his.

Across the top of the Continental Divide, with a sheer drop of forever on one side, Will Ross rode sitting up while staring at page 5F of "The Scene," the *Denver Post* entertainment section. Staring back at him were his daughter's eyes, under the headline, "In the Eyes of a Child—Death, Life and Rebirth: A Special Report on a Denver Tragedy by Beth Freeman. Sunday at 10 only on TV6 News."

Below and to the right of the copy and the picture of Elena's eyes was a picture of Beth, looking stern and serious, decidedly journalistic.

Suddenly he knew it wasn't just the altitude that was making him wheeze. His breath came in short gasps, as if he had barely made it to the surface after a prolonged dive. Will squeezed the paper into a gray lump in one hand, clutched the handlebars, brought himself back to the center of the road, and reached for his water bottle.

He drained it in two gulps, feeling the relief immediately.

None again until Grand Lake.

Not a drop.

I can do this. I can do this.

He rose up out of the seat and began to dig down, dig down for something he hadn't found in years, dig down for that spark, whether from desire or fear or anger, that had driven him forward to the finish in the past, drove him forward to a new sort of finish now.

Click … click … click … click … click … click … click. Click. Click. Clickclickclickclickclickclick …

He started to pour on the speed coming over the ridge, diving down into the descent, blind to what lay ahead, taking the first turns lazy and easy, in stride, watching ahead as they grew narrow and tighter. The few single riders in front of him were taking their time and great care on the west side of Trail Ridge, with good reason. There was still automobile traffic on the road, even this late in the season, even at this time on a Friday. And besides the danger, there remained the views and vistas and wildlife to see and admire and photograph on the stretch into the flatlands of the park.

Will didn't have the time.

"Hey, Will," the seniors on the tandem shouted. He waved a hand quickly, casually, and reset himself to the task at hand. Shift, lean, pedal, ride, keep the focus, and keep the line. Don't give up, don't slacken, don't go too wide on the turn or be ready to dig yourself out of the grillwork of a '98 Ford with Kansas plates.

The road grew narrow again as he dropped off the Divide into the western side of Rocky Mountain National Park, a collection of hairpins and short straights, aggravated by rock falls at odd intervals.

Around one turn, swing wide, avoid the rocks in the road, some gravel, and a chunk the size of a junior basketball. Lean in, leg up, take the turn, and don't lose the speed. He had never been good at descending because something in his soul lacked the necessary testosterone to point his body straight down and ride like a bat out of hell. There was too much survival instinct banging away inside of his head. He'd brake. He'd lie back. He'd make it, but behind everyone else.

Not this time. For some reason, some reason still unknown to him, Will's anger pushed him on—the notion of his being used, being fooled, being used as a chump in one reporter's game of "Gotcha."

Somehow, the thought of his daughter didn't figure into it at all.

CHAPTER TWENTY-FOUR

ONE IF BY LAND, TWO IF BY SEA

WILL STOOD DRINKING AT THE FOUNTAIN IN THE TOWN PARK IN GRAND LAKE for what seemed an eternity. It was long enough that a few people walked out of the town's community center to stare at him and his bloated, distended belly.

He gasped for air and lay on the grass for a moment to catch his wind and his bearings. Piercing anger can carry you only so far. It may get you up and over, but it burns quickly and can't carry you the distance.

It hadn't this time either.

As he had passed the visitor center at the western entrance of Rocky Mountain National Park, he felt as if someone had opened a valve in the side of his neck and released the anger to the wind, like steam escaping. Part of it was dehydration. He was feeling it now, and if you're feeling it, it's way too late. The bonk is on the way.

He kept up his pace as much as possible, swept around the last wide turn leading out of the park, and cut down the hard left to the town of Grand Lake. There were stores, Mountain Foods, Circle D, a nice little selection of bars. He wanted to stop but realized that his money was in the satellite truck. God, too many years of being taken care of on the road had turned him into a wimp. He couldn't even take care of himself.

He kept riding into the center of town and spied the stone drinking fountain. If only it hadn't been turned off for the season. It hadn't.

He rolled onto his side and stared at the town, all wood buildings and boardwalks. A sweet shop closed for the season. A jewelry store. A huge place on the corner selling what appeared to be home accessories. Will smiled. It reminded him of Saugatuck, about fifty miles down the road from his hometown in Michigan: touristy but hanging on to itself. He liked towns like that.

235

He stumbled to his feet and grabbed the water fountain for support as he watched the colored lights dance before his eyes. They passed, and he saw a phone at the corner of the park. Rolling the bike beside him for support, Will hobbled over to the phones, his feet unsteady from the cleats, his legs, especially the right calf, beginning to cramp like a mother.

Will slumped on the bench beneath the phone and dialed the 800 in-state number for the newsroom. It was one of the few numbers at the station he could remember, and it had taken him only seventeen miles of hard thinking to remember it.

"Hey, Bruce, Will Ross."

"Hi, Will. How's the ride going?"

Will's wheeze caught in his throat and carried up something ugly. He spat it into the grass behind the phones.

"That good, huh?" Bruce Mason laughed.

"Yeah, that good. Is Beth Freeman there?"

"Let me see, she's been hiding in editing the last few days, but—oh, you're in luck, I can see the tips of her horns just over the edge of her cubicle."

Will chuckled. "Cute," he said. Twelve hours earlier he would have defended her. "Let me talk to her, would you?"

"Ah, so you understand snake. A rare talent, I'm told."

"Just connect me."

"All right, Will. Here you go."

The line snapped, and he heard Tom Blakely's voice on a looped recording telling him to watch TV6 News at 10 with him and Martine, Fred March with the weather, and the latest sports news from Roger Flynn. If Roger Flynn felt like showing up, of course, Will thought. The loop ran twice before Beth picked up.

"Beth Freeman."

"Will Ross."

There was a pause before she said in her silkiest tone, "Will, my God! How are you?"

Her voice dropped in such a way at the end of the sentence that Will felt himself being pulled in again. Thoughts of her face, her eyes, and that inverted heart of a butt that simply cried out for a round of applause filled his head; exhaustion had replaced anger. His mind was off the mark.

"Fine. I'm fine, Beth."

"Good ride today?"

"Yeah, good ride. Until I saw a page out of the *Post* at the top of Trail Ridge Road."

There was a cold silence at the other end of the line for a long moment.

"What did you see?"

"I saw my daughter's eyes staring at me from the page, with the caption, 'In the Eyes of a Child.'" He read from the mangled, tattered ad he had carried in his fist from the top of the Divide. Some of the words in the subhead had smeared from his sweat.

"'A Denver Tragedy,'" Will read. "That wouldn't happen to be *my* Denver tragedy, now, would it, Beth? My Denver tragedy featuring my wife, my child, and my life?"

There was another pause, covered quickly. "Will, I'm only going to say this once," Beth said softly. "You've hurt me. You've hurt me deeply."

Will immediately sat back and felt defensive. "Hurt *you?* How the hell did I hurt *you?*"

"To think, to think for even a minute, that I would do something like that to you. That hurts. That hurts me. Deeply."

"Well, what is your story about if it isn't about me?"

"Good God, Will. Is it always about you?"

Will felt himself shrink on the bench. The bad boy suddenly realizing just how bad he had been and how disappointed he had made the world around him.

"God, I'm sorry—but what is it about?"

The pause had given Beth a chance to weave. "It's about Denver children. The tragedy is the growing abuse of children—plural—in the Denver area and how the local agencies aren't doing anything about it. Will, it's about many children. It uses JonBenet. It uses the Arvada case. It uses the story out of Aurora last week." She was pulling suburbs out of the air and adding them in, hoping he didn't know there wasn't an Arvada case or a story out of Aurora.

"But why ..."

"Elena? Talk to the newspaper. They created the ad," she lied. "They pulled the picture. I don't know where they got it, but you've got to talk to them."

Will was silent for a long time.

"I'm sorry."

She was silent, letting the line run out for a moment.

"I'm sorry too. I'm sorry you couldn't trust me. I'm sorry you jumped to that conclusion without thinking about how I felt for you."

"I don't know how you feel about me."

"Oh, come on, Will," she said sarcastically. "If we hadn't been out in the middle of Cherry Creek North the other night, there would have been some serious sex going on."

Will remembered the kiss. He began to stir.

"I'm sorry."

"Okay. This upsets me, though. This upsets me. We're going to have to have a long talk before I can trust you again."

"I'm sorry."

"You said that, Will. You said that already." She paused a moment to let it sink in again. "Why don't you finish your little race or ride or whatever, and when you get back next week, maybe we'll talk."

"Okay. I'm sorry I jumped like that."

"Well, take the time to ask me first before you start accusing me."

"I'm sorry, Beth, I will. Beth, I ..."

"I've gotta go, Will," she said, sensing the time to cut the line and let the fish run. "Ransford's waving at me, and I just don't want to stay angry with you. Bye."

Will said, "Okay, I understand," to a phone that had already been disconnected.

"Jesus," he said aloud to an empty street, "what an asshole I am."

❧

BETH FREEMAN SAT STARING AT THE PHONE, DROPS OF SWEAT BEADING HER UPPER LIP. She took a deep breath and tried to relax. That had been close—way too close.

She stood on shaking legs and walked as casually as she could to Hugh Ransford's office to report the problem, hoping he would take it upon himself to call Jeremy Paxton and chew him out for letting Will Ross see a morning paper.

Too close.

It was too damned close.

Still, a small smile crept across her lips. She had created a whole new story out of thin air, a good one too, maybe a story she wanted to do sometime in the future.

She had lied through her teeth and he had bought it, hook, line, and sinker.

Man, she was good.

So damned good.

❋

WILL CHECKED INTO THE SMALL HOTEL OVER THE BARBECUE JOINT ACROSS THE street from the park, carefully carried the Beast to the second floor, propped it up, then stripped down for a long, hot shower. Unless Paxton showed up with the satellite truck in the next few minutes, he'd have to change back into his riding clothes when he was finished, but after the ride, and especially after the call, he needed the shower.

He felt dirty somehow. He felt like shit.

He had jumped to a conclusion and hurt a friend. A good friend. A good friend that he wanted to become a better friend.

He sat naked on the edge of the bed and held his head in his hands.

Will Ross, consummate asshole.

The shame of the accusation grew to the point that he felt the wall in his head start to break down, releasing all the beasts and fears and tears that he had hidden behind it so many weeks before. He pushed them back again and stood up.

"Think of something else, jerk. Think of something else."

He went into the shower and thought of the 5 o'clock news and how he was going to build a story out of video he hadn't seen, that didn't include him, and that may not have even been shot.

Welcome to TV6 News.

As the hot water ran down his face, he began to laugh maniacally at the rank stupidity of it all.

❋

PAXTON ARRIVED THIRTY MINUTES AFTER WILL REEMERGED ONTO THE STREET. WILL asked where the hell he had been, and Jeremy, in no mood to argue after wrestling a satellite truck over Trail Ridge Road in the thick of a bunch of goddamned bicyclists, told him where he could put his video.

Will took his clothes and changed out of his riding gear, draping it over the back of a chair to dry before he stuffed it into his bag. When he returned they were both a bit calmer, able to discuss the video of the day. Jeremy had focused on vistas and riders, altitude and groups. Will nodded. He would work with that. He climbed into the satellite truck, rolled quickly through the video to see the images for himself, wrote the script for the 5 P.M. news, and tracked the narration. He tossed the audio track to Jeremy and let him take the seat in front of the suitcase editing station. It was his turn to be the wizard.

Will climbed out of the truck without saying a word to Jeremy, who didn't say a word to him. The silence said it all. Will went in search of more water and a phone.

Screw him, he thought.

Which was exactly the sentiment coming from the truck toward Will.

❁

"YOU MISSED THE TURN," WHITESIDE SAID AS THE US-40 EXIT AT EMPIRE PASSED by in a seventy-five-mile-an-hour rush.

"Yeah, I know, but Berthoud is all torn up and there are lines and waits and one lane at best, then they close it all at 9:30."

"It's only 4 now."

"It's just easier to go through Silverthorne," Timmons said, gripping the wheel a bit tighter. He didn't like having his driving choices questioned.

Ray Whiteside noticed the tension and decided to move on to something else. There was nothing on the radio. The valleys that I-70 was carved into made reception a hit-or-miss affair. He looked down and picked up the sheaf of reports, photos, and clippings in an old dark brown folder that Chuck Vernon had insisted Timmons take with them.

Whiteside glanced over. "Do you mind?"

"Not at all," Timmons said. "I have no idea why Vernon thought that damned thing was so important in the first place."

On the front was clipped a photo of the TV6 parking lot from yesterday morning. It was taken from a vantage point about ten feet above the ground.

How did they get that shot? he wondered. Maybe the bed of a pickup truck. The burned car was off to the left of the picture, and eyewitnesses and sightseers were gathered along the side. Vernon had circled one of them and put a question mark next to the circle. Why the mark? Whiteside wondered.

I know this guy.

Ray Whiteside opened the file and began to read.

"WHERE WERE YOU THIS MORNING? I TRIED TO CALL." WILL REALIZED HE WAS WHINING.

Rose soothed him as best she could. "I went to mass. Elena went with me. Your uncles were out and about, trying to find what Stanley called a new contact."

"I don't know what that means," Will said.

Rose laughed. "Believe me, I don't know either. They don't say word one to me."

"Okay. Are you watching? How do the stories look?"

"I'm sorry. I've only seen one. It looked good. You look tired."

"I am. It's a long haul."

"Not that kind of tired, Will," she said quietly.

"Ah, well, I do my best."

"Yes," she said. Will could hear resignation in her tone. "Yes, you do."

"How are the dogs?"

"Buggin' me," Rose said sharply. "They're whining and pacing and drooling all over the baby. They're unhappy about something, but for the life of me, I can't figure out what."

"How's, uh …"

"Elena? Your daughter?"

"Yes, Rose," he said, exasperation creeping into his voice. "How is my daughter?"

"She's fine." There was a pause. Will could sense her stretching into the living room arch to take a look at the baby.

"You'll be surprised at how fast she's coming along, Will. She's even starting to grasp and shake her rattle."

"Ow!" Will shouted. It was as if a huge bumblebee had flown, full bore, into the back of Will's head, bounced off, and flown away. He spun his head to both sides but saw no bee.

"You okay?"

"Yeah, something just hit me in the head. A bug of some kind."

"Well, you go look for it and teach it a lesson. I've got dinner started here. Your *daughter* ..." she emphasized the word "... and I will watch you at 5."

"All right. I'll call you later tonight. Take care, Rose."

"You too, Will."

"Kiss her for me, will you?"

"I will. Bye."

The phone went dead in his ear, and Will hung it up. He stared at the street for a while, silently watching the clumps of riders wander into town. The support van he had been so desperately searching for earlier in the day followed at the back.

That was a great goddamned place for it.

He rubbed the spot where the bee had hit him. It was sore, but it hadn't raised a bump. It was like the feeling he had had when his mother fwapped him with a thimble as a kid.

An aimless thought was rattling around in his head, broken free by the sting. Slowly it crawled to the front, where he could get a grasp on it. It was simple. It was clear. But somehow it didn't make any sense at all.

"What rattle?" he said aloud.

❋

THE TRAFFIC GROUND TO A STOP INSIDE THE EISENHOWER TUNNEL.

Whiteside looked up from the report.

"What's going on?"

"Aw, who the hell knows?" Timmons groused. "This damned road. One accident, one stall, one idiot going too fast or too slow, and the whole thing collapses. God, I hate it."

Marking his place, Whiteside put the folder beside him and stepped out of the car.

"Let me walk ahead a bit. I'll see what's going on."

"I'm sure the State Patrol will appreciate you walking down the road and checking things out—encouraging everybody else to do the same."

"I just want to get this done, Paul. I don't want to spend tonight in an old Ford—a cold Ford—in the Eisenhower tunnel with you."

"You used to love nights like that," Timmons said.

Ray Whiteside slammed the door and started walking toward the light at the end of the tunnel.

❖

THE FIVE WENT WELL, WILL THOUGHT.

The energy was high, the pictures were great, and Jeremy Paxton went up on the bird and turned on the IFB a full segment early. Will was able to listen in on a report about Zorro's condition, which had been upgraded, to the amazement of the doctors, and just before his shot heard the promo for Beth's story again.

In his shame, he tried to ignore it. The words they used somehow didn't fit her explanation, but Will couldn't bring himself to doubt her again. He forced the feelings behind the wall as Flynn introduced him, "live from Grand Lake."

Will opened his mouth and, without referring to his script, got into the piece smoothly.

Even the sports producer, who didn't say anything at a volume less than a scream, jumped into Will's ear to say quietly, "Nice job."

Will sighed. Now, that—that was worth it. He suddenly saw and felt the appeal of the job.

He dug his earpiece out of his right ear, unplugged it from the IFB box, and tossed the receiver back to Jeremy.

"I'm going to dinner," Will said.

"Where you going?"

"There's a Mexican place just down the street here, thought I'd try it."

Jeremy paused for a moment. "Mind if I join you?"

Will considered the request for a second, then finally said, "Sure, why not?"

He helped Jeremy pack up the truck, and together they walked off toward Pancho and Lefty's.

❖

"WHAT IS IT?"

"There's a major-league accident just down the stretch here leading into

Silverthorne. Some jerk was doing ninety on the slope and lost it. Closed the entire highway. Both directions. It's a mess, and the Smokeys say there's not a damned thing they can do for us."

Timmons laughed. "Smokeys? Jesus, you're dating yourself."

Ray Whiteside grinned and slipped back into his seat, closing the door behind him. They were going to be here for a while.

He picked up the dark brown folder and continued to read.

❂

STAN TURNED AWAY FROM THE TV SET AND WALKED INTO THE KITCHEN, WHERE Rose was putting the finishing touches on dinner.

"Will looked good tonight."

"Will was on? Why didn't you call me?"

"I didn't know you wanted to see him."

"No," Rose said slowly, "you didn't hear me say I wanted to see him because you weren't listening to me."

Olverio came out of the bathroom rubbing the last of the water off his hands. "Who wasn't listening to you?"

"My brother, for one," Rose said, "but your ears are usually plugged too."

"Sweet, isn't she?" Stanley said.

"So, Will did well? Looked good?"

Stanley nodded. "Yeah. He looked like Will and didn't throw up on the camera. I guess that's good."

"Thank you for the review. You're as good as that Elliott Green idiot."

"No, he did fine. Nice-looking pictures. Looked like a hard ride today."

"Well," Rose said, "Will wasn't looking forward to this one."

"Hey, I've got a question," Stanley said.

"Yes?"

"Why was Elena on the TV?"

"Elena wasn't on the TV. She was on her blanket in front of the TV."

"No." Stanley shook his head. "That's not what I meant. Her picture. Her face. Her eyes. They were on the TV. Some story they're doing?"

"Some story Will is doing? About Elena?"

"No. Some dame. Talking about children's eyes."

Rose and Olverio looked at each other.

"Let's eat dinner in front of the TV tonight, shall we?"

Olverio nodded.

"Good idea, Rose."

❋

TRAFFIC DIDN'T BEGIN TO MOVE AGAIN UNTIL ALMOST 9, AND EVEN THEN, IT MOVED at a crawl.

Timmons had stepped out of the car and relieved himself twice on the wall of the Eisenhower tunnel. Once he had, people up and down the line started doing it. After all, if a cop pees on a wall …

Whiteside shook his head.

"Classy, Paul."

"That's me. Mr. Class."

As they pulled out of the tunnel, Ray Whiteside had just finished the report, marked and noted and hand-delivered by Chuck Vernon back in Denver. As they crept forward in darkness, Whiteside leaned his head back and tapped the top of the hard brown file. The old-timers, he thought, they never got enough credit. They've been there, they've seen it, they remember the cases, the cases that keep coming back like bad pennies.

He kept tapping the file.

The jigsaw puzzle in his mind kept moving and shifting and reordering itself. If you thought it was a picture of Will Ross, some of the parts simply didn't fit, no matter how determined Paul Timmons was to force them into place. The Detroit hit men? They didn't work. The FBI had had them under surveillance until just days ago. My God, the government was their alibi.

He tapped the file.

But this, this was a new wrinkle.

He tapped the file.

Chuck Vernon had seen something. Chuck Vernon had put together the pieces. Chuck Vernon had finished the puzzle. Chuck Vernon knew.

But Chuck Vernon didn't know what he knew.

Raymond Whiteside suddenly did.

"Well, I'll be a son of a bitch."

"What?"

"Get through this traffic. …"

"Yeah, by magic, maybe," Timmons snorted.

"Paul," Whiteside said sternly, *"get the hell through this traffic. We've got to get to Grand Lake."*

"That's where we're going, Ray."

"You don't understand, Paul," Whiteside said, holding up the file. "Will Ross is in danger. He's next."

✿

WILL WANTED TO BE AFTER WEATHER IN THE TEN, BUT THEY HAD SHIFTED HIM into sports. Too bad, he thought. If he was on at 10:20, then he and Jeremy could be wrapped, packed, in the Lariat Saloon, listening to Steve Cormey, and royally drunk by 10:30, 10:35 at the latest.

But no—the great gods of TV news had decreed that he was sports fodder tonight.

He waited through the break after weather. The commercials weren't punched up in his ear, so all he heard was a quiet, distant static, followed suddenly by a burst of theme music. Will reached behind him and adjusted the IFB volume.

Tom Blakely began.

"Roger Flynn is feeling under the weather tonight …"

"I'll bet," Will muttered.

"… so Art Jackson joins us now with sports. Tough night in town for everybody, wasn't it?"

Art started low, as if commiserating with the Rockies, the Avalanche, the Broncos, and the Nuggets.

"Oh, a tough night, Tom. A bad night for Denver sports."

It wasn't what he said, it was the tone of his voice that chilled Will to the very core.

"All the bad news you can use in just a minute, but first, let's head up to the mountains, where Will Ross took a ride to the sky today. Will? Did you see God?"

Will stood in shock for a moment, shook his head, smiled, and picked up the line.

"No, Art. Not on Trail Ridge, even though I was riding through his backyard. I may have just seen him now, though. It was some ride today."

That was close enough to the roll cue for the producer. She was out of time. The director gave the call, and they punched up Will's short recut of the 5 P.M. package.

Will stood still, staring at Jeremy's camera. In the five feet between him and the lens, he noticed snowflakes beginning to fall. He listened intently for his cue. The producer called into his ear, "Keep it tight on the back side." Will nodded, listening.

He heard the cue.

"That was some day of riding. More comes tomorrow as we head down the road toward Breckenridge. Art?"

He listened. Art acknowledged the ride, told Will what a good package it had been, and went on to other stories.

The producer said, "You're clear," in his ear.

Will stayed still, continuing to listen to Art.

He listened not to the words but to the tone, the quality of Art's voice.

The satellite link went dead in Will's ear.

He stood still for another moment.

"Are you okay?" Jeremy asked.

Will nodded, then mumbled to himself, "Well, I'll be a son of a bitch."

❀

ROSE LEANED OVER AND SMILED AT THE BABY.

"Daddy's doing a good job tonight, Ellie."

The baby smiled at the attention and shook her rattle in a wobbly way in the general direction of her grandmother.

Rex paced and whined beside the couch. Shoe lay on the floor and stared at the baby, watching her every move.

"Rex! Knock it off! I'm trying to watch," Rose barked. The dog stopped whining but kept pacing, never taking his eyes off Elena and the rattle.

At the other end of the couch, Stanley leaned forward, staring at the TV screen.

"What, you see Will with a pimple or something?" Ollie said sarcastically.

"No," Stanley waved him off, "just a second."

He was intent on the end of Will's report, then kept watching as Art Jackson swung into the rest of the day's sports coverage.

"Well, I'll be a son of a bitch! I'll be a son of a *bitch!*"

As Stanley shouted, the baby jerked and cried, throwing the rattle. Rex was already moving, snatching the toy in midair and racing in a great circle toward the dog door that led to the fenced-in backyard.

There was a *bang!* as he hit the door, followed shortly by a *pop!* and a cry.

"What the hell is going on?" Olverio said, getting up and running to the back door. Rose crouched down to soothe the baby and looked up at Stanley.

"What in God's name, Stan …"

Stanley stared back at her with huge eyes.

"That's him, goddamn it. I'm telling you …" he pointed at the TV screen, "that's him!"

❈

RAY WHITESIDE WAS SHAKING FROM THE REALIZATION. THE FINAL PIECES OF THE puzzle, delivered to him in a traffic jam in the middle of the Eisenhower tunnel by a cop who had been with the force since Noah wore a badge.

"I don't get it, Ray. We were going to investigate Will Ross, remember?"

"No, Paul, no. It doesn't fit because he's not the player. He's the fucking target. He has been all along, but this asshole is such a crappy shooter that he keeps missing the target and hitting everybody around him. We've gotta stop by a phone. I've gotta call downtown. We need full coverage on that baby and the old lady. Son of a bitch! Why didn't I see it?"

"Why didn't you see what?"

"Paul." He held up the file. "Petey. That's what Vernon was trying to tell us. Petey is back in town—Little Petey who lost his family in an unexplained car explosion fifteen years ago. A car explosion that matched the one we saw yesterday. Little Petey—who went to live with his grandparents in Adams County. Five years later, they died in a propane tank explosion at their farm. Unexplained. His whole damned life is unexplained!"

"Little Petey, come on, Paul." He was almost begging Timmons to make the connection. "He became a very rich little boy. And then he just plain disappeared."

"Yeah, so?" Timmons still didn't see. Whiteside, Paul Timmons thought to himself, was just plain losing it, trying to clear a man who couldn't be cleared: Will Ross.

❋

OLVERIO WALKED BACK INTO THE LIVING ROOM FROM THE KITCHEN, HIS FACE ASHEN.

"That's the guy, Ollie," Stanley said, pointing madly. "That's the guy!"

Olverio stared blankly at him, then turned to Rose. "The rattle. It was a bomb. It blew up. Rex knew. He took it." Olverio pointed blindly toward the back door. "We've got to get him to the vet. He's hurt."

Shoe started to howl.

"Christ, I'm telling you, Ollie, that's the son of a bitch at the drop. He's the guy with the Semtex."

Ollie nodded. "I know, Stan. I know."

As Olverio stood in shock and Stanley kept pointing at the TV set filled with the face of Art Jackson, Rose bent down, scooped up the baby, and turned to her family.

She nodded toward the TV set.

"That man was in my house," she hissed. "That man killed my daughter. He just tried to kill my granddaughter. Now he's going to try again. And he's going to try and kill my son-in-law.

"I want you two to find him and kill him."

"Done," Ollie said quietly.

"Done," Stanley agreed.

"So," Rose whispered, "let's get the dog to the vet and find ourselves someplace safe."

Without another word, the three began moving as one.

WHITESIDE WAS GROWING EXASPERATED. HE REACHED OVER IN THE DARKENED CAR and started slapping Timmons on top of the head with the file folder.

"Goddamn it, Ray, stop it!"

"You stop it, Paul. Stop trying to force the pieces to fit. Think about it. Little *Petey!*" Whiteside shouted. "*Little Petey!* You've heard of him. *The darling of the press! Little Petey.* Tragic life filled with unexplained explosions! *Peter the Great!* Paul! Look at it!" Whiteside shook the file madly. "*Little Petey! Arthur Peter Jackson!*"

"Oh, Christ," Timmons whispered.

"Christ is right," Whiteside said. "Motive, opportunity, and history—Little Petey is back."

Without another word from Whiteside, Timmons pushed down on the accelerator and spend off into the night, driving too fast along the dark two-lane road to Kremmling.

WILL STILL STOOD ON HIS MARK IN FRONT OF WHERE THE CAMERA HAD BEEN. JEREMY Paxton walked up and quietly pulled the microphone from Will's hand, then reached behind him for the IFB box.

"You with us, Will? You ready for a drink?"

"Naw. Naw," Will said distantly, waving Jeremy off.

The snow was beginning to fall more heavily now.

"I've got to get back to Denver."

CHAPTER TWENTY-FIVE

MIDNIGHT RUN

WILL TURNED HIS FACE TO THE SKY AND LOST HIMSELF FOR A MOMENT in the gathering fall of flakes. The back of summer was breaking. Winter was making itself known in the high country with a vengeance.

Aside from Jeremy Paxton putting the last of the cable and gear away before putting down the dish on the top of the truck, the street was empty and silent. Streetlights were on, but the rest of the town was dark, with the exception of the Lariat, which was doing a booming Friday-night business. Each time the door opened, Will heard the singer in the distance, the lyrics just across the border of blue, adding to the raucous atmosphere of the place.

The snow grew heavier. It was going to slow them down.

"We've got to go, Jeremy," Will said as Paxton locked down the sat dish.

"Right enough. Sounds like they're having a good time in there."

"No, I've got to get back to Denver tonight. Right now," Will said flatly.

"What? No. We've got a 9 A.M. start tomorrow. I want to drink a bit and get some rest in my warm little bed right up there." He pointed at the corner room of the small hotel.

"Naw. I'm calling the ball on this one, Jeremy. We're going back tonight. I've got people to see. People to see tonight."

"Can't do it, Will. My job is to shoot this race and keep you …" He caught himself.

Will paused. "Keep me what?" he asked.

"Just to shoot this …"

"Keep me what?" Will insisted.

"Look," Jeremy held up his hands, "I'm just doing what I was told. My job is to keep you on the road and shoot the pictures and do the live shots. I'm keeping you on the road." He paused and sighed. "Hugh thought you might try to bag it halfway through," he lied, "so I was told specifically not to give you a lift on the road or back home if you decided you couldn't hack it."

"Couldn't hack it?"

"Couldn't hack it. Those were Ransford's words. Not mine. Those were his orders, Will. I'm sorry if his being a jerk hurts you, but I can't help that. I'm a freelancer, and he's the one paying me. I'm sorry. Come on. Forget about it. Let's go get a drink."

Will fumed, then popped.

"I can hack it, you little Nazi. I can fucking hack it."

"Yeah, well, I'm sure, Willie Boy, that's why you want to bag it and run home tonight."

"I told you …"

"I don't care what you told me, asshole. You're on the road until Sunday."

Will's anger drove him a step forward, which made Jeremy drop back instinctively into a martial arts fighting stance.

"Don't fuck with me, Will. I'm a second-degree black belt."

They stared at each other, Will's chest heaving with anger. After a momentary standoff, Will took a deep breath and took one step to the side, backing down, holding up his hands. Jeremy Paxton relaxed. He made the mistake of looking up the street toward the Lariat.

"Will, look, let's just get a drink and talk. …"

Will snatched the galvanized steel lid off the garbage can and slammed it, with all his weight, full force into Jeremy Paxton's face, catching him just as he turned back to finish his sentence. The lid rang in the cold, dark air, sending a shock wave racing up Will's right arm. Jeremy's nose exploded in a spray of blood, dotting the snow around his feet. Will leaned in close, grabbed Jeremy's arm, and hissed into his ear, "You're a second-degree black belt, Jeremy—but I'm the garbage man. Give me the goddamned keys."

Jeremy broke Will's grasp and rolled away, grabbing his nose and shouting an unintelligible yet seemingly endless string of curses in what sounded like a foreign language. Blood seeped through his fingers.

"You … you … you … fawck!" The blood continued to pour. Even Will was surprised by the amount. This guy was a bleeder.

Reaching into his back pocket with a bloody hand, Jeremy Paxton pulled out a set of keys and dangled them at Will.

"You want them, asshole? You want them? Go get them!" He leaned back and threw them with all his might into the curtain of snow falling on top of the hotel. Will watched them go, the silver catching the light once, then twice, before disappearing into the darkness.

"Son of a bitch," Will muttered.

"Sonofabeetch is right, you stupid shit."

The anger grew inside Will. This guy just wasn't getting it.

"Look. You don't understand, Jeremy. My family is in danger," Will growled. "I've got to get home tonight."

"And you don't understand, you backstabbing prick," Jeremy answered. "You're not going anywhere until Sunday night, when you can't do a goddamned thing about it."

"Do a goddamned thing about *what?*"

The brakes were off. His nose bleeding, his anger rich and full, Jeremy Paxton forgot the detailed instructions from Beth and Ransford about keeping his mouth shut. He opened it and let Will Ross have it right between the eyes with both tonsils.

"You are such a stupid son of a bitch, Ross, you know that? Stupid. What did she tell you? What did Beth tell you that story was about?" He spat blood in the snow. "You called her today. Then she called me and read me the riot act. What the hell did she tell you that story was about?"

"Child abuse in Colorado."

"Well, the only child being abused is you, asshole. She and Ransford both called me today saying you were getting wind of ..."

"Wind of what?"

"She give you tongue on Monday? When she kissed you? Did she make your willie tingle? She's good at that, you know, she's really good at that."

"What are talking about, how did you ..."

"Because I was behind the screen at the restaurant. I got the entire interview on tape, you stupid shit!" Jeremy stepped forward and angrily punched Will in the shoulder. *"While you were spilling your guts about dead wives and babies you don't care about and no future and not having any feelings anymore—all your emotional turmoil—wahwahwah—I was rolling tape! Ha!* Christ, she reeled you and that baby in like a huge damned fish."

Will stood stunned, as if he had been the one slammed in the face by the garbage can lid.

"Oh, man," Jeremy whistled, happy with Will's reaction, "she got you good. She got you good. She's done well before, but I've never seen anybody fall like you did. Hoo! And you even brought along your daughter as the centerpiece. What a *thoughtful* daddy you are! Come Sunday night, when you're finishing this little ride and sitting in your living room, drinkin' a beer, you're going to see six and a half minutes of highly charged emotional TV, laying out your so-called life and your short-changed daughter.

"You, my boy, are royally fucked up. You're an emotional basket case who doesn't even know it yet. And Beth Freeman got it all on tape for all of Denver to enjoy."

The snow continued to fall around Will, heavier now. He hadn't moved. It was beginning to gather on his shoulders.

"'In the eyes of a child,'" Jeremy intoned, covering his heart with his hand, "'there is hope and there is love, and therein lies the future. A future made all the more difficult by the death of both parents—one physically, one emotionally—on a rainy Colorado night not so very long ago.'"

Will stared at him.

Jeremy smiled. "'Beth Freeman, TV6 News.'"

The snowflakes in the darkness provided a curtain between the two. Paxton couldn't quite see the reaction on Will's face anymore, or the pain in his eyes. Battered, drained, and defeated, Will turned without another word and began to walk across the edge of the park toward the street and, in the distance, the door of his small hotel. There was no truck. There was no car. There was no way to stop what was going to happen.

"Aren't you going to give me another shot, Will? Come on, let's fight fair and see who walks away with the bloody hydrant this time. Come on! How about it, asshole?" Jeremy bounced on the balls of his feet and punched the air around him.

Silently, without any reaction at all, Will crossed the street, opened the wooden door of the hotel's small lobby, and walked up to his room.

Jeremy stood waiting in the park.

Opening the door, Will stepped into his room, sighed, and switched off the single light switch. The Western motif table lamp beside the queen-sized bed went off, plunging the room into darkness. Will closed the door, locked it, kicked off his tennis shoes, and began to move around the room as quickly and quietly as possible.

Jeremy Paxton watched the lights in the room go out from his position in the park. He leaned down, scraped up a handful of newly fallen snow, and pressed it against his face.

"Cry your eyes out, you little bastard." The bleeding had stopped. He wiped the drying blood from his face, smearing it across his cheeks. "Cry yourself to sleep on your enormous pillow while I go gets meself a drink."

As he walked toward the lights of the Lariat, Jeremy looked toward the roof of the corner hotel and wondered how the hell he was going to get the keys to his rental car—currently sitting in the parking lot of TV6 in Denver—back off the snowy roof. The keys to the satellite truck remained in his pocket.

Jeremy sighed. He'd worry about all that tomorrow morning.

WILL WATCHED JEREMY GLANCE HIS WAY, THEN WALK DOWN THE BOARDWALK toward the bar.

"Let's hope," he whispered, pulling the long-sleeved T-shirt over his head. It was cotton, not a specialty fabric, which meant it would hold the sweat next to his body as he went up and over the Divide. His red-yellow-and-black Haven jersey went over that, with a thin, hot-pink nylon jacket for top cover. Will shook his head. This was going to be one cold damned ride.

Sliding into white padded shorts, he then pulled on a pair of black riding tights. Without a light on the bike, and wearing black tights, only the pink jacket would be visible. In a snowstorm. In the reflected headlights of fast-moving cars.

Will put his odds at 60-40. Maybe 40-60. But what else could he do?

He dug in his riding duffel and found two pairs of socks. The thin cotton socks went against his skin to pull the moisture and stop the blisters. The second pair of socks made him smile: a long, strange, red-and-white-striped pair, woollies he had stolen from his sister years before. Good-luck socks.

He hadn't worn them in years.

Then again, he thought, he hadn't had good luck in years either. Will pushed the thought away and continued dressing in the darkness of the room.

The balaclava was next, followed by gloves, stuffed into a pocket, and a helmet slung over the headset, riding shoes buried in the jacket until he was downstairs, outside, and ready to ride. As a car passed on the street, Will caught a glance of himself in the mirror. In the shadowed darkness, the jacket stood out.

He looked like a hot-pink Batman.

As quietly as possible, he filled the water bottles, then scooped up the Beast, his stolen professional-model Colnago, shouldered it, walked to the door in his stocking feet, and paused to quietly ask the Madonna del Ghisallo to grant him the ride of his life.

He took a breath and felt an odd sense of calm rise within him.

Will Ross opened the door and stepped out, silently and unknowingly saying good-bye to the last two months of his life.

◉

"THIS SNOW REALLY SUCKS."

"No," Timmons said, "the snow doesn't suck. This car sucks. The tires on this car suck. The snow is nice. It's the car."

"Just keep driving, Paul, just keep driving."

"Hey, Byers Canyon, Hot Sulphur Springs, a stretch into Granby, and we're there. Thirty minutes max."

"An hour, easy."

Paul Timmons smiled. Anything to break the tension of a nighttime drive in snow.

"You're on."

❁

THE ENTRANCE ROAD TO THE VILLAGE OF GRAND LAKE WAS DARK, EMPTY, AND silent. Will had to concentrate and use every available light source to know where he was on the road. There were few, if any, reference points.

There was a short climb up to the junction with Highway 34. Will stopped. To the right were Rocky Mountain National Park, Trail Ridge Road, Estes, Boulder, and home. To the left were Granby, Winter Park, Berthoud Pass, Empire, I-70, Idaho Springs, and home. Berthoud was all torn up for construction, he knew, but Trail Ridge was higher and more open, with a greater chance of being plugged with snow. Berthoud they kept fairly clean. It was the major route in and out of town.

And it was shorter: 100 miles versus at least 120.

God, where was the argument?

Better to ride full bore into a construction pit on Berthoud than be found next spring as a Popsicle on Trail Ridge. Will turned left and began to build his stroke into the silent night.

❖

Four miles down the road, passing a log church that seemed to have given birth to a big new church beside it, Will began to wonder if he had overdressed for the ride. It was cold and it was dark and the snow continued to fall, making the road wet and slick and often invisible all at once, but Will realized that he was sweating heavily within the layers of clothing. He reached down for a water bottle, slipped, caught himself, and continued on. He'd get water in a minute. On a stretch of road that seemed a little more stable.

He was about to unzip his jacket when he came over a rise near a dry-docked marina and was hit by the first blast of wind off Lake Granby. It shot through him like microwaves through frozen vegetables. The knife edge of the cold took his breath away, and Will suddenly began to wonder if he had underdressed and if it was a good idea at all to be doing what he was doing, when he was doing it, how he was doing it, and where he was doing it.

He had been stupid before, but this ... good Lord.

He rode between two ridges that ran alongside the lake. The wind died, and Will caught his breath again. He stretched his fingers to force the circulation back into them. He bent back down over the headset. The ridges were coming to an end, the frozen lake blast pushing the snow sideways at a 30-degree angle not sixty, fifty, forty feet in front of him.

He gritted his teeth and burst through the curtain.

"Jesus," he screamed, as much a cry for help as a curse of despair. The road swung in a lazy arc to the right, away from the lake. The wind moved behind him and pushed him forward at a frightening pace into yet another long drop and an endless straightaway through the pitch-black valleys north of Granby. The valley behind him acting like some kind of gigantic natural flue, Will continued to feel the great relief of a tailwind, bitter as it might be. Twice he touched the brakes, frightened by the lack of visibility in front of him. Darkness and snow closed in the world around him until at times he felt as if he was riding rollers in a gigantic meat locker, himself just another side of beef.

He had been lucky so far: there had been little or no traffic. He could wander back and forth across the road, feeling out the shoulders like a blind man in a race car, without too much fear of winding up as a hood ornament on a Dodge Durango. Twice cars had passed, heading toward Grand Lake. He had inched over to the right and thanked them for the moments they turned on their brights, giving him the chance to see, for a second, anyway, where he was and what in the hell he was doing.

This was misery. This was misery in the cold and wet and snow. Around the last lazy left-hand curve, Will could make out yellow shadows ahead. They were clearer if he looked off to the side and used only his peripheral vision. Lights. He was approaching Granby and the junction with Highway 40. As he rode past the darkened Texaco station, he brought his right knee high and dove down into the sweeping left-hand turn into town. A quick glance to his right showed a lone set of headlights approaching. Will didn't care. He'd be across the road and up the hill before they got anywhere close.

He stood up out of the seat and began to pump in a big gear toward the top of a long hill. A white trailer with a red-light readout stood beside the road about halfway up the hill. It was calculating speeds in the thirty-mile-an-hour zone. As Will passed, it flashed "17."

I'll have to do better than that, he thought. I'll have to do a lot better than that. Up ahead, he saw the lights of an all-night gas station. Time enough, he thought, to pull in, pee, and have a cup of coffee.

At least his stomach could be warm and his head awake.

❋

"There's the sign—Granby, straight ahead. Junction Highway 34, Grand Lake, left."

Ray Whiteside squinted into the night. He couldn't see much of anything through the snow.

"Got it, got it." Paul Timmons began to slow down and feel his way toward the turn. He didn't want to break a wheel or bend an axle driving over a hidden traffic island.

Whiteside squinted again. "Use your low beams. It's easier to see."

Timmons flipped from high to low. "Not much easier."

"No, not much."

"And you tell me that one thousand people, including our boy, are going to ride in this tomorrow morning toward Breckenridge?"

"That's the plan."

"Idiots. Complete and total idiots."

Slowly, Paul Timmons took his foot off the gas and turned the wheel to his left, hoping to just slide through the turn onto the road toward Grand Lake.

The two police detectives were silent as the car moved in its unstable arc onto Highway 34.

Whiteside looked at his watch.

"You owe me. We're just passing an hour now."

Paul Timmons didn't say anything; he just stared into the driving snow that seemed to be coming right toward his eyes.

❋

The stop in Granby had been a mistake. As soon as he walked into the light and the heat, he could feel himself begin to stiffen. The T-shirt next to his chest was soaked. His knees were wet and frozen from the road spray. His eyes were shocked back into reality by the greenish hue of the fluorescent bulbs overhead.

Sixteen miles. Forty minutes. Had to do better. Had to do better.

The lady behind the counter stared at Will, then held up her hand when he tried to pay for half a cup of coffee.

"Where you riding to?" she asked.

"Denver. By morning."

"The coffee's on me."

Will smiled. "Thanks."

He took a long draw and turned toward the door. The thick java burned a path down to the top of his stomach and then spread its warmth around the edges. God, that felt great.

As he stepped out the door, he waved back at the woman. "Thanks again. Have a nice night."

"Good luck," she called after him. When the door closed, she said aloud, to no one in particular, "Geez—what an asshole."

❁

THE COFFEE GREW COLD QUICKLY OUTSIDE AND WENT RIGHT THROUGH HIM, BUT FOR those minutes, those precious few minutes, he had felt warm and alive and awake.

Maybe someday he'd feel that way again.

He followed the lights onto the gentle descent out of Granby, passed the movie theater, and rode off into the night.

The snow grew light. The road grew wet. Will settled in and tried to find his pace. The miles passed slowly.

A long straight out of Granby curved into a long climb leading up and over to Tabernash, then on into Fraser and Winter Park. He felt hungry. Oh, Christ. Bonk.

He hadn't even thought about it. He had been eating everything in sight since he had landed in Grand Lake, from pasta to chicken wings to a burrito the size of a battleship shell at Pancho and Lefty's. The plate had had a picture on it when he started. It didn't when he finished.

Still, for a ride like this, he needed more. He passed Snow Mountain Ranch, which he realized only by feeling the climb drop away and from the glow of a snow-covered light that lit a portion of the sign.

Winter Park. Maybe he could stop in Winter Park to buy something to eat.

He reached into his fanny pack. There was a Haven energy bar there, but the thing was frozen solid. He pulled it out and slipped it into his pants to thaw it.

The serious chill just above his package woke him up as much or more than the coffee.

Maybe that would work. Maybe that would keep him going. He crouched over the headset, scanning ahead for indications of just where in hell the road might be. There were moments in the flurries and the splatter that he had, honestly, no idea at all.

And still, he drove himself forward to increase the pace, always increase the pace.

He took another drink of water and finished the first bottle. He'd have to get more. That he knew as well. Winter Park. All good things happen in Winter Park.

All for the good in Winter Park.

Everything happens for the good.

He shook his head. What a stupid goddamned thought.

His own life was proof of that.

✿

PAUL TIMMONS AND RAY WHITESIDE PULLED UP OUTSIDE A STORE CALLED CABIN FEVER in downtown Grand Lake. It was directly across from the Tumbleweed Restaurant and the Three Sisters Inn, the small hotel where TV6 News had told Whiteside Will Ross and Jeremy Paxton would be staying.

They trudged silently across the street, past the TV6 News satellite truck. It was a few minutes before 1 in the morning. The silence in the street was so loud they could hear it.

The snow along 34 heading toward Rocky Mountain National Park had only intensified, blowing, drifting, blinding Paul Timmons until he was forced to pull off the road and wait half an hour until the storm began to abate.

Autumn had been skipped. Winter had arrived.

Paul Timmons was exhausted.

"Can't we just wait until morning and talk to him over breakfast?"

"No time, Paul," Whiteside said, shaking his head. "We've got to talk to him tonight. I can drive the three of us back to Denver if you want."

Timmons looked up at the sky. Snowflakes dotted his eyebrows.

"We ain't going anywhere tonight, Ray."

Whiteside shrugged and walked up to the door leading into the tiny lobby of the hotel. He rang the bell. Again. And again. And again. Finally a man appeared, tucking in a red flannel shirt.

He opened the door and grunted, "No vacancies. Sorry."

"No, sir. We're not here for a room. We're here to see someone who is staying here. I'm Detective Whiteside, and this is Detective Timmons of the Denver Police Department."

The man's eyes grew wide. "Well, sure, sure, gentlemen. Won't you come in?"

"Thank you."

"Thanks," Timmons said, hustling in from the cold. "Where are the Three Sisters?"

The man laughed. "You're lookin' at 'em. People might not stay at a place called the Grizzled Old Fart Hotel. This sounded better."

Timmons nodded. "Good point. We're looking for Will Ross."

"Oh, the TV guys? They've got two rooms. Second floor front and then right at the top of the stairs. You want me to come along? I'm pretty good in a fight."

"Oh, God," Whiteside sighed, wiping the melting snow from his face with his hand, "a fight is the last thing we're going to have. You can come along if you want. No fireworks."

"Great."

He looked like a kid with a new puppy. The three walked to the top of the stairs and stood on the landing in the darkness.

"Which room?"

"Don't know which one he took. Front room has the best view."

"Front it is, then." The three walked to the door of the front corner room. Whiteside began to knock.

"Will? Will Ross? Ray Whiteside. We've got to talk. Will?"

He knocked harder.

"Will?"

He heard a shout in the room, then silence. Whiteside knocked again. Finally there was a thump and a shuffling of feet, combined with a grunt, a belch, and assorted grumbles. The door opened.

"Who the hell are you?" Paul Timmons asked.

"I'm fine, thanks. Who the hell are you?"

Whiteside held up a badge. "Denver Police. Could you identify your-self, please?"

"I'm Jeremy Paxton from Ohio. Why?"

"Do you know Will Ross of TV6 News in Denver?"

"Yeah. I'm working with him. I'm driving the truck. Jesus, don't ask so much. I've been drinking."

"Sorry. Do you know where Will is?"

"No idea. Isn't he in his room?"

"Which is?"

"Right down there." Jeremy pointed at the next door. "He went in right at 10:30, and I haven't heard a peep out of him since."

Ray Whiteside nodded. "Thank you, sir. We're sorry we bothered you."

"Yeah, no problem." Jeremy scratched his head and gave a dull-eyed smile. As the three men turned away from his door, he leaned against the doorjamb and watched in gleeful anticipation of whatever fresh hell had come to find Will Ross.

Whiteside knocked at Will's door. He called out, then knocked again. Timmons was growing tired of it all—the drive, the search, the new angle, the wait. He leaned forward and bashed his hand three times on the door.

"Ross, goddamn it! Wake up."

"Hey, watch it," the owner wailed. "Those are brand-new doors."

There was no sound from inside the room. Whiteside thought for a minute. Timmons leaned back in, but Ray stopped him. He turned to the owner.

"Do you have a passkey on you?"

"You bet. Always. Want me to open 'er up?"

Whiteside waited for a second, then nodded. The man dug in his pocket, pulled out a master key, fitted it into the lock, and turned the deadbolt.

The door swung open. The owner flipped on the light.

There were clothes strewn all over the floor. The bed hadn't been slept in. The duffel bag was torn open as if someone had been searching for things hidden in its deepest, darkest recesses.

Whiteside looked around the room. What wasn't he seeing? Something wasn't right. Something wasn't there. But what? What?

Look, think, see. And then, and then …

"What is it, Ray?"

"What don't you see, Paul?"

"I don't see Will Ross, that's for damned sure."

"Besides that."

"I dunno. What?"

"I don't see a bike."

◎

ANGELA VALDEZ WALKED BACK TO THE NURSES' STATION AT THE BURN UNIT ICU at University Hospital. She glanced over the charts one last time, amazed again by the seemingly miraculous recovery of that TV reporter caught in a car fire.

Second- and third-degree burns on arrival, upgraded to serious first- and minor second-degree burns within twenty-four hours. The doctor had barely seen the guy but still marched around the unit saying, "Mygood, mygood, mygood." Jesus, she thought. Just what we need. Another one who thinks he can walk on water.

She looked up but couldn't see into the darkened corner where—she checked the record to get the name right—Clyde Zoromski was sleeping. She shook her head, not knowing who this Zoromski was or where he worked. She knew he was on TV, but she always watched Channel 4.

Someday, she knew, Larry Green was going to call and she was going to win ten thousand dollars. She had daily answers to the quiz going back to 1986. She'd get the money. No doubt. She looked up over the edge of the station again. She stood. She still couldn't see the patient.

Maybe she'd recognize him if she looked at him.

Angela Valdez quietly walked around the desk into the unit itself, trying to get a look at this Zoromski from a distance so as not to take a chance on waking him. She crept closer, then closer again, finally stepping into the darkness surrounding his bed.

She looked down at the lump in the bed and realized immediately that the lump wasn't the patient at all but blankets and pillows stuffed into a shape that looked like a somewhat lumpy forty-two-year-old man.

The yelp caught in her throat. Her heart raced. She didn't know what to do in a situation like this. People in the Burn Unit didn't just get up and go wandering around the hospital—never had in the twenty-five years she had worked this shift, this unit, this hospital.

Neither had Clyde Zoromski.

At that very moment, he was not wandering the hospital but shuffling under full steam away from it, trying to hitch a ride in the dead of night.

He had to get home, then to the station.

If Bruce Mason's inside info from the assignment desk had been right, Zorro had a lot of dirty work to do this weekend, whether Will Ross appreciated it or not.

❀

NOTHING HAD BEEN OPEN IN WINTER PARK. HE HAD FOUND A WATER FOUNTAIN AND coaxed two full bottles out of it, but beyond that, the city was dead. One forty-five on a Saturday morning, and even the bars were closed. At least those he passed.

He reached into his pants and pulled out the energy bar. His body heat had softened it. His sweat had given it an unusual aroma.

He didn't have the option of being picky. He started riding again toward Berthoud Pass and chewed the end off the wrapper. Before he realized it, he had swallowed the silvered plastic. He laughed stupidly. It would make some interesting stools over the next few days. He began to bite and hack and chew at the bar, which was taking on a consistency somewhere between rubber and wax teeth. He chewed and chewed and chewed some more until the piece was a lump that seemed small enough to fit down his throat. He swallowed, gagged as it caught at his larynx, swallowed again, and felt it pass all the way down.

He wrapped the rest of the bar and stuffed it back into his tights. Such a treat, he thought, should be savored slowly.

❀

THE UNMARKED POLICE CAR SAT AT THE JUNCTION. ONE MILE BEHIND IT WAS THE Village of Grand Lake. Immediately in front of the grille was US Highway 34. Right took you to Estes Park, while left took you to Granby and either Berthoud or Silverthorne.

"What do you think?"

"Well, you know, we didn't see him on the road from Silverthorne."

"Okay," Paul Timmons said. "And we didn't see him on the road from Granby. So—"

"He might have made it there before us."

Timmons shook his head. "Not with this snow and wind. No way. Besides, Berthoud's closed tonight for construction."

"Then you're saying …"

"Right. He turned right. The idiot is trying Trail Ridge tonight."

Ray Whiteside nodded. The car turned right and headed into Rocky Mountain National Park. They had been practical and logical about the direction they were sure Will Ross had ridden, and both men cursed the choice.

Five minutes later, a heavy satellite truck pulled up to the same stop sign at the same intersection. Jeremy Paxton spat into his hand and slammed his thumb down on the glob. In the golden light of the instrument panel, he saw the spit jump to the left.

That was the way he turned.

＊

AS WILL PASSED THE TURNOFF FOR OLD WINTER PARK, HE TOOK A GULP OF WATER, replaced the bottle, put his head down, and started building up his pace for the run up to the pass. He wasn't looking forward at all to the next ninety minutes. Crossing under the information sign for Berthoud Pass, Will realized that the final lights he would likely see until Empire were telling him that the pass was closed.

He sighed. No time to worry about that now.

Putting his faith in nothing more than his nose and a sense of when he should back away from the cliff, Will Ross rode on through the night, the sensation gone in both his fingers and his toes.

＊

THE ROAD KEPT CHANGING IN FRONT OF HIM, RISING UP, SLIDING TO THE SIDE, AND then straightening out again. He hit the shoulder, piled high with snow-covered dirt, and wobbled back into the middle of the road.

He shouldn't have had those last two shots. This truck was a bitch to handle even when he was sober. He took another drink from the pint to even himself out, squinted into the darkness beyond his headlights, and drove faster in search of the man who might cost him his career.

※

THERE WERE LIGHTS ONLY IN THE DISTANCE. THERE WAS NO LIGHT HERE. WILL was completely blind, riding hard enough that he bounced off the guardrail or the mountain with each new switchback like a pinball going for a triple score.

His tires slid on the pavement, now wet, now cold, now snowy. He had lightly treaded tires, designed for wet, not for cold. He didn't know if anything was designed for cold, especially this cold, the kind of cold that reached in and tickled your heart and after a while separated you from the very things that made you human: your touch, your sight, your mind.

Will kept pedaling.

The little man inside his head was there, flannel shirt and coveralls, wielding not his hod and mortar but a hammer—a big hammer—a sledgehammer. He swung it back and forth, back and forth, as if he was about to strike the wall and bring his two months of hard labor to the ground in a pile of rubble.

Will shook his head to clear the image.

He kept pedaling.

The man was gone, replaced by a new image: a daughter who was reaching for him, crying for him in the night, smiling at him in the hope that he might, just might, this time, stop for a moment and reach for her.

Will squeezed his eyes shut. The tears burned in the cold, ran down his cheeks, and froze to the edge of the balaclava.

Oh, God, he thought. What have I done?

Inside his mind, the little white-haired man swung the hammer, back and then forward, the head bouncing off the brick. Will heard the strike echo off the stillness of the valley around him and resonate around him in two golden pools of flashing light.

Will kept pedaling.

✵

THE TWO MEN HAD BEEN DOZING IN THE HEATED CAB OF THEIR TRUCK. THE MAN BEHIND the wheel jerked awake and peered into the distance. He nudged his partner.

"Hey! Did you just see a guy on a bike ride by?"

"Wha? God, you're dreaming, man. Leave me alone."

He curled up and went back to sleep. The man behind the wheel peered behind him at the two barriers with their flashing signal lights. He turned back and closed his eyes. He had been dreaming.

After all, who in hell would be riding a bike on a night like this?

He fell back asleep as the snowfall filled the single track, less than an inch wide, left by two bicycle tires heading up the mountain.

✹

THE NEWSROOM WAS DARK AND QUIET. ONLY THE SATURDAY-MORNING PRODUCER SAT sleeping at the assignment desk under a single bank of track lights.

Clyde Zoromski moved quickly between the cubicles to the door of Hugh Ransford's office. He slipped the plastic jimmy between the door and the jamb and slid it through the lock. The door popped open. He closed it behind him and went directly to the credenza behind Ransford's desk.

Mason had said the finished story and the raw tapes were in the upper credenza. He worked the jimmy between the wooden panels, felt the lock, and tugged. It held. He tugged again, and it popped open.

He opened the door, looked in, grabbed the tapes, and walked gingerly toward the computerized edit station buried deep in the back of the building. He could have all this material digitized and saved on disk, hidden in the system, and returned to Ransford's office in less than an hour. Then, Saturday morning, he and Tony Carver would begin to work their magic.

✺

THE CLIMB TO THE TOP OF BERTHOUD WAS ENDLESS, STROKE AFTER STROKE AFTER stroke and nowhere closer to the top. Will came around a tight U-turn, lost his balance, and fell onto the snow-covered road. He lay there for a moment on the shoulder, his elbow ringing and the breath knocked out of him.

He stared at the sky—the flakes were only sporadic now—and wondered what in God's name he was doing.

As if in answer, he saw the man in his mind again, swinging the hammer with more force now against his own handiwork. Cracks began to appear in the wall, the mortar growing dark gray.

Will shook his head, carefully rolled to the side, picked up the Beast, swung a leg over, and pushed off again toward the top of the Continental Divide at Berthoud Pass. He was struggling now for every foot.

And yet Will kept climbing.

Will kept pedaling.

❋

LESS THAN TWO MILES DOWN THE PASS, THE SATELLITE TRUCK RUMBLED AROUND A tight corner and plowed through two plastic barricade barrels topped by flashing yellow lights. Jeremy Paxton shouted, "Shit!" and went for the brake. He missed and hit the accelerator.

He laughed and kept driving up the mountain.

In the cab of the truck at the barricade, the man in the passenger seat woke up, shook his head, and looked into the night.

"Hey, did a big goddamned truck just drive by here? Knock down our lights?"

"Huh?" the man behind the wheel muttered. "Naw. If it did, it was one of ours. Go back to sleep."

So they both did as the snow filled the double tire tracks left by a satellite truck heading blindly up the mountain.

❋

THE CRACKS GREW DEEPER AND MORE WATER POURED THROUGH AS THE MAN CONTINUED to hammer on the wall.

"I miss you," Will whispered. "I miss you, Cheryl, I miss you, love."

He pushed the crank around. With each turn he said the words again, a mantra to push him up the frozen mountainside. He could see lights ahead in the distance, just around a turn. Not many, just some. A few stray mercury bulbs burning themselves blue in the black night.

"I miss you, love. I miss you, Cheryl. No one else. No one else. Oh, Christ, I'm sorry if I hurt you. I'm sorry if I hurt … God. Oh, God. Why did you leave me, Cheryl? Why did I let you die? Why did I let you die?"

The man hammered at the wall. One brick, then two, broke free, and the water began to pour through the holes, filling the room around his feet.

The cranks turned slowly, one after another after another after another. The cranks continued to turn. As he turned the corner, Will had been in darkness so long that the blue mercury vapor lights of the Berthoud Pass Ski Area parking lot burned his eyes. He squinted and his eyes teared, the drops hot again on his cheeks, frozen by the time they reached the balaclava, the edge now sticking to his face. He reached up and pulled it away, taking a chunk of frozen skin with it.

The cranks continued to turn.

Will continued to pedal.

And suddenly, it was all downhill.

✧

ON THE FINAL STRETCH TO THE SUMMIT OF BERTHOUD PASS, JEREMY PAXTON SAW a man on a bicycle, wearing a pink nylon jacket, cross slowly over the crest, not more than two hundred yards ahead. He smiled and took one last pull from the pint.

It couldn't be anyone else. Beth had said not to let Will get back to Denver, and by God, Jeremy Paxton wasn't going to let Will get back to Denver.

He blinked hard to clear his eyes.

"You're mine, sucker!" Jeremy shouted and urged the truck up the icy side of the pass, crossing over quickly into a sharp and dark descent.

✦

THE DROP CAUGHT WILL BY SURPRISE AND WOKE HIM UP LIKE A HARD SLAP AFTER a cup of coffee. It was sharp and fast, the road not snowy but wet, with a hairpin turn at the bottom. He had left the snow on the other side of the Divide.

He glanced above and saw a few stars but still plenty of cloud cover. It remained pitch dark in the distance, but if that was so, why could he see the wall rushing up at him so very clearly?

He shot a glance over his shoulder, sensing rather than hearing the truck rushing up behind. Will turned back and pulled close to the shoulder, slowing down and moving sideways to give the driver plenty of room to pass.

He looked ahead and saw the lights on the retaining wall shift, not out and away from him but in, to the point where his shadow was directly between the beams. Will glanced once more, shouted, and dug in, cutting across the road into the opposite lane, tight on the curve, shifting to a big ring in a bad place and pumping for all he was worth to put some distance between himself and the lights behind him.

The diesel roared in acceleration, the lights catching Will again on the straightaway.

Will had been on the bike, on the road, for nearly three and a half hours, drained by cold and hunger, thirst and fatigue, yet, now, suddenly, he was energized.

The road went from pitch black to bright yellow each time the truck's lights caught him, throwing his shadow, pumping, racing, working, before him.

"Stop it!" Will shouted. "Stop!"

He looked back. The truck was catching him, moving faster and faster toward an inevitable collision. Will crouched and bit into the gear, pumping for his very life. He looked up and screamed.

Not twenty feet in front of him the pavement ended—the road went from asphalt to grind to hard-packed dirt and gravel to mud, a single lane without a guardrail or protection or a solid riding surface. He was going in a heartbeat from velodrome to cyclocross, and there wasn't a damned thing he could do about it.

He rose just enough to take the shock of the drop in his knees. Sailing off the asphalt, the Beast bounced along the hard dirt for ten feet before the front rim hit a pile of soft gravel, cranked sideways, and flipped directly right. The bike, still attached to his feet by the cleats, flew through the air directly behind him. All Will heard was the roar of the wind, mixed with the scream of the diesel. His shadow flew in a hundred different directions before his eyes.

As he hit the ground and skidded through the mud, rather than feel the pain or the fear of sliding toward the cliff, he remembered Peter Pan and how he had lost his shadow.

Will felt something tear away from him. He wondered if he would ever find it and get it sewn back on again.

❀

THE SATELLITE TRUCK BOUNCED HARD AS IT LEFT THE PAVEMENT RIGHT BEHIND Will Ross. Jeremy Paxton instinctively let up on the gas, gained control, then floored it just as Will hit the gravel. He roared up behind the rider, then watched dumbfounded as Will's front wheel cranked to the side and bike and rider flew out of the path of the truck and back into the darkness.

"Woo! Shit!" Jeremy screamed with delight, looking back over his shoulder. That asshole wasn't going anywhere.

He turned back and stared into the darkness just beyond the headlamps. The road turned sharply to the left. He was drifting right, he was going too fast, and he wasn't going to be able to stop.

If they had finished the road, if they had finished the guardrails, Jeremy Paxton might have had a chance, bouncing back and forth across the road until he regained control.

But the road wasn't finished, and by the time Jeremy realized that fact and processed the information, the TV6 News truck known to the crew as Challenger had already left the road and was airborne.

Jeremy couldn't bring himself to realize that pumping the brakes at that point would never have any effect on these particular tires again.

❀

AS HE AND THE BIKE SLID INTO A PIT AT THE EDGE OF THE CLIFF, WILL HEARD A scream of brakes on dirt, a moment of silence, then a tremendous crash—the sound of wood and metal in heavy collision. It sounded like a train wreck. Then, silence.

Slowly, Will peeked up over the edge of the pit and looked down the road. He saw nothing. No truck. No lights. He twisted his feet out of the frozen pedals and picked himself up out of the hole, dragging the bike behind him.

Down the road, he could see a car coming from the other direction, drawn by the sound cascading down the mountain. A flashlight poked out the window, as if searching for the crash site.

Will stood on shaky legs. The sky was clear on this side of the Divide. By the light of the moon, he could see the tracks race off and disappear in a straight line. Will pointed groggily toward the edge of the cliff, following the path the truck had taken.

"There he is."

He looked back up the mountain; he was over the worst of it, he knew. He had to keep going. Denver was just over seventy miles away, almost all downhill or flats. There was just Floyd Hill to deal with, and that could be done. Will crouched painfully beside the Beast and ran his hand over the rims. Both seemed fine. He was amazed sometimes at what he could put a bike through, and what this particular bike seemed able to take.

He pulled himself up, stiffly threw a leg over the seat, and snapped his right foot into the pedal. He pushed off slowly and rode the brakes down, feeling his way gingerly along the wet hardpack. He came around the second corner wide and passed the car as silently as possible. The two occupants were down the roadside somewhere, their flashlights snapping back and forth across the landscape in search of the truck and the driver and whatever life might be left in both.

Will quickly cut back through two more construction zones, the workers ignoring him as he passed. He returned to pavement, which was drying. In the moonlight, he could clearly see the yellow center lines running off into the distance. Will released the brakes and started to fly.

The man in his head was gone. There were no more walls. Will's head and heart were filled with the pain he had pushed away for so many weeks, creating new realizations that he had tried to ignore: Cheryl was gone, he knew, now and forever. But there was still Elena. His daughter. Their daughter.

He had been a fool, a terrified and pompous fool, hiding away as if being close would make him love her and as if loving her would sentence her to death.

Will could see that now. And he could see Elena too. He could see her, hear her, smell her in his mind.

Will had failed her mother.

He was not about to fail her.

A new rage filled him with a new energy.
The tattered pink nylon jacket flapped in the wind behind him.
Will continued to pedal.
Home. To his family. To his daughter.

❁

AT SEVEN O'CLOCK THE NEXT MORNING, TWO THINGS HAPPENED.

First, the brown unmarked police car carrying Detectives Raymond Whiteside and Paul Timmons of the Denver Police Department limped into Estes Park after a snowy, white-knuckled ride across Trail Ridge Road in the middle of the night. As they left the eastern entrance of Rocky Mountain National Park, they were greeted by the shocked look of park rangers who informed them that the road had been closed overnight owing to heavy snow and hazardous driving conditions.

They nodded in agreement and went in search of breakfast and clean underwear.

Meanwhile, in Denver, Oliver Cangliosi quietly let himself into the home of Will Ross, looking for a diaper bag that his sister Rose had left behind in her rush to leave the house the night before. He found the bag. He also found, stretched out and asleep on the kitchen floor, his nephew, Will Ross, soaked to the skin and covered with dirt, his jacket and pants torn, his smell foul, two empty liter bottles of water rolling slowly across the floor beside him, a half-eaten energy bar, covered with hair, in his hand.

Ollie picked up the phone and called Stanley.

He was going to need help with this one.

CHAPTER TWENTY-SIX

GEARING UP

T HE DARKNESS HELD HIM IN A WARM HAND.

His last memory was finishing the second liter of water on the hardwood floor of the kitchen, just before falling into a hard face plant and oblivion. Now the floor was soft on his face and the air of the kitchen dark and warm on his back.

Will's hand ran down his side, and he slowly realized that somehow he had undressed himself and piled the clothes—quite evenly—over his back.

Damn. He was good.

He drifted off again.

The door to the room in the downtown Holiday Inn cracked open. Olverio reached up from inside and pulled it open for his sister-in-law.

"Elena needs a nap. She's getting cranky."

"She didn't sleep last night?"

"No. She fussed all night long, which means I didn't sleep either."

Olverio smiled. Rose was the one sounding cranky.

"He's still out. Why don't you put her down beside him?"

Rose nodded and carried Elena over to the bed. The two-month-old didn't fuss but looked toward the bed with wide eyes and understanding beyond her years.

Rose thought, "This one has an old soul." She put the baby down next to Will. Elena rolled halfway over into the crook of Will's arm and was immediately asleep.

"That's all she needed," Olverio said from the door. "She needed her father."

❄

ALL RAY WHITESIDE COULD SEE WERE FLAKES. HUGE FLAKES OF SNOW, WHITE AND golden in the headlights of the car, dashing themselves to pieces against the windshield of the police Ford.

He jerked awake. For a moment he didn't know where he was, then he realized, slowly, that he was in his office, in Denver, a full twenty-four hours after leaving this very same chair and with nothing to show for his travels.

Paul Timmons slept under the next desk, his head balanced on a pile of phone books.

Everything he had ached. His legs trembled from the drive, his fingers hurt as if he had his grandmother's arthritis in full bloom, his eyes stung, and his tongue felt as if it were wearing a dirty wool coat left over from the World War.

The first one.

He stretched, then leaned back, wondering what his next step might be. Will Ross hadn't been on Trail Ridge. Will Ross wasn't at his home. Will Ross might have gone over Berthoud after all, but Whiteside still couldn't see the sense of such a move.

He didn't know. He closed his eyes. Ray Whiteside suddenly didn't care.

As he began to drift off again, a weekend-duty desk sergeant popped his head in the office door, staring at Whiteside, sleeping head back in a chair with his mouth open like a bass on a line, and Timmons, only his feet showing from underneath the desk.

The sergeant stepped in, picked up a brass shell-casing pencil holder, and banged it against the rubberized plastic top of the desk nearest the door.

Whiteside's eyes jerked open, and he sat up quickly. Timmons sat up quickly as well, banging his head on the underside of the desk drawer.

"Shit!" he cursed.

"Enough of that, Mr. Paul," the sergeant said. "You guys have been traipsing the state looking for Will Ross, right?"

"Yeah," Whiteside answered, rubbing his eyes with the tips of his fingers.

"You shouldn't do that, Whiteside," the sergeant said. "It's the easiest way in the world to pass a cold."

"Thanks, I'll remember it. What do you want? What's this about Will Ross?"

"Well, we may have found him. There's a TV6 News truck at the bottom of Berthoud Pass."

"Stopped?"

"No. Crunched. One transported. The driver. Pretty broken up. Young guy carrying an Ohio license. Station says he was a freelancer working with Ross and that Ross was likely riding with him."

"That guy with the satellite truck last night in Grand Lake," Timmons said.

"Appears so."

"Why do you think Ross was riding with him?"

The sergeant shrugged. "EMTs on the scene said the passenger-side door was popped open, and whoever was sitting there was likely thrown out."

Whiteside sat back and stared at Timmons. "You wanna go along?"

"No."

"Great. Get your stuff."

THE ROOM WAS STILL DARK. WILL NOTICED THAT THE CURTAINS WERE PULLED. He could see a vague outline in a chair behind the door. It looked like Ollie, but he couldn't be sure, and he couldn't seem to make himself care. After all, Elena was asleep in the crook of his arm, her head against his chest.

Will felt warm and safe, secure in the knowledge that he had made it and had won a chance, just one more chance, to be a father.

"WHERE ARE THE ORIGINALS?"

"They're back in Ransford's office credenza."

Tony Carver nodded. "Good, good. They're trying to send me up the road to Berthoud today, but I think I talked them out of it."

"What happened?"

"Jesus, Zorro, where you been? Hiding in some burn unit?"

"Cute."

"No, some damned freelancer that Ransford hired drove Challenger off the pass in the middle of the night at a high rate of speed."

"Jesus …"

"Best of all, he was blotto."

"… Christ. That's not going to look good on his permanent record."

"Well, he lived. He's over at Denver Health now, busted to flinders. But they think he's going to make it."

"Goody, goody." Zorro thought for a moment, then asked, "Was Will involved?"

"Not as far as anybody knows. Will has just plain disappeared off the face of the earth, at least according to Ransford. The cops want him. Beth has been screaming that she wants to talk to him. Ransford keeps calling his house. He's very popular, but nobody can find him."

Zorro sighed. "Well, he's a big boy. Let's get to work."

"You got it, C. Z."

They both laughed a graveyard tune, knowing their prank could easily send them both packing in a world where pranks were rarely appreciated—especially when they belittled a station or a highly promoted story.

Then again, Zorro thought, is it a prank or nothing more than poetic justice?

⬤

THE ROOM WAS STILL DIM, LIT ONLY BY A SMALL LIGHT IN THE BATHROOM. WILL looked around at Rose, Olverio, and Stanley. He pulled Elena close and smiled down into her eyes.

"She is a wonder, isn't she, Will?" Rose said.

Will nodded, then answered in a soft tone, "Even more than that, Rose, even more." He buried his head in the baby's neck, and she gurgled at the scratches from his beard.

Stanley said quietly, disappointed to have to break the mood, "We know who he is, Will."

Will looked at Stanley with tiny little eyes and smiled.

"So do I, Stanley. So do I."

"How did you find out?"

"I heard his voice on the satellite last night—it was just last night, wasn't it?—and somehow I just knew. I just knew the voice. He didn't hide it. How about you?"

"When I saw him last night on the tube, I knew. I recognized him. Then there was the rattle. ..."

"What rattle?" Will asked suspiciously, sitting up higher in bed, pulling the baby closer to him.

Stanley froze, realizing he had gone too far. Olverio held up a hand.

"Will, ever since that guy picked you up on Wednesday morning, the dogs have been nervous around the baby. They wouldn't leave her alone. Rex and Shoe both kept whining and pacing. They knew something was up. About the time Stan recognized our friend, Rose realized that she had never seen the rattle Elena was shaking. Before any of us could move, Rex snatched it and flew out the back door. When he jumped to the ground, it exploded in his muzzle."

"Oh, my God."

"He's alive. He's missing some teeth, but he's alive. That's a great dog you've got. Very loyal. Very loyal. Wouldn't mind having a dog like that myself."

"God bless him, that's all I can say," Will whispered.

"Indeed," Rose answered. "I was never comfortable leaving the baby with those two until last night when I saw what they would do to protect her. Well, let me just say they've got my vote."

"What about Art?"

Stanley shook his head. "Disappeared. His house on the South Side is cleaned out completely. Not a hair in the sink. Interesting workshop in the basement, I thought. Ollie, what did that room smell like to you?"

"Smell like?"

"Yeah, smell like."

"I dunno. I don't get you. What?"

"It smelled like a gun shop. No, really. It smelled—it smelled like ammo."

"Good. Glad you thought that," Ollie snapped, "but that doesn't help us find the asshole."

"Don't curse," Will and Rose said simultaneously.

Stanley laughed. "Great. About time somebody else got to say that to him."

Olverio wasn't amused. "Well, until Jackson shows up at the station or someplace else, we don't have a chance in hell of finding him or tracking him back to his supplies.

"He's gone."

Will shook his head. "No, I don't think so. This has all been part of a plan to get rid of me. Then Zorro, when I wasn't going. Cheryl got in the way. And seeing what Cheryl's death did to me, he's thinking that if he gets the baby, I'm toast."

"Okay …"

"Okay, so there are two targets in this room right now. The baby and me. We've got to get him. And it's got to be tonight."

"So you're saying, let's call the police, lay out what we have, appear at the station tonight, and arrest him?"

Will stared off into the darkness of the room and said in a quiet, menacing tone that made even Ollie sit up and take notice, "No. No cops. No arrest. No trial. No newspaper columnists whining about how his life was so rough that we have to understand him. No. We go to his house, I put a gun to his head, and I pull the trigger."

"It's not that easy, Will."

"It's not that easy."

Rose was the only one in the room nodding her head. "Yes, right. Exactly, Will."

"Are you out of your mind, Rose?" Stanley sounded frantic. "One, Will could get killed. Two, it's not that easy to kill somebody, especially a nut who does it for fun. And three, there's a great chance that Will himself will get killed."

"And we don't know where he is."

Will looked at Rose and said in a whisper, "Will you look after our daughter?"

Rose smiled. "Now and forever, Will."

"Thank you. Guess that takes care of your concerns. At least two of them. I'll handle the one in the middle."

Olverio shook his head. "No good, Will. We don't know where the asshole is, remember? You can't just walk up to him in the middle of a sports report and pop him twice in the head. We've got to get him with the stuff, with the materials, with the things that will tie him to you and Cheryl and the Lone Ranger …"

"Zorro," Will corrected.

"Whoever," Ollie said, waving his hand so as not to lose his point. "We've got to find him, follow him, go home with him. Get in close, and then we'll …" he pointed between Stanley and himself, "we'll do the hit."

"Well, Ollie, I appreciate that, but the missing piece you need is the one I've got. You forget. Art has a big mouth. He likes to talk. Dance around himself. And I've been doing a lot of riding, especially out on the plains. And I've put two and two together, and you know what I got?"

"Four?" Stanley offered.

"Two, Stanley. I got one asshole and where he lives. Tonight he is mine. He'll be home about 11:15. At 11:35, he'll be dead and my daughter will be safe."

"We should …"

"No. You can help, but it's my game. I'll need your help, but I'm going in alone."

"Will, I …"

"*No!*" Rose barked. "Will is right. This is his. He goes in, he goes in alone. If you're going to sit around and discuss this like a bunch of old men, then you go ahead, and Elena and I will help him. Otherwise, put a sock in it."

The two men, both feared in their neighborhoods, town, and state, sat quietly. Rose had spoken. She didn't speak up often, but when she did, it carried a weight that carried the day.

Ollie finally agreed. "All right, Will. We'll get you there, we'll get you a gun, and we'll back you up. It's your show. But I'll also tell you—if this doesn't go down just right, we're coming in there and taking him out, no matter what you say. Understood?"

"Understood."

"Good." Ollie and Stan stood up. "It's 3 now. Why don't you take a shower and get dressed. Dark clothes. Do you have any black tennis shoes?"

"Gray."

"Those will work. Nothing showing."

"Understood. I'll have to go home for those."

"We can do that. We'll go in the back."

"Where's Shoe?"

"He's with a neighbor. Do you want to see Rex?"

"Yeah. Let me have a shower and shave," Will said, passing Elena to Rose. "Give me twenty minutes and I'll be ready to go."

"Done."

Will rolled off the bed and stood up stiffly. He smiled at Rose and the baby.

"I liked that," he said quietly.

She smiled back.

"I thought you would."

❁

"COME ON, JUST LET ME PUT IT IN."

"You can't put it in—it will undercut everything else we've done with the story."

"We haven't done anything with the story," Tony Carver said, "except exchange a few shots here and there—wide for close—close for wide—and add a new tag. That's it."

"I know."

"So can't I add the *Looney Tunes* theme?"

"No. I want this to have an impact, Tony. Not be a joke."

"All right. All right." Carver surrendered and went back to editing the story the way Zorro wanted to see it done.

❁

PAUL TIMMONS LEANED BACK AGAINST THE HOOD OF THE CAR HE HAD SPENT THE majority of the past twenty-four hours in and slept, his head balanced precariously on a single finger propping up the middle of his forehead.

He looked ridiculous, but no one laughed. Both he and Whiteside looked like they had just finished the siege of Bastogne in shirt and ties. Timmons slept, and Whiteside wandered.

"Have you found any trace of a passenger yet?"

"No," the State Patrol officer said, stepping upwind of Whiteside to get clear of his breath. "We've been all over this chute and can't find anything. I'm wondering if he was in the truck at all. Maybe the door just popped and we're on a wild-goose chase."

"Has anybody walked back up the road?"

"We've worked the shoulders but not the road itself. There was no body on the road."

"Understood. Mind if I wander up there?"

"Help yourself, Detective." The officer swung his hand up the road in a gesture that seemed to offer Whiteside the entire mountain.

Whiteside turned and began to trudge up Berthoud Pass to the point where the TV6 satellite truck had left the road. Will had been here. He could sense it. He could feel it.

Either that, or he had a really bad headache.

❁

"There you go," Tony Carver said with a smile, adjusting the in-cue for the last bit of sound. "Finis. And it looks good."

"Thanks, Tony. By the way, keep your mouth shut. You had nothing to do with this."

"Hey, I hate that bitch. I want to stand with you on this one."

"You've got the boys. I'm free to screw up my life."

"But I want to stand with you."

Zorro shook his head. "Not this time, my friend."

Carver couldn't fail to see the logic in the argument, despite the fact that he wanted desperately to stick it to Ransford and Freeman, if not TV6 News in general.

"All right. So. How are you going to switch tapes?"

"When you're done, we'll dub off the story on her tape, right over her story, so her story doesn't exist anymore. I've bulk erased the raw tapes and replaced her master tape in the credenza with an exact duplicate, right down to her chicken-scrawl code on the front. I'll just come back in tonight after midnight and switch them again. Nothing will exist of this story, with the exception of our handiwork."

"Some handiwork, Z. She's going to shit."

"That's the idea."

❁

As drugged and in pain as Rex might have been, as soon as Will opened the holding cage and stepped in, the dog's tail began to wag furiously, and he tried to rise.

"No, no, Rex. You stay down. You stay down," Will whispered soothingly.

The dog stretched out on the mat. Will crouched down beside him and took the licks while scratching him behind the ear.

"Be careful with your muzzle, my friend. Be careful. You've been through a lot."

Rose held a sleeping Elena just outside the cage. She turned to notice that, beside her, Ollie had tears in his eyes.

"You—tough guy …"

"Hey, what can I say?" Ollie mumbled. "I love that dog."

❁

RAY WHITESIDE DRAGGED HIMSELF UP THE HARD-PACKED ROADWAY TOWARD THE END of the pavement. The point where the truck had left the road was a straight line shot out into oblivion. The driver hadn't even hit the brakes. Whiteside looked over the side. The guy was damned lucky to still be alive. Whiteside turned up the road and started to move along the shoulder, following the cluttered trail of footprints. This ground had been covered thoroughly by the State Patrol. He moved closer to the center of the road, where a single lane of traffic was being allowed to pass. As he walked up toward the start of the pavement, he noticed a faint single line of dried mud that left the pavement directly between the tire tracks of the truck.

Shocked awake, Whiteside turned, followed the line of the truck back to make sure, then walked fifty feet up the pavement to make sure of the other direction. The line between the truck tires was perhaps half an inch wide. It left the pavement, hit the hard pack, then stopped at a small, soft pile of dirt and gravel. There were odd footprints all around the pile as if someone wearing bicycle shoes had tromped around in a circle, then walked casually, given the stride, over to the opposite lane, now filled with traffic, where the half-inch line picked up again before being destroyed in a continuous line of cars heading for the hills.

Whiteside looked back one more time, then walked quickly down to the State Patrol command center. He could bring the search to a halt right now because he knew Will Ross had not been in the truck. He had been on his bike. The driver of the truck had been trying to run him down.

Will Ross had survived to ride to Denver.

Whiteside smiled. He was impressed. That took guts, especially last night.

That realization, however, led to a new and more troubling problem. He and Timmons had to return to the city on the fly and decide what to do. They had started out the day before to protect Will Ross from Art Jackson.

Now Whiteside wondered if that situation had suddenly gotten turned around.

❋

"This is a Colt .38 snub-nose," Stanley explained. "It's missing all its numbers, but even if it wasn't, it would take God himself to track this one down."

"Don't blaspheme."

"Well, it would," Stanley argued. "This one has been through more hands than a deck of cards in Vegas."

"We need to get Will some range time," Ollie said.

"Why?" Will asked.

"You can't just walk up and shoot the guy without knowing how the gun reacts. How it feels just before you pull the trigger. How it sounds. We need some range time."

"I've got a couple of indoor ranges from the phone book."

"No. Let's try outdoor. The weather's a little cranky. Crowds will be down. The fewer people who see Will with a gun in his hand, the better off we'll be tomorrow."

"There's an outdoor range at Cherry Creek. Zorro did a story about it a few weeks ago."

Olverio smiled.

"Then Cherry Creek it is."

❋

"You've left the first three minutes of the story the same, though, Z— can't I add the *Looney Tunes* theme?"

"No cartoon music. This has got to be serious."

"Well, shit. You're no fun."

They sat silently as the story was dubbed over from the digital editor to the master tape, obliterating Beth's original.

Carver turned toward Zorro, turned away, then turned back again.

"Go ahead, ask me."

"Ask you what?" Carver said as innocently as he could.

"Ask me why."

"Hey—I gotta—I mean—why are you doing this? Are you doing this because she left you?"

Zorro stared at Carver for a moment, then shook his head.

"No, Tony, I'm doing this because some poor sap got used just when he didn't need to be. I'm doing it because the story is staged—it isn't real. It's a ratings grabber based on bullshit. It's unethical, Tony. It's immoral."

"So you're doing this because of *your* high journalistic standards?"

"Naw, Tony. I'm doing this because it's right."

❈

"WELL, BETH," HUGH RANSFORD WHINED INTO THE PHONE, "I'M JUST SAYING THAT all of this has turned to shit."

"Not yet. Not yet—the story is still golden. We'll be heroes once it airs."

"*You* will be, Beth. Just so you can get your story on the air, I've sacrificed a satellite truck."

"Don't forget Jeremy."

"Oh, I haven't forgotten Jeremy. I've got the union crawling up my butt because I sent a freelancer out in a major piece of equipment that he drives off a mountainside while blasted out of his mind."

"They're not sure of that yet, Hugh."

"Oh, come on, Beth," he argued. "The bottle, the stink, the puke. All he was missing was a neon sign saying, 'Hammered.' The blood tests will be back this afternoon. The State Patrol put a rush on them."

"So, that's him. Not us."

"No, Beth, that's me. Not him. Not us. I'm responsible. I authorized his freelance hire for you. I authorized him to go out and drive the truck for you. I authorized him to hold Will Ross, physically if need be, in the mountains.

For you. Barbara Gooden has been on the phone all night with me and Andropoulos. I'm toast here, no matter how hot your story is, Beth."

"Well, I'm sorry to hear that, Hugh."

"Oh, oh, don't give me that shit, Beth. I've got a broken-up guy in the hospital—that I've got to pay for, by the way—who might just start singing. Did you ever think of that, Beth? And when he sings, who do you think he's going to be singing about? What do you think his lyrics might be? Who will be the female lead in his little song, Beth? Hmm—could it be—*you?* You're in this as deeply as I am, Beth. Don't you forget that."

"The story is going to make it all worthwhile, Hugh. Besides, we can shut Jeremy up."

"Oh, shit. I don't want to hear this. Good-bye, Beth."

Ransford hung up the phone.

❦

DESPITE THE FOAM EARPLUGS, THE GUN WAS LOUDER THAN WILL ANTICIPATED. IT jumped in his hand as his surprise let it fly into exaggerated recoil.

Olverio leaned in close. "Don't be afraid of it. You're not Dirty Harry, and you're not shooting a .44 Magnum. It's loud, but it's not the jumper you've made it out to be. Take your stance and just do it."

Will nodded, scratched his lip under the masquerade mustache they had bought at a Halloween store in Littleton, then went back to the target.

He saw a face. He pulled the trigger.

This time the gun did not jump.

CHAPTER TWENTY-SEVEN
HELLZAPOPPIN'

T HEY POSITIONED THEMSELVES IN A CLUMP OF COTTONWOODS JUST PAST THE house by the side of the stream. The three had hiked in from the car, which they left hidden on an irrigation service road half a mile away. Will looked at his watch. It was 9:45.

Despite his determination to do what he had set his mind to do, his palms were wet. He wiped them on his pant leg.

Olverio noticed the move and smiled.

"We can do this, Will."

"No," Will replied with no tremor in his voice, "this one is mine."

"All right. But all you have to do is wave."

"I understand, but I want you to understand as well: no matter what you hear—you stay out. If I die, I die. You take Rose and Elena and go."

They were silent again. They could hear the rustle of dried cornstalks in the distant wind. The weather was breaking down on the plains, just as it had in the mountains, from extended summer to a short autumn, to be followed soon by the gray clutch of winter.

Stanley looked around the clump of trees. With the exception of the cottonwood trunks and a few low bushes, there was very little cover. They crouched down. The way it was, even the moon could give them away.

"Don't worry," Will said, noticing Stanley's nervousness. "The house is empty. There's no one around for miles. His grandparents used to own all of this."

Olverio turned to Will.

"How did you know about this place?"

"See that road over there? I rode that last week. I rode it any number of times into any number of headwinds. I passed this place. I read the mailbox. *Jackson.*

There was nothing else to see out here. When Art drove me to the station on Wednesday morning, he told me about how he was an only child and his parents died in a car accident and he lived with his Grandma Jackson in Adams County. He even told me which county road. I didn't think about it until this morning. ..."

"It was afternoon," Stanley offered.

"... this afternoon." Will smiled. "When you told me his house was empty, I realized he had booked. He moved it. He moved it to stay clear of the law and the neighbors and anybody else who might come snooping around. Here and there, here and there. One step ahead."

"Now here," Ollie said.

"Now here," Will agreed. He smiled at Olverio and calmly wiped his right palm on his pant leg again.

The branches began to rustle in the wind, and the few leaves that remained started to rain down on the three of them.

They continued to wait.

❄

THE POLICE CAR SAT QUIETLY IN FRONT OF ART JACKSON'S MODEST SOUTH SIDE home. The only sound on the street was the occasional passing car and the *tick-tick-tick* of the cooling engine.

"Why don't we just pick him up at the station?"

"You know, Paul, I'm not in much of a mood to give him a heads-up on what is going on. I want Little Petey just as much in the dark as we are. I'm tired, I'm cranky, and I stink. I want to finish this one up so I can go home and sleep more than forty-five minutes at a crack."

"So let's just go pick him up at the station. Arrest him."

"With what? I want to catch the bastard red-handed. I want to catch him with the stuff. Otherwise nothing sticks."

"So we pick him up and get a search warrant."

"And he gets a hotshot lawyer like Will's who shuts us down before we can even scream 'probable cause.'"

Paul Timmons nodded, then opened the car door.

"Where are you going?"

"I'm going inside," Timmons said matter-of-factly. "I'm going inside to investigate the cry for help I just heard emanating from this house as we just happened to be driving past."

"That's illegal, Paul."

"I know. Oooh. Did you hear that cry?"

Whiteside sat silently for a moment, then smiled. "Yes. As a matter of fact, I did."

He got out of the car. Timmons walked around the Ford to join him.

"Don't worry, Ray. We find anything, we drive to TV6 and pick the bastard up right in the middle of his newscast. We'll be heroes, and he'll be shit on a shingle."

They walked quietly to the back door of the house.

"Got your picks?"

"Don't need 'em," Timmons said.

"Why not?"

"Door's open."

❁

"But I'm scheduled to anchor tonight, Zorro. Ransford told me."

"I've got it, Art. I've got it."

"But you're hurt. You're supposed to be in the hospital."

"Go home, Art. Just go home. I've got it, and I'm going to do it tonight. End of argument."

Clyde Zoromski gingerly stood up, picked up his sports coat, and shuffled out of the office toward the studio. Art Jackson watched him go, then angrily picked up his bag and swung it over his shoulder.

Not good enough, he thought. Not good enough by half. Zorro had to go now too. He had saved himself once; he wouldn't come next time.

And next time was tomorrow.

Jackson stomped across the atrium and out of the building, slamming the door as he left.

Clyde Zoromski might anchor Saturday, but he wouldn't see the Sunday-night news.

Except perhaps as the subject of the lead story.

The mere thought made Art Jackson smile.

❀

THIRTY MINUTES LATER WILL FINISHED PEEING NEXT TO THE STREAM AND TURNED back to the trio's observation point. Stanley held a hand up and Will froze, silhouetted in the darkness.

"Car," Stanley whispered, his voice covered by the rustle of the leaves.

Will nodded.

The car turned into the driveway from behind them, the lights illuminating the house rather than the cottonwood trees. Lucky them.

The car pulled up to the side of the house, and the lights snapped off. In the darkness, Will could see someone, a man, step out of the car and walk angrily toward a work shed set perhaps forty yards from the main house. He unlocked the door, stepped in, and turned on a light. When the door closed, the light disappeared. The windows were shuttered.

Olverio looked at Will.

He pointed at his eyes, then pointed at the shed.

Will nodded. Stanley nodded.

They had both recognized Arthur Peter Jackson.

❧

"SOMEBODY HAS CLEANED OUT THIS PLACE," WHITESIDE SAID.

"You couldn't find a cat hair in here," Timmons agreed.

Carefully Whiteside opened the door to the basement and turned on the light.

"Hello? We heard a cry for help and came in to investigate. This is the police," Timmons called out softly.

Whiteside rolled his eyes and walked slowly down the steps.

The basement was unfinished and empty except for an extensive work area. Whatever had been done there was gone as well. On top of a Formica shelf, Whiteside noticed an oily, circular residue as if a jar or coffee cup had leaked. He ran his finger through it and sniffed.

"Don't go licking it," Timmons warned.

"What do you make of that?" Whiteside said, offering Paul his finger.

Timmons raised his eyebrows and sniffed.

"My nose is pretty much gone tonight, Ray. What do you think?"

"I think it might be nitro," Whiteside said quietly. He looked around the empty basement. "Problem is, our buddy has booked. Come on. We've got to run."

"Where?"

"The TV station," Whiteside said, halfway up the stairs. "We're going to pick up Jackson on probable cause and find out where he's hiding the rest of his stuff. When we get in the car, call downtown. I want this house sealed off so nobody else can wander through and wipe away what we've found."

"You've found," Timmons muttered. "I haven't found shit today."

WILL SLIPPED AS QUICKLY AND QUIETLY AS POSSIBLE THROUGH THE FIELDS, HIS movements covered by the wind crossing the plains, announcing a new weather front passing across the Front Range.

Twenty feet.

He snapped the safety off.

Ten feet. He brought the gun up to his right shoulder.

Five feet. He began to reach for the doorknob. He placed his hand on it, took a deep breath, and turned it slowly. It gave.

The door wasn't locked.

Will pushed open the door and stepped into the dim light of the work shed.

Art Jackson sat on a stool, hunched over a block of Semtex and a string of wires.

Will brought the gun to bear. Art Jackson, Arthur Peter Jackson, Peter the Great, didn't move from his work.

"Hello, Will," he said.

"WHAT DO YOU MEAN HE'S GONE?"

"He's gone. Left. Outa here for tonight. Gone home. Dee-parted, as it were," Zorro said.

"He was supposed to do the sports tonight," Whiteside said. "That's what Ransford told me earlier today."

"Ransford doesn't know shit," Zorro answered. "It's my Saturday-night sports report, and I'm going to do it unless I'm dead."

"Be careful, Mr. Zoromski," Timmons said. "Your lips to God's ears."

Zorro shrugged.

"Do you know where he went?" Whiteside asked.

"Home. I told you."

"We were there. He's not home."

"No, he's moved out to his farm in Adams County," Zorro said as if it were common knowledge. "He said the city was closing in on him."

"It was … still is," Whiteside said hotly as he turned and ran out the door. Timmons followed in a rush.

Zorro watched them go and smiled.

"Squeeze the little prick," he shouted after them.

"I KNEW YOU WERE COMING, WILL," ART SAID, TURNING TO LOOK AT WILL THROUGH eyes made obnoxiously large by his lighted, oversized double loupe, "but I'm sorry, I didn't bake a cake."

He turned back to his work.

"You're a dead man, Art."

"Oh, I've known that for a long time, Will." Art said, the soldering gun smoking in his hand. "But I also know that you won't be the one to do it."

"Say good-bye, Art." Will raised the gun.

"WHAT THE FUCK IS TAKING HIM SO LONG?"

"Olverio Cangliosi, I'm shocked by your language."

"Shut up, Stanley. We should already be on our way back to the car."

❧

"No, Will, you see, I know you won't shoot me. And you won't shoot me for a couple of reasons."

Will paused. "Like what?"

"Well, that, for one," Art answered. "You're looking for a way out. Can I give you a good enough reason not to shoot me?"

Will cursed himself. He tightened the tension on the trigger.

"Hear me out, Will. You won't kill me because you're a nice guy. Nice guys need extraordinary circumstances to kill. Soldiers, for instance. That first one is by far the hardest."

It was as if the safety were still on. Will glanced. It wasn't. The trigger wouldn't move.

"Then again, think of your wife. She's hovering around you right now, Will. She's hovering around you and stopping you from pulling the trigger—because of her goodness and her concern for you. Pulling the trigger makes you just as bad as me. Dooms you to hell, right beside me, rather than heaven, right beside her."

As Art talked, Will swore he could feel Cheryl's hand on his shoulder.

"See? Told you so. Also, she's trying to tell you that if you don't put the gun down on my workbench—*right now* ..." he reached into his pocket, "... I'm going to press this button on this garage-door opener, which will set off that charge of C4 and nitroglycerin that sits just above your head. Go ahead—look. I won't try to take your gun."

Will glanced up at the ceiling. There was a box with a detonator attached. The light on the detonator was red.

"If I push this white button right now, that red light will be the last thing either one of us sees." He slid the opener back into his pocket, then turned and stepped up from the stool, removing his overhead loupe as he did.

As Will looked back at Art, the bomber swung the loupe in a lightning arc that caught Will's gun hand and snapped the gun away from him. It bounced off the opposite wall.

❉

"LET'S GO, LET'S GO," OLVERIO SNAPPED.

Stanley put out a hand.

"No, not yet. Will said don't."

❧

"OLÉ," ART SAID, WALKING BACK TO THE WORKBENCH. HE SAW WILL EYE THE GUN. "Don't even think about it, man. You'll be dead before you take a step. Your daughter will be an orphan. For a while anyway."

"What's that supposed to mean?"

"Loose ends. The world is made up of loose ends. You see, Will, she's got a rattle that will more than likely blow off her hand in the next few days as she gets to whipping it around. Sorry about that. ..."

"You fucker."

"Yes, I am, Will. Yes, I am. Always have been. My father called me that, among other things. Saw a movie with a great idea for an accident in it and made the accident happen to my dad. My mom and my three sisters just happened to get in the way. Tragic. Made me rich, though."

"I thought you were an only child."

Art laughed. "Well, that's how I became one."

Will stood frozen, using his peripheral vision to glance over at the Colt sitting at an odd angle against the wall.

"Then, when my grandparents started to question my, well, my hobby, they had to go as well. Grandpa hated it when I blew up that cow. So I blew him and Grandma up. Made it look really accidental."

Will began to lean toward the gun.

"Eh! Don't do it." Art poised his right hand over his jacket pocket.

"You don't think I'd sacrifice myself to save my daughter?"

"You won't. It's not in your nature. Besides, you've got to race home and try to keep her from shaking that rattle."

"Okay. I'm standing," Will whistled through clenched teeth. "Why me? Why Cheryl? Why us?"

"Because, you asshole," Art Jackson laughed, "you got in the way. Remember Jay, the guy who worked the Sports Department before you? He had to go because he had the job I wanted. I was in the day before applying for it—again. But after he ran away, Sessions gave the job to you—to you, asshole. No experience. No credentials. No 'J' school. That was why I was so upset. That was why I wanted a thank-you. 'Thank you, Mr. Bomber, for giving me my job,'" Art said sarcastically.

Will nodded. "Thank you, Art."

"About time, Ross. Too late, though."

"Why Cheryl? Why my wife?"

"Oh, I don't know. If any one of those other bombs had gone off, I wouldn't have set the secondary. But you kept tripping all over them. You and what's-his-name, Whiteside. Trip, trip, trip, so I had to do something. Something to drive you away from Denver. Wasn't quite sure what would happen with that—who it might catch. But man, it caught you good. Gave me almost six full weeks to make my name after Hugh Ransford hired me on before you came wandering back with all the sympathy in the world."

"Sorry."

"I would have left you alone if you had just left. But you didn't just *leave*. You stuck around and pushed me into the background again. You and Zorro. There."

The final wire smoked, and he sat back, the soldering gun still hot in his left hand. He put the device in a safety rack and admired his handiwork.

"Like it? Simple but deadly. I can tell you right now that Mr. Zorro isn't going to like it tomorrow."

"Wait a minute. If you set that thing off," Will said, pointing to the ceiling, "you kill yourself too. And all your little enemies in the world get away." Art's head bounced in agreement.

"I know, Will. That's why I'm not going to set it off."

He swung around, slipped off the stool, and scooped up the .38 from the floor.

"I've got a .38 and a shovel here, Will, plus plenty of acreage. They won't find you until they start building condos way out here. Twenty years. Easy."

He raised the gun and pressed the short barrel against Will's forehead. "Good-bye, Will. Nice to know you."

✦

"FASTER, PAUL, FASTER!" WHITESIDE SHOUTED, PEERING OUT THE WINDOW INTO the night. "There, there! There's the damned turn!" he screamed.

Paul Timmons was too tired to react quickly. The car roared past the poorly marked turn in the heart of Adams County. The tires screamed and the transmission grumbled as the Ford went into high-speed reverse. Timmons stopped the car.

"Are you sure, Ray?"

"I'm sure."

"No, Ray—are you sure *this* time?"

"Yes, Paul, I'm sure. Go. Just *go!*"

The car turned slowly, drunkenly, onto the narrow county road and roared off into the night.

✿

WILL CLOSED HIS EYES IN PREPARATION FOR THE GUNSHOT THAT WOULD END HIS LIFE. A heavy-grain .38 slug that would go in small and come out large, leaving a hole the size of a grapefruit where he used to keep his hair.

Will listened for the *tink* of the spring that he had noticed the first time he pulled the trigger on the firing line. He was already twisting his head when that sound hit his ear. His left hand went up and pushed the gun away while his right pulled the knife from the loop of his belt and slashed it across Art Jackson's left cheek.

The gun exploded in Will's ear, and he felt a burning punch to his face. He opened his eyes to see shock on the face of Arthur Peter Jackson, a local TV sports star who now had two mouths: one where it should be, the other just above and to the left. Jackson began to turn the gun back toward Will. Without thinking, Will rushed him, pushing the gun aside. Art fired again, into the floor this time. Together, they flew back across the shed, Jackson crashing with the force of Will's 165 pounds into the heavy, free-standing shelving unit that held cases and bottles and timers and fuses.

The two scrambled for control of the fight, shifting their feet and throwing wild punches like second graders. Will moved his hands all over Jackson as if trying to grab some piece of fabric for a judo throw. Jackson felt a shift in weight and pushed, sending Will stumbling back across the room. He stood up and away from the shelves, not noticing that Will had pulled them off balance as he fell.

Taking one step forward, the man who liked to call himself Peter the Great raised the gun. Before he could bring it to bear, he was forced to the ground as the shelves, piled high with the stuff and nonsense of a serious demolition hobbyist, fell down upon him. Art felt his face slam into the floor, the gun going off again, wild, the weight of the shelves pinning him to the plywood floor. He scrambled an inch, perhaps two, then found himself caught. A metal rod, brought home to cut up for use as shrapnel, had rammed itself through his thigh and nailed him to the floor.

Arthur Peter Jackson wasn't going anywhere—at least, not anytime soon.

"Aw, shit," he moaned.

Will leaned back against the door and wheezed. "Oh, shit, indeed." He took a breath and forced himself up to his full height.

Art Jackson looked at Will through shuttered eyes. He slowly glanced to his side. The .38 was just beyond his fingers. At least two shots remained. Maybe three.

"So, you've got a knife. Why the fuck don't you just come over here and kill me?"

"No," Will said softly.

"Then all I can tell you is that you are dead, Will Ross. You and your baby and everyone you hold dear."

"Hhmph." Will laughed. "Okay. But I'm not going to kill you."

"Good, Will. You'll turn me in, I'll get time—prison or the funny farm—then I'll get out, and I'll come after you. Five years or fifty years, it doesn't matter, Ross. I'll be there, and one day your life will go *boom*."

He stretched out the word. As he did, he stretched out his fingers toward the gun.

Will wiped the blood off his nose and looked away.

Art Jackson went for the gun. The knife flashed in the air, hit the barrel a carom shot, and knocked both over to the wall. Will walked over and picked them up. He slid the knife back into its belt-loop scabbard and pointed the snub-nosed barrel of the Colt .38 directly at the middle of Art Jackson's forehead.

"Go ahead. You still haven't got the balls. Your wife is over your shoulder right now, holding you back. She was all sweetness and light. You failed her, and now you're doing it again."

Will laughed.

"Oh, man—you sure as shit didn't know my wife." He swung the barrel hard against Art Jackson's ear.

"Ow! Son of a bitch!"

"Yep. Son of a bitch."

Will stood and faced the door. He took one step and turned.

"Thank you for the lovely evening, Art."

"I'll fucking kill you, Ross!" Art screamed.

"I don't think so. You appear to be stapled to the floor like a gigantic roach in a sophomore biology project, and I've got the gun. I guess I win. Good-night."

Will opened the door and stepped outside, walking slowly but with resolution toward the cottonwood trees. He slipped the gun, still warm from its shots, into his left jacket pocket.

Stan and Ollie stood beside the trees, their faces drained white, fearing the worst from the shots and crashes and screams they had heard. Will walked toward them, his hands at his sides.

He didn't run. He didn't hurry. He didn't waste any time either.

He walked closer and closer to the trees.

"Get down," Will said in a loud, determined voice.

There was a pause before Stan and Ollie dropped to the ground.

INSIDE THE SHED, ART JACKSON IGNORED THE PAIN IN HIS SHOULDER AND FORCED his right arm around the shelves and down his side. He could feel the top of the pocket. He leaned to his right and kept forcing his hand farther into the jacket. He reached the bottom. The control, the switch, the detonator wasn't there. He moved his hand frantically around the pocket, then looked madly across the floor for where it might have fallen.

It hadn't fallen.

It was, at that very moment, seven feet in the air, ten yards from the trees, held aloft by Will Ross, who knew enough not to fire a .38 in a room full of unstable explosives but had no problem at all with the morality of pushing a button on a dark and lonely Saturday night in the distant reaches of Adams County.

"Like I said, asshole," Will hissed, "I win."

He pushed the button.

Art Jackson heard the detonator click but never had time to comprehend what happened to him. The pressure forced the air out of his lungs, separated his molecules, and vaporized them and the floor on which they rested. The fury of the explosion pushed him down into the earth, found resistance, then threw everything upward in milliseconds, pushing the mass of debris through the roof and into the evening air.

THREE MILES AWAY, RAY WHITESIDE AND PAUL TIMMONS SAW THE BLAST, HEARD the explosion, and felt the shock wave, in that order.

The car rolled to a stop as they stared in disbelief.

"Oh, Jesus," Whiteside said. "Let's go. Hurry, Paul."

"We're too late, Ray."

"Just hurry!"

THE LIGHT OF THE BLAST, WARM ON HIS BACK, WAS FOLLOWED IMMEDIATELY BY A crack of thunder and a gigantic hand throwing Will toward the trees and then face down into the hard dirt of a Colorado farm.

He felt the pressure wave crest over him and hit the trees, pushing him beyond his own life as it passed.

WILDERNESS

"Is it you? Are you there?" he whispered.

"It is me, Will. I am here," she answered.

Will picked his face up out of the dirt and in the golden, flickering light of the burning shed saw Cheryl glide over the grass to him.

"Hi, babe, how are you?" he mumbled.

"I'm good, Will." She smiled. "Better than you."

"Ha, yeah. Yeah. But I got him. I got the son of a bitch."

"Yes, you did. I'm proud of you. Now, watch your language."

"Oh, sorry. I guess your new friends don't care much for it."

"No, it's just not necessary here."

"Oh, yeah. Well, guess I'm not going there, huh?" He wheezed. "Oh, God. Am I dead, Cheryl? Am I dead? Does it really hurt this bad?"

"Well, love, it does hurt that bad, but that's only because you're not dead. You are seriously messed up, I can say that, but no, you're not dead. You've got lots of years left. I'd love to take you along right now, but I can't. Fate has a different plan for you. A new path. And there is another reason why you know I can't. You know, don't you?"

"I'm sorry. I'm sorry, Cher." Will began sobbing, his tears leaving streaks in the dirt ground into his cheeks. "I'm sorry. I was so scared, I was so scared that if I," he gasped, "loved—her ... like I loved you, that somebody would come and take her from me, just like, just like, just like he took you. Just like he took you."

His chest tightened and strained. His stomach clenched, and the tears that had hidden themselves behind the walls inside him for two months now poured out. Berthoud had been a breakthrough, but this, this was the flood.

"Awwwww, God! My God, Cheryl—I miss you. Oh, God, I miss you. I'm sorry. I'm sorry. ..."

"Shhhh, shhhh, love. There's nothing to be sorry about. I'm gone, but you'll never be without me. You will never lose me, Will, because I left you a part of me."

"Your mother?" he asked.

"No, you idiot," she laughed. "Our daughter."

"Oh, yeah." He giggled stupidly.

"*Oh, my Lord, you're a mess, Will. Such a mess. Time's running short, Will. Just know, love, that I'll always be nearby—part of your life, part of your heart, part of your memory. Elena is not me, but she is my gift to you. I'll be there, with her, with you—always.*"

"*I'm sorry about … about …*"

"*Beth?*"

"*Yeah,*" he said, collapsing with the word and the weight of the embarrassing memory.

"*Will, you'll find someone new to love, I know you will, I promise you that. But,*" she said, leaning in close to whisper in his ear, "*Jesus Christ—show some taste, would you?*" She shook her head. "*Not her, for heaven's sake—find somebody decent.*"

"*There's nobody like you.*"

She smiled.

"*I know, but find her anyway.*"

Will raised her head to look at Cheryl, to see her one last time, but all he saw in front of him was a mist, and through that mist came Stanley and Olverio, moving fast and low.

Without a word, they scooped Will up under the armpits and dragged him into the cottonwoods, across the stream, and back toward their hidden automobile.

As they did, a dirty brown Ford pulled into the driveway. Paul Timmons and Raymond Whiteside got out of the car, stared at the flames, and both slid down to the ground in sheer exhaustion.

Another day late.

Another dollar short.

CHAPTER TWENTY-EIGHT

OPENING NIGHT

SUNDAY NIGHT IS, TRADITIONALLY, THE HIGHEST AUDIENCE VIEWING NIGHT in local TV news. What is the weather going to be like next week? Is the world going to blow up before Joey's soccer final on Wednesday? What the hell happened to the Broncos?

In fact, the potential audience is so high that many of the stations worked their main news teams on a Sunday-through-Thursday schedule. Not TV6. Not because it wasn't a good idea but because Tom Blakely had told them to go piss up a rope. He wanted Sunday off, and by God, until he retired, the main news team at TV6 would work Monday through Friday.

Still, that hadn't stopped Barbara Gooden, and now Hugh Ransford, from at least attempting to put TV6's best foot forward. Sunday's anchor team was an Irish blond from New Jersey with a wicked jaw and a spine of spring steel named Mary Katherine O'Hara—Katie—who had worn her way through a progression of coanchors over the years. The latest man in the barrel was a Studly Dudley from a minuscule market in Illinois named Francisco Cortez. His real name was Frank Cook, but his great-grandmother had been Hispanic and he had taken her name. It was a wise move, racing him up the market ladder toward the big time. And the big time was where he was headed, weekends in Denver being only a stepping-stone.

So, while the faces kept changing beside her, Katie O'Hara stayed, a pillar of stability in the maelstrom of market change

And though Tom might not make an appearance on Sunday night, even when the Pope was in town, it was still the night to step forward into the week with the best stories, the audience-grabbing series, the barn-burner reports that would have people talking for days to come.

Perhaps that was a bad choice of words in the case of TV6 News on this particular autumn Sunday.

On Friday the station had lost a satellite truck on a mountain pass. No one seemed overly concerned about the driver, now neck to toe in a body cast at Swedish Hospital, wearing a halo that made him look like the biggest badass angel among the pantheon of heaven. But in a way, some should have been. When he finally sobered up and decided to come out of his coma on Sunday morning, Jeremy Paxton not only discovered a whole new world of pain but found God.

He hissed at the nurse through the clenched teeth of his broken jaw, and soon he had an audience of two tired, grungy police detectives as well as the two TV columnists from the *Denver Post* and the *Rocky Mountain News,* all listening in fascination to a halting story of news, sex, betrayal, and flying trucks.

Still, the freelancer was far from the station's thoughts at the moment. More pressing was the news, the lead-story news, that Art Jackson, up-and-coming sports reporter at TV6, had been up and coming mainly because he had been trying to kill his competition. One had been scared away, one had been seriously burned, and a third had foiled three attempts on his life but had lost his wife in the process.

The shed had still been burning when the first news trucks arrived. It made spectacular pictures, compelling video, all bright colors and flashing lights. On that basis alone, it would have been the top story of the day, but this had more to offer—and it dug into the soul of a competitor at the same time.

It had "lead story" written all over it for five different stations. Six if you counted the one that had hired the mad bomber in the first place.

NOW, ON A SUNDAY NIGHT IN AUTUMN, TWO OF THE THREE SURVIVORS OF THE TV6 sports office came together in the TV6 newsroom.

Clyde Zoromski couldn't wait. He had arrived at noon, a full ninety minutes before his shift began, two hours before the Broncos game. The transfer had gone without a hitch. Now he couldn't wait to see if he had pulled it off.

He watched the game and blindly strung together some highlights. He didn't much care. He wondered if the newscast would even get to him that evening. He watched the game and paced, checked the wires occasionally for other scores, and paced some more.

At 10:05 he was standing in the newsroom, waiting for the story, waiting for reaction. He tried to appear calm and unconcerned. He glanced over at Ransford's office. Beth was sitting with the news director, cool and distant. It was her attitude whenever she had a story to tell.

No worries, but don't get within fifty feet of me.

That Zorro knew.

Barbara Gooden was in the newsroom that night, talking with reporters, getting as much information on the various weekend debacles as she could. Andy Andropoulos, the general manager, was there as well, standing beside her, asking for information and explanations that he could pass on to the Stoval Station Group lawyers in Chicago.

He looked sick. He looked pissed.

Zorro gave him a wide berth.

As he turned the corner of the assignment desk, determined to wait in the atrium until the story aired, Clyde Zoromski was shocked to see the newsroom doors swing open and Will Ross hobble in, his face a mass of scrapes, one eye blackened, and supporting his right side with a cane. Behind him walked an older woman carrying a baby and two men, one tall and thin, the other short and round.

"Hey, Z," Will said.

"Jesus Christ, Will," Zorro said in shock, "what the hell happened to you?"

Will smiled.

"That Ride to the Sky thing was a lot tougher than we thought."

"A lot tougher," the round man said.

"A lot tougher," the skinny man mimicked.

Zorro's eyes shot back and forth between the two, then returned to Will.

"Will, what the hell are you doing here?"

"I'm here to express my displeasure concerning an upcoming story on TV6 News."

"What?"

Will grinned. "Well, essentially, Z, I'm here to kick Hugh Ransford's ass and squeeze Beth Freeman into a tomato-paste can."

Zorro nodded in understanding, then leaned forward to Will.

"I know what you're thinking, and I agree. Completely. But before you go in there and drill them between the eyes, could I take just a second of your time and tell you a little something?"

Will turned and looked down toward Ransford's office. The news director and Beth were still deep in conversation. They hadn't noticed he was there.

He said, "Sure," and began to follow Clyde into the dispatch room behind the assignment desk. Rose, Elena, Stanley, and Oliver followed. Zorro stopped and looked at them for a moment, realized immediately that they weren't about to leave, waved his hand in invitation, and began to explain in whispers what they were about to see.

When he finished, he looked at Will.

"You can stomp them when it's done, Will. You can stomp them. All I'm asking is that you stand back and let this happen. Don't stop the story. Please. We're dropping the big one here, Will, and it's got my fingerprints all over it. There's gonna be a lot of collateral damage. Trust me on this."

He glanced at Rose.

"Ma'am, I don't want to hurt you or Will or the baby in any way, but when it's done, believe me, there won't be much stomping that has to be done."

Will stared at Zorro for a long moment, then agreed.

"Okay. How long does the story run?"

"Six minutes."

"Okay. You've got six. Then I hit her with my stick."

"I'll hold you up when you do it, Will. Just wait 'til after the fireworks."

"You've got it, Z. I'll wait."

The six of them walked out of the dispatch room just as Beth carried her story toward the tape room. Will and Zorro stopped and stared. Beth stopped and stared. Then she smiled tightly and walked out through the newsroom doors.

Rose made a gesture with her right hand toward the departing figure.

Will turned to her. "You know, you keep doing that. What is that?"

"My grandmother used to do that in the old country. People upset her and she would make the sign and they would drop dead."

"Really?"

"Well, that's what she said. When I was a girl, nobody in our neighborhood wanted to test it."

"Ross!" Ransford screamed from across the newsroom. He marched, quickstep, over to Will and Zorro. "What the hell are you doing here, and where the hell have you been? You've got one hell of a lot of explaining to do."

Will rose up but felt Zorro squeeze his left arm. He forced himself to relax.

"We'll talk, Hugh. I'll let you know everything about what happened to me this weekend ..."

Barbara Gooden came up behind Ransford. Will glanced at her and smiled.

"... if, of course, you'll tell me everything about what happened to you."

Ransford felt Gooden's presence and blanched. Andy Andropoulos stepped up behind Ransford as well, took one look at Will, and rolled his eyes.

"Oh, Jesus, what happened to you?" he wailed.

The newsroom doors opened again. The group, now of nine, turned as one and stared at Beth Freeman as she walked back into the newsroom. She smiled again, tightly again, and walked over to the largest monitor in the newsroom. She stood before it in anticipation. One minute away from her story. It didn't matter that the subject was standing right there. It didn't matter what it had taken to get the story to this point in terms of people and lives and shattering both.

She had another award winner to embrace, and Denver would likely never forget this one.

Which, oddly enough, was exactly what Clyde Zoromski was thinking at that very moment.

Ransford turned and walked toward Beth, standing behind her. He was part of this as well.

Andy Andropoulos turned to join them. Clyde Zoromski quickly put out a hand and grabbed Andy's arm. Andy looked at the hand and then at Zoromski. Zorro shook his head and rolled his eyeballs toward the smaller monitor at the corner of the assignment desk. Andy squinted suspiciously for a moment, then followed Zorro's lead.

Eight people gathered around a sixteen-inch monitor as Katie O'Hara introduced a story of loss and heartbreak, a man who, in his pain, turned from his own child, denying his love in order to search selfishly for himself, his own future.

Will felt his face flush. The opening "Beth Freeman Reports" animation began, followed by violin music and video of that night, so many weeks before, when Cheryl had died.

"She lived her life for others, and in the end, she gave her life to save her only child. The only child she would ever have. The only child that would carry her memory into the future."

The violins rose again.

"Her loss crippled her husband emotionally. Did he blame himself for her death? And—what of the child? Could he face her? Could he emotionally reach out across the gulf that he himself had formed in order to be her father?"

The pictures of Will, Cheryl, and the baby, culled from earlier news reports, were replaced by the inside of Frisco's. Will closed his eyes. He didn't want to see himself made into such a fool.

Zorro put a hand on his shoulder.

"Courage, my friend. It will be done soon."

"In my exclusive interview with widower Will Ross, I asked him why— why did he feel so emotionally distant?"

"It's been a tough six weeks. I haven't slept. I can't focus. Beth, I can't even seem to cry—and the baby—I don't know, I just don't know ..."

Will waited for the quote to continue, remembering that he had said something about being afraid that loving someone might mean that person's death, but the line had been cut from the story. It explained a lot. But it wasn't there. He turned away from the screen and looked at Beth. She felt his gaze, turned, smiled, and went back to watching the monitor.

Will looked back again, but the scene had shifted.

Rather than a tight shot on Will's face or a close-up of Elena from over Beth's shoulder, there was a wide shot from a different angle.

"Jesus," Will muttered, "how many cameras did she have in there?"

"Four," Zorro said quietly. "Just watch."

The questions continued, probing, insightful, personal, digging deeply into

Will's loss of Cheryl and his fear of loving Elena, his terror of being left old and alone, dribbling peas and watching ancient reruns of *Friends*, but now the viewers saw Beth and watched her reaction, the dead look in her eyes that lifted only when Will looked up at her, and the left hand under the table, making a series of small gestures, almost as if she were directing the camera to move in close, take the baby, pull out, take Will, two shot, wide, tight, freeze.

There was a sudden sense of manipulation in watching the video, as if Beth Freeman were pulling the audience along by the nose to see this man whom she was pulling along by the nose spread himself emotionally across the videotape.

It was horrifying and fascinating all at once, a backstage look at human misery as presented in living color by blind, thoughtless ambition.

Rose turned and looked at Beth Freeman again, ready to zing her with another of her great-grandmother's terrible gestures, but paused when she saw the look on Beth's face, a look of shock and utter horror as the video-tape rolled on over her career.

Rose turned back to the monitor, caught Zorro's eye, and nodded. He smiled in return.

The story rolled on to its end, with Beth reaching out a hand to Will. He took it.

"*Thank you, Beth. I appreciate just, well, getting to talk.*"

"*Thank you, Will, for sharing this with us.*"

Problem was, you couldn't see her saying that. Her mouth was away from the camera. What appeared next was the same moment from a different camera, this one tight on Beth's face. Will repeated his line.

"*Thank you, Beth. I appreciate just, well, getting to talk.*"

Her true response, however, now seen face on, was different. Very different.

"*Oh, Will, just know—I'm here for you. Always.*"

Beth and Ransford both stiffened.

The scene shifted abruptly again to yet another camera. The wide shot again. The taping was over. The main camera had been shut down, but this one, showing the secluded restaurant booth from a different angle, continued to run. The audio was tinny and distant, picked up now by a shotgun microphone.

Jeremy Paxton emerged from a corner and began to tear down his camera blind. A few moments later, a door in the rear of the restaurant was heard opening and Beth Freeman walked into the shot and over to Jeremy.

The sound was muffled, but the sound could be heard and understood.

"Did you get what you wanted?"

"I think so," Beth answered.

"Did he?"

"Well, I scraped his tonsils for him a good one. Christ, I just thought," she laughed, leaning up against one of the tables, *"if I don't have enough emotional spew on this tape, I'll have to sleep with the dweeb to get him to talk again."*

They both laughed.

The scene faded to black, then rose to a shot of Elena and Beth Freeman's closing line.

"In the eyes of a child there is hope and there is love, and therein lies the future. A future made all the more difficult by the death of both parents—one physically, one emotionally—on a rainy Colorado night. In the eyes of a child lives the hope of reaching across the emotional chasm to the distant father who can no longer find it in himself to love."

The picture of Elena faded to black.

Will took a deep, shaking breath.

Then he heard something more, an instantly recognizable bit of music, completely out of character with the tone of the story: the *Looney Tunes* theme.

A starburst background rushed forward, followed immediately by a black-and-white still photo of Beth Freeman. Her eyes bugged cartoonishly and her mouth moved like a cutout dummy, in the manner of Monty Python.

Zorro jumped. Carver. Damn.

"Tha-tha-tha—that's all, folks!" the picture shouted, and the camera dissolved back to Katie O'Hara and Francisco Cortez. They stared at the monitors built into the news desk and remained silent for a moment until Katie looked up at the camera, smiled, and said, "We'll ... be right back."

The camera held on her a moment and then went to black, but not before she burst into peals of laughter.

"Aaaaaaaaaaaah!" Beth Freeman screamed, pointing at the monitor and unable to find her voice.

Around the newsroom, people were either shaking their heads in embarrassment or stifling laughs. Barbara Gooden was red with the shame of what one of her reporters had done to get a story. Andy Andropoulos was red with fury at more shit to deal with on a Sunday night, this crisis played out on his leading newscast.

Rose, Stan, and Ollie were red from laughing. Elena was red from pooping.

Will and Zorro showed nothing at all. They simply turned to face Beth Freeman.

"You!" she screamed. *"You!"* She pointed at both Will and Zorro. "You did this to me! You trashed my story! You did it!" She pointed between the two, unsure whom to blame. "You!" She finally stopped, pointing at Zorro.

Ransford was right behind her, even more furious, if such a thing were possible. "Clean out your desk, Zoromski! You're finished." He turned on Will. "You too, Ross!"

Will heard a tremor in Ransford's voice that told him the news director was both angry and frightened at once. He had seen his whole career pass before his eyes in the final moments of that news story. The only way to save it was to fire all the witnesses.

Andy Andropoulos held up a hand. Ransford immediately grew sullenly silent. Beth Freeman continued to wheeze but didn't say a word.

"Did you do this, Zorro?"

Clyde Zoromski nodded.

"Yes, I did, Andy. I did it with my little hatchet. I just wanted to prove to *her* and *him*," he jerked his head toward Ransford, "that this is not the way we do news here at TV6. This is not how we get stories, this is not how we talk to people, this is not how we report. In the dark, behind a series of lies, using sex and threats to gain advantage."

Andy nodded.

Will stepped forward.

"I did it too, Andy. I was right beside Clyde. We did it together."

Bruce Mason stood up at the assignment desk. "I did it too, Andy."

"And me, Andy," Tony Carver said, leaning over the opposite end of the assignment desk.

Suddenly there was a chorus of "And me," "Me too," and "I did it," from around the newsroom. The room grew quiet again.

Andy Andropoulos pursed his lips and stared at the floor.

"Me too, Andy," Barbara Gooden said. "It's my newsroom. I did it too."

Beth Freeman angrily shook her head. "Goddamn you all."

Katie O'Hara burst through the doors of the newsroom, still chuckling over the images in the story. Seeing Beth, she shouted, "Hey, Freeman! Nice story! Hope to hell you at least got laid out of it. Haw!" She kept walking.

Andy smiled, watching her go, then turned his eyes down to the floor, then looked back up at Beth Freeman.

"Whether you got mud for your turtle or not, Beth, does not matter. This was underhanded and unethical, and it will not wash. As soon as TV6 Sports Wrap is done, you will go out on the set and tape an apology for our viewers. Then you will consider yourself fired.

"Clear out your desk immediately. I want you gone as soon as you are finished taping."

He nodded at Barbara Gooden, and they started to leave. Ransford followed them. Andy stopped and put up a hand.

"Not you, Hugh. Not now. Barbara and I have to talk. The people you've brought in have, in one weekend, ruined what we've worked toward for the past ten years. We'll talk tomorrow morning, but I'd say that you'd best go looking for a new job."

Andropoulos and Gooden pushed open the newsroom doors and walked out.

Ransford stood in complete and utter shock, staring at where his bosses, his former bosses, had last been standing.

Beth Freeman broke the silence. "Fuck them. Fuck you. I'm not doing any apology, I'm leaving, and I'm leaving now."

"Miss Freeman?" called a gritty voice from the other end of the newsroom. "I hate to disagree, but I will this one time."

Detective Ray Whiteside stepped out of the shadows, his face lined, tired, and unshaven, his suit rumpled beyond hope of pressing. Paul Timmons stumbled behind him. Tony Carver brought up the rear, making faces and swiping his hand past his nose. They had arrived before the story aired, but Carver had begged them to hold back until after the drama had played itself out.

"Whoa, Detective Whiteside!" Zorro called to him. "Interesting look. You didn't happen to see Nurse Nancy's story last week on the importance of good hygiene, did you?"

"Screw you, Mr. Zoromski."

"Guess not," Clyde said quietly, looking at the floor.

"Beth Freeman, I suggest you call a lawyer. We are taking you downtown to question you in the matter of conspiracy with one Jeremy Paxton to commit murder upon the person of one William Edward Ross on Friday last on the eastern slopes of Berthoud Pass. You have the right to remain silent. ..."

"I thought you guys only did that on TV," Will said.

"Shut up, Ross," Timmons moaned as Whiteside continued to Mirandize Beth Freeman. "You have no idea what we went through for you this weekend."

"Well," Zorro smiled, "at least we know it wasn't a shower."

"I don't watch you. I don't like you," Timmons said flatly.

Clyde Zoromski only laughed.

❁

TIMMONS HAD TAKEN BETH FREEMAN OUT TO THE CAR. SHE HAD ALREADY called a lawyer. For a quick moment, Will had considered giving her Felix Ramirez's card, but then he realized that getting her solid legal representation was not high on his priority list. The card stayed in his wallet.

Whiteside was talking to Ransford, telling him the detectives wanted to talk to him on Monday afternoon. After 2 P.M. because there was no way Whiteside or Timmons was showing up before then.

Whiteside looked over at Will, nodded at Hugh Ransford, and sauntered over to the edge of the news desk.

"I need to talk to you alone, Will."

Will looked at Rose. She and Elena stepped away. Whiteside leaned in close.

"Um, you wouldn't happen to know anything about an explosion at a farm in Adams County last night, would you?"

Will shook his head. "No. Not a thing."

"Do you have an alibi for your whereabouts last night?"

"Yep." Will pointed at Stanley, Oliver, and Rose. Elena waved an arm in the hope of being included. "I was with them. They took me to the hospital after I fell down the steps." He held up the cane.

"I see," Whiteside said. "I see.

"Then you wouldn't happen to know anything about a .38 Colt snubnose found near a stand of cottonwoods on the scene."

"Nope."

"It had fingerprints on it."

"Really?" Will's gut clenched. He tried to keep his face uninterested. "Amazing."

"Yeah. What's even more amazing is that between the discovery of the gun and its arrival at the evidence room downtown, the fingerprints were carefully wiped off and the gun was mistakenly placed in the meltdown bin. As of 4 this afternoon, it's an ingot."

"Really?"

"Really, really."

Whiteside put out his hand.

"Have a nice life, Will. I never want to see you again."

"Thank you for everything, Detective. Same goes."

They smiled and parted.

As they did, Hugh Ransford shambled past them, heading back to his office. At least, the room that had been his office.

"Hugh—a second," Will called after him.

Ransford turned with tired, empty eyes.

"What now, Ross? Haven't you caused me enough problems?"

"Just one more, boss—I quit." Will grinned wide, despite the pain of the scratches and scars on his cheeks, and turned back to his family.

They were free of the shadows.

Finally free.

EPILOGUE

So, WHAT ARE WE GOING TO DO FOR A LIVING?" ROSE ASKED, BOUNCING A bubbling Elena on her knee.

Will chuckled as he continued to pack the boxes.

"Don't know yet. House sold in forty-eight hours. We close next week. I guess just move back to a quiet, small-town life in Detroit."

"Oh, to be as dim and optimistic as your daddy," Rose whispered into Elena's ear.

The baby cooed, then spat up a bubble of formula.

"I heard that," Will said. He picked up a photo album and flipped through it. Him at Paris-Roubaix. Cheryl and him together at the start of Le Tour. Hootie, Nancy, a photo of Hootie with Marjorie Stump hovering in the background. She made a sour face for the camera, which brought a painful smile to Will's face.

"You've pretty much shot yourself in the foot as far as TV goes," Rose said. "So—any idea what you're going to do to support your daughter in the style to which she has become accustomed?"

"I thought I'd leave that to you," he offered.

"Oh, my, no," Rose whistled. "I need a good night's sleep."

"Don't we all," Will said honestly, knowing he had been sharing the late-night duties for the past two weeks. "It's kind of fun when you think about it."

"I've had better," Rose laughed. "You tell me that in two months, when your lower eyelid is bouncing off the hardwood floor. Yes, yes," she said in a funny, high-pitched voice that made Elena laugh, "you're a nighttime party girl, aren't you? Aren't you?"

The phone rang in the kitchen. Shoe jumped up and howled. Rex slept in one corner and opened an eye, assessed the threat, and promptly went back to sleep.

"Aha! See? Job offers," Will shouted, pointing in large, wild circles toward the phone. "They're coming in now. In a rush!" He hurried toward the kitchen.

"Bet it's the lawn guy," Rose called after him.

Will answered the phone and within seconds was talking urgently into it. Rose strained to hear what he was saying, but a neighbor's major-league Harley drowned out the words. She cursed the neighbor and gave him the sign. Just to be sure, she took Elena's hand and formed the baby's fingers into a rough approximation of it, index and little fingers extended, and pointed Elena's arm in the general direction of the neighbor as well.

"It worked at the station on that Beth woman," she whispered. "Maybe it works on motorcycles, too—eh?"

The motorcycle stopped. The neighbor shouted, "Shit!"

Elena burbled.

Rose heard Will hang up the phone. He walked back into the room, looking as if he'd been hit in the back of the head with a two-by-four.

"What is it, Will?"

He turned to her. His expression didn't change.

"What is it? Bad news?"

He shook his head.

"Good news?"

Will nodded.

"*What, then?*" Rose shouted. The baby turned her head up to look at her father.

"Well, you remember Richard Bourgoin with Haven in France?"

"No. I wasn't there."

"Oh, yeah, well—he was the team leader when I rode the Tour. He's off the bike now. Running a team in Germany. He just called and wondered if I could come and run it with him."

"In Germany?"

"In Germany."

"What did you tell him?"

"I told him I'd have to talk with you. …"

Rose stared at her son-in-law for a moment, then at the baby, then back at Will.

"Sure, we'll go, won't we, Ellie?"

Will smiled.

"I'm glad you said that. So I said yes."

THAT EVENING WILL STOOD ON THE SMALL DECK IN THE BACK OF THE HOUSE, holding Elena bundled in his arms.

He looked at the sky for a long moment and sighed.

"Thank you, Cheryl. Thank you, love."

The baby stirred in his arms. He looked down. As he looked back up again, a shooting star streaked across the entire night sky.

He watched it go.

His eyes filled with tears, but Will Ross smiled.

The Moody Cycling Murder Mystery Series

Two Wheels

American Will Ross attempts to fill the late world champion's shoes, but also discovers the death wasn't an accident.
1-884737-11-0 • VP-MTW • $14.95

Perfect Circles

Drugs and murder at the Tour de France.
1-884737-44-7 • VP-CIR • $14.95

Derailleur

Will Ross and Cheryl Crane leave European road racing for mountain bike racing in Colorado, but trouble follows.
1-884737-59-5 • VP-DER • $14.95

Deadroll

It's a case of shifting lives and serial bombers for Will and Cheryl Ross, who always find danger waiting just around the next hairpin turn.
1-884737-92-7 • VP-DRL • $14.95

Tel: 800/234-8356
Fax: 303/444-6788
E-mail: velopress@7dogs.com
Web: velopress.com
VeloPress books are also available from your favorite bookstore or bike shop.